URRVENSKEYR MOUNTAIN

LAKE SKYLLIVRENG

ELDR

ISLAND OF ICHIL

SEA OF ICE

TAINS

SILBER RIVER

VALLÉ DE LUMÉ

THE CHRYSÓS SEA

SÚNDRAILLE

LLORENYAE

THE SHADOW QUEEN

Also by C. J. Redwine

Defiance

Deception

Deliverance

Outcast: A Defiance Novella

THE
SHADOW
QUEEN

A Ravenspire Novel

C. J. REDWINE

Balzer + Bray
An Imprint of HarperCollins*Publishers*

Balzer + Bray is an imprint of HarperCollins Publishers.

The Shadow Queen
Copyright © 2016 by C. J. Redwine
All rights reserved. Printed in the United States of America.
No part of this book may be used or reproduced in any manner whatsoever without
written permission except in the case of brief quotations embodied in critical articles
and reviews. For information address HarperCollins Children's Books, a division of
HarperCollins Publishers, 195 Broadway, New York, NY 10007.
www.epicreads.com

Library of Congress Control Number: 2015938955
ISBN 978-0-06-236024-3

Typography by Sarah Nichole Kaufman
16 17 18 19 20   PC/RRDH   10 9 8 7 6 5 4 3 2 1
❖
First Edition

For Dad,
who taught me that I could do anything I set my mind to.

For Mom,
*who brought me to the library every week so I could check out yet another book of
Grimm's fairy tales and who encouraged my wild imagination.*

And for Heather,
my real-life sister who is also the sister of my heart. I owe you an orange Spree.

THE SHADOW QUEEN

ONCE UPON A TIME . . .

NOTHING HAD BEEN right in the castle since her mother's death. Her father's smile had disappeared, and a brittle imposter had taken its place. Her younger brother had begun screaming in the dead of night, trapped in nightmares he couldn't remember upon waking. And the faint tingle of magic in the princess's palms that her mother had laughingly told her would one day make flowers bloom and birds sing had become a fierce burn of power that stung her veins and shook the ground if the princess wasn't careful.

She'd been desperate for a change—for some way to return the castle to the happy place it used to be. So when the king of Morcant began pressuring her father to marry another Morcantian of the king's choice in order to keep the alliance between Morcant and Ravenspire strong, and her father announced that he was marrying the princess's aunt Irina, a woman who'd never set foot in Ravenspire until her sister was buried, the princess began to hope.

At first, it seemed the princess's wish had been granted. Irina charmed the young prince into calling her Mama, and his nightmares all but disappeared. She coaxed smiles out of the king, and his hollow cheeks grew round again as she tempted his appetite with lavish feasts nearly every night. And she took the princess under her wing, sharing the secrets of the magic that ran through their blood.

It was almost like having a mother again. Almost like being happy.

But it was all a lie.

Understanding dawned slowly, like prickles of pain in a limb gone numb. The princess began noticing things that shouldn't be. Apples that gleamed beneath the candlelight but spilled rot once the skin was punctured. Apples her father, her brother, and the castle staff ate nightly until every bit of them had disappeared.

Apples Irina said were for those without magic in their blood.

As the king and his staff became glassy-eyed puppets, dependent upon Irina for their every thought, the dungeons filled with those who refused to give Irina what she wanted. Ambassadors from other kingdoms left in anger at the king's refusal to speak to them unless he first asked Irina what to say. And whispers of magic threaded throughout the castle, a web of deceit it seemed only the princess could detect.

Scared that she was losing her father, the princess decided to find a way to break Irina's control over the castle and everyone in it.

The princess chose her moment carefully. The warmth of day still lingered outside, but the air in the castle's entrance hall was cool and comfortable, and the family often spent their evenings watching through massive windowpanes as the stars came to life. The princess's father sat beside Irina, dull and vague, while they watched the prince play with the pet snake the queen had given him for his seventh birthday. Members of the royal guard stood watch nearby, their eyes focused on the queen they somehow adored more than life itself.

The faint aroma of apples filled the air, and the lingering stain of rot smeared the teeth of those who smiled at Irina.

The princess's bare hands trembled as she wrapped them around Irina's arm, and fear left a bitter taste in her mouth. Her magic burned through her veins and pooled in her palms, and she felt the heart of the queen—vicious, determined, and strong—surge against her hands.

Her pulse pounding, her legs trembling, the princess said the incantor that would change everything.

"*Nakh'rashk.* Find the threads of Irina's magic and scatter them to the four winds."

The queen jerked her arm free, but it was too late. Power leaped from the princess's palms, slammed into the queen, and then shot to the gleaming marble floor where it exploded into a thousand tendrils of brilliant light. The light snaked over the floor, touching the palace guard, the prince, and the king before streaking throughout the castle to tear into pieces the fabric of lies Irina had built her new life upon.

The king, his eyes clear, his memory of the last six months restored, shouted for Irina to be put to death for treason. The palace guard, released of their bespelled adoration, rushed to do his bidding. And Irina, one hand reaching to punish the princess who had betrayed her and one reaching to bespell the king again, hesitated for a split second between the two.

In a heartbeat, the guards were upon her. The king pushed the prince and princess behind him. Swords flashed. Screams rose.

And then Irina began to laugh.

The princess shivered deep within as the guards closest to the queen fell back, clutching their faces while their skin peeled away from their bones and their blood bubbled like soup left too long on the fire.

"Take your brother and run!" the king shouted as he put the prince's hand in hers. "Protect him."

The princess snatched her brother's hand and pulled him toward a small doorway that led to the servants' hall.

Irina scooped up the prince's pet snake and with a whisper turned him into an enormous black viper. The snake slithered across the bloodstained marble and sank his fangs into the king.

"No!" The princess turned back for her father, but Irina raised her arms above her head and slammed her palms into the wall behind her.

Instantly, the stone shuddered and twisted. The princess screamed as the floor buckled, heaving upward and throwing her against a pillar that was quickly disintegrating into dust. All around her, the walls were crumbling, the floor was cracking, and the snake was attacking anyone still left alive.

The princess locked eyes with the queen, a lake of blood and horror between them, and Irina smiled as the wall behind the princess exploded outward to crush the girl into dust.

Chunks of stone crashed around the princess, leaving her

a small circle of space full of acrid dust. She was trapped, the debris above her creaking and sliding as the floor shuddered. She was going to die, and there would be no one left to protect her brother from the monster who'd taken Ravenspire's throne.

A large dark hand reached through a space in the debris, wrapped around the princess's wrist, and pulled her through the narrow opening between the pile of rubble and the servants' hall. Gabril, the head of her father's palace guard, crouched before her, his brown eyes steady on hers, his voice calm.

"Can you run?" he asked as he scooped the prince onto his shoulders.

The princess didn't want to run. She wanted to see her father. She wanted to stay in her home.

She wanted to fight.

But though the queen had said that the princess was the daughter she'd never had, Irina had kept the knowledge of how to use magic as a weapon for herself alone.

And so, as the walls caved in behind them, the princess put her hand in Gabril's, told her brother everything would be all right, and ran.

ONE

"WERE YOU SEEN?" Gabril asked, his dark skin gilded with the last rays of the setting sun as he motioned Lorelai and Leo into the barn. The former guardsman had gray sprinkled throughout his short black hair now, and tiny lines were etched around his eyes. He still carried himself like a soldier, but the cost of trying to keep the queen from discovering that the prince and princess were still alive showed in the slight stoop of his shoulders and the worry that filled his eyes when he thought no one was looking.

"No." Lorelai Diederich, crown princess of Ravenspire and fugitive at large, hurried into the dim interior. The barn was tucked away at the edges of an abandoned farm just outside the mountain village of Felsigen and was so dilapidated, a good stiff wind might flatten it.

"You're sure?" Gabril's voice was urgent as he stepped past the princess to help her brother, Leo, pull a heavily loaded hay cart into the barn.

"Please. You're talking about the Royal Rogues. Nobody sees

us unless we want to be seen." Leo gave the hay cart one last push inside and then pulled the door shut. He glanced down at his filthy trousers and heaved a sigh. "Although we really should rethink these disguises."

"I told you, we aren't calling ourselves the Royal Rogues. And our disguises are fine." Lorelai's gloved fingers fumbled with the buttons of her ragged coat.

"If by fine you mean hideous, then, yes, they are." Leo rubbed at the dirt he'd smudged on his face earlier in the afternoon—part of his attempt to look like an unkempt farm boy in case anyone caught sight of him waiting beside the road that led from Felsigen to the queen's northeast garrison. "And I have several other excellent suggestions for names. The Plucky Pair. The Royal Robbers, though personally I think that makes us sound too much like criminals—"

"We are criminals." Lorelai folded up her coat and laid it beside her travel pack. "At least in the eyes of the queen."

"A minor detail." Leo ran his hand over the sacks of loot that were neatly stacked on the hay cart.

"We made good progress tonight," Lorelai said as Gabril counted the sacks full of the village's meager food supply—a food supply Irina had demanded as taxes, even though her garrison already had enough food to feed every village in the Falkrain Mountains for several months. Not that the starving villagers would see a bit of it. Irina would use some of it to feed her army, and let the rest of it rot as a message to remind everyone that she owned Ravenspire down to the last stalk of wheat. "That makes six robberies in two months. Six villages of people who are now loyal to us and will support me when I go after the throne. If we keep up this pace, we'll have gained the loyalty of the entire Falkrains by spring."

Leo gave her a charming, lopsided smile. "Think how much easier it would be to earn the peasants' loyalty if we had a name to go with our reputation. We could be the Daring Duo—"

"You could be hanging for your crimes if we don't move on to the next village," Gabril said quietly. "Now let's focus on what needs to be done so we can leave at first light, just in case you were seen."

"We weren't," Lorelai said as her white gyrfalcon soared in through the open loft window and perched on the princess's shoulder, her talons digging into the leather harness Lorelai had fashioned to be worn on her shoulder. A dead mouse dangled from the bird's beak.

"I hid in the treasury wagon before it left Felsigen. Sasha distracted them with a fake attack when they were an hour outside the village." Lorelai ran a gloved finger down her bird's back. "And Leo—"

"Did the most incredible impression of a Morcantian farm boy you've ever heard." He sped up the cadence of his voice, hitting his consonants hard and running all the sounds together. "I was a Morcantian peasant angry that the blight in Ravenspire is seeping across the border and killing my goats."

"He yelled at the treasury officers long enough to give me time to hide in the wagon, but they never got a good look at him." Lorelai shoved the dangling mouse away from her face.

Gift. For you. Dinner. Sasha's thoughts flitted through Lorelai's mind with quick precision.

Thank you, but I don't eat mice. Lorelai's throat closed as the little body brushed against her hair while images of Sasha's beak enthusiastically shredding the mouse's skin to get to its internal organs blazed from the bird's mind into hers. She swallowed hard to avoid insulting Sasha's gift by gagging out loud. Most of the time she was grateful for the day nine years earlier when she'd found the dying baby gyrfalcon and sent her magic into the bird to heal her. But sometimes the telepathic link that had formed between them as a result gave Lorelai far too much information about the inner workings of her bird's mind.

Strange human. Delicious mouse. Sasha spread her wings and glided to the barn floor, where she tore into her prize with relish.

"My performance was impeccable." Leo looked smug as he wiped dust from his curly black hair.

"I don't know how you do it," Lorelai said as Gabril finished inspecting the bags and then limped over to a sizable crack in the barn's wall to peer outside. "You've never even been to Morcant. You overheard one conversation three years ago, and you sound like you were born there. I couldn't do that if you aimed an arrow at my heart."

Leo grinned. "That's because you're good at magic, and I'm good at everything else."

Gabril turned from the door. "Enough talking. Lorelai needs to practice while there's still light left to see. Leo, take the sacks up to the loft. My contact in the village will collect them and distribute the food to those in need."

Leo looked aggrieved. "I'm always the one who has to do the heavy lifting."

Lorelai's smile was smug. "That's because I'm good at magic, and you're good at everything else."

"That was cruel, Lorelai." Leo sighed dramatically and hefted the first sack. Gabril fetched a bundled-up blanket from the corner of the barn and laid it on the floor. When he opened it, several items lay beneath the dim light filtering in through the cracks in the walls. There was a length of rope, a tinderbox, and a brilliant green jewel half the size of Lorelai's palm.

Lorelai's stomach clenched, and the air felt too thick to breathe as she slowly crouched beside the blanket and pulled off her gloves. The fabric stuck to her suddenly clammy skin.

It wasn't enough to rob treasury wagons and build loyalty among the peasants. It wasn't enough to escalate the robberies and gradually move farther south—closer and closer to Konigstaadt, the capital of Ravenspire—to widen her base of support while she weakened the queen's.

Confronting the most powerful *mardushka* to come out of Morcant in a century required a careful, step-by-step plan. Nine years ago, Lorelai had challenged the queen, and her father had paid the price because Lorelai hadn't thought through every possible way her plan could go wrong.

She wasn't going to make that mistake again.

"I bartered for these from an Eldrian refugee. None of them have touched Ravenspire soil," Gabril said.

Lorelai nodded and thanked the heavens that her voice didn't shake as she said, "So there's no chance the magic Irina is using to drain the land tainted these, and no chance that if I touch them, Irina's magic will recognize mine and tell her that I'm still alive."

"And exactly where to find us," Leo said in his I'm-being-helpful voice from the loft above. "Don't forget about that."

"I haven't forgotten," she said. The knowledge that if she touched something that was bespelled by Irina—which could be anything in Ravenspire considering how much magic Irina used to keep herself on the throne—the queen would come for them was the silent fear that crouched in the corner of her mind and kept her thinking, planning, and thinking some more every hour of the day.

The only way she could become stronger was to practice her magic whenever Gabril found items that couldn't possibly have been touched by the queen's magic, which threaded its way deep throughout the kingdom. Magic that was sucking the heart of the land dry, withering crops and destroying livestock as it forced the living heart of everything it touched to submit to the will of Ravenspire's queen.

"You don't have to do this," Gabril said softly as Lorelai hesitated, her hand hovering over the three objects on the blanket. "You've already had a long day. If you want to practice tomorrow night instead—"

"I'll practice now." Her voice shook a little.

"You know how to do this," he said. "Use the incantor that works best for what you want to do. Let your power do the work for you. You're as strong willed as they come. You can subdue the heart of any living thing, or any object made from a living thing. You don't have to fear what you are, Lorelai. Being a *mardushka* isn't a choice. It's how you use your power that matters."

She let him think she was afraid of her magic. Of being a *mardushka* in Ravenspire, where outside of Irina and the princess, practitioners of magic didn't exist. Where magic wasn't passed through bloodlines as it was in Lorelai's mother's kingdom of

Morcant, but was feared, and the rare *mardushka* who left her home country and traveled south into Ravenspire was cursed by peasants and nobility alike.

Letting him believe she feared her own power was better than admitting that she could still remember the warmth of Irina's arm beneath her hand and the shape of her lips as she spoke the incantor to undo all Irina's spells. Still hear the screams and smell the blood as the castle itself turned against everyone but the queen.

Still feel the weight of Leo's hand in hers as her father spent his last words telling her to protect her brother.

If she wasn't stronger than Irina, she wouldn't be able to protect Leo. She wouldn't be able to save her kingdom.

She'd fail.

Swiftly she picked up the green jewel. Its jagged edges gleamed in the dull light, and its weight was a solid presence. Her jaw clenched until it ached, and her power responded to the determination in her heart.

Magic rushed through her veins and gathered in her palms, sparking and burning and begging for release. The heart of the jewel surged to meet her power and put up no resistance to her will.

"*Rast`lozh!* Become the image that is in my mind." Her magic flooded the emerald. She threw it into the air, and it exploded into a hundred razor-sharp needles that hovered, all pointed toward the barn's door, waiting for a threat that wasn't going to appear.

"You called your magic much faster this time," Gabril said, approval warming his eyes.

"I thought of Irina." Or more precisely, how badly she wanted Irina to pay for killing their father and stealing their kingdom.

"Any residual weariness?" he asked.

"Plenty. Thanks for asking." Leo widened his eyes at the look Gabril gave him, then hefted another sack and started back up the ladder.

Lorelai slowly lowered her hand. The needles rushed together and fused into the stone again. "Not really. Jewels don't put up much resistance to magic. They like to change form. Now, if you really want me to test the limits of my magic and how much it will drain me to forcibly subdue something, you should let me heal your leg."

"Not a chance," Gabril said as he pressed his fist against his left leg. He'd broken it the night he'd rescued the two of them and hadn't taken the time to have a doctor properly set it because his priority had been putting as much distance as possible between the children and the queen. Lorelai's determination to heal him and his determination to refuse her formed the backbone of an argument that had worn a groove through their relationship for the past nine years.

"Gabril—"

"I spent months bespelled to follow Irina's every whim. I don't know how long residual magic lingers on someone Irina has touched, but we aren't risking it. If you use magic to heal me, and any of Irina's magic remains, she'll learn that you're alive before you're ready to challenge her for the throne, and she'll hunt you relentlessly." His tone warned her not to argue. "We aren't risking that for an old man's leg."

Lorelai locked gazes with him, magic burning in her palms.

"Now that we have that settled, who wants to help me with the last of these sacks before it's so dark that I misjudge the ladder and fall to my untimely death?" Leo asked.

Gabril leaned forward and brushed his hand over Lorelai's long, black hair. "I'm fine. My leg hardly bothers me."

"You're a terrible liar."

His smile was gentle. "So are you." He lowered his voice as Leo took the last sack up the ladder. "You're as strong as Irina, Lorelai. As a child of eight with only a few months of training, you were strong enough to undo the spells of a full-fledged *mardushka*. You've only grown stronger since."

"But I could miss something. I could make a mistake." Her heart thudded painfully as she forced herself to say, "I could lose, and then there will be no one left to protect Ravenspire."

To protect Leo.

"Is that why the plan you put into place this past summer is supposed to take eighteen months before you're finally ready to face the queen?"

"Eighteen months is forever," Leo said as he hopped off the ladder and walked toward them. "We could just head to the capital now and yell, 'Surprise, you slimy coward! We're not dead, but you're about to be!' and then you can turn her into a pile of fungus."

"And what if I can't?" Her words hung in the air, punctuated by Sasha cracking open the mouse's bones and pecking at the marrow.

Leo crouched beside her and met her gaze. His brown eyes, so like hers, were serious for once. "You can. You never let anything stop you."

"I just have to be sure of every contingency." She placed the jewel back on the blanket and reached for her gloves with trembling fingers. "I have to be sure I can succeed."

"You don't go into battle because you're sure of victory," Gabril said. "You go into battle because it's the right thing to do. Now get some sleep. We leave at dawn."

TWO

EARLY THE NEXT morning, they headed east toward the small village of Tranke. The town was built along the road that led east over the Falkrains and into the neighboring kingdom of Eldr. With an ogre war raging across Eldr, rumor had it that Eldrian refugees with pockets full of jewels were moving through Tranke, desperate to trade for food and drink. Gabril was hoping they might have other items to trade as well—items Lorelai could use to practice her magic.

The three of them walked in silence. Clouds scudded across the gray sky, and the crisp, wet bite of an impending snowstorm chased a shiver down her spine as they climbed the same road the treasury wagon had followed the day before. Sasha flew in lazy spirals overhead, her white wings blending in against the clouds.

Want food? Sasha sent an image of a small rodent scurrying along the underbrush.

I don't even know what that is.

All tastes the same.

Not to me.

Eat raw. Tastes the same. Try? Sasha dipped her wing and circled her prey.

I can't eat raw animals. Lorelai shuddered. *And stop sending me images of spleens and bones and other things I don't want to put into my mouth.*

Can give you some for brother. Sasha's amusement drifted into Lorelai's mind like a cold breeze.

Lorelai smirked at Leo, who raised a brow and then glared up at the sky. "The two of you are conspiring against me again, aren't you?"

"She just wants to share her lunch with you."

Leo blanched. "Last time she shared, I got a face full of rabbit guts from above. You tell your bird to keep her victims to herself."

He doesn't want any. Is the road ahead clear of soldiers?

No soldiers. Safe. Sasha dove for the ground and something shrieked as she found her prey.

Safe. Lorelai frowned as she walked past thick oaks whose trunks had large patches of rot clinging to them. Soldiers weren't the true danger in Ravenspire. If Irina didn't stop draining the land with the demands of her magic, there wouldn't be anything left of Lorelai's kingdom when she was ready to challenge the queen for the throne.

Ignoring Sasha's thoughts about her meal and Leo's attempts to come up with a name for their daring escapades, Lorelai mentally picked up each piece of her plan and examined it for weakness.

Step one: Rob the treasury wagons. Six robberies already accomplished without mishap.

Step two: Find a safe contact in each village who could distribute the goods to those in need. Gabril had taken care of that to mitigate the risk that someone untrustworthy might see the resemblance between Lorelai and the late king and curry favor with the queen by reporting it.

Step three: Let the rumors of the robberies become attached to the idea of the princess returning to claim her throne so that she could build a base of loyalty. She hadn't actually figured out how to do that yet.

She hadn't, but Leo had. She glanced at him and sighed. She was never going to hear the end of this.

"You're right, Leo," she said. Gabril and Leo turned to look at her as the road dipped between a stand of pines whose needles were turning brown and a meadow of brittle grass.

"Of course I am." He paused. "About what?"

"We need a name. Something that can give the villagers someone to be loyal to."

Leo's eyes lit up. "That's what I've been telling you. And I overlooked Gabril's involvement—my apologies—which opens up an entirely new list of possibilities. The Fearsome Threesome."

"Not quite," Lorelai said.

"The Triumphant Trio."

"No." Gabril turned on his heel and kept walking.

"We could always return to the Royal Rogues. No number specified."

"No," Gabril and Lorelai said together.

Leo huffed out a breath. "You two display such a staggering lack of imagination, it's a wonder I survive."

"We'll have to put some more thought into it," Lorelai said.

"Meanwhile, the two of you haven't been practicing courtly conversation like I asked." Gabril's voice was stern. "You can't interact with our nobility or that of Ravenspire's allies if you forget your etiquette."

"I never forget my etiquette." Leo looked wounded.

"You aren't the sibling I'm concerned about." Gabril gave Lorelai a meaningful look, and she huffed impatiently.

"Courtly conversation is tedious. I have better things to do."

"Better things than convincing our nobility that you can lead a kingdom, maintain its allies, secure new ones, and interact with royalty without bringing shame upon the kingdom of Ravenspire?"

"I was kind of hoping vanquishing Irina would take care of all that."

Leo grinned. "I could be your mouthpiece. Think of it! You'd be the mysterious *mardushka* who never speaks, and I'd be the voice of Ravenspire issuing orders, correcting fashion disasters—'Did you *see* what Lord Horst was wearing last time we were in his village? Ghastly.'—and assuring one and all that my sister can smite them where they stand if they don't obey."

Gabril raised a brow at Lorelai.

"Okay, fine. I'll practice courtly conversation."

She turned toward Leo, who gave her a cheeky grin. "You are looking most fetching this morning. Though I only have Gabril for comparison, so take that as you will."

Lorelai snorted. "Fetching? What kind of stupid compliment is that?"

"I'm pretty sure snorting is beneath royalty." Leo sounded smug.

"Fine. You also look most *fetching*. So fetching, in fact, that I might allow Sasha to share her meal with you after all." Lorelai laughed as Leo glanced uneasily at the sky.

"When I said courtly conversation, I meant it." Gabril swept a rotted branch from the road, sending it skittering into the ditch. "Enough foolishness."

"Pretend I'm a visiting ambassador from Akram," Leo suggested.

"Why do *you* get to be the visiting ambassador?"

"Because I thought of it first."

Lorelai glared. "Next time I get to be the visiting ambassador, and you have to come up with stupid conversation to pass the time."

"I had no idea Ravenspire princesses were so uncouth," he said in a near-perfect imitation of an Akram accent—long vowels, choppy consonants, and a mesmerizing singsong cadence that Lorelai found impossible to mimic.

Her answering smile bared all her teeth. "I hope your journey wasn't too arduous, my lord, and that you are in good health. When you have refreshed yourself with sleep, I would love to give you my undivided attention so that we may discuss various issues of interest to both our kingdoms."

"Better," Gabril said. "Now practice how to negotiate with brokers from Balavata. After that, we'll deal with the customs of Llorenyae."

Hours later, after practicing how to speak with the royalty, merchants, and nobility of all Ravenspire's allies, even Leo was tired of talking. They'd trekked through pastures full of yellow, dying grass and flocks of sheep too thin to face a winter, past forests full of crumbling tree trunks and soil that was losing its color, and past cottages that appeared to be abandoned. It seemed the only part of Ravenspire that wasn't dying as a result of Irina's magic were the rivers. They were coming up on another cottage without smoke curling from its chimney when Gabril suggested they stop for lunch.

Leo pulled out the last of their oat bread. Lorelai took a canteen from her pack and began moving toward the cottage, searching for its well. She was walking past a line of brittle rosebushes that edged the south side of the cottage when a thin, high-pitched scream pierced the air, raising the hair on the back of Lorelai's neck and sending a jolt of magic burning down her veins. The scream was coming from the backyard.

Lorelai dropped the canteen and ran, her palms stinging with magic. Skidding around the corner, she saw three small children, bellies distended with hunger, lying motionless on the frigid ground behind the cottage. A woman with sunken cheeks and desperate eyes was standing over a fourth child, holding a bloodstained knife in her hand.

Lorelai's heartbeat thundered in her ears as icy fingers of panic closed around her chest.

"Stop!" Lorelai shouted, but it was too late. The woman, her arms trembling, her face white with strain, plunged the knife into the fourth child's chest. The little girl slumped to the ground while the woman stood holding the knife with shaking fingers.

Lorelai raced over the grass and threw herself to her knees beside the child. The girl's blue eyes seemed to beg Lorelai for something, and her mouth moved as if she was trying to speak.

"It's all right." Lorelai's voice trembled as she pressed her gloved hands to the wound that was pouring blood out of the girl's chest with alarming speed. Her words were a lie—already the girl's heartbeat faltered, and her body shuddered with the effort it took to stay alive.

Leo raced past her to the other children who lay silent and still, blood soaking into the ground beneath them.

"They're dead." Leo's voice was a whiplash of anger as he looked up at the woman.

"I had to." The woman's lips were cracked and pale against her haggard face, and her bones stood out in sharp relief. Tears slipped down her cheeks, and she gripped the knife tightly. "My babies . . . my poor babies."

Beneath Lorelai's hands, the little girl's chest went still, and her blue eyes became dull and lifeless. Lorelai whispered, "She's gone."

Her throat closed over the words, and she had to swallow past the sudden ache of tears. She climbed to her feet, her gloves still covered in the child's blood. "How could you do this?" Her voice trembled with horror as magic gathered in her palms like lightning. She wanted to rip off her bloodstained gloves and speak an incantor that would punish the woman. That would hurt her the way she'd hurt her children. It would be justice.

No one else will give you what you want, Lorelai. You have to take it for yourself. You have the power. Use it.

Shuddering at the memory of Irina's words, Lorelai tugged her gloves toward her wrists.

The woman shook as she looked down at her children lying silently in the brittle grass. Her voice was hollow as she said, "I had nothing left to feed them. My husband died weeks ago—starved to death so that our food would last a little longer." She sank slowly to her knees. "It was an awful way to die. Slow and lingering."

She reached a hand out to smooth the tangled blond curls out of her baby's face. Sobs tore at her, and she curled over the baby's body. "I had to. I couldn't watch you suffer. I had to."

She repeated the words over and over while Leo stumbled away from her, his face pale and stricken. Gabril wrapped his arms around the prince, but his gaze was on the woman.

"How can we help you?" he asked, but the woman didn't hear him. She was crawling from child to child, repeating her chant, smoothing their hair and kissing their faces.

When she reached the oldest girl, Lorelai crouched beside her. Keeping her bloodstained gloves behind her back, she said softly, "I'm sorry. Will you let us help you?"

The woman looked at Lorelai as if suddenly remembering that she wasn't alone with her children and said, "There is no help left in Ravenspire. Not for the likes of us."

Lorelai opened her mouth to reply, but if words existed that would ease the mother's pain and offer hope, Lorelai couldn't find them.

How many of their people were facing the terrible choice between watching their children starve to death or killing them quickly as an act of mercy? The twelve bags of food she'd taken from the treasury wagon yesterday weren't enough for a need this big. They were a bandage on a wound that needed a tourniquet.

The woman made an awful, keening noise and then turned the weapon toward her own chest. Sun glinted sharply against the blade as it plunged toward the woman's heart. Lorelai lunged for her, but she was too late. With a soft groan, the woman slumped over the body of her daughter. Lorelai snatched her shoulders and pulled at the weapon as if she could somehow save her, but the woman had buried the knife deep beneath her sternum, and blood was a river that poured into the parched soil beneath her. It wasn't long until the desperate pain on the woman's face eased into stillness.

Lorelai's eyes stung, and her throat closed on the rusty-sweet smell of blood in the air. Wiping her gloves clean on a tuft of grass, she gently closed the woman's eyes and prayed that in death, she'd found the peace she couldn't find in Ravenspire.

Leo and Gabril joined her as she closed the children's eyes, tears streaming down her face. When she reached the baby, she sank to her knees and pressed her gloved hands to the dying ground. Leo knelt beside her and wrapped an arm around her shoulders while Gabril stood behind them, a hand on each of their shoulders.

"We have to do more." Lorelai's voice broke, and she looked at Leo. "We have to help them. We can't wait another eighteen months like I'd planned, or there will be no one left to rule even if I do take the throne. We have to do something *now*."

Leo's eyes burned with determination as he nodded.

"They need food. They need *hope*. We have to do something that makes a statement—something that will grow beyond rumors and into the kind of story that becomes a legend. Something that will give people like this mother a reason to turn away from . . ."

"From this," Leo finished for her. "I'm with you."

Gabril's hands tightened on her shoulder. "As am I."

"What's the plan?" Leo asked quietly.

The knowledge that she would have to face Irina earlier than she'd anticipated was a stone in Lorelai's stomach as she lifted her gaze from the baby's silent body, over the field of dying grass, past the dusty cobblestoned road, and looked east toward the carpet of evergreens that covered the mountain and the treasure they hid from her view.

"We're going to rob the queen's garrison."

THREE

Kolvanismir Arsenyevnek, second born prince in the kingdom of Eldr and recent expellee from Eiler's Military Academy (for what would surely go down in the record books as the single greatest prank to ever have been pulled by a senior cadet) was trying to have the time of his life.

"More mead!" he roared over the deafening noise of a party that had been in full swing in an unused storeroom within the castle's basement for over an hour.

Servants scurried to the far corner of the room, where an ever-shrinking stack of barrels waited for their turn to be emptied into the mugs of Kol's friends, acquaintances, and—he squinted in the flickering light of the torchlit chandelier, his stomach sinking—his younger sister.

His parents were already going to be furious that he'd been expelled (for the third time, though the first was for such a minor infraction, Kol figured it hardly counted) and that he'd chosen to celebrate this accomplishment by depleting the castle's supply of spiced mead. If he added "got his little sister drunk" to the long list of things-Kol-does-that-disappoint, he'd probably be sent to the front lines of the ogre war before he could get the words "I'm sorry" out of his mouth.

As he moved across the dusty storeroom floor, dodging raised mugs and bodies writhing in time to the thunderous beat of the drummers Kol had hired with the last of his monthly stipend, two of his best friends flanked him. Raum was still dressed in his cadet's uniform, bronze epaulets and all, but Mik had changed into a dress with dainty flowers and enough ribbons to make the royal seamstress jealous.

"Is that Brig?" Mik pointed toward the short girl with auburn hair who had her back turned to them. "Kol, I think that's Brig."

"I know." Kol muscled his way past a fellow senior and quickened his pace as Brig held out her mug to a passing servant.

"When your parents get back, they are going to kill you for this," Raum said.

"I *know*."

Kol reached Brig just as she was raising her mug to her lips. Snatching it from her hands, he said, "I'll take that."

His sister glared, her golden eyes a match for his. "Give it back, Kol."

He held it high above his head as she grabbed for it. She settled for smacking his shoulder instead.

"That's mine."

He started to laugh, but quickly swallowed it at the look of hurt that flashed across her face. "It's yours when you turn seventeen, Brigynaske, and not a single day before."

"I'm nearly seventeen."

He raised a brow while beside him, Mik crossed her arms over her chest, and Raum began tapping his boots against the floor. "You're fourteen."

"Close enough." Brig's tone was full of bravado and longing.

Kol remembered when he'd first sneaked into one of their brother's parties, hoping to pass as far more grown-up than he was. He'd learned two things that day. One, feeling grown-up enough to guzzle mead in a dark corner until one's older brother caught you wasn't the same as being grown-up enough to keep the mead down for any respectable length of time. Kol still shuddered when he remembered that particular bout of sickness. And two, Ragvanisnar truly did throw the most boring parties in the entire world. Who else would include a chess tournament and a dramatic reading of *Finlerbenske the Great* but forget to hire a band or invite any girls?

Brig reached for the mug again, and Mik deftly snatched it from Kol's hand and disappeared into the crowd. Before Brig's pout could finish forming, Kol looped his arm around her shoulder and steered her toward the storeroom door.

"You know the law, Brig. No mead until you come of age. No parties where I have to constantly watch to make sure you aren't sneaking some behind my back, either." He squeezed her close to take the sting out of his words. "Besides, I'm going to be in enough trouble as it is. Do you really want to be the final torch in my funeral pyre?"

She sighed heavily but didn't resist as he reached for the doorknob. "I just wanted to try it."

"You have your aerial defense exam tomorrow, right?"

She shrugged.

"I'll let you in on a secret. We Draconi might be able to shift into our dragons while hungover, but flying in a straight line is torture, and Master Eiler is going to ask much more of you than a simple straight-line flight. You can't pass your exam if you drink tonight."

"And *you* can't pass your final cadet exams when you've been expelled." She smirked at him.

He doubled over, clutching his chest. "You wound me, Brig."

She rolled her eyes. "Wait until Father hears about this. He was only able to get you reinstated the last two times because he and Master Eiler are friends."

"Because, sky forbid, we have a prince in the family who doesn't graduate from Eiler's." He deepened his voice to mimic his father's. "With honors. With honors *upon* honors."

Brig's face softened, and she wrapped a hand around his. "You could graduate with honors. You're smarter than everyone else in your class."

"I beg to disagree." Raum sounded offended.

Kol smiled, though it felt stretched too tight as Brig's words found their mark and burrowed deep. Leaning close, he said, "Why show them what they've never bothered to see?"

Before she could answer, he straightened and said sternly. "Now, off to your rooms where you will study for your exam or paint your talons or do whatever it is fourteen-year-old Eldrian princesses do when they aren't busy trying to sneak some of their brother's mead."

"Fine." She gave him one last glare, though there wasn't much heat behind it. "But I'm only going because you're already in enough trouble and I feel sorry for you."

He opened the door with a flourish, though her pity scraped at something he didn't want to acknowledge. How was it possible that his fourteen-year-old sister could see him so clearly while his own father never saw him at all?

As Brig disappeared down the hall, Kol wiped his expression clean and turned back to the party. He grabbed the closest mug, drained it, and shouted, "More music! More dancing! More mead!"

He had five hours before his parents returned from giving Rag a tour of the war front and called him to task for his actions.

He had no intention of showing up for that conversation sober.

The band played their last song at dawn. Most of the senior cadets had long since left for the dorms located on the spacious academy grounds just west of the castle's bulky stone exterior. Of Kol's closest friends, only Jyn and Trugg remained.

Determined to make the most of what would likely be his last hour of freedom, Kol turned toward his friends, executed a proper bow, and held out his hand to Jyn.

"May I have this dance?"

"Skies above, I thought you'd never ask." Trugg thrust his meaty palm into Kol's and slammed his shoulder into the prince in what had to be the worst attempt at a pirouette Kol had ever seen.

"Not you, you ugly lizard." Kol shook his hand free and laughed. "Her."

Trugg grinned. "I'm a better dancer."

"Your dancing could take out an entire row of innocent Eldrian maidens in one fell swoop." Jyn elbowed her way past

Trugg, swatting at him when he pulled on her short dark hair.

"Ah yes, but then I'd have impressed an entire row of innocent maidens, and Kol here would have impressed only the one." Trugg wiggled his brows at Kol.

"If your goal is to impress girls, save your moves for the sky, where you truly shine," Kol said as he took Jyn's hand in his and spun her into his arms.

"I am a beast in the sky, aren't I?" Trugg clapped his friends on their backs, sending Jyn into Kol's chest, and then wandered over to peruse the sad remains of the mead barrels.

The song was a blend of pounding drums and wailing violins, but Kol couldn't find the energy to keep up the pace. Not with the weight of his impending confrontation with Father sitting like a rock on his chest. Instead, he closed his eyes, held Jyn loosely, and swayed while his thoughts circled the situation.

Mother would frown, more because Kol had once again fallen short of what was expected of a prince of Eldr than because he'd been expelled, but later he'd make her laugh as he recounted the story of sealing Master Eiler in his toilet closet.

Rag would look silently superior, and Kol would be honor bound to punch him for it later.

And Father . . . Father wasn't likely to ask Master Eiler to reinstate Kol this time. Not when the chance to redeem himself and graduate with honors was no longer a possibility. No, Kol would be sent to the war front to learn responsibility or die trying. Father had threatened as much before, but Mother had intervened.

Kol was certain no intervention in the sky above could sway Father this time. He should be afraid of what was coming. He should be making plans to plead his case. Instead, there was relief—a sort of shaky calm at the thought of finally facing the threat that had hung over Kol like a blade for the past two years.

Behind him, the storeroom door flew open with a bang. Kol turned, his stomach rising up to meet the weight on his chest, his shaky calm evaporating, and met the gaze of a harried-looking castle page.

"The presence of His Royal Majesty Prince Kolvanismir is requested in the throne room."

He followed the page into the long stone hallway that bisected the castle's basement, his twin hearts pounding miserably in his chest.

What would Father say if Kol admitted he'd pulled the prank—the epic, legendary, worthy-of-record-books prank—because every other honor in the school had already been earned three years ago by Rag?

His boots scraped the steps as he ascended the stairs and entered the hall that led to the throne room. The long stretch of bronze stone, cooled by the breeze that entered through the open balconies lining the hall, overlooked the spacious castle grounds.

When the enormous throne room doors with their carved runes and golden handles loomed before him, Kol's spine snapped into the ridiculously rigid posture Master Eiler demanded of his cadets. The doors began to open, and suddenly the headmaster himself was there, stepping past the page and wrapping an arm around Kol's stiff shoulders. Kol jerked back, but the words he wanted to snap at the headmaster for interfering with the meeting Kol was about to have died when he looked into Master Eiler's face.

"Come with me," the headmaster said softly as he turned the prince away from the doors. A maid stumbled out of the room, her hands pressed to her mouth, and ran down the hall.

Kol's blood felt too thick for his veins, and his knees began to shake.

"What's going on?" Kol pulled away from the headmaster, his palms slick with sweat, his dragon heart kicking louder than his human heart as if it sensed a threat Kol had yet to identify.

Master Eiler's green eyes were puffy, his face pale. "You don't need to go in there."

"Why not? Father already convinced you to reinstate me?" Kol's voice was too loud, his breathing too hard as the dragon fire in his chest rumbled. More staff exited the throne room, their faces stricken.

The headmaster's voice held a wealth of grief. "I'm so sorry to have to tell you this, but ogres attacked the reserve unit while your family was asleep in their tent. Your father is dead."

Kol's ears thundered with the beat of his dragon heart, and it was difficult to breathe. "That's not . . . It can't be."

"I'm sorry." The headmaster's tone left no room for doubt. Kol's legs suddenly felt too weak to hold him.

"Where is my mother? She'll need me with her." Kol craned his neck, looking toward the throne room. "She'll need Rag, Brig, and me."

"Kol." Master Eiler sounded old for the first time in all the years Kol had known him. His rigid military posture sagged, and he leaned heavily against the balcony's railing. "They were all killed. Your father, your mother, and Prince Ragvanisnar . . . they're gone."

"No." Kol took a shaky step away from the headmaster. "There's been a mistake."

"I'm afraid not. I just saw their bodies." The headmaster

glanced at the throne room, and then whipped a hand out to stop Kol as he stumbled forward like he meant to see for himself. "You don't want to see them like that, my king."

King.

Kol shook his head, a violent denial that did nothing to soften the headmaster's next words.

"You are the king of Eldr now, Kol. I'm sorry."

Master Eiler said something else, but Kol couldn't hear him over the thudding of his dragon heart. The rush of scorching fire in his veins was a scream of agony. He couldn't stay here, trapped on the balcony, waiting for the grief to swallow him in front of the headmaster and the steadily growing crowd of servants and guards behind him. His skin rippled, an itch that started in his scalp and sped toward his toes, and the heat in his chest spilled out of his nostrils in a stream of ash-gray smoke.

Without bothering to shed his clothing first, Kol gave in to the pounding of his hearts and let his dragon take him. His bones flexed and shifted, his muscles expanding. The familiar pain was a welcome outlet for the awful grief that tore at him from the inside out. He shook his head and heard the ridges along his spine clattering into place as his skin hardened into the red-gold scales of his dragon.

He thought he heard someone cry out his name, but he was done with listening. His talons dug into the stone balcony beneath him as he roared, emptying his grief and horror into the skies above. Then he unfurled his golden wings with a snap and soared into the air, leaving the castle far behind him.

FOUR

KOL STOOD BESIDE Brig on the shore of Lake Skyllivreng, facing the vast expanse of water that stretched from the base of the
Urrvenskeyr Mountain far into the distant forests to the north.
Before him, floating on the water, were the funeral pyres of his
father, his mother, and his brother. Their bodies were wrapped
in gold silk and tied with a blue cord to symbolize the Sun
Mother and the Sky Father. Bronze chests filled with treasure
were placed at their heads while gold chests filled with mementos
from their former lives were at their feet—one guaranteed their
entrance into the afterlife, and the other helped them remember
the ones they'd left behind.

Kol didn't want to be left behind. He didn't want to be on
this shore, his arm around his sobbing sister, the entire kingdom
at his back waiting for him to say good-bye and take up the
responsibility for saving a kingdom no one truly believed could
be saved.

His twin hearts beat hard against his chest as Master Eiler

stepped to his side and held out a lit torch.

Brig shuddered, burying her face against him, and he leaned his cheek against the top of her head for a moment. It was the only comfort he could offer. He was a seventeen-year-old failure of a prince with the weight of an entire kingdom on his shoulders. He had no idea what to say or do that would give anyone—himself included—confidence that he could lead his nation to anything other than its final destruction.

Looking up, he met his former headmaster's gaze, expecting to see pity. Instead, he saw the same rigid expectations he'd always seen. That Kol would be the cadet—the Eldrian—Master Eiler had trained him to be.

Once upon a time, those expectations had felt like a noose around Kol's neck. Today, they were a road map for a journey Kol had never thought he'd have to take.

He straightened his spine and gave Brig one last squeeze. Stepping forward, he took the lit torch from Master Eiler with a steady hand and waded into the frigid water.

"From the Sky Father, life was granted." His breath hitched, and he cleared his throat. Raised his voice. Tried his best to do justice to the funeral chant. To his family. "And to the Sky Father, life returns. We thank him for your journey here."

His voice broke, and he blinked his eyes rapidly before continuing. "And we send you on your next journey with honor, with respect, and with love."

His choked on the last word, and he had to work just to breathe as the crowd behind him repeated, "With honor, with respect, and with love."

When their voices faded, Kol moved to his brother's pyre.

His chest ached sharply as he thrust the torch into the straw that cushioned his brother's body. The fire caught and ate greedily at the tinder.

Moving to his mother's pyre, Kol laid his hand on her raft and tried to speak. He wanted to tell her that nothing would be the same without her. The words wouldn't come. Instead, he simply whispered, "I love you best, and I'll miss you forever," as he lit her straw and turned away.

Firelight from his mother's pyre glinted against his father's golden shroud as Kol laid his palm against the wooden planks and took a deep breath. "I know I disappointed you." The words left a bitter taste in Kol's mouth. "And we never understood each other. But now I have the weight of Eldr on my shoulders, and I don't know how you did it all those years. All I can do is promise you that I will do my best. I won't disappoint you again."

His father's straw caught fire, and then members of the royal council were there beside him, pushing the pyres out into the lake until the current caught the rafts and sent them on their slow, stately journey toward the afterlife.

Master Eiler waded into the water. "The sun will be setting soon. It's time for the coronation. Eldr must see that they still have a king."

Kol nodded. It was the best he could manage. He was about to become king of a nation on her deathbed. Defending his people from the ogre invasion was now his problem and his alone. He faced the castle and clenched his fists. He would figure out how to lead his people. How to protect them. He would become the kind of ruler he could be proud of, or he would die trying.

◆ ◆ ◆

Two hours after he'd been crowned king and had met with the royal council to discuss the ogre war, Kol was ready to leave for the war front to assess the situation himself. All that remained was to tell Brig good-bye.

She stood in the middle of his room, watching him with tear-filled eyes. Kol crossed the distance between them and pulled her into his arms. "It's time."

"Please, Kol. I've already lost everyone else. Don't go."

He swallowed the sharp edge of grief that ached in his throat and said, "Brig, I'm the king now. The war is my responsibility. How can I figure out how to beat the ogres if I've never seen what they're capable of doing?"

Her voice rose. "You've seen what they're capable of doing! We lost *everyone* because of them. It doesn't matter if you go to the war front or if you stay here. No one can stop the ogres. Their skin is hard as a rock and immune to our fire, to our catapults—they're three times our size, and no weapon we use against them does anything more than slow them down." She glared at him. "You might *die*."

He had no answer for that, so he simply held her and wished he could turn back time to a week ago before he'd pulled his epic prank on Master Eiler, before his parents had taken Rag on a tour of the war front, before everything became so complicated. So impossible.

"What are we going to do?" Brig's voice was little more than a whisper.

Kol stepped back and lifted her chin so he could look into her eyes. "You are going to stay here and manage the castle for me with Master Eiler and the royal council. I'm going to assess the ogre situation and come up with a solution. And together, we're going to show our people how to face pain and fear with honor and strength."

"You sound like Father," Brig said, a shaky smile flitting across her face.

Kol had to swallow hard against the sudden tightness in his throat. "Who would've guessed I'd ever be capable of that?"

It took nearly a full day for Kol, Trugg, Jyn, and two members of the royal council to reach the war front by flying in their dragon forms. The craggy mountains and lush forests that surrounded Tryllenvreng, the capital of Eldr, slowly gave way to rivers that cut through the rocky hillside like ribbons. Eldrians fleeing the southern half of the kingdom for the safety of the refugee shelters in Tryllenvreng camped along the riverbank in clumps. Kol's human heart ached for them as he flew past. He understood now what it meant to have those you loved ripped away from you.

The land began to bear battle scars as Kol and his friends closed in on the war front. The evidence of a recent fight could be seen in shattered boulders, in trees ripped up at the roots, and in an entire hillside caved in as if an enormous creature had ripped the land to pieces.

Tearing his gaze away from the wreckage, Kol signaled the others to follow him to the highest hilltop in the area. Night was falling, and soon they'd be able to fly over the armies and assess the situation undetected.

Kol alighted on the hilltop, shook out his wings, and folded them back as the others came to rest around him, their talons digging into the rocky soil. Below him, the Eldrian army was positioned with the strongest flyers in the center, archer and catapult support just behind them, and secondary flyers hidden from the approaching army on both the left and right flanks. The third wave of flyers were hidden behind the archer and catapult support to provide either another wave of attack or defensive cover for the forward soldiers in the event of a retreat.

Kol had a feeling all the army had been doing was retreating, giving up Eldr in bits and pieces.

As he studied the army's position, there was a cry of warning, and then a pack of ogres swarmed over the rocky hills to the south. The ogres were immense thick-chested brutes—wide as four large oak trees side by side and double the height of the average Draconi—with no necks, round black eyes, and tough gray skin that matched the rocks they were scaling with incredible speed.

Immediately, the first wave of flyers rose into the air, and the catapults began pelting the incoming ogres with boulders coated in pitch and flame. A few of the ogres went down, crushed beneath the weight of the boulders, but for every creature who fell, another three took its place.

The ogres formed a V and stopped as if waiting for the arrival of the Eldrians. From his vantage point on the hilltop, Kol saw something in the middle of the V begin to glow like a brilliant blue sapphire. He squinted against the glare of the dying sun, and a pit of ice formed in his stomach.

What kind of weapon glowed like that? The ogres in Kol's history books—the ones who'd roamed Eldr and the southern kingdom of Vallé de Lumé in vicious packs centuries ago before a witch sealed them away in a prison deep beneath the southern mountains—had always used brute strength and violence to crush their opponents. Not weapons that glowed. Not formations that spoke of organization and strategy.

He wanted to scream at the flyers to get back, but it was already too late.

The flyers dove at the assembled ogres, fire spewing from their mouths—a cover for the poison-tipped arrows the archers sent just beneath the Draconi. A few of the arrows struck ogres in the eyes, but the rest glanced off the beasts' rock-hard skin and fell harmlessly to the ground.

The flyers banked a perfect turn, preparing for a second assault, when the ogres on the outside of the V dropped to the ground, revealing the creature who stood in the center. It may have once been an ogre but now it was something far worse. Its round black eyes were lit with sapphire flames from within. Its massive bulk was covered with so much knotted muscle, it resembled an enormous gray rock bound by gnarled tree roots. And in its hands was a ball of crackling blue light the size of a small horse.

What kind of monstrosity was this?

Kol's hearts thundered in his chest, and his stomach plummeted as he dug his talons into the unforgiving ground and forced himself to stay hidden. To stay safe because Eldr needed her king, even though her king had no idea how to save her.

The creature stretched to its full height, casting a long shadow over the ogres crouched below it. Kol lashed the ground with his tail, scattered bits of rock and dirt. His army was already struggling to contain the ogre onslaught. How were they supposed to fight a monster like this? How was *he* supposed to fight it? The kingship he'd accepted at last night's coronation ceremony felt too heavy to bear as his flyers banked, preparing to sweep the ogre lines again.

The creature drew its arm back and flung the sizzling blue light directly into the flyers as they completed their turn. It wrapped around the Draconi like chains of lightning and then exploded into a brilliant blue mist. When it dissipated, all that was left of the entire squadron were a few bloody scales that slowly drifted to the ground. Kol felt sick, his dragon's fire burning miserably in his chest.

Magic.

The ogres, released from their mountain prison by the dark enchantress who had ensnared the southern kingdom of Vallé de Lumé the previous winter, had somehow found a way to tap into her power and use it for themselves in their quest to once again dominate the lands they'd been cast out of so many lifetimes ago.

There was nothing Kol could do to stop them. Not without magic of his own. The realization was a blow Kol didn't know how to absorb. Focusing on the grief and desperation in his human heart, Kol released his dragon. His wings receded, his fangs drew back, and as his red-gold scales softened into his human skin again, he turned to find the others had shed their dragons too and were busy pulling clothing out of the travel bags Jyn had volunteered to carry for the group.

Jyn tossed Kol some trousers and a shirt and asked, "How did ogres get the use of magic?" She sounded shaken.

"A better question would be how do we stop them?" the councilwoman asked as she shrugged into a shirt.

"We can't stop them." Kol was grateful his voice didn't reveal the panic that wanted to steal his breath and paralyze his thoughts.

He'd promised to protect Eldr. How was he going to do that when his enemy was unstoppable?

"If we had magic of our own, it would be different," the councilman said.

"You're right." Kol looked at the councilman while his thoughts raced. "The only way to turn the tide of this war is if we have magic of our own capable of defeating the weapon we just saw. And I only know of one kingdom with that kind of magic—"

"You aren't seriously suggesting that we go to Morcant for aid, are you?" Jyn asked, her hands on her hips. "Have you forgotten what those magic wielders—those *mardushkas*—do to Draconi? For centuries, they've captured us with their cursed magic, forcing us to sniff out gems and veins of gold like dogs on leashes. There's a reason we have a law forbidding Eldrians from setting foot on Morcantian soil."

"We aren't going to Morcant for aid." Kol's hearts pounded as a plan just as bold and risky as any of his pranks took shape in his mind. "Negotiations work best when you have enough leverage to come to the table as an equal. Ravenspire is suffering from massive food shortages caused by a blight on their crops. There are reports of tremendous unrest and violence among the peasants."

"That's correct," the councilwoman said.

"Ravenspire's queen doesn't have enough resources to feed her people and stop the unrest. We, however, have an entire mountain full of treasure—enough to buy food from the merchants in Súndraille for the next ten years. We have the solution to her problem, and the queen of Ravenspire—"

"Is a *mardushka* from Morcant and married into her throne," the councilwoman finished, her eyes gleaming.

Kol shouldered his bag. "Let's go back to the castle. Master Eiler and the rest of the royal council need to know what we're up against and what I plan to do about it. I leave for Ravenspire in the morning."

"Why you? Let us go in your place," Trugg said.

Kol shook his head. "Queen Irina doesn't meet with ambassadors. She leaves all that to her castle steward, and I can't afford to be turned down. If I arrive at her castle, she'll have no choice but to receive me." He looked at the council members. "I need the council to keep the country running while I'm gone. Send a courier if there's an emergency, and I need to return. I should be able to cross the mountain border into Ravenspire in two days if I fly hard. After that, I'll be on foot—I don't dare anger Queen Irina by violating the treaty that prohibits Eldrians from using their dragon form within Ravenspire. I'll be easy for a courier to catch. Trugg and Jyn, I know asking you to leave Eldr in her time of need is a sacrifice—"

"We're with you, remember?" Trugg wrapped a hefty arm around the back of Kol's neck and squeezed. "To the sky and back."

"To the sky and back," Jyn repeated.

Kol pushed his grief, his fear that he would fail and all Eldr would pay for it, into the corner of his thoughts and focused on what he would say to the queen of Ravenspire to get her to agree to use her magic to save Eldr from certain destruction.

She was his last hope.

FIVE

LORELAI'S PULSE KICKED hard against her skin, and her breathing quickened as she crouched in an evergreen that bordered the southern wall around the northeast garrison, gripping the branch beneath her with gloved hands. Sasha perched above her, her bright black eyes fixed on the garrison.

It had been two days since Lorelai had seen the desperate mother kill her children to spare them death by starvation. Two days, and the horror was as fresh as the day it had happened.

Today's robbery wouldn't make that right—nothing could—but it was a step in the right direction.

The tree shook as Leo climbed up to join her. His curly black hair was hidden beneath a cap, and he carried their stash of burlap sacks rolled into a pack on his back.

"All set on the plan?" he asked quietly as they watched the garrison's patrol—a pair of guards in full uniform—march inside the western perimeter of the wall.

"Of course I'm all set on the plan. It's *my* plan." It would take the patrol fourteen minutes to complete the circuit around the inside of the wall. Fourteen minutes for Lorelai to get into place and be ready to create a distraction worthy of diverting the attention of every soldier inside the garrison.

"It's a terrible plan," Leo said, his hands clenching and unclenching within his gloves.

"You didn't think so yesterday when you and Gabril were putting your end of it together."

Thirteen minutes. She scanned the garrison for movement. The plan would work if the only soldiers out in the frigid weather were those required to be on patrol. Close to the northern corner of the wall—the spot where Gabril waited, along with the handful of trusted peasants from the surrounding villages who'd been invited to bring a wagon and load it down with supplies for their respective towns—a stocky structure housed the storehouse of food. The kitchens and the dining hall were close by, but the armory was on the southern side of the garrison, and the barracks were to the west. No one should be near the storehouse in the middle of the afternoon.

Lorelai was going to make sure of it.

"It's a terrible plan because you're taking most of the risk." Leo's voice was edged with worry. "If I'm seen carrying food from the storehouse to the wall, I can just scale the wall. By the time the soldiers get out of the gate, we'll have disappeared into the forest."

"I can scale walls too. I'll be fine."

"You can't scale walls if you get caught." He turned to her, and the mischief that usually lit his eyes was replaced by the kind of unrelenting fierceness Lorelai usually saw in Gabril. "If this works, every soldier in the barracks will be after you. If they catch you—"

"If they catch me, I have a weapon they can't take from me. That's why I'm better suited for this distraction than you are."

"No." He glared at her. "No magic. I know I'm always the one pushing you to practice so we can get rid of Irina one day, but you can't do magic here, Lorelai. This place is Irina's down to the last grain of dirt on the ground. She'll have bespelled it so she can keep an eye on her soldiers, or she'll have spies throughout the ranks, or . . . I don't know. *Something.* And if you use magic, she'll know that we're alive, and she'll know exactly where to find us."

"I'm not going to use magic. My weapon is Sasha." She smiled at him. "Remember how you wanted a name for us? Something that would give people hope?"

He gave her a tiny smile in return. "I finally convinced you to call us the Fearsome Threesome, didn't I?"

She snorted. "No. But I've been thinking about what that poor woman said."

"'There is no help left in Ravenspire. Not for the likes of us.'" Leo nodded. "I've been thinking about it too."

"I want people to know that they haven't been forgotten. That their problems matter, and that we are doing something about it." She met his gaze. "I think we should call ourselves the Heirs."

A slow smile spread across Leo's face. "I like it. But you know that if we make a name for ourselves as the Heirs, Irina is eventually going to hear about us and come looking."

Lorelai held her brother's gaze. "We can't hide from her

forever. Not if we're going to save Ravenspire. Now, we have ten minutes before the patrol returns to the western part of the wall. Time to get in position. Don't get caught."

"Don't get caught yourself." He gave her a one-armed hug and then shinnied down the trunk. He ran for the northeast corner of the wall where he'd scale it, rig a simple rope and pulley system with Gabril, and then break into the storehouse so he could start sending bags of food over the wall to the waiting wagons.

Where is the patrol? she asked Sasha, sending an image of the pair of soldiers marching inside the wall.

Sasha spread her wings, lifted herself out of the evergreen, and flew over the garrison. *Corner. Leo.* She sent an image of the soldiers approaching the northeast corner where Leo, Gabril, and their helpers waited.

It was time to send a message—not just to the villagers but to Irina—that there was help in Ravenspire for those who needed it most.

It was time to make the next big move in Lorelai's plan to weaken Irina and take back the throne.

Cover me. Lorelai sent, and then she was moving. Swinging from the branch, she dropped lightly onto the garrison's wall. Her boots, thin-soled and flexible, gripped the narrow lip of stone as she began moving west with quick, light steps. Sasha swooped through the air and flew beside her.

Nine minutes until the soldiers reached the place where the stables huddled just past the long, low-slung wooden buildings that housed the barracks.

Reaching the southwest corner, Lorelai pressed her hands

against the stone, gathered herself, and leaped for the ground. The rocky dirt seemed to rise up to meet her, and she tucked her body, rolling forward upon impact. She was running the second she got her feet beneath her again.

Eight minutes.

Check the barn. She glanced at Sasha as the bird surged ahead and began circling the distant stables.

Clear. Sasha sent. *Ready?*

Almost. Lorelai sprinted across the open space that stretched between the wall and the stables. She had to run past all three barracks to get there. Any moment a soldier could look out of a window and see what looked like a boy in a soot-stained cap and sound the alarm.

She hoped one would.

The barn loomed before her, a solid block of brown wood with white trim. Lifting the iron latch, she pulled the double doors open and went inside. The barracks were still quiet. None of the soldiers had any idea their security had been breached.

Time to change that.

Racing down the row of stalls, she flipped the latches and pulled open the doors. The horses snorted in alarm at her appearance, and a few shied away, but several tentatively left their stalls and looked toward the open door.

"That's right. You want out. Trust me, you aren't going to want to stay here." She used her most coaxing tone of voice, but the horses didn't look convinced, and Lorelai was out of time. Any minute, the patrol would be back, and they needed to see the kind of situation that required the attention of every soldier in the barracks.

Sasha, help. Get the horses out.

Lorelai reached the ladder that led to the hayloft as Sasha flew through the open doors. Her bird swooped through the air, pecking at hindquarters and shrieking as she drove the panicked horses out of the barn, and Lorelai raced up the ladder and into the loft.

Horses clear. Leo?

Yes. Tell Leo he can start.

Sasha flew out of the barn, and Lorelai shoved the loft doors open, letting in a slap of air that still carried a bite from the previous day's late autumn snowstorm. The patrol was approaching the section of the wall that flanked the barracks, but their attention was locked on the horses that milled about the stable yard. With a shout, the two guards broke into a run, heading for the barn.

"That's the least of your worries," Lorelai said as she assessed the stacks of hay that surrounded her. The bales were stacked three high and eight deep. More than enough to burn the whole thing down.

Another shout drifted up to the open loft doors, and Lorelai snatched her tinderbox from her pocket and flicked the lid open. Flint struck the glittering black stone inside the box, and a brilliant white flame leaped to life. Moving quickly, she swept down the line of hay bales, shoving the flame into the dried grass and then racing on when that bale caught fire. Soon, the loft was ablaze, fire greedily chewing through one hay bale and then leaping for the next.

The heat was nearly unbearable. Her skin felt dry and crisp as she hurried to the open loft doors. Flames crawled from the hay and raced up the wall. She grabbed the edges of the opening and peered out.

Soldiers were pouring out of one of the barracks while horses reared and shied away from those who tried to catch them. In the barn beneath Lorelai, someone shouted, and footsteps pounded up the ladder. She looked at the ground to assess her jump and locked eyes with a soldier who stood directly below her.

"Thief!" the woman yelled, pulling her sword and pointing it up toward the princess. Soldiers rushed to her side.

Lorelai's heart thudded against her chest, and magic burned in her palms.

She couldn't stay in the barn surrounded by fire.

She couldn't leap directly to the ground.

She had to improvise.

Sasha, help! she sent, and then she swung her body out of the loft doors, balanced on the edge of the opening, and prayed salvation would hurry up.

A sharp pain seared her neck, and she slapped her gloved hands against her coat as the fire that was consuming the barn wall came for her. Another pain, this time above her ear, had her ripping off her cap and throwing it behind her as flames chewed into it.

Hurry! She scanned the skies, but Sasha was coming from behind the barn, and Lorelai couldn't see anything but the steadily growing sea of soldiers below her, their swords ready to impale her when she fell.

"Surrender in the name of the queen!" the woman who'd first seen Lorelai yelled.

It was either burn to death or leap into the throng of soldiers. Lorelai was out of time. Grabbing the edges of the loft doors, she muttered a prayer and chose a landing spot to the left that appeared to have the smallest concentration of sharp weapons ready to punish her for her treason.

I'm jumping. She sent, and shook with relief when Sasha exploded over the top of the barn and dove for the soldiers.

Protect. Hurt. Kill. Sasha's thoughts vibrated with fury. She screamed her battle cry and swooped below the line of swords. Crashing into the soldiers closest to the barn, the bird tore at them with her beak and talons, sending them staggering back into those behind them.

It was all the opening Lorelai needed. Launching herself into the air, she tucked her knees, aimed for a soldier who'd turned his back to defend himself against Sasha's next attack, and slammed into him.

They went down hard, and Lorelai rolled to the side, narrowly avoiding the wicked slice of someone's sword, and then scrambled to her feet. Soldiers filled the stable yard and more were coming. Lorelai needed to get out while she still had a chance.

Wall, Lorelai screamed as Sasha tore into another line of soldiers, nearly getting impaled by a sword in the process. *Path.*

A full-grown gyrfalcon in hunting mode was a terrifying force to be reckoned with. As big as a buzzard, twice as fast as a cougar, and viciously focused on her prey, Sasha's shrieks batted the air as she dove, tore, and collided with anyone between Lorelai and the wall. Tucking her head, Lorelai raced behind her bird, somersaulting beneath a soldier who lunged for her and then flipping to the side to avoid another's sword.

The wall loomed in front of her. Soldiers were running behind her. Sasha surged upward seconds before a thin black arrow streaked through the sky, just missing the gyrfalcon.

Danger. Flee. Lorelai willed the bird to obey as she approached the wall without slowing. She aimed for the corner, the joint that marked the meeting of north and west.

"Stop in the name of the queen!"

"Kill her!"

"Forget the bird. Shoot the girl!"

The shouts rose behind her as Lorelai gathered herself. Planting her left foot, she launched her right foot toward the wall. The second it touched, she kicked outward, gaining height and leverage. Her left foot hit the wall, and she kicked outward again, forcing herself upward, defying gravity. Using the corner for additional leverage, she reached the top of the wall in four leaps. Slapping her palms onto the edge, she pulled her legs beneath her, touched her toes to the wall, and then leaped for the closest tree.

Sasha landed hard on her shoulder, talons gripping tight, her mind filled with furious worry for Lorelai.

Watch our backs. Lorelai took off running for the northeast corner where Gabril and Leo were finishing the job of emptying the garrison's storehouse. The wagons gathered in the forest were laden with bags of grain, beans, apples, dried vegetables, and spices. Gabril took one look at Lorelai's face as she sprinted around the corner of the wall and barked a command at those around him.

By the time the soldiers secured the horses and opened the garrison's gate to search for her, Lorelai, Leo, and the rest of the robbers—along with over half the food kept in the storehouse—were gone.

SIX

"BRING ME ANOTHER." Irina stood outside the castle's dungeon, a pile of bodies at her feet. "A younger one this time." The dungeon master hurried to comply.

The air was damp and chilly, but the queen was warm beneath the weight of the coat she wore. She ran her hands over the coat's thick gray-white fur and felt the hearts of the wolves who'd given their pelts surge against the magic in her palms.

Magic that still flowed easily through her veins, but that left her drained and weary at the end of every spell. Magic that caused her heart to stutter and her chest to ache with the strain of it.

"Your Highness." The dungeon master stepped out of the doorway, pulling a skinny girl of seventeen or eighteen behind him. Her dirty brown hair brushed the sharp edges of her collarbone, and her eyes were dull. The dungeon master yanked the girl forward until she stood in front of Irina.

The queen grasped the girl's chin and examined her face

under the fading light of the early evening sun. "How old are you?"

"Eighteen."

"And what crime sent you to my dungeon?"

"I was hungry." There was a thread of defiance in the girl's voice, though she wouldn't meet the queen's gaze.

Irina's long, polished red nails dug into the girl's face. "Being hungry isn't a crime. I will only ask you this once more." Her voice was hard. "What was your crime?"

"Stealing food," the girl whispered.

"And whom did you steal from?"

The girl swallowed audibly but didn't answer.

The queen's nails punctured the girl's cheek and tiny crescents of blood bubbled up. "Answer."

The girl's voice shook. "From my lord's kitchen. I was a maid in the Ranulf household."

Irina let go of the girl's face and rubbed a drop of blood between her thumb and forefinger. "Ungrateful peasant. If you steal from my nobility, you steal from me." She leaned close, her mouth a breath from the girl's ear. "Do you know what I do to those who betray the ones to whom they should be loyal?"

The girl's body trembled, and her knees gave out, but the dungeon master held her firm.

A thief. A betrayer. A girl who deserved her fate. And one whose heart might be strong enough to save Irina from her own.

The queen's open palm slammed into the girl's chest, her nails curving over the space that held her heart. "*Ja`dat*," she whispered, and the power burned in her hands. "Take what is hers and give it to me instead."

Irina's palm, wreathed in brilliant light, pressed hard against the girl's chest.

Her heart surged to meet Irina's magic, and the queen could feel the strength of her remaining years stored inside her like an apple ready for the plucking.

Her magic leaped into the girl and surrounded her heart. The girl cried out in agony and resisted, but Irina's will was fierce. Indomitable. Stronger.

Irina was always stronger.

The queen threw her head back as the girl's youth poured out of her. It was a flood of heat and need and restless ambition that abandoned the girl and rushed through Irina's veins instead. The girl's face aged, her hair grayed, and then she collapsed in a heap beside the other bodies.

Irina stood panting, her hand still outstretched, and waited for the band of tension around her chest to dissolve. For the weakness, the ache, to wash away.

The pain still throbbed dully along her sternum. Her pulse still fluttered like a bird trying to break free of its cage.

Nothing had changed.

If anything, the pain was worse—the heat of the girl's youth turning from something that energized into a poison that scalded the queen from the inside out.

The queen stared at the bodies before her—a man with the muscles of a blacksmith, a woman whose fierce attitude was written in every line on her face, a stable boy, a teacher, and the maid. All of them had submitted to Irina's will. All of them had given up their remaining years to the queen's magic.

And yet none of them had strengthened her failing heart.

"Clean up this mess," she snapped at the dungeon master as she turned on her heel and strode back toward the castle.

The spell wasn't the problem, she was certain. She'd had no problem sucking the remaining years out of her father's flintlike heart nine years ago and absorbing their strength and vitality. Doing the same to the criminals in her dungeon should've been an easy solution to her problem, even with the residual weariness that came from forcing another's heart to submit to her will. Instead, she felt weaker and the pain stronger, as if the youth she'd consumed was a slow-moving poison thickening her blood.

Taking the remaining years from the hearts of her prisoners wasn't the answer, but that didn't mean she couldn't find one. She always found one, because she never flinched from doing what needed to be done.

Waving pages, maids, and guards out of her way, Irina entered the east wing of her castle and strode toward her rooms. The plush ivory rug beneath her swallowed her footsteps, and all she could hear was the sudden hiss of candles being lit in the sconces along the walls as twilight fell.

Her personal guards opened the door to her rooms. She walked into her sitting room and turned toward the fireplace where her viper was coiled, his serrated black scales glowing red in the flickering light of the flames.

Come. She pushed the thought at Raz, and the viper uncoiled himself from his bed. Swiftly, he slithered across the gleaming cedar floor. When he reached her feet, she bent down, extending a hand. The viper moved up her arm and settled around her neck, his long black tongue flicking toward her face as if he meant to taste her. She ran a slim finger over his blunt nose, and he pushed his head against her hand.

Ssstill hurt, his rough voice whispered in her mind. *Ssstill weak.*

For now, but the spell will work. I just have to find the right person. The right heart.

And while she searched, she had a kingdom to run, a spate of violent peasant outbreaks to subdue, and an increasingly contentious nobility to bring into line. Moving to her vanity, she looked at the oval mirror hanging above her bottles of perfume. It was the size of a dinner platter with serpents and gilt-dusted brambles surrounding the glass—a gift from Irina's long-dead mother. The most valuable thing she'd left her eldest daughter, unless you counted the magic running through Irina's blood.

Magic that had taught her father and sister the terrible price of betrayal and that had removed every obstacle standing between Irina and the Ravenspire throne.

Unbidden, the thought of the white monolith resting in the center of the castle garden and her sister's body buried beneath it filled Irina's mind. Her heart lurched, tapping against her breastbone like an impatient fist. She pressed one pale hand against her chest and focused on the mirror.

It didn't matter what she'd done to secure the throne that would've been hers all along if her sister hadn't betrayed her. It only mattered that she remained strong enough to keep it.

Raz lifted his head and stared at the mirror with her, his golden eyes unblinking.

She held her spine straight and kept her voice steady as she asked, "Mirror, mirror on the wall, who is the most powerful of them all?"

The mirror's opaque surface swirled into a gray mist and then slowly resolved into Irina's own reflection—pale blond hair, a delicate face, and eyes as blue as the summer sky.

The queen smiled.

SEVEN

It took Kol, Jyn, and Trugg a little over three days to cross the border between Eldr and Ravenspire. They'd flown as fast as possible, stopping only when absolutely necessary. Kol wasn't sure how long it would take to fly to the capital, but he knew that they needed some food and rest before they attempted it. Spotting a little village on the road that wound down the Falkrain Mountains on Ravenspire's side, he signaled his friends to land in a meadow full of yellow, brittle grass just north of the village.

His dragon heart beat fiercely in his chest, but he ignored it and focused on his shift to human form. The spikes that lined his back receded, his muscles and bones shrank slowly into his human form, and his scales softened into skin again. Quickly, he pulled clothes out of his pack and put them on, the grass beneath him crunching with his every move.

"We need a decent meal and a drink," he said.

Trugg's eyes lit up. "A drink! I knew there was a reason I

agreed to follow you to Ravenspire. Do you think they serve spiced mead?"

"You're impossible," Jyn said as she wrapped a leather belt around her waist and pushed her short dark hair behind her ears.

"Look at this." Kol motioned at the ground. Bending close, he ran his fingers over the ground. The soil was pale and crumbled easily beneath his touch as if it was nothing more than air. The grass that clung to it was a sickly yellow that turned brown with rot at the roots. "If it's like this across the kingdom, Irina should be looking for a way to save her people." Kol clenched a fistful of dirt, and it dissolved into a trickle of dust.

"Come on." He wiped his hands clean and stood. "Let's go get a meal and a room so we can sleep in real beds tonight and be rested when we reach the capital."

"Do you think they have a room with three beds? Or will we be sharing?" Trugg raised a brow at Jyn. "I'm good at sharing."

"You get to sleep on the floor." Jyn stepped in front of Kol and began moving toward the village.

Trugg moved to Kol's side. "Somehow my considerable charms never work on her."

Kol and his friends entered the open gate that led into the village and moved down the main road toward the heart of the town. A handful of children playing in the dirt near the gate stared at the Eldrians, their eyes wide, and then took off running toward the village, yelling something about visitors.

"Their welcoming committee is kind of creepy," Trugg said as they passed rows of tiny cottages with thin wisps of smoke curling from their chimneys.

"Maybe they don't see many outsiders here," Kol said, but as they neared the village proper, a din of voices on the road ahead of them sent his dragon heart pounding. They rounded a corner, leaving behind the cottages for the brick and board storefronts that made up Tranke's main street, and a crowd of villagers was waiting for them. The children from the gate were standing off to the side, staring at the Eldrians as the crowd surged toward the visitors.

"Need some cloth?" A woman lunged in front of Jyn and held up a length of pale pink linen. "Make a trade for a jewel."

"I have buckets. And bricks." A man grabbed Kol's sleeve. Trugg growled and slapped the man's hand away. Kol's dragon heart pounded faster, and the fire in his chest burned.

"I can launder your clothes."

"I'll polish your boots."

"My family is hungry. You can spare some food, can't you?"

"I have a sword to trade. Please. A jewel from you might be enough to convince a merchant from Súndraille to take my family out of Ravenspire."

Villagers surrounded them, and more were coming. All of them were calling out, offering services, trying to trade, or simply begging for riches the Eldrians didn't have to give. Kol had brought a few bronze coins and some small jewels, enough to give them a night or two in an inn with a meal when they needed it, but with his army steadily losing ground to the ogres, he hadn't had time to make a formal request for funds from the royal purser. Instead, he'd taken what was left of Brig's monthly stipend and borrowed the rest from his friends.

"We can't help you," Trugg said gruffly as he pried yet another hand off Kol's arm.

"Let us pass or it will go poorly with you, humans," Jyn snarled as a man grabbed her hands and implored her to buy a pair of teacups from his wife.

The man reached for her again, and Trugg shoved himself between the two, his dark eyes glittering with his dragon's fury as he said, "Touch her again, and she'll destroy you. And if she doesn't, I will."

People surrounded them, pressing in from all sides. Above the gathering crowd, Kol spotted a sign that said White Wheel Tavern. Beneath the sign, a girl with curly dark hair and pale skin stood staring at the crowd, her gloved hands fisted in the skirt of her green dress. She met his eyes and jerked her chin toward the tavern. He frowned, and she lifted one hand to beckon sharply. Unlike the wild desperation he saw on the faces around him, she looked calm and focused.

It was trust her or deal with the mob himself without giving in to the violent pounding of his dragon's heart. He made a split-second decision and nodded to her. She whirled and disappeared inside the tavern. A boy with the same pale skin and curly black hair followed in her footsteps.

"Come on," Kol said as he shouldered his way through the throng, Trugg and Jyn at his side. "We're going into the tavern."

"Maybe we should just shift and get out of here," Jyn said.

"The second we stop to shift, this crowd will be all over us." Kol firmly pushed a man's arm aside and ducked beneath the outstretched hands of another. "And since we have to give in to our dragon hearts to shift—"

"Our dragons would attack," Trugg finished for him.

"Maybe that's a lesson these people need to learn." Jyn shoved past a girl who was holding a dirty rag doll up for trade, and motioned Kol toward the tavern.

"They're desperate," Kol said quietly. "They're just doing what they can to survive. We can't hurt them for that. Besides, if we attack Ravenspire citizens in our dragon form within their borders, we violate the treaty my father signed with Irina years ago, and we'd lose our opportunity to have any upper hand in the negotiations."

They reached the wooden sidewalk that ran in front of the tavern, and Kol immediately moved toward the door.

"If we go inside, we'll be trapped," Jyn said.

"I think there's a way out." And, skies above, please let him be right about the girl and her intentions. If he led his friends into a trap, they'd have no choice but to shift.

Behind them, the villagers shouted and begged, but the pleading had disappeared from their tone, and anger had taken its place.

Kol, Jyn, and Trugg raced into the tavern seconds before the mob of furious villagers began shoving through the doorway, their eyes wild as they screamed for the Eldrians' cloaks, boots, and coin.

"This way!" The girl waited by an open door in the far wall that led to an alley. "Hurry."

In the alley beyond her, a man with dark skin and graying hair stood with his hand on the hilt of the sword strapped to his waist while the boy who'd followed the girl into the tavern was looking both ways. "It's still clear. Let's go," he said.

The mob behind the Eldrians surged forward, and a man with sunken cheeks and a patched shirt that hung from his frail shoulders launched himself at Kol, his bony fingers grabbing at the small leather satchel tied to Kol's belt. Two more men leaped forward and snatched at Kol's cloak.

"Get off him!" Trugg roared and slammed into the men, sending all three of them flying into the closest wall.

More villagers—starving and desperate to get their hands on anything of value—poured into the room and surrounded Jyn while Trugg shoved his way to stand in front of Kol.

Kol's chest burned with dragon's fire, and pain rippled over his muscles as his body fought to shift. He drew a deep breath, tasting smoke at the back of his throat, and focused on keeping his human form.

Jyn's laugh raised the hair on Kol's neck. "You picked the wrong girl to mess with today, humans." Her fingernails lengthened into talons, and a shudder rippled across her skin as it began hardening into scales.

"Who wants a piece of this?" Trugg shouted, smoke pouring from his nose as the crowd pressed in on all sides. Some of them raised crude weapons—planks of wood, butcher knives, and hand-carved spears—and waved them at the Eldrians.

"No!" Kol shouted, panic slicing into him. "Don't shift. I forbid it."

Over the heads of the mob, he spied the girl in the dress. Her dark eyes met his, and then she whistled sharply.

Something sharp jabbed Kol in the back, and he stumbled forward. The crowd surged against him, and its weight shoved him to his knees on the dusty floor. Smoke began pouring from his nostrils, and his dragon raged.

Then a piercing shriek split the air, and an enormous white gyrfalcon swept into the room and slammed into the people surrounding Trugg and Jyn. The bird circled, raked the mob with its talons, and then screamed a battle cry.

"Get up. Up!" A small gloved hand wrapped around Kol's arm and hauled him to his feet. Before he could take a single step, the girl locked her arm around the back of his neck, leaped against his chest, and slammed both of her feet into a group of villagers, sending them sprawling. Falling back against him, she whirled around and pulled his shoulders toward her while another plank whistled through the air where his head had been.

Skies above, she knew what she was doing in a fight. He supposed he should be embarrassed—the king of the Draconi needing rescue from a human wasn't exactly the kind of story the bards would turn into song—but he was too grateful for her help to bother.

Trugg and Jyn, their attackers momentarily driven back by the gyrfalcon, hurried toward him. The mob quickly rallied in their wake and came after the Eldrians with renewed fury.

"Follow me." Without waiting for a response, the girl looked at the gyrfalcon. As if obeying some unspoken command, the bird shrieked and flew toward the door. The girl hiked up her skirt and ran forward, the Eldrians on her heels.

They burst out of the tavern and into an alley covered in sodden leaves and clumps of almost-melted snow, the crowd of villagers right behind them.

"Gabril, get Risa and anyone else who will be reasonable and see if they can talk sense into their neighbors. Promise them we'll rob the next treasury wagon and give food to everyone." The girl turned from the black man with the sword and looked at the boy who'd entered the tavern with her.

"Leo, find a clear path out of the village," the girl said. The boy disappeared around the corner, and then reappeared on the roof of a building close to the street.

"North and then west," he called.

"You three, follow me!" the girl said as she sprinted down the alley, leaving the man with the sword behind. Kol obeyed without hesitation.

The bird swooped low and slammed into a pair of women who were chasing Jyn, rusted knives in their hands.

"I like this bird," Jyn said, and though her skin still shimmered with her dragon's silvery sheen, her eyes were human again. "It has good taste."

"I think the girl is controlling the bird. She has it trained to obey her movements or something," Kol said as he raced with his friends toward the mouth of the alley where the girl was . . . skies above, she was yanking off her dress.

"Then the girl has good taste, and, *hello* there," Trugg said with appreciation as the poufy green dress was dumped unceremoniously on the dusty cobblestones, leaving the girl in a pair of fitted dark brown pants, a white jerkin that left her pale arms bare, and a pair of boots.

A thick jug went sailing past Kol's head and slammed into the ground, and the crowd behind them screamed for money, for food, as Kol snarled, "She just saved our lives. Stop looking at her like she's next in the try-Trugg-on-for-size club."

"I'm one size fits all," Trugg said as they reached the mouth of the alley and tumbled into the street where the girl was already moving north.

"You're a fool," Jyn snapped.

The mob of villagers poured out of the alley in the Eldrians' wake and came for them.

"We have to get out. *Now.*" The girl sprinted up the street and skidded around the corner of a squat little brick building. The boy appeared on the rooftops to their left and kept pace with them, leaping from building to building like a mountain lion.

"We'll have to use the north gate," he said. "It'll be locked."

"Meet us there," the girl said. Her bird arrowed into the sky and flew in the opposite direction.

"Hey! We might need that bird," Jyn called out.

"She needs to find Gabril and make sure he's safe," the girl said as she practically flew over the cobblestones. "There's nothing more she can do for us."

Kol sped up—the girl was *fast*—and came abreast of her as she whipped into another alley. "How far to the gate? And why is it locked?"

"Just past this alley. And it's locked because when the gate watchers warned the village about your arrival, several of them ran to bar the gates shut from the outside. Makes it easier to rob you if you refuse to barter when you have nowhere to run," she said as she reached the end of the alley and launched herself into the street.

"If the gate is *locked*, how—"

"She led us into a trap." Jyn grabbed Kol's shoulder as they rounded the alley's corner and found themselves facing a brief cobblestoned walkway leading to a closed gate. The wooden beam used to bar the gate from the inside was still propped against the wall, which meant the girl was right—the villagers had locked the gate from the outside to trap the Eldrians.

"Watch your backs and wait for me." Flexing her gloved hands, the girl took a deep breath and ran for the wall.

Kol's jaw dropped as the girl seemed to run straight up the wall, kicking upward and out, lightly touching the wooden planks, and then flying upward again.

"Skies above, now *that* is a worthy human." Trugg clapped his meaty hands once and glanced over his shoulder. "Trouble coming. Better hope that girl can open a gate as fast as she can climb a wall."

"My sister can do anything." The girl's brother leaped from the roof of a building to Kol's right, rolled forward as he hit the ground, and came up to his feet like jumping off a building was as easy as walking down the street.

The gate swung open, and the girl met Kol's eyes. "Hurry up."

He didn't need to be told twice. The Eldrians raced through the open gate, followed by the girl's brother, and then she shut and locked it behind them. In moments, she'd led them deep into the trees where the shouting from the village couldn't make a dent against the forest's hush.

As soon as she stopped moving and turned to face them, Kol dropped to one knee and touched his brow in the Eldrian gesture of fealty.

"Why are you bowing to me?" The girl took a step back and

gave her brother a look Kol couldn't decipher. "You don't bow unless you're before royalty." A thread of worry wrapped around her words.

Kol slowly raised his head. "I'm not—this has nothing to do with royalty. You saved our lives. We owe you an incredible debt."

The girl glanced at her brother again, who spread his arms in a grand gesture and said, "We humbly accept your fealty on behalf of the— Hey!"

The girl punched his shoulder and glared at him.

He frowned and rubbed at the bruise. "I was just—"

"About to say something you shouldn't." She gave him a look that must have meant something to the boy, because he dropped his eyes and kicked the ground with the toe of one boot. The girl met Kol's gaze. "You don't owe us anything. You should leave. Now."

"That's kind of rude," Jyn said.

"Be quiet, Jyn. Have respect for the human who can run up walls," Trugg said.

"May I have your names?" Kol asked.

"We're nobody." The girl's brown eyes were guarded. She had a smudge of dirt on one pale cheek, and her long dark curls were tangled from her sprint through the village, but even so, she was beautiful in a way that made Kol want to keep looking. He smiled to show her he'd meant no harm and slowly rose to his feet.

"You need to be much more careful. The people are starving, and they still owe taxes. Taxes they can't pay. Unless they find another source of coin or food, they'll either starve to death or be thrown in one of Irina's dungeons. The last Eldrian refugees who came through here paid for food with jewels worth fifty times the price of their bread. The lucky people who gained those jewels were able to take their families and escape Ravenspire. Walking into one of the poorest villages in the kingdom looking as rich as Eldrian royalty is a tremendous risk."

Trugg cleared his throat and stepped forward. "We look as rich as Eldrian royalty because he"—Trugg pointed at Kol, who suddenly felt like his collar was too tight—"*is* royalty. I present to you King Kolvanismir Arsenyevnek, son of Ragvanisnar III, holder of the sky scepter and supreme ruler of Eldr."

EIGHT

Lorelai stared at the Eldrians, her cheeks heating. The handsome boy with the golden eyes and wild hair was a *king*? What would a king be doing walking into Tranke with only two escorts, both of whom looked no older than Lorelai herself?

The boy seemed just as uncomfortable as she felt. He waved a hand in the air like he could swat his title away. "There's no need for formality, really. I'm just Kol—"

"You're not old enough to be the king of Eldr, Kol." Lorelai crossed her arms over her chest and glared at him. Did he think she was stupid? She didn't know what the Eldrians hoped to gain by making such a ridiculous claim, but they weren't going to get it from her. She'd spent years learning everything there was to know about the kingdoms that surrounded Ravenspire, and the king of Eldr was old enough to be this boy's father. "I don't know what you want here, but it's time for you to go."

"You dare speak to him this way?" The girl with the short dark hair and sharp green eyes stepped toward Lorelai, but the huge, dark-skinned Eldrian boy put a hand on her shoulder to hold her back.

Kol met her gaze, and grief lurked in his. "My father died in the ogre war. My older brother and my mother also." His gaze drifted from hers as he opened his cloak to reveal the Eldrian royal seal—a bronze dragon with emeralds for eyes and wings studded with rubies—pinned to the inside just above his heart. "I'm the king of Eldr now."

She believed him. "I'm sorry for your loss." And she was. But more than that, she needed to understand why the king of Eldr was in Tranke and whether that posed a danger to her people or to Leo, Gabril, and herself.

She waited until he looked at her again before saying, "What are you doing traveling through Ravenspire with such a small escort? And why would you bother stopping at a village like this when Nordenberg—which is a far wealthier town—is just north of here and its people are used to nobility—"

Leo nudged her with his elbow and whispered "manners" before giving Kol a huge smile. "Forgive us, my lord, for you have us at a disadvantage. My sister is frankly deplorable at conducting courtly conversation. The only thing worse than her ability to make appropriate small talk with royalty is her attempt to let a man lead her on the dance floor. Your timely interruption has saved me from the chore of attending dance lessons with her. My feet thank you."

Stepping back from the Eldrians, Lorelai snatched Leo's shirt and pulled him close so she could whisper, "We aren't royalty here. We're supposed to pass as peasants. That means—"

"We aren't peasants. We're the Heirs—"

"Not to him. We need to send them on their way and go meet up with Gabril and Sasha to make sure everyone in the village is all right."

"This is getting weird," the female Eldrian called out.

Leo flashed her a smile. "It's our first time meeting royalty in the woods. We really don't have a precedent to call upon." Turning to Lorelai, he whispered, "One day Irina won't be on the throne. You will, with me as your charming and lovable assistant. And when that day comes, you'll need a working relationship with the king of Eldr. It might be best if he didn't remember you as the girl who saved his life and was then unspeakably impolite."

He was right. Plus, she wanted to know why the new king of Eldr was in Ravenspire instead of in his own country where he belonged, and she wasn't going to get that information without trying to use a little bit of Leo's charm. Mustering a smile, she let go of her brother's shirt and stepped toward Kol again. Behind her, Leo whispered "courtly conversation" as she reached one gloved hand toward the king as if offering him a dance.

Kol took her hand in a gentle grip. She looked up and found his amber eyes fixed on hers, while the wind teased his red-brown hair and the sun glowed against his golden skin. The corner of his mouth quirked in a half smile, and heaven help her, every lesson she'd ever learned on proper etiquette for Eldrian royalty flew right out of her brain.

Leo made a sound behind her, and Lorelai realized she'd been staring into Kol's eyes, her hand resting in his palm, for who knew how long while the king's escorts frowned at her, waiting for her to break the silence.

She should bow—no, *curtsy*. She was a princess. Princesses

curtsied. She should curtsy and say . . . something.

The king's half smile grew, and he opened his mouth as if to speak. Hastily, Lorelai swept into an elegant curtsy—no small feat considering her current attire—and said the first thing that popped into her head.

"You look most fetching today, my lord."

The large Eldrian boy snorted. Kol's eyes widened, and his smile froze. And Leo—curse his miserable hide—made the kind of strangled choking noise that meant he was trying desperately not to laugh.

"Oh no." Lorelai pulled her hand from Kol's, her skin prickling with heat from absolute humiliation. Maybe if she prayed hard enough, the forest floor would open up and swallow her. If there was any justice in the world, it would swallow Leo too.

"I . . . thank you?" Kol glanced at his escorts, but they were both smirking at him.

"This is *your* fault." Lorelai glared at Leo, who stopped trying to swallow his laughter and sagged against the closest tree trunk so he could truly enjoy her embarrassment. "You and your stupid courtly conversation jokes, and now look what happened."

"I myself have always found Kol quite fetching." The Eldrian boy stepped forward and held out a hand twice the size of Lorelai's. She gingerly placed her hand in his. "I'm Trugg and that beautiful but surly Eldrian is Jyn. We're both grateful for your help." His brows rose. "You can call me fetching as well, and then allow me to demonstrate my gratitude by—"

"That's enough, Trugg," Kol said. Trugg grinned at Lorelai, his teeth a slash of white against his dark skin.

"Why is the king of Eldr traveling through this part of

Ravenspire?" Lorelai asked because even though she'd mangled her attempt at making a good impression as a princess—not that Kol even knew she was a princess—she was determined to get the information that mattered.

"I'm on my way to see your queen. We stopped, hoping to find a decent meal and a bed in one of the mountain villages—a mistake I won't make twice."

"You're going to see Queen Irina?" Lorelai stepped back, icy calm washing over her as Leo stopped laughing and moved to her side, his eyes guarded.

"I am."

Lorelai's hands slowly closed into fists as magic raced down her veins to gather in her palms. "You said you owed me a debt."

He inclined his head graciously, though a watchfulness had entered his gaze.

"Then do me a favor and forget any of this ever happened." She leaned toward him. "Forget this village. Forget my bird. Forget the two of us. Don't mention any of this to the queen. She punishes those who displease her, and this village has enough problems without adding the queen's wrath to the list."

Kol touched his brow again, and said quietly, "I owe you a much greater debt than simply omitting today from my conversation with Irina. You saved our lives."

She met his gaze. "And by keeping silent, you will save ours." She glanced at the village again. "Ours and hundreds of others."

He held out his hand. "You have my word."

She slowly laid her palm over his. He pulled her closer and slid his hand up her arm to cup her elbow in the traditional Eldrian greeting. Heat unspooled in her stomach, and her heart quickened—a foolish response she had no time for.

Casting about her lessons for a polite way to say good-bye to an Eldrian, she said, "May the skies grant you protection on your journey."

Kol's eyes widened as though surprised that she knew the phrasing, but he responded, "And may heaven watch over you on yours."

She gave him a tiny smile as she pulled away from him and then turned to disappear into the forest with Leo.

"One more word about courtly conversation from you, and it will be the last thing you ever say," Lorelai said as they hurried through the woods toward the village.

"I wasn't going to say a thing!" Leo protested as they leaped over a fallen evergreen. "Though I do think the entire conversation was very—"

"Leopold Arlen Wolfgang Diederich, don't you dare."

"Fetching."

She opened her mouth to insult him—not that she could ever think of an insult that could get the best of him—when Sasha's thoughts arrowed into her own, a silver-quick image of Gabril sagging against the back wall of the pub, blood pouring from a wound in his chest and puddling on the cobblestones at his feet.

The breath left Lorelai's body, and panic curled through her stomach. Not Gabril. Not like this. Her lips trembled as she started running for the village.

"What are you doing?" Leo demanded as he caught up to her.

A rush of magic burned down Lorelai's arms, and she clenched her fists. "Gabril is hurt."

Bleeding fast, fast, fast. Big wound. Sasha's thoughts darted through Lorelai's mind, showing Lorelai an image of a crudely made spear lying beside Gabril, its sharp tip covered in blood.

A homemade spear one of the villagers had thought to use against the Eldrians but had used against Gabril instead. Why? Because his wards were helping the Eldrians escape? Because Gabril had tried to stop the mob himself instead of going to the mayor's wife, Risa, for help?

It didn't matter how Gabril had been wounded. All that mattered was that they get to him in time to save his life.

Lorelai leaped over a tumble of stones and skidded around an oak with drooping brown leaves still clinging to its branches. Leo sprinted past her, his longer legs eating up the ground. He reached the gate ahead of her, threw the bar to the ground, and heaved it open, his eyes full of the same desperate fear that pounded through Lorelai with every beat of her heart.

Gabril was all the family they had left. He was their surrogate father, their protector, their mentor, and the rock-solid foundation upon which they'd rebuilt their lives.

He was *not* going to die.

It only took a few moments to run from the north gate to the alley behind the pub, but it felt like forever, the distance stretching endlessly before them while Gabril's blood poured out of him with every passing second.

Leo reached him first and wrapped his arms around Gabril as the older man stumbled toward him on legs that shook.

"We'll take him to Risa's. She can send for the physician," Lorelai said as she put her arm around Gabril and helped Leo support him.

"The physician left town a month ago," a woman said from the pub's doorway.

Lorelai turned to find the owner of the pub standing behind them, her watery blue eyes full of anger.

"Then Risa will know where to find medical supplies." Lorelai turned away. "Come on, Leo."

"There be no medical supplies in Tranke. And even if there were, you wouldn't be getting any of them." The woman spat on the cobblestones and crossed her arms over her chest as Lorelai turned to stare at her again. "Best be leaving now, girl."

Magic stung Lorelai's fingertips, and it took effort to sound calm as she said, "We can't leave. He's badly wounded. Risa will know—"

"Risa won't have anything to do with you after what you just did. Not if she knows what's good for her." The woman's voice was as hard as the look in her eyes.

"But we'll help you. We'll get food for the village, I promise. Just as soon as Gabril is stable, we'll—"

"What good is your promise to help us sometime later on when you just denied us help we need now? You get out of here before I stop telling my husband he doesn't get to kill all three of you and take your possessions as payment for the Eldrian riches you just stole from us."

"You think you can kill us?" Leo's voice vibrated with fury. "Do you have any idea who we are?"

"You're the fools who chose loyalty to a pack of Eldrian strangers over your own people." The woman spat again, only this time she aimed the spittle at Lorelai's feet. "If you aren't out of this village in the next few minutes, I won't be held responsible for what happens to you."

Leo opened his mouth, but Lorelai beat him to it. "We're leaving. Come on, Leo."

"But Gabril—"

"Will die if we don't get out of here." Lorelai's hands burned, her power begging for release she wouldn't give. The woman was right. Lorelai and Leo had taken the possibility of Eldrian riches out of the villager's hands, and the desperate people in Tranke weren't concerned with the morality of saving innocent strangers when it meant condemning their children to starve to death.

The only way to help Tranke and villages like it was to step up her plan to take down Irina. Hit another garrison and steal more food. Break loved ones out of dungeons where they were rotting away for the crime of being unable to pay taxes to the queen due to the blight.

But she couldn't do any of that until she saved Gabril's life. Without another word to the pub owner, Lorelai and Leo helped Gabril back to their tent outside the village, bandaged his wound as best they could, and then quickly left Tranke behind.

NINE

"Do you have a description of the thieves who robbed my northeast garrison?" Irina's voice was cold as she turned to face her castle steward. Viktor stood framed in the doorway between her balcony and her sitting room, his pale skin and exquisite cheekbones gleaming in the faint light of dawn.

"Only one was seen—a girl who created a distraction by burning down the stables. She had a gyrfalcon helping her." His blue eyes were steady as they met hers, but his fingers worried with the perfectly tied cravat at his throat. He hesitated before handing her a piece of parchment with a drawing of the girl.

Irina stared at the drawing, her heart thudding painfully and her chest squeezing until she thought the pain would send her to her knees as she looked into the face of a ghost with long curly dark hair, pale skin, red lips, and brown eyes.

"This can't be." Her voice shook. "She's dead."

Viktor reached up to brush his fingertips against her cheek. "It could be anyone. If the princess was still alive, we'd have heard something by now. It's been nine years. This is just some mountain girl who bears a faint resemblance to your sister."

Her nails dug into the parchment until it tore.

"The garrison is on Kiffen land. A robbery that big required a team of people, which means someone somewhere is talking about it. Lord and Lady Kiffen arrived in the capital yesterday. Bring them to the front gate within the hour. They'll tell me what they know, or they'll regret it."

He caught her hands before she could walk away. "Don't use magic. Please. I see the strain it causes you. There's no need to make an example of anyone."

Because she wanted to lean against his touch the way she always had since she'd been a lonely girl of fourteen and he'd been the impoverished son of the tutor her father had hired, she stepped back and straightened her spine. Met his gaze and drove the warmth from hers until all that was left was the single-minded purpose it took to be queen.

"Never assume that because you sometimes share my bed, you also share my throne. You are dismissed."

Irina arrived at the castle's front gate as the sun cut through the morning clouds and bathed the capital in its hazy morning glow. Raz curled around her shoulders, his forked tongue tasting the air as they swept past the guards who stood at attention in a half circle around Lord and Lady Kiffen.

Irina locked eyes with Lady Kiffen, whose puff of gray hair framed a stern brown face with unflinching dark eyes. "A girl helped rob the garrison on your land three days ago. She had a gyrfalcon with her. Who is she?"

"I wouldn't know, Your Highness." Lady Kiffen's voice was steady.

Beside Lady Kiffen, her husband clenched his jaw and stared at his polished boots.

Raz uncoiled himself from Irina's neck and hissed.

The queen stepped closer. "What rumors do you hear of the thieves?"

Lady Kiffen held her gaze boldly. "I don't listen to rumors."

Irina's smile could cut stone. "Tell me what you've heard, or die for your silence."

Her husband glanced between his wife and the queen and then said, "There are rumors the prince and princess roam the Falkrain Mountains—"

"Frederick, no!" Lady Kiffen whirled to face her husband.

Irina lunged for Lady Kiffen. Snatching the woman's gown, the queen drove her to her knees. "You dare stop him from answering his queen?" Irina's voice was lethal.

Lady Kiffen raised her eyes to glare at Irina. "You are *not* his queen. You are a Morcantian *mardushka* occupying a throne that isn't yours."

Irina leaned down and said quietly, "You have just committed treason, Lady Kiffen."

Turning to her guards, Irina pointed toward a section of the castle's wall that stood next to the edge of the apple grove. "Put her there."

Lord Kiffen threw himself at Irina's feet, grasped the hem of her gown, and sobbed out, "Please, my queen. Spare my wife, and the Kiffens will be your staunchest allies. I beg of you."

Irina shook the man free of her skirt and turned to look at the castle, its thin spires and scalloped balconies silhouetted against the dawn sky like slivers of shadows slowly crystallizing into something solid.

She'd had allies once, or so she'd thought. She'd all but secured a betrothal to the king of Ravenspire, and she had a crowd of admirers who fell over themselves to be near her. But Arlen had broken protocol to ask for her sister's hand in marriage instead, her uncle had betrayed his eldest niece by agreeing to Arlen's request, and the crowd of admirers had abandoned Irina for her sister because it was power they truly craved, and Irina suddenly had none.

For ten years, she'd waited. Refusing marriage requests from Morcantian dukes and earls, turning a deaf ear to her uncle's increasing ire at his niece's refusal to cooperate, ignoring her father's complaints that the daughter he'd loved had abandoned him for Ravenspire, and throwing herself wholeheartedly into the kind of dark magic her uncle had long ago forbidden Morcantians to practice.

And when the opportunity came to right the wrongs, to seize the life that should've been hers, Irina hadn't needed her uncle, her father, or a crowd of admirers. She'd only needed herself.

She wasn't about to falter now.

Irina turned back toward Lady Kiffen, once again shaking off the grasping fingers of the woman's husband as he begged for mercy. "I have heard your request, Lord Kiffen. Don't worry. Soon, you will be the most loyal man in my entire kingdom."

The power in her palms burned like fistfuls of live coals as she walked toward Lady Kiffen. Irina smiled as she met the woman's defiant gaze.

She moved to the apple tree beside Lady Kiffen and grasped the closest branch. The blight had yet to reach the capital, and the apple tree's heart—soft and light as a summer breeze—surged upward to meet Irina's palm.

"Rast` lozh." Her voice was a whiplash of strength and power.

The branches of the tree curled toward Irina, brushed against her skin, and then unfurled and stretched long slender fingers toward Lady Kiffen.

Irina stepped toward the woman, whose eyes were fixed on the apple branches as they grew rapidly, twisting into something that resembled wooden vines with clawlike twigs at the ends. The branches reached the wall, crawled along it, and then slid down to wrap themselves around Lady Kiffen.

"No! Please, I beg you." Her husband rushed forward. A branch as thick as one of the pillars in the castle's entrance hall wrapped around his wife's chest, slowly lifting her off the ground as she struggled. Two more tendrils unfurled from that branch and whipped around the woman's arms while another two branches grasped her feet and pulled until she was pinned to the wall, eye to eye with Irina, her arms and legs spread-eagled against the cold gray stone.

Slowly, the queen wrapped her palm around the woman's neck. Lady Kiffen's pulse beat frantically against Irina's skin.

"If you want your wife released from her punishment, you must do one thing for me. After that, if you still wish it, I will release her and forgive her of her crime."

"Anything, Your Highness." His voice trembled.

The queen leaned close to Lady Kiffen and put her other hand on the branch that surrounded the woman's chest. In one palm, she felt the thunder of Lady Kiffen's pulse. In the other, the willing, compliant heart of the apple tree. Gathering her power, the queen whispered, *"Tvor,"* and poured her intentions, her desires, into the word as the heat in her palms exploded into Lady Kiffen and the tree, wrapped around the heart of each, and then joined them as one.

The woman's back arced, and the cords of her neck stood out. She opened her mouth to scream, but choked instead. Her cheeks bulged, her eyes grew wide with panic, and for one long moment, she didn't breathe. But then, her jaw dropped open, wider than should be possible, and a perfectly formed apple slowly tumbled out of her mouth and into the queen's hand.

Irina gave the apple to Lord Kiffen.

"Eat this," Irina said. "And then if you want me to free your wife, I will. I swear it."

Lord Kiffen stared at the apple, its glossy red skin glowing in the morning sunlight. He raised his eyes to his wife's, but she was in the throes of pain again, her throat open in a silent scream as another luscious apple slowly emerged from her mouth and into the queen's hand.

Quickly, he raised the fruit to his mouth and bit deep. His teeth pierced the skin, but instead of crisp, sweet apple, the center was fermented, and thick black rot oozed onto his tongue. He didn't seem to notice. Instead, he chewed quickly, his eyes glazing over as he ate the apple, licking his fingers clean like a starving man afraid to leave a single bit of food behind.

Irina had two more apples in her hands, and Lady Kiffen was already stretching her jaw wide to produce a third, when Lord

Kiffen finished. He stared at his hands as if he couldn't understand where the apple had gone.

"Do you believe that traitors to your queen should be punished?" Irina asked him.

"Oh yes, my queen." Black rot smeared his teeth and lips as he stared at Irina.

"Frederick!" Lady Kiffen's voice was hoarse, and tears leaked from her eyes as she began choking on the next apple. Lord Kiffen never looked away from his queen.

"Do you have news of the girl's whereabouts?" Irina asked.

Lord Kiffen shook his head. "I know only that some believe the mountain girl with the gyrfalcon could be the princess, and the boy who is with her could be the prince. They are sometimes on our lands with a man who acts like their father, and there are those in our village who have dedicated themselves to protecting their location in case the rumors are true." He blinked as an idea occurred to him. "Your Highness, it pains me to confess that I have not questioned those traitors as I should have. I beg you to allow me to rectify that error."

Irina's smile stretched wide enough to hurt as she leaned closer to the man. "Oh, I think I'll come along and question them myself."

Another apple fell from Lady Kiffen's mouth and smashed against the ground, spreading a circle of black rot that instantly destroyed every blade of grass it touched.

"And your wife?" Irina asked as she took Lord Kiffen's arm. "Should I let her down and forgive her of her crimes against me?"

Lord Kiffen never even glanced at the woman pinned to wall. "Traitors must be punished, my queen."

"Indeed." Irina stepped away from the wall, Lord Kiffen by her side.

"Frederick?" The woman's voice shook, but Lord Kiffen didn't look back.

Irina looked at one of her guards. "I'm traveling to Lord Kiffen's lands by the end of the day. Send for a coach and have my maid pack a trunk. And have someone gather several barrels of apples as she produces them. I'm going to need them."

TEN

KOL AND HIS friends shifted out of their dragon forms in the Hinderlinde Forest just north of Ravenspire's capital. After dressing in their finest travel garments and procuring horses from a livery at the edge of town, they entered the capital with Jyn riding point and Trugg bringing up the rear.

The streets wound neatly among well-kept homes with steeply gabled rooftops and brightly painted shutters. A cobblestoned road cut a wide swath through the center of the city. Carriages of polished wood were filled with ladies dressed in bright silks and fancy hats. Ravenspire men in silk cravats stood outside shops, smoking pipes and talking. A few nobles from the western kingdom of Akram, their white robes edged in scarlet rope, were scattered here and there, doing business with tapestry shops and fabric weavers. Occasionally Kol caught a glimpse of merchants with olive skin and dark hair driving wagons loaded with crates that all bore a likeness of the Súndraille flag. And over it all, the majestic spires of Queen Irina's castle rose toward a sun-kissed sky.

The poverty and violence that Kol had seen in Tranke had yet to truly touch the capital. Kol was grateful. The Eldrians couldn't afford to be the cause of a mob here.

"Ready?" Jyn asked as they reached a steep hill bisected by a road paved in white gray-flecked stones. At the top of the hill was the gate to the castle.

Kol felt sick to his stomach as his spine snapped into the rigid, academy-approved posture he'd spent so much of his last four years mocking. If Irina wouldn't see him as an equal, wouldn't listen to his request, or wouldn't accept his terms, he would be out of options.

Eldr would be out of options.

He lifted his chin and assumed the formal royal expression that had always made Father seem so distant and difficult to understand.

Irina would listen. She would negotiate. She would use her magic to save Eldr.

Kol wasn't leaving this castle until she did.

"Jyn, you do the talking. Announce me by my full title. Request a meeting with the queen on a matter of dire importance." His voice, thank the skies, didn't shake. His hands remained steady on the reins.

Years of pretending indifference to being confronted about his actions had finally come in handy.

No one spoke as their horses trudged up the steep hill from the city to the castle. Behind them, cathedral bells tolled the hour in deep, sonorous tones that echoed across the entire countryside.

"What in the skies above is that?" Jyn sounded horrified as she crested the hill.

Kol spurred his horse forward and then pulled it to a stop beside Jyn as he tried to understand what he was seeing.

A woman old enough to be Kol's grandmother was pinned to the castle wall beside the gate by what looked like unnaturally long, limber branches growing out of a nearby apple tree. The branches were lashed around her wrists and ankles, holding her spread-eagled against the stone.

"She must have done something against Irina." Jyn's voice was taut.

The woman began to convulse, her mouth gaping wide as something large and round pushed its way up her throat.

"Oh, now that's just not right." Trugg looked away as a shiny red apple slowly worked its way out of the woman's throat, rolled across her tongue, and fell from her lips to land in a pile of apples beneath her feet. "Skies above, I'm never going to be able to eat another apple twist."

Kol slowly tore his gaze away from the woman and found two guards standing on either side of the gate, their hard expressions daring the Eldrians to make a wrong move.

"Who approaches the queen's castle?" the guard on the left, a woman with wide shoulders and green eyes, called out to them.

"King Kolvanismir Arsenyevnek, son of Ragvanisnar the Third, holder of the sky scepter and supreme ruler of Eldr, requests an audience with Queen Irina of Ravenspire at the queen's earliest convenience to discuss a matter of dire importance." Jyn's voice carried over the awful choking sound of yet another apple rising out of the woman's throat, but still Kol flinched inwardly.

What kind of crime did this woman commit against her

queen that she deserved a punishment so horrific?

"Greetings, my lord. Please come inside the gate while I alert the castle steward," the guard said.

Moments later, a tall man with black hair, blue eyes, and a calm, inscrutable expression met them on the wide drive that led from the gate to the castle's entrance. The man's brow furrowed as he studied Kol for a moment. "*King* Kolvanismir?"

Jyn took a deep breath. "It is with deep regret that we inform Ravenspire of the untimely passing of King Ragvanisnar the Third, along with his wife, Queen Linneayaste, and firstborn son, Prince Ragvanisnar."

The man nodded slowly. "My deepest condolences on such an unfathomable loss, King Kolvanismir. My name is Viktor. The queen is scheduled to leave for our northern lands shortly, but she can give you a few minutes."

Moments later, Viktor led the Eldrians into a long rectangle of a room with candles lit in bronze sconces along the walls and a huge table surrounded by chairs in the center of the floor. Queen Irina sat in a high-backed chair at the far end of the table, her spine stiff enough to make Master Eiler proud and her pale hands pressed flat against the tabletop on either side of a sheet of parchment. There was an enormous black viper loosely coiled around her shoulders, his golden eyes staring at the Draconi.

Even with the creepy snake as a necklace, Irina was beautiful—the kind of beautiful that stole a boy's words and made it hard to remember how to walk without tripping over his own two feet. Hair like sunshine, eyes like the midday sky, and pale skin that glowed against her delicate bones—it seemed impossible that someone so dainty and pretty could have used her magic to force an old woman to choke on apples all day long.

Irina smiled warmly, and Kol's hearts kicked hard against his chest.

"Please come in, King Kolvanismir, and be seated at my side." Her voice was soft and welcoming. "Your dignitaries may take any seat along the left side of the table. My official witnesses will be on the right."

She gestured toward Viktor, who sat at her right hand with a quill, an inkpot, and a few more sheets of parchment. Two other men, both dressed in guards' uniforms, sat down across from the Draconi as well.

Once everyone had taken a seat, Irina folded her hands on her blank sheet of parchment and turned to Kol, her blue eyes intent.

"I am deeply saddened to hear of the loss you recently suffered. I suffered a similar loss years ago. It was devastating." Her gaze slipped from his as if looking at some faraway moment of her own. One warm hand reached out and covered his, and then her gaze snapped back to his. "But we are royalty. We cannot grieve as others grieve. We must move forward and take up the mantle of leadership for the good of our kingdoms, yes?"

He nodded and then realized that if he wanted to be treated like an equal, he had to act like one. Pulling his hand from hers, he said, "It is for the good of our kingdoms that I've come to you."

She inclined her head as if waiting to hear more.

Kol's posture matched Irina's, and his voice was clear and strong as he said, "For the sake of time, I'll be blunt. Ravenspire's people are starving because of the blight that is plaguing your country. Your people, driven by starvation and desperation, are becoming violent toward one another and toward you."

Irina's eyes narrowed.

He softened his tone. "I know you've done everything in your power to help them, but you cannot produce food where none exists."

Trugg made a noise in the back of his throat, and suddenly Kol was sure everyone in the room was thinking of the woman lashed to the castle wall, gagging on apples as they rose from her gut and tumbled out of her mouth.

He hurried on. "You need resources to meet your people's immediate need and to deal with the subsequent food shortages over the coming years as you rebuild your agriculture."

"Is that what I need?" Irina's voice was still quiet, but there was a note of power that hadn't been there before, and Kol didn't have to glance at his friends' strained faces to remember that he was dealing with a *mardushka*.

"Eldr has need as well." He looked Irina in the eye. "We are being invaded by an army of unnaturally strong ogres. We believe they were unleashed by the dark magic that has enslaved the kingdom of Vallé de Lumé to the south of us. The ogres are overcoming our armies because they have somehow managed to master use of that magic and are turning it against us. Without powerful magic of our own, Eldr will be overrun."

"And so you propose a trade?" Irina asked.

"Yes." And, skies above, *please* let her agree to it. "We will give you enough of Eldr's treasure to purchase goods from Súndraille to feed your kingdom for the next ten years in exchange for you using your magic to flush the ogres out of

Eldr and seal them back into Vallé de Lumé."

Viktor made a small noise, but Irina didn't even look at him. Instead, she said, "You are wrong about what Ravenspire needs."

Kol frowned. "The blight, the starvation—it's common knowledge. Your people—"

"My people have no idea what this kingdom needs. I do. If you want my help, you must meet my terms."

"What are your terms?" Kol asked, desperately hoping it was something he could give.

"It's simple. You must agree to hunt down a traitor and bring her to me. Once I have her, I will save your kingdom."

Dread pooled in Kol's stomach as he asked, "Who is the traitor?"

Irina's smile sent a chill down Kol's spine. "Princess Lorelai."

A heavy silence fell in the wake of Irina's words. Kol knew about Princess Lorelai. Even with his less-than-ambitious approach to his schoolwork, the story of the night the king of Ravenspire had died, along with the prince and princess, had stuck with him.

"I thought the Ravenspire heirs died the same night the king died," he said.

Irina's voice was hard. "As did I, but I have new information."

"How am I supposed to find her?" He frowned. "You're the most powerful *mardushka* to come out of Morcant for generations. If you can't find her, what makes you think I can?"

Her smile disappeared. "The princess is a *mardushka* as well and is cloaking herself from me. She might be able to hide from magic, but she can't hide from a predator who tracks his prey by scent." Her gaze pinned him where he sat.

His mouth went dry. "People aren't prey."

Her lip curled. "The only people who aren't prey are those smart enough and strong enough to become the predator." She leaned toward him. She smelled of vanilla and apples. "You're a *king*. You don't have the luxury of turning away from what must be done. Not if you want to save your kingdom."

She was right. Skies curse her, she was right, and Kol knew it.

"I attended a wild boar hunt hosted by your father years ago. I saw how fast the Draconi cornered their prey once they had the scent. It was magnificent." She lowered her voice, as if confiding a secret. "I couldn't understand then why Eldr hadn't conquered every other kingdom in the land. Why you weren't ruling the entire world with the terrible strength of your dragon selves. But then I learned about your dual hearts."

She reached out and pressed her palm to his chest. His hearts leaped beneath her touch, and he jerked away from her. She smiled.

"Your dragon heart is fierce. Monstrous. It wants the unfettered freedom to rule the skies, to burn the land, and to subjugate everyone else to its whims. It's the perfect predator, but your human heart tempers your dragon self with demands for honor, compassion, and justice. Your people have dealt with this duality by rigorously training your dragon heart to bow to your human heart, but deep within you are the instincts required to be the most terrifying predator in the land. I have no doubt you'll quickly hunt down the princess and save your kingdom."

A band of tension wrapped around Kol's chest as he slowly got to his feet. "Draconi don't hunt people."

"Especially when that person is a *mardushka*." Jyn stood as well, her expression furious. "We will not accept our king putting himself in such danger on your behalf."

Irina rose to her feet, and though she was small, she seemed to fill the room with her presence. "He does this for Eldr, not for me. You came to me because you're desperate." Her tone was sharp. "You have no other options. Where else can you go for help defeating the ogres and their magic? Morcant?" Her delicate laugh was filled with scorn. "King Milek, fearing the true depth of power a *mardushka* can achieve with time and training, outlawed all but the most benign forms of magic decades ago. None of the *mardushkas* in his service will admit to being capable of stopping one ogre, much less an entire army. Those in Morcant who *could* help you are no friend to the king."

"You've still not given us reason to believe that asking him to hunt down the princess, who is also a *mardushka* like yourself, is safe." Trugg glared at the queen.

"The princess is a mere fledgling *mardushka*, and I will give him a means to protect himself from her magic," Irina said as she bent to retrieve a wooden chest from the floor. Placing it on the table in front of her, she lifted the lid. There were two items inside the box—an oval mirror with golden serpents and brambles surrounding the glass with swirling gray clouds on its surface and a circular collar made of thistle and bone. Irina picked up the collar and laid it on the table next to Kol.

"He will wear my magic—my protection. This collar was created years ago and has been bespelled by my strongest magic." Irina looked at Kol. "No harm will come to you while you are in my service. Simply retrieve the princess, and I give you my word I will destroy every ogre within Eldr's borders. In fact, I will make a sacred blood oath to you so that my magic will be forced to keep my promise once you keep your own end of the bargain."

Viktor made another sound of protest and gripped his quill with white-knuckled force. Irina picked up the mirror. "Shall we check on Eldr for you?"

Kol leaned toward the queen as she said, "Mirror, mirror in my hand, show me the state of Eldr's land."

"Why does it have to rhyme?" Trugg muttered. Jyn shushed him as the mirror's surface swirled, the gray clouds moving faster and faster until colors began to bleed through, and then Kol was looking at Eldr.

Or more specifically, at the sizable city of Frenellskyre, a city Kol and his friends had flown over in their quest to see the war front. Frenellskyre had been safe and whole, far north of the war front.

But not now.

Now it was overrun with ogres. The brutish creatures loped through the streets and smashed through storefronts and work-shops. They scaled homes, ripped off the roofs with one swift movement, and dove inside.

Kol gripped the edge of the table and then sank slowly into his chair as Eldrians—many of them children or the elderly left behind to care for them while the able-bodied joined the war effort—spilled out of the homes, their mouths gaping in terri-fied screams the mirror wouldn't allow him to hear. His throat closed in horror as children too young to fully shift tried any-way, desperate to flee. Elderly Draconi shifted and tried to scoop their young charges in their talons, but the ogres smashed wings, broke spines, and tore his people limb from limb.

Kol made a strangled sound as he tried to breathe, tried to think beyond the tragedy playing out in front of him.

Where was his army? Why hadn't the city been evacuated?

The answer hit him like a swift blow to the stomach. The only reason his army would fail to defend Frenellskyre was because his army was *gone*. His army was gone, and since Kol hadn't received word from the royal council, the ogres must have destroyed the army so swiftly, none survived to get a message to the castle.

Nothing stood between the capital and the ogres but rivers, rough terrain, and more villages full of innocent Draconi who had no warning that ruin was about to reach them.

How long did his people have? How long did Brig have?

Irina laid the mirror back in the box and pushed the collar closer to Kol. "Do we have an agreement?"

Kol stared at the collar while his pulse roared in his ears and his hands shook. He wasn't a predator. The princess wasn't prey.

But Eldr was falling, and Queen Irina was its only hope. Could he really balk at hunting down the princess when the alternative was the destruction of his kingdom?

He tore his gaze from the collar and found Irina watching him intently while the snake around her neck met Kol's gaze and hissed. Behind him, his friends, who hadn't seen the surface of the mirror, were talking over the top of each other, their voices rising as they argued.

"He can't go up against a *mardushka*, I don't care what protection he has. That's madness." Jyn emphasized her point by slamming her fist against the table.

The ogres were already in Frenellskyre.

"The queen has nothing to lose if Kol fails or if the princess kills him." Jyn glared at Irina.

His army was gone.

"She said she'd make a blood oath." Trugg's voice was sharp. "That means she's bound by her magic and can't break her promise."

"It also means *Kol* would be bound by her magic. What if he can't find the princess? What is the penalty for failure?" Jyn demanded.

The brutes tore his people limb from limb. No one in their path stood a chance.

"He won't be paying any penalty for failure, because he isn't going to do it," Trugg said. "Queen Irina, one of us will take our king's place."

Irina never looked away from Kol. "Such loyalty. Admirable. But Eldr is his to save. He has the most to prove." She leaned forward to press her hand lightly on Kol's hearts, and he felt a jolt of almost pain. "His dragon heart won't allow him to fail."

Jyn sounded frustrated. "None of us will fail. Simply pick one, and we'll—"

"I'll do it." Kol met Irina's gaze as his friends erupted into angry protests. He whipped a hand into the air and gave them a look that begged them to listen. "She showed me the ogres. They're already at Frenellskyre. The town was full of children and the elderly. The ogres . . . no Eldrian left there will survive the night."

His friends stared at him in horrified silence.

He turned to Irina. "I'll make the blood oath. I'll hunt down the princess. And then I want every last ogre inside Eldr obliterated."

The brilliant light of triumph in the queen's eyes made something hard knot up in Kol's chest, but he was out of options, and Eldr was out of time.

Irina cut the center of her palm with a quick slice of her fingernail. Blood welled to the surface. Quickly, she sliced open Kol's hand as well and then pressed her bloody palm to his. This time there was no mistaking the jolt of power that struck him. It burned against his skin and tingled in his blood. The queen met his eyes and said, "I vow that when you have completed the task I set before you, I will use magic to destroy every ogre inside Eldr's borders."

He swallowed hard as the tingle of her magic surged up his arm and flooded his chest like a swarm of bees beneath his skin. "I vow that I will complete that task in exchange for your help in destroying the ogres within Eldr."

Irina's smile was hard and bright as she placed the collar around his neck. It lay against his collarbone, cold and rigid. "We will begin today. The coach is waiting. We're going hunting in the Falkrain Mountains."

ELEVEN

PANIC WAS FRAYING the edges of Lorelai's thoughts, chewing away at her minute by minute until she thought she'd go mad if she couldn't settle on a plan that could save Gabril's life.

In the four days since Gabril had been stabbed, the wound had festered. His body, wracked with fever and pain, continued to weaken. There were no medicinal plants anywhere near their campsite. There were no villages within a day's walk except Tranke, and no one would help them there even if they could. And despite Lorelai's relentless pleas, Gabril refused to allow her to heal him, convinced that any lingering trace of Irina's magic would immediately report Lorelai's whereabouts to the queen.

Not to mention that healing Gabril would require her to expend all her energy to force his stubborn heart to yield to hers, leaving her too weak to fight the queen once Irina did find them.

Gabril would die anyway, and Leo with him. It was a chance Lorelai couldn't take.

Instead, she'd cobbled together a plan out of the only alternative she could think of. Leaving Sasha at the campsite to guard Gabril, Lorelai headed to the huge village of Nordenberg with Leo—who refused to let her go alone since she'd been seen at the garrison—where she hoped the apothecary would have supplies that could save Gabril. The Kiffen lands stretched across much of the eastern Falkrains, but their estate was in Nordenberg. If any village still had the means to buy medical supplies, it would be Nordenberg.

Leo had volunteered to go alone, but she'd argued him into silence. Soldiers would undoubtedly be searching for the garrison robbers. How would his charm and recklessness help him if he got caught? Or if someone recognized him and decided to turn him in to the queen in exchange for enough food to last the winter?

He was her responsibility—he had been since the moment her father had placed Leo's hand in hers and told her to get him to safety. Nine years later, she was still doing her best to obey her father's last wish.

The journey took a day and a half. When at last the snug, tidy cottages of Nordenberg appeared in the distance, the sun was approaching its midpoint in the sky. The town was arranged in neat rows and gentle curves at the base of the northernmost Falkrain mountain, its wood and brick buildings following the swell of the land as it began its ascent to the sky above. A wide lane bisected its heart, and most businesses were located either along that lane or one street over.

The apothecary shop was on a side street that was paved in

buckled cobblestones with patches of wild grass pushing through the cracks. After stopping behind an outlying barn to change into their peasant outfits, Lorelai and Leo pulled caps low over their foreheads to keep from being recognized and entered the village. Lorelai was so focused on their destination that the heavy silence within the village streets didn't penetrate her thoughts until they was already past the first block of shops.

A chill brushed her skin as she grabbed Leo's arm and pulled them both to a halt. She looked around, but the streets were deserted. It was as if every person in Nordenberg had simply disappeared.

Slowly, she spun on her heels and looked for something to tell her what was happening.

"Where is everyone?" Leo whispered.

"I don't know, but something's not right."

It was time for the midday meal—had everyone gone to their homes to dine? Had Lady Kiffen called a town meeting on the grounds of her estate?

"I can go to the rooftops to check it out," Leo said.

"You do that. I'll keep going toward the apothecary's. Whistle if there's trouble ahead of me. I don't care what's going on; we can't leave here without those supplies."

If the apothecary was as empty as the rest of the businesses around her, she'd take what she needed and leave the dagger on his counter as payment. Gabril's situation didn't give Lorelai the luxury of waiting for the villagers to return.

Leo scaled the closest wall and moved swiftly across the rooftops while Lorelai hurried forward, every nerve straining to recognize the first sign of trouble.

Her brother's soft whistle—a perfect mimic of a canary—drifted through the air as Lorelai was halfway through the intersection of the next street. She turned to look up at the rooftop behind her but then froze, her heart thudding rapidly as she stared.

Parked on the side street, just beyond the bakery, was a coach with the Ravenspire crest painted on its doors. The street beyond the coach was packed with villagers who were slowly eating handfuls of glossy red apples while staring at the royal vehicle.

And standing on top of the coach facing the villagers, a large red and gold dragon on the street beside her, was Queen Irina.

Lorelai stood, halfway into the road that cut between the bakery and the livery stables, and stared at Irina, her heartbeat slamming against her ears, her mouth going dry. For a moment, her vision wavered, and her knees shook.

Magic stung her veins and gathered in her palms, and a brilliant flame of rage lit her from the inside out. In her mind's eye, she saw Irina laughing while the castle came to life and tried to crush Lorelai. She saw her father's blood on the marble floor while Irina's snake slithered away.

She remembered her father telling her to protect Leo.

Protect Leo.

Fighting Irina like this—without thinking it through, without a backup plan—was a good way to get Leo killed. She'd learned that lesson the hard way nine years ago.

The thought of losing Leo galvanized her into action. Clenching her gloved hands, she eased back a step and forced herself to wall off the fear that flooded her. Fear would cause her to make a mistake, and making a mistake now would cost her everything.

She tore her eyes from Irina and stared at the dragon that stood still as a statue facing the crowd of silent, vacant-eyed villagers. Magic burned her palms, and she had to work to breathe past the band of panic that wanted to crush her. What was a *dragon* doing with Irina?

As Lorelai backed up another step, she had the sinking feeling that it had been a mistake rescuing the Eldrians from the mob of peasants. There was nothing she could do to change that now. Nothing but run, hide, and get Leo out of Nordenberg alive—with Gabril's medicine safely stowed in her pack.

"Who is your rightful queen?" Irina demanded of the crowd. Her voice had a cruel edge. It was as if the Irina who'd smiled so warmly at Lorelai years ago had never existed.

"You are our rightful queen," the crowd answered, their voices blending together in a singsong rhythm that made the hair on the back of Lorelai's neck rise.

Her fingertips began to itch, and fire burned through her veins as she kept backing away, moving toward the corner of the bakery so she could hide against its south-facing wall, just out of the queen's sight, while she figured out how to get to the apothecary's without getting caught. A quick glance at the roof showed her that it was empty. Either Leo was lying flat to stay out of sight—unlikely, since he knew his sister was in danger— or he was on his way down to the street to help her.

"And what about Princess Lorelai?" Irina's voice crackled with power.

"Death to traitors! Death to Lorelai!" The crowd's voices rose to a fevered pitch, and Lorelai shrank as the chant echoed throughout the streets until it seemed she was surrounded by a thousand people screaming for her demise.

Whatever magic Irina was working, Lorelai and Leo needed to outrun it.

And they would. Once they had medicine for Gabril.

She took another two steps back, moving with silence rather than speed. All the speed in the world wouldn't save her if she attracted the queen's attention. Her pulse beat a frantic tempo against her skin—the powerful heat of the magic in her blood making it hard to think. And the bone-deep fear of Irina that filled Lorelai's nightmares in the dead of night had become a monster that threatened to swallow her whole now that she was seconds away from coming face-to-face with the queen in the broad light of day.

She was within four steps of the bakery's corner when Irina whipped a hand into the air, instantly silencing the crowd. In the sudden quiet, the soft shush of Lorelai's steps was faint but clear. Irina's shoulders stiffened, and she turned to look over her shoulder.

Lorelai twisted toward the bakery and lunged for cover. Her boot caught the uneven edge of a cobblestone, and she fell forward. She rolled with the fall, but she was off balance. Before she could correct her trajectory, she hurtled past the corner of the building, just out of sight of the queen, and slammed into the wall.

Instantly she leaped to her feet, her breath caught in her throat, her hands suddenly shaking. She'd made a mistake.

Irina was going to do everything in her power to make sure Lorelai paid for that mistake with her life.

"Come out, come out, wherever you are." Irina's voice was sugar-coated knives.

Desperately, Lorelai scanned the nearest buildings. Where was Leo? They needed to hide before Irina or one of her guards rounded the corner.

Or, heaven help Lorelai, the dragon.

"How many of you are hiding from me? Come out, and you will face a merciful queen." The sugar disappeared from Irina's voice. "Or, if you refuse, I will find you, and you will face a judgment more terrible than any you can imagine."

Another canary whistle, this time from half a block back down the street she'd already traveled.

Lorelai started running.

She flew past the tailor's shop, her boots barely touching the cobblestones beneath her.

"Find them!" Irina's voice rang with authority. Instantly Lorelai heard the rough scrape of talons against the street.

The dragon was coming.

She ran faster.

The cordwainer's shop held a few displays of her finest leather shoes, fit for the upper gentry or the Kiffens themselves. The tools of her trade lay neatly on her workbench, but Leo wasn't there.

Lorelai's pulse thundered as loud as her thoughts as she raced past the cordwainer's and closed in on the smithy. There would be a brick forge. A table for his tools. Nothing they could hide behind for long. Nothing that could save them from what was coming.

Her hands felt like they were coated in fire beneath her gloves.

Her breath was a desperate sob in her chest. Where was Leo?

Any second now, the dragon would round the corner and see her, and it wouldn't matter how fast she ran or where she hid. He'd find her. Her only hope was to get out of sight and pray that without being given her specific scent beforehand, the combined scents of everyone who'd been on the main street today would require the dragon to search every building.

She raced toward the blacksmith's doorway, her ears straining to hear sounds of pursuit past the thudding of her heart and the ragged tear of her breathing.

A hand reached out of the smithy's doorway, snatched her coat, and hauled her inside.

"I've got you," Leo whispered, and she threw her arms around him even while she scanned the room, looking for a place to hide.

"Come out in the name of the queen!" A man's voice thundered into the air, and Lorelai shrank from the smithy's doorway as Leo put a finger to his lips and jerked his chin toward the back of the shop.

Lorelai followed him as the soldier in the street yelled, "We'll have to search the shops. The dragon doesn't know which scent to follow. I need all guards—"

"Oh, I have a much better idea." Irina's voice echoed down the alley behind the shop as Lorelai skirted the large brick belly of the forge, its embers still glowing from the smithy's morning fire.

"Come on," Leo whispered as he gestured toward a slim iron staircase that spiraled into the ceiling in the far corner of the shop.

Lorelai climbed the stairs, which shifted and creaked with every step, and followed Leo into a narrow room with a small cot, an unlit oil lamp resting on a tiny desk, and soot staining the walls from the bellows in the shop below.

"Stand clear of the buildings." Irina's voice drifted in through the room's tiny window. "I know how to flush them out."

"Skylight above the bed." Leo breathed the words as he nodded toward the cot resting in the far corner of the room.

Lorelai followed him as quietly as she could, all the while listening for sounds of pursuit, Irina's voice—anything that would tell her where the threat was coming from.

Leo hopped onto the bed, his scuffed boots barely sinking into the thin mattress. "The villagers are under her control. I don't know how she—"

"It's the apples." Lorelai climbed up next to him. "She did the same thing to everyone in the castle after she married Father. They've been bespelled to make them mindlessly loyal to her."

"If everyone was eating those nasty things, then how were you able to stand up to her?" he asked as he reached up and pressed his fingertips against the low-slung ceiling. A square of wood twice Lorelai's width slid quietly to the side, revealing a slice of the cloudy, pale blue sky.

"She never gave me any. She said they weren't for people with magic in their blood. Plus, she trusted me because she thought we were the same."

"Proof that she's a fool." Leo smiled at her, though there was worry in his eyes. "All the roofs are joined by narrow catwalks." He cupped his hand for her foot. "If we stay low, the chimneys might hide us from anyone who happens to look up."

"Unless she's got the dragon circling the sky above."

"You have a better plan?" He nudged her with his cupped hands, and she placed her foot in the cradle of his palms.

She didn't have a better plan. She had Gabril's implacable voice in her head giving her instructions, expecting her to heed him, refusing to let his princess do anything less than survive and keep Leo alive as well.

Use your environment to your advantage.

Surprise your enemy. Be unexpected.

Don't get caught.

Don't get caught. Lorelai looked up through the hole in the ceiling and took a steadying breath. If anyone could survive fleeing from the queen and her dragon over slanting rooftops and narrow catwalks, it was Lorelai and Leo.

Lorelai wrapped her fingers around the edges of the hole above her and climbed out onto a gently sloping roof made of weather-stained shingles pierced with copper ventilation pipes and a massive brick chimney to her right.

Dropping quietly to her knees, she reached down to help Leo onto the roof and then gestured toward the chimney. They began sidling toward it, careful not to let their boots slip against the shingles.

Lorelai's heart beat painfully as panic wrapped tight bands around her chest. Her palms burned with the need to rip off her gloves and protect herself. She pulled at them, making sure not a single sliver of skin was showing.

The power in her blood might believe it could protect her, but Lorelai knew better. She didn't feel capable of facing Irina on her own, much less Irina with a dragon and a horde of slavishly devoted villagers at her beck and call.

"You cannot outrun me." Irina's voice echoed down the street. "You cannot hide from me. You can either surrender or die."

"Your Highness, the dragon needs a scent to follow," a man said.

"I don't need a hunter to follow a scent when my prey is so close. I can find them myself," Irina said.

"Ready?" Leo whispered as he nodded toward a narrow iron catwalk that bridged the distance between the alley-side corner of the smithy and the brewery next door.

"Ready." Taking a deep breath, she found her balance and ran lightly down the sloping roof, onto the iron catwalk, and across to the brewery's roof in seconds.

Irina's voice rose. "You have chosen death."

The catwalk creaked, and then Leo was behind her, moving quickly across the brewery's roof, staying low and hugging the chimneys for cover. Lorelai followed, her stomach churning as Irina's voice echoed across the alley below them.

"*Nakhgor. Kaz`prin.* Find the ones I seek."

A light as brilliant as fire shot into the air, arced, and then plunged deep beneath the alley's cobblestones.

Lorelai's palms blazed with heat in response. She grabbed Leo's hand and yanked him forward, their boots sliding dangerously against the brewery's shingles as they fought to get to the next catwalk.

"*Nakhgor,*" Irina shouted as the cobblestones shook violently.

Lorelai and her brother reached the catwalk that led to the harness maker's workshop as long jagged cracks split the cobblestones beneath them.

Sprinting across the catwalk, Lorelai scrambled up the harness maker's roof and half slid down to the other side, Leo right at her heels.

"Kaz`prin." Irina's voice filled the air. The cobblestones cracked and crumbled as her spell gained strength. "Bring them to me to face their punishment."

Lorelai was halfway across the catwalk that led from the harness maker's to the weaponsmith's when a score of thick black vines exploded out of the ground.

TWELVE

Lorelai froze on the catwalk, Leo right behind her, as the vines of Irina's spell burst out of the cracks in the cobblestones, rushed toward the buildings, and plunged through windows and doorways, leaving shattered splinters of wood and glass on the ground. The shops shook, joints creaking, as the vines surged forward, scouring the insides for anyone foolish enough to be hiding from the queen.

The catwalk shook as well. Lorelai braced herself and looked back to meet Leo's gaze.

They weren't going to make it to the apothecary's. They weren't going to get help for Gabril. She absorbed the blow and swallowed against the grief that thickened her throat.

She couldn't save Gabril, but she could still save Leo.

Her voice nothing more than a breath on the wind, she said, "Stay with me, Leo. Don't fall behind, don't veer off course, and don't look back. Just stay with me, and I'll protect you."

His voice shook at the edges. "We'll protect each other."

More vines exploded out of the ground, but instead of

rushing toward the buildings, they shot straight up until they were nearly eye level with Lorelai. The band of fear around Lorelai's chest felt like it might crush her as the vines hung in midair like muscled snakes with serrated leaves. Slowly, they turned, each bulbous end lifting slightly as if testing the wind, searching for its prey.

Lorelai took a frantic gulp of air, her gaze glued to the vines, her body trembling. These weren't the snakes from her nightmares. These weren't the things that had killed her father, and yet the screams she heard in her dreams seemed to echo inside her head as she watched the vines twist in the air.

Leo wrapped his hand around hers, his grip steady. He nodded at the path in front of her, and she slowly nodded back, pretending she didn't hear screams inside her head. Pretending she could breathe past the panic.

Lorelai took a single step forward and then froze as the vines closest to the catwalk swung toward her and cocked their heads. Like they could hear her. Like they were waiting for another sound to give them her exact location.

The band of panic around Lorelai's chest felt like it was crushing her, and her hands were burning with magic she didn't dare let loose. She reached for Gabril's voice, for the instructions he'd mercilessly drilled into her over the past nine years.

Don't get caught.

The band loosened a little as she focused on the goal.

Be unexpected.

Irina thought she was hunting a few rebellious villagers. She had no idea what Lorelai and Leo, even without magic, were capable of doing.

Use your surroundings.

Rooftops. Catwalks. Chimneys. Pipes.

Vines.

Lorelai catalogued the options without taking her eyes from the snakelike things that were still facing her, waiting for one wrong move.

Fear still clutched at her, but Gabril's voice had broken through the worst of it.

Lorelai looked at her brother, who was staring at the vines with fierce determination on his face, and added one more instruction to Gabril's list.

Save Leo.

Slowly, hardly daring to breathe, Lorelai met Leo's gaze and then looked pointedly at the solid square chimney on the weaponsmith's roof. If they could sprint to the chimney and hide behind it as the vines struck, they'd have a few seconds to get to their next hiding spot before the vines could strike again.

She hoped.

Leo nodded. Lorelai tensed, practiced the run in her mind once—leap from the catwalk *there*, plant her foot *there*, avoid that loose shingle *there*—and then she sucked in a deep breath and ran.

The catwalk screeched in protest as Lorelai sprinted, Leo right at her heels.

The vines whipped toward the pair and struck, slamming into the iron catwalk, wrapping around it, and tearing it from its moorings with a deafening shriek of metal being ripped asunder.

As the catwalk disappeared beneath their feet, they lunged for the weaponsmith's roof. The second her feet touched the shingles, Lorelai raced forward, her boots flying over the rooftop, her eyes on the chimney. Behind her, Leo took a running leap and was knocked to his stomach by the vicious swipe of a vine.

"Roll!" Lorelai yelled as she slammed into the chimney, grabbed it for balance, and then watched, her heart pounding in terror, as Leo heaved himself to the side seconds before a trio of black vines burst through the roof right where he'd been lying.

"Get up!" She ducked, and a vine smashed into the chimney where she'd been standing, scattering shards of brick. The vine wrapped itself around the chimney, its bulbous head whipping from side to side as if looking for her before snapping its black jaws around the hem of her coat. She shrugged out of the garment and leaped to the side as another vine burst out of the workshop below her and began slithering over the roof. A quick glance at the path between the chimney and the next catwalk made her stomach sink.

The roof was crawling with vines. Their thick black skin made a hissing noise as it scraped across the shingles. Soon, the entire roof would be covered, and there would be nowhere left to go.

"Run!" Her brother lunged past one questing vine and then ducked beneath another as he struggled to reach Lorelai. Blood seeped from a cut on his face. "Lorelai, *run!*"

She wasn't leaving him behind. Jumping over a vine, she reached for him as the vines that hung in midair began writhing, swaying toward each other until they touched and fused together to create a new vine—twice as thick, twice as strong.

As the new, thicker vines fused together once again, Lorelai reached Leo, who was struggling to his feet, the reckless light that usually gleamed in his eyes replaced with fear. Wrapping her gloved hands firmly around his, she hauled him toward the last open space between the chimney and the catwalk.

"She's making one large snake thing," Leo said as they stumbled and slid toward the next catwalk. "I give her points for flair, though black is a dull color choice." His voice shook, a blend of bravado and terror. He clung to Lorelai's hand, steadying her when she needed it, and using her as his anchor when his feet began to slip.

"Don't look back." Lorelai assessed the catwalk, her heart pounding as beneath the hiss of the vines behind them, the building groaned and shuddered. "Just run."

"This is the last building on the street. We'll have to jump and run the rest of the way on the ground."

"Stay with me," Lorelai said as the hanging vines finished fusing together and became an enormous, monstrous thing as wide as the weaponsmith's shop and nearly twice as tall. "Go!"

They ran, feet pounding over the iron catwalk as the vines behind them hissed and snapped and the enormous thing in the alley stretched toward the sky, its skin sounding like fabric tearing as it doubled, then tripled in size.

Lorelai's boots hit the roof of the next shop, following instantly by Leo's. She was already running, heading for the chimney as the vines behind them ripped the weaponsmith's apart, rending wood and brick like they were paper and scattering the pieces to the cobblestones below.

Leo rushed to her side, and together they skidded down the eastern edge of the roof while the vines burst into the building beneath them. "Hurry!"

The monstrous thing above them writhed and stretched, its

bulk casting a long shadow across the rooftops of Nordenberg. Beneath their feet, the shingles buckled and cracked as smaller vines pushed their way through the shop and onto the roof.

Lorelai reached the roof's edge first and launched herself into the air. She rolled as her feet touched the ground, and came up to find Leo right beside her. A short distance away, vines snaked across the alley, rushing toward them in the shadow of the monster that now towered over the entire village.

"I never thought I'd be grateful for all the land sprints Gabril makes us do," Leo said.

"*Nakhgor. Kaz`prin*," Irina shouted, her voice raw with power but edged with weariness.

"She's tiring. We just have to outrun these things a little longer," Lorelai said, and hoped she was telling the truth. Maybe Irina's magic stopped when she grew exhausted from the strain of overpowering the heart of Ravenspire for her own uses.

Or maybe her magic, once unleashed, took on a life of its own.

They ran toward the edge of the village, their boots pounding the cobblestones as the vines closed in behind them, hissing and writhing with incredible speed. Leo held himself back, keeping pace beside her, his brown eyes wide as he glanced over his shoulder to assess the towering threat behind them. Buildings flew past, and Lorelai could see the sloping meadow of wild grass that hugged the village entrance, and beyond that, the line of trees that seemed like a beacon of safety to the princess.

They'd hide in the trees. Wait out the remnants of Irina's spell, and when it was over, they'd do what they'd come here to do: go to the apothecary's and find medicine for Gabril.

They were almost to the gate, almost to the meadow, when Leo cried out and stumbled to a halt. Lorelai whirled to find a vine wrapped around his ankle, its serrated edges slicing through his trousers and drawing blood.

"Leo!" She grabbed the dagger from its sheath at her ankle as another vine slammed into her, sending her skidding across the cobblestones. She rolled to her left before it could wrap around her arm and sent the dagger sliding toward Leo. He snatched it and stabbed at the vine's bulbous head. A viscous black liquid foamed out of the vine, over his glove, and onto the bare skin of his wrist.

He screamed, a terrible wail of agony that sent a shaft of desperate panic into Lorelai and had the magic in her hands blazing. She lunged for him, dodging vines and buckled cobblestones. Slipping her hands beneath his arms, she pulled with all her might.

He slid toward the gate.

The vine slid with him, its grip unchanged by the gaping wound in its head. The black liquid wrapped around his wrist and burrowed in, a shackle beneath his skin.

The monstrous vine that towered over the village trembled violently and then, with a tremendous crack, unfurled hundreds of glistening snakelike tendrils that arced through the air toward the edges of the village.

"Oh no. It's a *cage*." The air felt too thick to breathe as Lorelai's pulse pounded against her skin in frantic beats. It was a cage, and it was going to trap them here with Irina if Lorelai couldn't get them free. Digging her boots into the ground, she pulled with all her might. Leo slid closer to the gate as the vine around his ankle stretched thin. "We have to leave *now*. Help me, Leo. Push with your feet. Slide back."

The black in his veins spread over his collarbone, heading for his heart. The truth was a heavy stone in Lorelai's stomach. She couldn't save him without using magic.

If she used magic, Irina would know. She'd come for Lorelai and stage a battle Lorelai had no idea how to win. Lorelai would probably die, but Leo didn't have to. She'd use her magic to send him into the forest, far from where she would be facing the queen alone.

It didn't matter what she had to sacrifice. It only mattered that she save Leo.

She let go of him and reached for her gloves. Something whipped around her waist and flung her away from Leo. She struggled, trying desperately to keep the head of the vine from biting her.

Trying desperately to reach her brother.

The vines overhead moved faster.

"Go." Leo's voice was weak with pain, but the look he gave her was fierce. "Get out of here."

"I can't . . . you're trapped. I can't pull you free." Her breath was a ragged sob of desperation as she tore at her gloves. As the vine around her snapped its teeth toward her heart.

The black liquid beneath his skin spread to his veins and turned them black as well. The snakelike bars of Nordenberg's cage reached the top of their ascent and hurtled down toward the village border.

"Leo!" She stopped fighting the vine and stretched her arms toward her brother.

The vine sank its teeth into her chest and shrieked in agony as her blood touched it. It hissed and released her, slinking back, its gaping mouth sizzling as if it had swallowed acid.

The cage streaked toward the ground.

She ran for Leo on shaking legs and smeared blood from the wound in her chest onto the vine that held him.

It let go.

"I've got you, Leo. Come on." Scooping her arms beneath his, she pulled with all her strength, and he slid toward the gate.

Almost there.

The vines dropped down with a hiss.

She sobbed out a prayer to the heavens and staggered out of the gate with him seconds before the falling vines slammed into the ground.

She pulled him back a few more steps before stumbling, the pain in her chest a throb of agony that turned her knees to water. Breathlessly, she said, "Can you run? Or at least walk? We have to get away, Leo, and I need you to help me."

He was silent.

"Leo?" She laid him on the meadow grass and dropped down beside him.

The blackness in his veins had spilled across his chest, up his neck, and into his eyes. The pulse that beat along the side of his neck was still.

"No!" She yanked her glove off, tore at his shirt, and slammed her hand against the bare skin of his chest where Irina's dark magic had spread across his body—a web of death that had stolen her brother.

"Please," she whispered, her power gathered and waiting for

his heart to surge toward her so she could tell it what she wanted.

So she could bring her brother back.

"Leo!" She tried to push her magic into him—to find one shred of life left in him that could respond to her. That could come back to her.

His heart remained still.

He was gone.

THIRTEEN

LEO WAS GONE.

Three simple words that tore into the foundation of Lorelai's life and left ruins in their wake.

Leo was gone.

Her best friend. Her greatest antagonist and staunchest ally. Her brother, who'd believed in her with every fiber of his being.

And whom she'd failed to protect.

She stumbled over the bumpy roots of a sugar maple and fell to her knees. The forest was too quiet, the world too vast, without Leo in it.

He was gone.

Something sharp and hot surged through Lorelai's chest and seized her throat. She curled over her knees, dug her gloved fingers into the ground, and opened her mouth in a soundless wail as tears streamed down her face. Grief swelled within her, pressing against her skin until she thought she would burst from the strength of it. It stole her voice, her breath, and gave her agony instead.

She hadn't saved him, and now he was gone.

Sobs shook her, and she let them take her. Let everything Leo meant to her cut her into pieces.

Gone.

Not gone . . . *taken.*

Slowly her tears dried, and the awful strength of the grief that consumed her gave way to one burning thought.

Lorelai hadn't lost Leo.

Irina had taken him, just like she'd taken their father.

Just like she'd taken Ravenspire.

Without Irina, Lorelai and Leo would be happily arguing in the castle while her father ran his kingdom with a firm and steady hand.

Irina was to blame for the wreckage that surrounded Lorelai's life. For the woman who'd killed her children to spare them starvation. For the mob of desperate peasants that had attacked the Eldrian king. For the death of Ravenspire.

For Leo.

It was time Irina paid the price for all she'd taken.

It was time Lorelai stepped out of the shadows and became the queen Ravenspire needed—the queen Leo and Gabril had always believed she could be.

She got to her feet, a hard, bright light of purpose burning in her heart. She was through hiding. Through with robbing coaches and cautiously working her way up to someday confronting the queen.

She was a strategist. A planner. And she could be as daring as her brother when she had to be. Irina would rue the day she'd ever set foot in Ravenspire.

But first, no matter the cost, she was going to save the only family she had left.

She took off running east toward the distant campsite where Gabril lay dying.

Lorelai stumbled into their camp at sunset the next day, her legs shaking, her body shivering since she'd lost her coat on a rooftop in Nordenberg, and her eyes burning from tears. Her boots crunched over dead leaves and brittle pine needles as she approached the tent where she'd left Gabril. It was dark. Silent.

Miserable heat spread from her chest to her throat, and she swallowed against the grief that thickened in her throat.

Was she too late?

Her heart aching, Lorelai lifted the tent flap quietly and braced herself for what she'd find.

It was empty.

She froze, and the ache of loss disappeared beneath a rush of heart-pounding fear. Where was he? Had someone taken him?

Lorelai dropped the tent flap and whirled to scan the area, trying hard to see a human-sized shape in the gathering dusk. Her hands shook as she called out, "Gabril? Are you here?"

There was no reply.

Sasha? Sasha!

For one agonizing moment, silence met Lorelai's words. She was already moving, searching the ground beside the tent for any signs that could tell her where Gabril had gone.

Help. Hurry, hurry, hurry. The cold, precise thoughts of her bird arrowed into Lorelai's mind, and she wanted to cry in relief.

Where are you? She sent back.

Sun.

Sun. Lorelai glanced at the quickly darkening sky and started moving west, following the last trace of sunlight as it slowly disappeared from the mountain. She walked for several minutes before she heard a soft thump-thump of wings, and her gyrfalcon swooped through the trees and perched on her shoulder.

Where is he? Lorelai asked as Sasha burrowed her face against Lorelai's neck, her beak scraping against the princess's skin.

Follow. Sasha's talons dug into Lorelai's shoulder as the bird pushed into the air and flew southwest.

Lorelai ducked low-hanging branches and skirted clumps of withered underbrush as she struggled to keep up with Sasha. Her heart thundered in her ears, but it couldn't drown out the terrible thought that Gabril might already be dead.

Her bird crested a small hill and disappeared over the other side. Lorelai raced forward, afraid she was going to lose sight of Sasha in the shifting shadows of the day's twilight. She reached the top of the hill, and then skidded to a stop as she saw Gabril lying on his back, his eyes closed, his chest bare despite the frigid weather.

"Gabril." She choked on his name as she ran to him and dropped to her knees. He was burning up with fever, she could feel it even through her gloves, but his teeth were chattering. His eyes remained closed, his breathing shaky and faint.

She looked at Sasha. *How did he get here?*

Sasha cocked her head, her bright black eyes catching the first hint of starlight. *Walk. Run. See things.*

What things?

Things not there. An image of Gabril, wild-eyed and afraid, staggering from the tent, batting at the air as if fending off a foe, and then running in short, halting steps through the forest accompanied Sasha's words.

Lorelai put the image and the words together and came up with the truth—hallucinations brought on by his high fever.

"Please," she whispered as she laid her head against his shoulder, wincing at the heat of his skin. "Don't leave me. I have no one else."

She had no one else. The truth of that statement hit hard, stealing her breath and sending a bright shaft of pain through her chest with every heartbeat.

Her parents were gone. Leo was gone. All she had was Gabril, the man who had protected her and taught her how to protect herself. Who loved her and believed in her and was ready to sacrifice himself for her.

Lorelai wished with everything in her that she could sacrifice herself for him instead.

"Ada?" Gabril's voice was nothing but a wisp of sound floating past his lips.

She lifted her head and found him gazing at the sky, a look of longing on his face. She frowned. Who was Ada?

"It's me," she said softly. "Lorelai."

He blinked, a slow, dragging motion as if he barely had the strength to keep his eyes open, and then slowly focused his gaze on her. His smile was full of love and pride and confidence, and it broke her heart.

"My . . . queen," he whispered.

Lorelai couldn't speak. Couldn't breathe.

His queen, whom he'd sacrificed everything for. Whom he'd rescued, protected, and raised to be the kind of ruler Ravenspire needed.

His queen who hadn't been able to stand up to Irina long enough to save her brother.

She wasn't going to make that mistake twice.

"Lorelai." His voice was nothing but a breath now. "Stronger . . . than you think. Love you," he whispered, his eyes closing.

Lorelai stared at him, her mouth working, trying to form the words "I love you" in return, but her mind was racing. Only a miracle would save him now, but miracles didn't happen in Ravenspire.

Miracles didn't happen, but magic did.

Lorelai tore off her gloves with quick, vicious movements as Gabril's chest rose sharply, his breathing quick and shallow.

She laid her bare hands against the fevered skin of his chest and immediately felt the heart of him—the core of implacable strength and resolve that fueled him—surge weakly against her palm. It was faint. He was almost gone.

She refused to let him go.

The risk of her touch triggering a latent spell and revealing Lorelai to Irina was a risk she was willing to take.

"*Nakhgor.*" Her voice shook, and her fingertips began to itch. "Find the sickness in his blood."

Gabril's breath rattled in his throat, and he choked weakly.

"No!" She pressed her hands harder against his chest and felt the sting of magic surge down her veins to pool like lightning in her palms. "I forbid you to die. I forbid it!"

Gabril's chest rose once more and then slowly deflated until there was nothing but a faint, irregular heartbeat slowly fading away.

"Gabril!" Her tears dried. Her hands stopped shaking. There

was nothing but the burn of magic and a fierce resolve to save him. "*Nakhgor.* Find the sickness in his blood. *Kaz`prin.* Bring it through me and into the ground instead."

For a moment, her magic seemed to hover against Gabril's skin, holding fast to the heart of him but refusing to obey Lorelai's command and enter his body.

Unbidden, she saw a memory of Irina crouching beside Lorelai so she could look the child princess in the eye as she said, "You have to mean it. The heart knows if you are worthy to command it. Allow no doubt. No room for dissent. Speak what you want and mean it with your whole heart, and every other heart will obey yours."

Lorelai glared down at Gabril's chest and focused. She was a warrior. A survivor. She was everything Gabril had taught her to be.

She was his queen, and his heart would obey hers.

"*Nakhgor. Kaz`prin.*" Her voice rose, filled with grief and power and fury. "*Nakhgor. Kaz`prin.*"

His chest shuddered. His heart thumped once against her palm.

She threw back her head as the magic flooded her, as its heat pressed against her skin from the inside out until she thought she might explode from the pain and the freedom of it, and yelled, "*Nakhgor! Kaz`prin!*"

Power burst from her palms, pierced Gabril's chest, and surged into his body, a tide of white light that hurt Lorelai's eyes when she stared at it in wonder.

The light rushed through Gabril's veins, and then Lorelai could see his thoughts the way she could see Sasha's. With Sasha,

Lorelai heard a few words and saw a simple image here and there. With Gabril, it was a flood of memories threaded through with words, sentences like ribbons weaving in and out of a moving canvas. She glimpsed the castle, her mother holding her father's hand, a pretty woman with dark skin and two young boys on her hips, the cruel slant of Irina's mouth as she screamed at Lorelai while standing in a pool of the king's blood, and an old mountain woman whispering that if Lorelai wore her gloves, she would be safe from the queen. The images spun on in rapid succession, but the light had finished scouring Gabril's blood and was returning to Lorelai bearing every bit of Gabril's fever and sickness.

As the light surged back into Lorelai, she screamed in agony. Pain was a creature with teeth and talons that raked at her from within. It was heat and swelling and unbearable anguish. Her bones felt like they would dissolve. Like she would split wide open at the seams and come apart.

Gabril's chest rose and fell in even measures. The arrow wound knit back together, the skin smooth and healthy. His eyes flew open as his princess sobbed in agony, her bare hands still pressed to his chest.

"Lorelai!" He grabbed her arms and sat up, but she couldn't see him. Couldn't hear him.

Nothing existed but the unending pain.

She'd told the magic to take the sickness from Gabril, bring it into her, and then send it into the ground.

Why wasn't it going into the ground?

She gnashed her teeth and then bent double as her stomach clenched.

"No!" Gabril wrapped his arms around her and held her

against him. "Don't touch the ground with your gloves off, Lorelai."

Touch the ground.

Her fevered mind latched on to the words as the pain scraped her raw.

The magic was trapped inside her until she released it the same way she'd called it. By touching her palm to the heart of the thing she wanted.

Gabril was rocking her, whispering things she couldn't hear. She struggled frantically, and he gentled his hold as if to help her get comfortable.

The moment he loosened his grip, Lorelai lunged forward, her breath a ragged sob in her chest, and slammed her open palm down onto the forest floor.

The light exploded out of her hand and plunged deep into the ground beneath the Falkrain Mountains. The pain receded, draining out of her and into the dirt as her magic ebbed. Exhaustion swamped her—a profound weariness that instantly sucked her down into the darkness of sleep as Gabril snatched her away from the ground and desperately tried to shove her gloves back on her hands.

He was too late.

Beneath the surface of the mountain, tendrils of Irina's magic sent to spy on the outer reaches of her kingdom, wove a web under the land. The threads of Lorelai's magic struck the web, and in a heartbeat, the princess's location was on its way to the queen.

FOURTEEN

THE DREAM ALWAYS began in the same place—on a snow-capped hill overlooking the road that cut through the Falkrain Mountains to join Ravenspire with Morcant. Irina's legs were knee-deep in snow that crested the fur-topped edge of her boots as she stared at the Ravenspire carriage slowly making its way across the Morcant border, bringing her younger sister, Tatiyana, to their father's funeral.

In the dream, Irina never opened her mouth. Never spoke the incantor that ripped the fir tree from its roots and sent it plummeting down onto Tatiyana's ebony carriage. But even if her dreaming mind refused to reenact her sister's death as it had truly happened, Irina couldn't escape the truth.

The carriage crumpled beneath the weight of the tree. Her sister's maid screamed for help. And in her dream, the snow around Irina turned to blood. She sank slowly, the blood an implacable force that demanded its due. When the blood coated her palms, hot and sticky, she felt the thunder of her sister's heartbeat pounding against the magic that had taken her life.

Flailing, Irina struggled to keep her palms away from the blood, but the moment she pulled her hands free of it, she sank like a stone. The blood surged over her mouth and nose and covered her head. She remained trapped, her sister's heartbeat thundering against her ears.

"Irina, wake up. Please. Come back to me." A familiar voice cut through the dream, dissolving her sister's heartbeat, and Irina swam sluggishly through thick clouds of gray-black darkness. She was shackled to weariness with chains that felt like the residue of her magic. In her mind's eye, the chains resembled writhing black snakes—like the snake that had killed Arlen and that she'd thought had killed his children too.

Her heart pounded, and she sucked in a breath as the pain hit—a sharp jolt of anguish that sliced through the darkness of her slumber and dragged her toward consciousness.

The clouds shifted and swirled, the weariness tugged at her, and she began to sink again when she felt something new.

A brush of power at her fingertips. An itch of pain that began to burn.

Something was wrong.

Lorelai.

She tore through the heaviness by sheer willpower, and her eyes snapped open as the magic surged through her veins.

It took a moment to realize that she wasn't in Nordenberg where she'd collapsed from the strain of the spell she'd used to catch the villagers who'd tried to run—she was lying on her own bed, propped up on pillows and covered in silk sheets.

How long ago had she been here? Had the girl who'd helped

to rob the garrison already been found?

Was it Lorelai?

Power stung her fingertips at the thought of the princess. Her hands twitched against the silk sheets, but the rest of her was still cocooned in weariness.

She blinked, her eyes feeling scoured with sand, and saw that the sky outside her window was a carpet of stars, that Raz was coiled at her feet, his golden eyes focused on her, and that Viktor was slumped in an armchair beside her bed, his fingertips pressed against his closed eyes, his clothing thoroughly rumpled.

She made a noise, and Viktor's eyes flew open. He lunged to his feet, his blue eyes finding hers. His shirt was untucked, his collar hanging to one side, and his cravat missing entirely.

Raz slowly uncoiled himself and slithered up the sheets to nestle against Irina's side. *Long sssleeep. Worry.*

Viktor fell to his knees beside the bed and gathered Irina in his arms. Her head tipped against his shoulder, and he buried his face against the crook of her neck as he tightened his hold.

Her hands burned, and the certainty that something had happened filled her.

"I thought you were going to die." His voice shook.

For a moment, his worry, his desperation, felt like love, and Irina let the warmth of it touch her. But then the burn of her magic surged through her veins, and she struggled to move her arms. To sit up.

Gently, he slid his arms beneath hers and lifted until she was propped against her pillows. She looked away from the searing intensity of his gaze as the magic spread down her arms and warmed her hands. He sat down on the sheets beside her, placed a finger beneath her chin, and gently turned her face toward his.

"How are you?" he asked.

Maybe it was the unfettered devotion in his actions or the fact that he was the one person she'd never had to bespell to ensure his loyalty. Whatever the reason, Irina found herself saying, "I'm so tired."

He ran a hand through her hair, tugging gently at the tangles he found. When he reached the base of her neck, he cupped it with his hand and squeezed the tension away.

"You overworked yourself," he said quietly. "You always do. You act like if you delegate too much, the kingdom will fall to pieces."

She smiled a little. "I have you to make sure that doesn't happen."

His eyes darkened. "The spell in Nordenberg . . . that was an enormous outpouring of energy, and it cost you so much." His voice cracked, and he looked away as he drew a deep breath.

"I'm fine."

"You are *not* fine. You keep using your magic as if there's no cost demanded of you, but there is. There is and I can't . . . You almost died, Irina. I almost lost you this time." He was back to searing her with his gaze, and an uncomfortable sense of guilt heated her cheeks.

"That's ridiculous."

"How would you know? You've been unconscious for three days. Three days!" He pulled sharply at his already crooked collar as if it was choking him. "Your heartbeat was irregular. Your breathing grew so shallow the second day, the physician told me to have the maids pull out the black crepe to make mourning bands for the staff."

"Well, he was wrong. Remove him from his post and—"

"He wasn't wrong." The finality in his voice silenced her. "You expended so much energy and caught one boy. Was it worth almost dying?"

"I had to." She found the strength to sit up straight and leaned toward Viktor until she could feel the warmth of him against her skin. "Viktor, I *had* to. The rest of the village was loyal to me. They were ready to help me find the mountain girl. But this boy ran. Why would he do that if he wasn't going to warn her? If he didn't think she was the princess? I'd lose her and have to start all over, and I *can't*. If Lorelai is alive, I have to find her and destroy her before she tries to destroy me."

Slowly, so slowly she could've moved away if she'd wanted to, he leaned forward and pressed his lips to hers. Her body swayed toward him, finding a home against his chest where she fit perfectly within the circle of his arms. Warmth that had nothing to do with the burn of magic rushed through her, sparkling like champagne in her veins, and she grabbed his mangled collar and pulled him closer.

He made a rough noise, tilted her head back, and kissed her with a desperation he only ever showed her when they were alone. Gone was the calm, unflappable Viktor who managed the castle's affairs with a steady hand. In his place was a man full of fierce longing and need who kissed Irina like she was the air, and he was drowning.

For a few heartbeats, she let herself feel it. Let herself believe it. This could be hers. All she had to do was say the word, and she wouldn't be alone.

She wouldn't be alone, but there would be a price for that. There was always a price. Her father, who had loved her sister best, had taught her that. Her uncle, who crushed her dreams by breaking Morcantian protocol that stated the eldest daughter was to be married first and letting Arlen have Tatiyana for his bride instead of Irina, had reminded her. And Lorelai, the little princess with the power so like Irina's own, had carved that lesson deep into Irina's heart with the knife of utter betrayal.

She pulled away from Viktor.

He looked at her, the desperate longing still raw in his eyes, and said, "What do you need? Just tell me what you need."

Her fingertips itched. Her palms burned. The memory of Lorelai's betrayal obliterated the warmth she'd felt while kissing Viktor, and the awareness that tingled at the edge of her power rushed forward.

Lorelai.

"Bring me my mirror, please."

The moment her palm touched the mirror's surface, magic sparked from her fingertips and the swirling gray depths of the mirror began to move faster. Her hands shook, her skin clammy as she gave the command.

"Mirror, mirror, your depths I scry," she said as power gathered in her palms and leaped toward the glass. "Show me the princess Lorelai."

The white light of her magic spiraled into the swirling gray of the mirror, and suddenly there she was—lying on a blanket inside a tent, her eyes closed, a black man with his back to the mirror bending over her, and an enormous gyrfalcon perched just inside the tent's entrance. Her skin was as white as snow, her lips as red as blood, and her long hair as black as ebony.

"*Lorelai*," the queen whispered. She looked up at Viktor, her voice shaking. "She's alive."

FIFTEEN

KOL STOOD ON the balcony of his room in Ravenspire's castle and stared at the midnight sky. How was Brig faring without him? How much ground had his army lost to the ogres while he'd been gone? The council hadn't sent word for him to return, so he had to believe the ogres had yet to threaten the capital, but that could change in an instant. His people needed saving, and so far his desperate mission to get help from Queen Irina had been a spectacular failure.

He couldn't hold up his end of the bargain without a specific scent to follow. The trip to Nordenberg had been as terrifying as it had been unproductive. It was one thing to know he was dealing with a *mardushka* of extraordinary power. It was another to see it in action.

All that power, however, had been for naught. No princess caught in the queen's web. No scent for Kol to track. And at the end of the spell, Irina had simply collapsed. He'd been ensconced in the visitor's wing of the castle for days now with no word on when Irina would be well enough to meet with him. In fact, judging by the somber looks on the faces of the maids and pages who served the Eldrians, many in the castle no longer believed Irina would recover at all.

Which meant Eldr and everyone in it was doomed.

He began pacing the stone balcony, his eyes tracing familiar constellations in the sky above. Did his sister wander her balcony at night staring at the stars while she worried over him?

Did his people fear their second-rate king had abandoned them in their time of need?

Most important, could he come up with a plan to save Eldr that didn't involve Irina before the ogres destroyed what was left of his kingdom?

The cathedral bells tolled the hour—twelve strikes of a hammer against the bells. Twelve reminders that Kol was running out of time. Eldr was running out of time.

Maybe he could go to Morcant and beg King Milek for favor. Despite what Irina had said about *mardushkas* in Morcant obeying the laws restricting the use of magic, he bet he could find a price that would tempt Milek into finding a *mardushka* capable of helping. He doubted Milek would need reminding that Draconi were able to sniff out veins of gold and caverns of jewels buried deep under the ground. It was tantamount to agreeing to enslave himself to the king as a treasure hunter for the rest of his days, but it was better than allowing Eldr to fall.

His friends would never let him do it. He'd have to shift into his dragon and leave the castle without a word to them.

The thought of not saying good-bye—to his friends or to Brig—hurt, but he didn't have a choice. He didn't have the energy to argue with them, especially when nothing they said would sway him. Eldr was *his* responsibility, and he'd made a promise on his father's funeral pyre that he wouldn't be a disappointment again. He refused to break that promise.

He also couldn't risk his friends shifting into dragons and following him to Morcant, which they would do without hesitation. King Milek would agree to loan Eldr a talented *mardushka* in exchange for the servitude of one dragon. He didn't need to know there were two more potential treasure hunters at his disposal.

Kol stopped pacing and sagged against the iron railing as a frigid breeze chased dead leaves across the wide expanse of the castle grounds. Facing the flight to Morcant alone was harder than he'd anticipated, but it was what a true leader would do.

His mind made up, Kol unbuttoned his shirt with swift fingers and shrugged out of the garment, letting it fall in a heap on the balcony. He'd leave enough signs for his friends to realize he'd shifted and flown away on his own, rather than let them worry someone in Ravenspire had done him harm. By the time they realized he was gone and tracked him by scent to Morcant, he'd have already struck a deal with King Milek, and it would be over.

He stepped to the edge of his balcony as he reached for his belt.

"Going somewhere?" Jyn asked from the balcony to his right.

He jumped and whirled to face her as she stepped out of the shadows beside the door to her room.

"Planning to shift into your dragon and go make a deal without us?" Trugg asked from the balcony to his left as he too stepped out of the shadows and into the starlight, his meaty arms folded over his chest while he glared at his king.

"What are you two doing out this late?" He forced himself to sound casual, like the fact that he'd been stripping in the moonlight was of no consequence, but the looks on his friends' faces said they weren't convinced.

"What do you think we're doing? We're guarding you." Trugg sounded furious.

"Guarding . . . I never instructed you to guard me." He returned Trugg's glare with one of his own while his hastily constructed backup plan disintegrated into dust.

"Good thing we didn't ask your permission, then." Trugg stepped closer.

"You're our king." Jyn rolled to the balls of her feet and shrugged out of her shirt, leaving nothing but a thin camisole and her pants. "And our friend. Did you really think we wouldn't be watching over you day and night?"

Something hot and thick rose in Kol's throat as Trugg's shirt hit the balcony as well. They were preparing to shift. They weren't trying to talk him out of his decision. They weren't arguing with his reasons. They were simply ready to throw themselves into danger because where he went, they followed.

"You can't come with me," he said, and, curse the skies, his voice shook.

"I dare you to try to stop us," Trugg said as he dropped his pants.

"You don't understand." Kol's voice rose. "I don't have time to wait for Irina to get better—*if* she gets better. Eldr needs help *now*. I'm going to Morcant to offer myself to the king in exchange for a *mardushka* capable of defeating the ogres. If you come along—"

"*When* we come along." Jyn's pants followed her shirt.

"*If* you come along, King Milek will try to enslave you in exchange for the *mardushka* instead of just enslaving me. I can't allow that. I won't. It's my job to protect Eldr. All of Eldr. And I'm not going to fail my people. Do you hear me?" He grabbed the balustrade with shaking fingers. "I'm not going to fail my people anymore. This is my sacrifice to make."

"And we aren't going to fail you, Kol." Jyn's dark eyes gleamed. "You think you have to be strong for Eldr, and you're right. You do. But so do we. So does every single Eldrian threatened by the ogre invasion. You have the responsibility of saving Eldr, but we have the responsibility of saving *you*."

Kol stared at her while the thickness in his throat became the sting of unshed tears in his eyes. "I don't need to be saved."

"Don't be an idiot," Trugg said gruffly. "Eldr needs a king, not another loss. And you are the king Eldr needs, even if you pull stupid stunts like trying to fly off on your own to deal with the king of Morcant because sky forbid you should ask for help."

Gratitude and fear settled into Kol's chest like a burning stone. He slammed his fist against the balustrade and yelled, "If I ask for your help, I'm condemning you to enslavement in Morcant for the rest of your lives!"

Trugg lunged forward until only the thin space between their two balconies separated him from Kol. "No, you great ugly lizard, *I'm* condemning myself to enslavement in Morcant for the rest of my life because Eldr needs a *mardushka* and a king. Now shift or shut up about this plan and go back into your room where I don't have to worry about you."

A tense silence fell between them. Kol was trying to swallow past the thickness in his throat and come up with words that would shoulder the weight of his feelings, but if the words existed, he couldn't find them. Trugg raised a brow and stood in his undergarment, his arms crossed over his chest while he waited for his king's decision.

Before Kol could choose whether to continue with his plan to petition King Milek at the expense of his friends or whether to give Irina one more day to recover from her illness, someone knocked sharply at his door.

Instantly, Jyn disappeared into her room as if rushing to check the hallway outside Kol's door. Trugg backed up, took a running leap, and landed beside Kol on the king's balcony.

"I'll answer that," he said.

"I can answer my own door." Kol decided to save himself the humiliation of trying to push past Trugg and into his bedroom first. "Besides, you aren't wearing any pants."

"I don't need pants to deal with whoever has decided to disturb my king at this unholy hour of the night." Trugg strode through Kol's chambers and wrenched open the door.

Viktor stood on the other side, his hair damp as if he'd just finished bathing, and his clothing impeccable. He glanced once at Trugg's lack of clothing and then looked pointedly over the boy's shoulder.

"Queen Irina has recovered and requests an audience with King Kolvanismir," he said, his measured tone giving no indication that he was face-to-face with a mostly naked Eldrian warrior.

In minutes, Kol and his friends were appropriately dressed and standing before the queen as she reclined on a white couch in a cozy office. A torn once-white coat lay on her lap, and her creepy snake was coiled by her side.

"I'm pleased to see that you're recovering," Kol said, though *pleased* hardly covered it. Eldr still had a chance, and Kol hadn't had to sell himself into slavery to King Milek to accomplish it.

Irina leaned forward, her eyes lit with zeal. "We're both about to get what we want, my dear boy."

The queen lifted the coat, and Viktor hurried forward to bring it to Kol. It smelled like burned wood, spicy evergreens, and crisp snow with a hint of something softer underneath.

Something about the scent was familiar.

"Whose is this?" he asked.

Irina's smile was fierce. "It was left on a rooftop in Nordenberg by someone fleeing my spell."

"How does that help us?"

"Because the person fleeing my spell was the princess. I've recently seen the body of the boy who was caught by my spell. It was her brother. My magic just discovered her location in the Falkrain Mountains, and now we have her scent."

Kol stared at the coat in his hands, his hearts pounding. Slowly, he raised his head to look at the queen. "Our blood oath still stands. I'll bring the princess to the castle, and you seal the ogres back into Vallé de Lumé."

Irina's smile disappeared. "I don't require all of the princess, huntsman."

A chill raced over Kol's skin. "I don't understand. Our oath said—"

"Our oath said that once you complete the task I set before you, my magic will deliver Eldr from the ogres. The exact wording of the oath itself must be obeyed, or your blood will turn to poison, and you will die."

"I agreed to bring the princess back to the castle." Kol met the queen's gaze and worked hard to hold it.

She leaned forward, her eyes pinning Kol where he stood. "You agreed to do whatever I asked of you. And I am asking you to bring me the princess's heart."

The breath left Kol's body, and his fists dug into the coat while his dragon heart pounded fiercely. "I can't . . . I don't hurt people."

The queen's voice was lethal. "Hurt one person, or lose your life and the lives of everyone in Eldr. It's your choice."

It was no choice at all. His kingdom was in shambles. His people were dying. Even now, the ogres could be at the capital. And if he refused, if he broke his oath, he would die, and Eldr would fall.

Kol turned on his heel and left the room to hunt.

SIXTEEN

LORELAI'S EYES OPENED slowly. The canvas ceiling of their tent stretched above her. For a moment, she expected to hear Leo complaining about how early Gabril had awakened them, but then the truth hit with a fresh wave of pain.

Leo was gone.

Her chest was a hollow, empty space that ached with loss, and she wanted to close her eyes again and let sleep take her.

Wake up, wake up, wake up, please Lorelai. Please. Just wake up.

She blinked, and tears stung her eyes as she turned to see Gabril kneeling beside her, his shoulders bowed, his face pressed into the blanket next to her shoulder. She opened her mouth to tell him that she was awake, but he was already speaking again.

I don't know what to do. What do I do, Ada? Leo, my precious boy, didn't come back, and Irina must know where we are since Lorelai touched the ground. Where do I take her when I can't carry her? How do I keep her safe now?

Lorelai frowned. It was Gabril's voice, but it wasn't like anything he'd ever say to her. And he was talking to Ada, the woman he'd mentioned when he'd been out of his mind with fever. Was he feverish again?

The queen will be coming. I know it. What do I do?

He sounded desperate. Lorelai tried to lift her hand to lay on his shoulder, but her body didn't want to obey her yet. She settled for saying, "Gabril."

Gabril slowly raised his head. "You're awake." His voice shook with relief.

How do I save her, Ada?

"Who's Ada?" Lorelai asked seconds before an image of a beautiful black woman with two boys who looked remarkably like Gabril filled her head.

Lorelai's mouth dropped open, and she shook her head in rapid denial as Gabril's eyes widened in horror. She hadn't been hearing him speak. She'd been hearing his *thoughts*.

"Oh no. I sent magic into you, and now I can hear your thoughts like I can with Sasha." Her voice trembled. "I don't want to be inside your head."

His mouth tightened, and suddenly where his thoughts had been there was a blank wall of nothing. A frown pinched her brows together as she pushed to feel the connection between their minds and came up with nothing.

"Better?" he asked quietly.

"How did you do that?"

"I don't know if you remember the Morcantian mountain woman we stayed with for a few weeks after we left the castle. I'd met her a few times before when I accompanied the king to Morcant. She gave me a rudimentary understanding of your magic and taught me how to block a *mardushka* from using a mental bond in case the magic Irina used to bespell me had given her the ability to hear my thoughts."

"A bond is only created when a *mardushka* sends her magic into you and commands your heart," Lorelai said. "Like what happened when I healed Sasha. I don't think Irina would dare create a mental bond because it works both ways. She'd never let anyone know what she's really thinking."

"Better safe than dead." His dark eyes studied her intently. "You've been asleep for two days. Thirsty?"

She accepted the water he offered.

"Leo . . ." Her voice, husky from disuse, cracked over her brother's name, and then she was in Gabril's arms, sobbing.

"He's dead?" Gabril's voice wavered. Tears gathered in his eyes as she nodded.

"How?" he asked, and the edge in his tone promised terrible things for the one who'd killed his prince.

"Irina." Her eyelids were already drooping again, and weariness that was half grief and half weakness from having had to overpower Gabril's implacable will to heal him turned her thoughts to wisps of smoke.

"Sleep," he said softly. "We need to leave first thing in the morning. You can tell me about it then."

By morning, Lorelai was strong enough to get up and eat breakfast without help. Gabril boiled a small pot of beans and sliced the last of the apples they'd stolen from the queen's garrison. She ate the beans but ignored the apples.

After seeing the villagers eat Irina's rotten apples in Nordenberg, Lorelai wasn't sure she'd ever be able to eat the fruit again.

Hunt but don't bring your meal back to share with me. Lorelai pushed the thought at Sasha and watched the gyrfalcon spiral into the sky and disappear from view.

Gabril eased himself down beside her, his hand massaging his aching left leg in the early morning chill. He peered at her half-eaten breakfast, his expression inscrutable.

"Do you want to tell me what happened?"

Her stomach churned, and her voice was hollow as she told Gabril about Nordenberg. The grief that had consumed her from the moment she realized she couldn't save Leo was burning in her chest. A wound that swallowed the words she still thought to say to him before once again remembering that he was gone.

She leaned against Gabril as he held her, and then he said gently, "Better finish eating. We need to leave. We'll figure out what to do next once we put some distance between us and this part of the mountain."

She looked at her boots, at the worn toe on the left one where she used it to push off walls or tree trunks to propel herself upward, and took another bite of beans. The food tasted like ashes in her mouth, and her stomach rebelled at the thought of eating, but she didn't have the luxury of allowing her grief to make her weak. She chewed viciously, magic threading through her veins and stinging her palms as the terrible grief within her focused on its target.

She had a queen to destroy.

She remained silent while she ate, her thoughts a tangle she had to unknot so she could make a plan. Irina was a master at using her magic like a weapon, and she knew where to find Lorelai. That was a significant disadvantage. Plus, Lorelai was used to being part of a team—Leo dreamed bold and big, while Lorelai planned down to the smallest detail to keep them both safe.

But Leo hadn't been safe. She shoved another bite into her mouth and forced herself to focus on the task in front of her.

Lorelai swallowed her last mouthful of beans and something hard and bright filled her chest as a plan came to her. The plan was bold and daring, like Leo, but used the battle strategy that came naturally to Lorelai. She'd send the kind of dramatic message that would have put a sparkle in Leo's eyes, but she'd plan down to the last detail to make sure every single risk she took brought Irina one step closer to total destruction.

And at the end of it, Lorelai would pit her will—her heart—against the heart of Ravenspire's queen, and only one of them would survive.

Minutes later, they were ready to leave. Gabril turned east, but Lorelai put a hand on his arm.

"We're going to the far northwest mountain."

He frowned. "That's Duchess Waldina's land. She's loyal to Irina."

"I'm counting on it." Lorelai's voice was cold.

"I thought we had another six months of working our way through the mountain villages, robbing the queen's treasury offices and building loyalty by giving it back to the people."

"I'm done being cautious and safe, Gabril. Irina has destroyed my family and my kingdom. It's time I repaid the favor."

A fierce light burned in his eyes. "Agreed. How does Duchess

Waldina factor into your plan?"

"She's loyal to Irina and often stays at the castle. I need to know the gossip. The rumors. Anything that will show me a weakness I can use against Irina as I form a battle strategy for taking her down."

"I'm not sure the duchess will be willing to give you that information."

Lorelai's jaw clenched until her teeth ached. "She'd better rethink that position before I get there." Flexing her gloved hands, she said, "Once I have what I need, I'm going after Irina. No waiting. No hiding. Just a full-force attack that will end with one of us dead. It will be dangerous. Risky even by Leo's standards." Her voice broke, and she made herself look away so he wouldn't see how desperately she wanted him to ignore her next words. "You don't have to come with me. You've already risked so much. I release you from your service."

He took two steps forward and pulled her against his chest. "You aren't releasing me from anything. Where you go, I go." She gripped his coat with desperate hands as relief warmed the pit of ice that had been forming in her stomach at the thought of facing the rest of her journey alone.

"What about Ada?" she asked as she released him and stepped back. "I didn't mean to pry into your thoughts, but . . . is she your wife? Were those your boys?"

The loneliness that clung to him when he didn't think she was watching filled his eyes, but his voice was composed. "Yes, that's my family."

"You never told us about them." She tried hard not to make it sound like an accusation.

"Because you'd just lost everything. My choices, my grief, weren't yours to bear."

"Where are they? Do you ever see them?"

"They're still in the capital. I got a message to her as I fled with you and Leo, and we've managed to exchange a few messages since then, but, no, I don't see them. She buried me—the entrance hall collapsed on all the guards who were on duty that night. She simply claimed that I had died along with the others and held a funeral. Irina attended. I've stayed away because as long as Irina believes I'm dead, Ada and the boys are safe."

Lorelai's hands curled into fists. "You should have your family back."

"So should you," he said gently.

Her eyes burned with unshed tears, but she lifted her chin. "It's too late for mine, but it isn't too late for yours. Let's get moving. We have a lot of ground to cover, and I have a lot of planning to do if I want to have a chance against Irina."

"Oh, you have more than a chance." He picked up her travel pack and handed it to her. "Do you know why I'm willing to follow you into this battle without hesitation?"

"Because I'm Arlen's oldest child, and that makes the throne of Ravenspire rightfully mine."

"Wrong." He held her gaze, his eyes fierce. "Bloodlines and birthrights don't make someone worth following. Neither does the appearance of power. I follow you because you have the courage of a true warrior."

"I don't feel courageous." She turned toward the west. "I just see what needs to be done, and there's no one else to do it. No one else who can fight Irina with the weapon she's used to destroy Ravenspire. It has to be me. That doesn't make me a warrior. That just makes me the best tool for a necessary job."

As they left the campsite behind and moved through a grove of trees with crumbling trunks and bare, shriveled branches, Gabril said, "A warrior doesn't focus on the odds stacked against her. She focuses on her heart, on her will to face the evil in her world and defeat it, and then she finds a way to do it."

Lorelai grabbed his arm to help him over a fallen evergreen. She should've healed his leg when she healed his sickness, but she hadn't been thinking clearly.

She was thinking clearly now. The first order of business when they stopped for lunch would be restoring his left leg. She refused to hear an argument from him over it, either. His heart would submit to hers to make the cost of magic light enough to easily bear, or . . . well, she didn't know what she'd do to overpower the will of the man who'd been like a father to her for the past nine years, but she'd think of something.

"I want to tell you a story." Gabril reached for her gloved hand, and she held on to him while the morning sun filtered in past the bare branches and hung in the air like pale gold dust.

"Once upon a time, there was a princess who was unlike any other princess."

She made a sound of disbelief, and he glared at her. "You may be my queen, but I can still assign you an hour of land sprints if you aren't listening."

She gave him her full attention.

"Other princesses were raised in castles with maids to clean up after them, cooks to bake their favorite treats, closets full of fancy dresses, and parents to watch over them and love them."

Lorelai's heart began to ache, thrumming in the hollow space that grief had carved into her. Other princesses also had brothers who were teasing them or starting arguments or defending them at any cost. She drew in a sharp breath and focused on Gabril's words before the empty space inside could consume her.

"Those princesses had soft hands and peaceful sleep. They had the luxury of knowing what every day would look like, since every day was the same as the one before it, and of knowing what their future would hold. They would grow up, dance at balls, flirt at royal functions, and then marry into another kingdom or assume the crown and rule their own."

"Sounds very exciting," Lorelai said in a tone that implied the exact opposite.

"We'll pity those other princesses and send them our condolences for their boring, ball-filled lives later." Gabril pressed a fist against his left leg as they began to climb the steep incline that would bring them back to the road that dipped and curved around the Falkrains, joining the eastern edge of the range with the lands in the west.

"Now, the princess in our story didn't live in a castle anymore. She'd lost her home, her family, and her kingdom to a wicked queen who wanted the world at her feet more than she wanted anything else. This wicked queen destroyed the princess's life and broke her heart. For some princesses, all that pain, all that loss, would break their strength of will."

The ache in Lorelai's chest spread, and she wrapped her arms around herself.

Gabril leaned forward and captured her gaze with his. "Not this princess. For you see, it was the princess's extraordinary strength of will that had first caught the attention of the wicked queen. The queen thought to bend that will to her own. To tempt that will into believing a lie. But the princess was not so easily deceived, even when everyone else was. Though she was a child, and though she had no allies, no one to help her face the evil queen, she found the strength to do so on her own."

Lorelai bent her head and studied the leaf-covered ground as she walked.

"She almost succeeded, and that terrified the wicked queen, for nothing scares the wicked so much as the realization that someone has chosen not to surrender, even when the cost of defiance is almost too much to bear."

"The cost was too much for others to bear too," Lorelai whispered.

"Who is telling this story?" Gabril demanded.

"You."

"That's right. Now, as I was saying, the wicked queen was terrified of the princess's strength, and she did everything she could to break the princess's will, but the princess refused to be broken. She stood up to the queen, revealed her for what she really was, and escaped the castle—"

"Because you helped her."

"Interrupt me one more time, and you will have both cooking *and* cleanup duty for a month."

Lorelai pressed her lips closed.

"The princess could've let her grief turn into bitterness, but she turned it into kindness instead. She could've let her terror turn into paralysis, but she used it to fuel her courage. She learned how to climb walls, how to fall without being injured, how to disguise herself, how to sprint through the forest without leaving a sign—she learned how to survive, but she never allowed her own survival to mean more to her than the survival of others."

His voice grew husky. "She'd been trained to flee at the first sign of trouble, but instead, she stayed. She fought an entire group of soldiers because she didn't look at her odds of winning; she looked at her reasons for fighting. She trekked through the forest to Nordenberg with her brother even though the entire northern army was looking for her because she didn't look at the reasons not to risk the trip. She looked at her reasons for going."

Lorelai flinched at the mention of Nordenberg.

"And when the princess realized that she and her brother were in terrible danger, she didn't freeze. She didn't surrender. She fought to save him, leaving herself open to attack."

Lorelai's pulse pounded, and her palms burned as the wound where the vine had sunk its teeth into her chest throbbed faintly.

"And when tragedy struck once again, the princess didn't wallow in it. Didn't let it break her. No, she came back to her mentor, saw that he was about to die, and"—his voice broke, and he cleared his throat—"she disobeyed his most important rule, knowing it might bring the wicked queen straight to her to finish what she'd tried to do nine years ago. The princess healed her mentor, at great cost to herself, because she didn't look at her odds of survival. She looked at *his*."

Slowly Lorelai met Gabril's gaze.

"Now you tell me, Lorelai Rosalinde Tatiyana Diederich, does that sound like a courageous warrior to you?"

She couldn't speak.

He took her hand again as they neared the top of the steep rise. "Thank you for saving my life, Lorelai."

"You're welcome." Her voice was small. The spot beside her that Leo would've filled with joking about what costumes they'd wear as they took the fight to Irina or with congratulating himself on surviving the seriousness of Gabril and Lorelai was achingly silent.

Gabril's voice was strong and sure. "I believe in you, and I've fought for you, because in a world full of people who crumble before an evil too terrifying to comprehend, you put up your fists and fight."

Before she could reply, a strange sound shook the forest—a steady thump-thump that reverberated from the air above and caused the trees to shiver. A shadow blocked the sun, and Lorelai looked up to see Irina's red and gold dragon—longer than a horse-drawn carriage and twice as tall—fly over the top of the hill and plunge straight toward her.

SEVENTEEN

"Down!" Lorelai shoved Gabril to the right and took off running in the opposite direction. "Chase me. Come on, chase *me*," she whispered as she dove between two thick-trunked pines and sprinted down the hill. Her heart thundered in her ears and a vise squeezed her chest as visions of Gabril being consumed by dragon's fire or crushed between the creature's monstrous jaws filled her mind.

Branches exploded into the air, and a tree crashed to the ground and tumbled past her to disintegrate into chunks of debris at the bottom of the hill.

She risked a glance over her shoulder as she tossed her travel pack to the ground and leaped between another pair of trees.

The dragon had flown past Gabril, who was struggling to his feet, his face a mask of terrified fury. The beast was heading straight for her, its enormous wings shattering treetops as it came.

"Run, Lorelai!" Gabril yelled.

She *was* running—flat out sprinting faster than she ever had—and the dragon was closing the gap between them like it was nothing.

Hurtling over a boulder, she dove beneath a low branch and whipped toward the left as the crackle of dragon's fire exploded into the tree behind her and sent it plunging to the bottom of the hill.

She couldn't outrun a dragon. Couldn't climb trees and leap through the forest when the dragon could just light her on fire the second she was in range.

There was only one way out of this, and the power was already flooding her veins.

She skidded down the rest of the hill, her pulse beating a frantic tempo against her skin as the dragon roared and fire strafed the ground behind her. The heat licked at her skin, and she rolled forward, coming to her feet at the bottom of the hill, where she was surrounded by smoking chunks of the trees the dragon had destroyed.

She wasn't going to die here—incinerated by Irina's pet dragon while the queen stayed safe and sound in her castle, content in the knowledge that she'd destroyed the last of the Diederichs.

Kill overgrown lizard. Eat the eyes, tear out the heart. Sasha's thoughts, vibrating with rage, broke past the thunder of Lorelai's heartbeat and sent a shaft of panic down the princess's spine as the gyrfalcon, returning from her morning hunt, streaked through the air, heading straight for the dragon.

No! Lorelai tore off her gloves as the beast reached the bottom of the hill, the wind from its wings slamming into Lorelai until it was hard to keep her footing. *Don't attack. Don't come closer. He'll kill you.*

Kill it first. Sasha shrieked and dove for the dragon.

No! Lorelai screamed, but Sasha ignored her.

Her bird was going to die, and then she was going to die unless she changed her odds. Lorelai locked eyes with the dragon, magic burning like lightning in her palms, and sprinted straight for the beast.

The dragon's eyes became slits as Sasha slammed into its head, and it shook her off as easily as a horse dislodges a fly.

Smoke poured from the beast's nostrils as Lorelai closed the distance between them, and it opened its mouth.

Fear tore at her, threatening to turn her thoughts into a whirlwind of panic, but she was acting on instinct now. She twisted to the side, kicked off the ground, slammed her feet against the closest tree trunk, and launched herself into the air. Arcing, she flipped and landed on the dragon's back, just behind its head.

Sasha flew at the creature's face, aiming for its eyes, and narrowly missed getting incinerated. Heat from the fire that poured out of the dragon's mouth warmed the scales beneath Lorelai, and she grabbed its neck with her bare hands, her mind frantically scrambling for an incantor that would force the dragon's heart to obey hers instead of Irina's.

The dragon's skin shuddered, a ripple that nearly dislodged Lorelai.

Sasha banked hard and shrieked as she came for the beast.

Something crashed behind Lorelai, and she glanced back to find two additional dragons smashing through the trees—a silver and black dragon that was slightly smaller than the one Lorelai clung to and an enormous all-black dragon whose wingspan was wider than a peasant's cottage.

Sobbing a desperate prayer that she could somehow figure out how to defeat three dragons at once, Lorelai dug her fingers into the scales on the dragon's neck, an incantor on the tip of her tongue.

Except she wasn't gripping scales.

She was gripping skin that was rapidly softening into something human.

The dragon dropped to the ground, sending Lorelai tumbling. Its ridges and wings receded, and its bones made an awful grinding sound as its body shrank.

Sasha slammed into the dragon-turning-human and knocked him to his side. The silver dragon roared and lunged toward the bird, but then a boy with wild red-brown hair picked himself up off the ground and held up his hand, palm out.

The other dragons slowly settled onto the ground, their eyes watchful.

Sasha perched on a branch and watched them as if waiting for one of them to make a wrong move.

The boy turned to face Lorelai, wearing nothing but a strange collar of thistle and bone. The breath left her body as the sun glinted against his wild hair. His amber eyes locked on hers, and the empty space carved into her by Leo's death filled with fury as she stared at the Eldrian king she'd rescued from the mob in Tranke.

"You!" She spat the word at him as she raised hands that shook with anger, power sparking in her palms and begging for an incantor that would send her magic into the boy and kill him where he stood.

"*You're* the princess?" He sounded shocked and horrified.

She trembled, and there was a buzzing in her ears that made everything but the need to hurt him seem inconsequential. She stalked toward him, her eyes locked on his. "I should've let the villagers kill you. Or let you break the treaty by shifting into your dragon so that Irina would have nothing to do with you."

"I didn't know when I agreed to hunt down the lost princess that it was you." He held his hands up in a placating gesture as if somehow his words would make amends for anything.

"You were with Irina in Nordenberg." Magic burned against her skin, and incantors designed to punish and destroy balanced on the tip of her tongue, desperate for release. "You were hunting us there."

"I didn't know who I was hunting—"

"Leo died there!" Her hands slammed into his chest and sent him to his knees. "My brother is dead, and you were there helping Irina kill him."

The black dragon roared, smoke pouring from its nostrils, but Kol held up a hand to stay it. His eyes were stricken as he stared up at her.

Lorelai leaned down. "Oh, you're going to want his help. Not that he can save you from me. You owe me your life, remember? And now you owe me for Leo's, even though it was Irina's spell that killed him. What do you think my brother's life is worth, Kol? Is it worth the life of a king who would enslave himself to a monster and kill the innocent?"

"I'm so sorry." He breathed the words, every syllable full of pain and regret.

Lorelai's heart pounded, and magic seared her veins with the power to make him truly sorry. To make him pay for his part in Leo's death.

Behind him, the black dragon began shifting to his human form, but Lorelai ignored him. Let him plead for the life of his miserable king. Let him threaten to kill her for laying a hand on Kol. Lorelai didn't care. The terrible pain that had filled her when Leo died had found a purpose in hurting the king of Eldr. It would be justice, and Leo deserved that.

No one is going to give you what you want, Lorelai. You have to take it for yourself. Use your power and take it. Take it!

Irina's voice, quiet as a breeze but hard as iron, filled Lorelai's memory as she flexed her fingers and held Kol's gaze. Beneath her anger, beneath the awful need to make him pay for Leo, a voice whispered that she was on a precipice. If she took the leap—if she used her magic to take the life of a boy simply because her pain begged her to without first making sure that it was justice, how could she look Irina in the eye and say that the queen was wrong for doing the same thing?

"Nothing I say can make up for the loss of your brother," Kol said with quiet sincerity. The grief in his voice matched the pain that lived inside Lorelai. "Or make up for the fact that I was trying to kill the girl who saved my life."

"No, nothing will ever make up for losing Leo," she said, and though anger still shook her, she slowly curled her hands into fists, ignoring the burn of her magic. "My first mistake was to rescue you. My second was to believe that you had honor."

"I didn't mean to violate the debt I owe you. As soon as I recognized your bird, I put my human heart back in control and shifted. I don't want to be a killer." There was desperation behind his words. "I don't expect you to believe me after all that's happened, and I have no right to ask you for mercy—"

"No, you don't."

"I don't ask mercy for myself. Only for Eldr." His amber eyes held hers as the black dragon finished shifting and became the enormous boy—Trugg, if Lorelai remembered correctly—who instantly started running toward them. "You're a *mardushka*, like Irina. You could save Eldr. You're a good person—you wouldn't have helped us in Tranke if you weren't. Please, do what you want with me, but say that you'll save my people now that Irina won't."

She frowned at him. "What are you talking about?"

"Don't hurt him." Trugg threw himself between Lorelai and Kol, his arms held wide to block her from being able to touch his king.

"He tried to kill me." She glared at Trugg. "And he is part of the reason my brother died."

"He had no choice. Not really. Irina twisted his words—"

"I can speak for myself, Trugg." Kol put a hand on the boy's shoulder and then slowly climbed to his feet, his eyes still on Lorelai. Still full of regret. "But if it's okay with the princess, I'd really like to put on some pants before we have this conversation."

For the first time, Lorelai realized that she was facing two boys who didn't have a stitch of clothing on. Her cheeks warmed. "Yes, please put some pants on."

Kol turned toward a bag that was still strapped to the back of the silver dragon, but Trugg stood there, his arms crossed over his chest, staring her down as if convinced she would hurt his king the second Trugg turned his back.

"Pants." She flapped her hands at him.

"I'm good."

She glared. "I'm not."

"Trugg, get dressed. We need the princess's mercy, not her wrath." Kol returned with clothes for his friend while the silver dragon began to shift into the girl with the short dark hair and narrow green eyes.

Lorelai took a step back and looked at Sasha, still perched on a branch, her thoughts a steady litany of death threats toward every Eldrian in the clearing. Just behind the Eldrian girl, Gabril limped toward them, his sword out, his expression the kind of icy calm that meant someone was about to die.

"Why are we worried about her wrath? We can shift and kill her if she becomes a threat," the girl said.

"If she *becomes* a threat?" Gabril reached the bottom of the hill. "Do you have any idea whom you attacked? There isn't a single moment that she isn't a threat. The only thing keeping her from bringing this entire mountain down on your miserable heads is her commitment to becoming a just queen."

Trugg and Jyn bristled, but Kol inclined his head toward Gabril. "I'm grateful for the opportunity to explain my actions."

Gabril gave Kol a long, cold stare. "You'd better pray she accepts your explanation. Dragon or no, I will kill you for putting my princess in danger."

"Understood— Hey!" Kol whipped his arms above his head

as Sasha swooped low and yanked at his hair with her talons.

Let him speak, Sasha. I want to hear what he has to say, Lorelai sent, and Sasha reluctantly left Kol and perched on the princess's shoulder instead, her black eyes locked on the king.

"Thank you," Kol said to Lorelai.

"I don't want your thanks. All I want is an explanation for why you tried to kill me and why you've asked for my mercy for Eldr."

He straightened and met her eyes. "Eldr is overrun with ogres—ogres that are unlike anything we've ever seen. The dark enchantress who has ensnared the kingdom south of ours let them out of the mountain where they were imprisoned, but it also changed them. They're huge, bigger than our biggest dragon, and nothing we do stops them. Their skin is impervious to fire, to boulders, and to blades. My army was simply slowing them down, not stopping them. Even our best warriors—like Trugg, who is a *beast* in the sky—"

"Ladies." Trugg raised his brows and gave Lorelai and Jyn a little smirk.

"This is not the time," Lorelai said as Jyn muttered, "You're a pig."

Kol took a step toward Lorelai, and she raised her hands.

"So your kingdom is in trouble," she said. "That doesn't explain why you got in bed with the devil."

He flinched, but held her gaze. "Here's the truth." He swallowed hard, and closed his eyes for a long moment before finally looking at her again. His voice was quiet as he said, "I was never supposed to take the throne. My father was a strong, fair ruler, and he was training my brother to follow in his footsteps. I wasn't even a very good prince. I spent all my time pulling pranks and skipping school. But now . . ."

His voice broke, and he looked at the sky.

"Now I'm all that's left. Me and my little sister. I'm all Eldr has, and I can't save my people. I can't stop the ogres. Every week brings a new flood of refugees from southern Eldr into the capital. Every day brings the ogres closer to the capital as well, and we have nowhere left to run."

Despite her anger with him, a small thread of compassion entered Lorelai's heart. She knew what it was like to be desperate. To see the people you were supposed to protect lose everything and to be powerless to stop it.

Kol looked at her again. "I was out of options. I can't fight magic. So I came to Ravenspire to offer Queen Irina a deal— enough of my kingdom's treasure to buy food for her people for the next ten years in exchange for using her magic to seal the ogres back into Vallé de Lumé."

Lorelai's voice was grim. "You made the mistake of believing Irina cared about the fate of her people."

"Yes." Kol reached up and ran a finger along the thistle and bone collar that wrapped around his throat. "She made a counteroffer."

"My life for the lives of your people." Lorelai held his gaze and dared him to justify his choice.

"No." He shook his head. "She told me to return you to the castle. That's all I agreed to do. But then she required a blood oath, and she changed the wording to say that I agreed to do whatever she asked of me—"

"You made a blood oath with Irina?" Lorelai asked sharply.

"Do you have any idea what she can do to you if she thinks you failed to uphold your end of the bargain?"

Kol's shoulders drew back, his chin lifted, and suddenly he looked every inch a king. "I die. Horribly. Which is why I'm asking for your promise to show mercy to Eldr."

Jyn's face paled, and she stepped forward. "Kol—"

"I'm not going to hold up my end of the bargain," Kol said. His expression was resolute. "I'm not going to cut out the princess's heart and give it to Irina. Which means Eldr still needs someone to save it from the ogres."

"It means you'll die," Lorelai said, "and Eldr will be without a king."

"Better that than for Eldr to have a murderer on the throne." He knelt before her and touched his forehead in a gesture of fealty. "I have nothing to offer you. I will spare your life no matter what your answer. But I beg you to use your magic to stop the ogres in Eldr and save my people."

"You aren't going to die," Jyn said, her small frame vibrating with anger. "I'll kill the girl myself, and—"

"Try it, and you'll have a sword through your heart before you can even finish shifting." Gabril held his blade steady.

"You can't kill two dragons in one blow, human." Trugg sounded furious. "And if you want to hurt either Jyn or my king, you'll have to go through me."

"This is the only way." Kol sounded stoic, but his hands trembled, and Lorelai could see the fear in his eyes as he looked at her. "Please. Promise me you'll save Eldr."

The others erupted into arguments and protests while Lorelai's thoughts raced. If she promised to help Kol with her magic and let him die for betraying his blood oath, Irina would know that her huntsman had failed, and she'd search for another way to find the princess. Lorelai didn't need the distraction of staying one step ahead of the queen when what she really wanted to do was put into place her plan to honor Leo and take Irina down.

She needed a way to make Irina believe Kol had succeeded in killing her. If Irina believed Lorelai was dead, she'd send her magic through the used-up, dying Ravenspire ground into Eldr, which might weaken the queen, and that would give Lorelai an advantage she couldn't afford to pass up.

She studied Kol, his eyes full of determination and regret, his spine straight though his hands shook, and admitted that while she was furious with his choices, she couldn't truly blame him for them. She didn't like him, but he didn't deserve to die for Irina's treachery.

"All of you, be quiet. Quiet!" Lorelai whipped her hands into the air, and white light blazed in her palms. Jyn's mouth snapped shut. Gabril hefted his sword a bit higher and watched his princess. Trugg stared at her hands and whispered a curse.

"Nobody is going to die," Lorelai said. "And Irina is going to honor her side of the blood oath. Now listen carefully. I have a plan."

EIGHTEEN

KOL WATCHED LORELAI pace the clearing, her bird swiveling its head to maintain eye contact with him no matter where the girl went. Skies above, the bird's unblinking gaze was creepy. He looked away from the gyrfalcon and asked, "What kind of plan do you have?"

"We're going to trick Irina," Lorelai said without looking at him.

"That's suicide," Jyn said, her voice rising. "At least for Kol. Nobody tricks a *mardushka*—"

"Except another *mardushka*." The princess gave Jyn a look that would've made a lesser Draconi tremble.

The gyrfalcon caught Kol's gaze and snapped its beak at him, its intentions clear. He did his best to ignore the bird, but he couldn't ignore the mess he was in. He had been reluctantly willing to honor his blood oath when he'd thought Irina was Eldr's only salvation. But he wasn't going to kill the girl who'd saved his life. And he wasn't convinced she could trick Irina.

He appreciated her attempt to once again spare his life—the thought of dying made his hearts ache miserably—but what he really needed was the princess's promise to help Eldr. He had no leverage, nothing to offer, but he'd seen the rage in her eyes when she realized he'd been in Nordenberg helping Irina the day her brother was killed. He'd seen the sparks of power glowing in her palms as she stalked toward him while he was defenseless.

And he'd seen the moment she pulled back from her rage and decided to let him live long enough to explain.

The furious man with the sword who watched Kol every bit as closely as the bird did was right. Lorelai was a threat who held her power in restraint because she was just. She was kind. She was committed to doing the right thing, even when it cost her.

He had to make her believe that helping Eldr was the right thing.

"How do you plan to trick Irina?" the man with the sword asked without lowering his weapon.

"And what will it cost Kol if you fail?" Jyn snapped.

The princess lifted her chin. "If the trick fails, he'll pay with his life. It's the same price he was willing to take from me."

"He doesn't deserve to die," Trugg said.

"Neither do I. Neither did my brother." Lorelai's tone dared anyone to argue with her. "But Irina doesn't care about any of that. She only cares about power. And because of the blood oath, she owns Kol."

Lorelai looked at the man with the sword. "I have to test a theory before I know if this plan will work. Gabril, I'll need your help."

The man nodded and limped carefully across the wreckage

of the trees Kol had destroyed as he'd chased the princess through the forest. As he walked past Kol, Gabril said quietly, "Don't let the bad leg fool you, son. If you hurt my princess, I will be the nightmare you never see coming."

"I understand the lengths to which we'll go to protect those we love," Kol said. He didn't add that those lengths were what had put them all in this situation to begin with. Or that he wasn't through fighting for Eldr.

The older man studied him for a moment, his expression unreadable, and then the princess said, "Gabril, let's get started."

Gabril turned from Kol and approached the princess as her bird lifted from her shoulder and flew into the sky.

"Where's Sasha going?" Gabril asked.

"Hunting." The princess turned to face Kol as Jyn and Trugg flanked him, their arms crossed over their chests and their expressions grim. "A *mardushka* uses her magic by calling to the heart of the thing she touches. Every heart feels a little different—the best way I can describe it is that it feels like the characteristics of the person, animal, or thing I'm touching. I'm going to see if I can trick my magic into believing the heart I hold is Gabril's."

"Whose heart do you plan on holding?" Kol asked, half afraid the answer would be his, though he thought he was far enough away from her to have a chance at shifting before she could hit him with her magic.

"An animal's," the princess said. Sasha returned, carrying the limp carcass of a rabbit in her beak. She swooped past the Eldrians and smacked Trugg in the head with the rabbit's body as she passed.

"Stupid bird," he muttered as he scrubbed a hand over his hair.

"My bird can drive her beak straight through your neck and into your artery in less time than it takes for you to draw a weapon, and she already dislikes you intensely. If I were you, I'd do my best not to antagonize her any further," Lorelai said.

"I thought the bird obeyed you," Trugg said.

"Better not antagonize me either." Lorelai knelt as Sasha laid the rabbit at her feet.

"I'll have you know that I am a Draconi warrior who graduated from the academy with honors befitting a cadet who— Oh skies, that's disturbing."

Trugg fell silent as Sasha tore the rabbit's chest wide open with one strike. Her second strike ripped the heart free, and then the bird cocked her head and glared at the Eldrians, blood dripping from her beak.

"I see your point," Trugg said.

The princess held out her hand, and Sasha deposited the rabbit heart onto her palm.

"Can you tell it was a rabbit's heart?" Kol asked, stepping forward despite the forbidding look the princess aimed at him.

It was his fate on the line. His life, his kingdom. He had to see the magic at work for himself.

Brilliant white light shot from her palms and surrounded the heart. "It feels like a rabbit."

"I should think so," Jyn said.

The princess stared at the heart. "No, I mean the essence of the heart is very . . . rabbitlike. Arrow-quick thoughts, wariness, and speed. It would never pass for human, even if the size and shape were right." She looked at Gabril. "Would you be willing to cut your hand and put your blood on the heart so I can see how that changes the essence?"

Kol took another step forward. "Let me. This is my problem to fix. There's no need for him to have an injury, no matter how small."

The princess locked eyes with him, and the disdain in her expression was worse than the disappointment he'd become used to seeing in his father's face. At least with his father, he could tell himself he'd been misunderstood, or that something his father had done justified Kol's behavior.

There was no misunderstanding here, and the justification that he was desperate to save Eldr didn't change what he'd nearly done to the girl who'd saved his life.

"My magic has already touched Gabril's heart. I know what his feels like." She cut each word into sharp little pieces. "I'm not interested in having anything to do with yours, even if it could pass for human and not Draconi, which it can't."

He absorbed her words and held her gaze. She didn't have to have anything to do with his heart, but he wanted her to see it in his eyes anyway. Regret for what his choices had nearly cost her. Regret for being at Irina's side when her brother was killed. And desperation to change the fate of his people without making the princess pay the price for their salvation.

Something soft flickered through the princess's gaze, but then she turned away as Gabril said, "Ready when you are, Lorelai."

Swiftly, Gabril nicked the fleshy side of his palm against his sword. Lorelai placed the heart on a nearby rock and watched as Gabril allowed his blood to drip over it. When his cut began to clot, he reached down with his other hand and smeared the heart on all sides, covering it completely with his blood.

"Now try."

She reached for the heart and cradled it in her palm. The same white light surrounded the heart, and the princess frowned.

"Did it work?" Kol asked.

Lorelai's frown slowly eased into fierce smile that had Kol's dragon heart thumping hard in his chest.

"It worked. Now instead of rabbitlike thoughts, wariness, and speed, I feel quick intelligence, speedy reflexes, and a stubborn sense of duty." She looked at Gabril. "If I hadn't recently felt your true heart for myself, I'd believe that this was yours."

"Except for the obvious problem that it doesn't look anything like a human heart," Jyn said.

"No, but a deer's heart would." Lorelai looked at Trugg. "How fast can you hunt one down and bring it back to me?"

Trugg looked to Kol, and the king nodded.

"Fine. I'll go find a deer. That's exactly why I excelled at flying and battle strategy at the academy. So I could hunt down a deer." Trugg stabbed a finger at Lorelai. "My king had better be in one piece when I get back."

"I'm not the *mardushka* he needs to worry about."

As Trugg shifted and Gabril cleaned his sword on a clump of dying underbrush, Kol took another cautious step toward Lorelai. When she didn't snap at him to back up, he came close enough to say quietly, "Thank you."

"I'm not doing this for you." The wind tossed her curly black hair over her shoulders and the sun painted her pale skin gold as she looked at him. "I'm doing this because if you fail, Irina will just keep trying to find me. And because if Irina uses Ravenspire land to send her magic into Eldr, it might weaken her, and I can use that to my advantage."

"That's more than fair, but—"

She laughed sharply, and beneath it he heard the kind of fathomless loss that had opened up within him the day his family had died. "None of this is fair. My father should be ruling the kingdom. Leo shouldn't be gone. . . ." Her voice wavered and broke.

"I'm sorry. I know more than most how useless those words are when you've lost so much."

She closed her eyes as if his words hurt, and when she opened them again, there was a hint of compassion on her face. "It isn't fair that your people are dying because of choices someone made in another kingdom. And it isn't fair that you felt you had no option but to tie yourself to Irina because that was better than losing absolutely everything."

"I have no right to ask this, and I will have no way to repay you the debt I owe, but if this fails, and I die—"

"I'll send my magic into Eldr and put a barrier between the ogres and your people. Once I'm through fighting Irina, I'll be able to afford expending the kind of energy it will take to seal them back into Vallé de Lumé." She said the words simply as if she hadn't just lifted a weight that was crushing Kol from the inside out. "Now listen, here's what we're going to do. Irina will test the heart with her palm. It's been nine years since she's laid her hands on me, so my blood on the deer heart should fool her. But she also has a scrying mirror."

Kol nodded. He'd seen the destruction of his kingdom in that mirror.

"She can't find me with it unless I've recently touched something tainted with her magic with my bare hands. I'll put my gloves on in a moment and leave this place far behind, and I won't take them off for five days. That gives you enough time to get to the capital and then meet up with me if you're still alive."

He swallowed hard at the matter-of-factness in her voice, and said, "And if I don't show up?"

"Then I'll know we failed, and I'll send my magic into Eldr to form the barrier while I deal with Irina."

"If that would weaken Irina, won't it weaken you?" he asked.

"Look around you." She gestured toward the rotting trees and the dry, crumbling soil. "When a *mardushka* uses a willing heart to do magic, there's very little cost to either the heart or the *mardushka*. But when you have to overpower the heart and force your will, you drain the heart of its strength and vitality, and you drain yourself. Irina's been forcing Ravenspire's land to do her will for nine years, and the land is dying because of it. Irina has to be suffering the cost of that. I, on the other hand, am young and strong, and I will use the one thing in Ravenspire that isn't dying because of the queen—the rivers."

"Irina will know where to find you once you use your magic, won't she?" he asked because it was clear that once again, Lorelai was willing to do the right thing even though it was going to cost her.

Her smile reminded him of the way it had felt to watch the ogres while his dragon's heart thundered for their blood on his talons.

"Irina is going to know where to find me at the end of those five days no matter what happens with you and Eldr."

"Where should I meet you?" He didn't add, "if I'm not dead," but the words hung in the air between them.

"It's better if you don't know where I'm going. I don't need Irina to get the information out of you before I'm ready to reveal myself. Just come back here and start tracking me. You're much faster than me in your dragon form. You'll catch up soon enough."

Trugg returned with the deer, and soon Kol had the animal's heart covered in Lorelai's blood and secured in a pouch. Before he left for the castle again, he met Lorelai's eyes.

"Thank you."

"Try not to die," she said, and then she pulled her gloves on and watched him shift into his dragon and head for the capital.

NINETEEN

IT TOOK KOL and his friends a little more than a day to fly back to Irina's castle. They'd pushed themselves, stopping only twice to drink before rising into the sky again.

He had a heart covered in Lorelai's blood. The princess had her magic-cloaking gloves on.

Irina would be fooled. Eldr would be saved.

He would still be alive.

Skies help him, he wanted to be alive.

When they arrived at the castle, they were quickly ushered into the same room where days ago he'd pledged himself into the queen's service with an oath that would kill him if this trick didn't work.

"Come to me, huntsman. Your friends may stay in the hall," Irina said.

Irina stood at the far end of the table, waiting, her eyes gleaming, her mouth curved into a tiny smile.

He walked in slow, measured steps, bowed with perfect

etiquette, and then handed her the pouch. His hands were steady, but the dragon fire in his chest was blazing and the air in the room felt like it was closing in on him as Irina unknotted the rope that held the pouch closed.

She opened it, and the deer's heart, coated with Lorelai's blood, fell into her hands. For a moment, she closed her eyes, and white light blazed from her palm and into the heart. A slow smile spread over her face.

Her eyes snapped open. "Well done. It seems our little Lorelai was no match for you, *mardushka* or not."

He took a cautious breath, the band of tension around his chest easing. It had worked. He was going to live, Eldr was going to be saved, and he owed the princess of Ravenspire a debt far greater than he would ever be able to repay.

He waited for Irina to lift the collar and send her magic into Eldr. Instead, she placed the heart on the table, wiped her hands clean on the pouch, and picked up her scrying mirror.

"Mirror, mirror, your depths I scry. Show me the princess Lorelai." The queen stared at the opaque clouds that swirled across the mirror's surface, her knuckles white as she gripped the mirror.

The hope that had flared within him waned as Kol's hearts slammed against his chest. His knees felt incapable of holding up as the mirror's surface spun faster.

What if Lorelai had taken off her gloves? What if she'd been wrong about how the mirror found her?

What if he was about to die?

His chest burned with dragon's fire as he fought to keep his expression calm. If he was going to die, he would face his fate with courage befitting a king.

Moments passed, but the surface of the mirror remained unchanged. Irina gently placed the mirror on the table and picked up the heart again. Kol caught himself before he sagged against the table in relief.

The heart had passed its test. The mirror had been fooled. Eldr was about to be saved, and he was going to be alive to rule it.

"One last test." She met his gaze as she sliced into the muscle with a sharp fingernail and withdrew a single drop of blood.

The relief that had filled him drained away, as she placed the drop of blood on her tongue. Lorelai had said nothing about a *mardushka's* ability to read blood with her tongue. Maybe Lorelai didn't know. Or maybe she'd hoped the queen would take a drop of the blood that covered the outside of the heart.

Irina rolled the blood across her tongue and looked at him, her smile sharp around the edges. "Do you know how I've stayed in power all these years in a kingdom full of people who'd love to see me lose my throne?"

He stared at her in silence, his knees shaking while he clenched his jaw and struggled to look composed.

"I've stayed in power because I always expect people to betray me." She moved closer to him. "And because I expect betrayal, I'm always ready."

Her smile became a shard of ice. "You are going to pay for your betrayal, huntsman."

She slammed her hand into his chest, and his blood sizzled and churned with white-hot intensity. Before he could pull away, she threw back her head and yelled, *"Kaz`ja.* Take what is human, and give me control over what remains."

The magic in his blood rushed for his hearts as Trugg and Jyn leaped into the room and ran toward him.

He tried to wrench away from Irina, but then the pain hit—an unbearable burning that blistered his chest as if he'd swallowed fire itself. He clutched at his hearts as they beat louder, louder, *louder* until their frantic rhythm drowned out everything else.

Irina threw out her hand, and the stone floor beneath them shook. Pillars as wide as Trugg's waist shot out of the floor, blocking Kol's friends and creating a cage around Irina and Kol.

Pain was a fire-coated blade that kept stabbing Kol with every heartbeat. It stole his breath and turned his knees to water.

He fell to the floor, clawing at his chest, ripping at his shirt and his skin as if he could somehow let the magic out and stop the agony.

Trugg and Jyn threw themselves at the cage, but the pillars didn't budge.

Irina sank to her knees beside him, one hand on the collar of bone and thistle she'd given him.

Kol doubled over and screamed as the fire inside him coalesced into a single, excruciating bolt of pain that felt like it was ripping him in two.

The queen leaned close to the collar and whispered something to it.

Kol shuddered. His hearts pounded.

And then her hand was against his chest, and her voice was rising above his as she repeated her incantor over and over again.

His friends threw themselves at the stone cage. Kol writhed on the floor as the collar shrank against his skin until it fit him like he'd been born with it. Irina kept chanting, her palm pressed to his chest.

Then his human heart seemed to leap toward her hand, tearing free of its moorings with a sickening lurch that left Kol gasping for air.

Irina smiled, cold and vicious, as Kol's human heart appeared in her hand, shimmered like a mirage for an instant, and then became solid.

The pain stopped, and in its place was an insatiable need to hurt, punish, hunt, and destroy.

Kol lay on the floor, shaking with the desperate need to shift. His muscles ached to stretch, his bones to re-form, but it was as if his human skin had become an iron cage that refused to allow his dragon out.

Irina reached beneath the table and pulled out a small gold box with a black stone set in the center of its lid. She placed his heart inside the box, sliced her palm with one long, polished nail, squeezed three drops of her own blood onto it, and then turned to him.

"What have . . . you . . . done to me?" His voice was raw from screaming. His tongue felt clumsy, his words foreign things he struggled to speak. Rage was the strength that got him to his feet.

She lifted the box, and he could hear his heart—his human heart—beating within its golden walls.

"I've made you the perfect predator." Irina ran her fingers lightly over the stone on top of the box. "Now nothing stands between you and your dragon's instinct. Just don't try to shift. The collar won't let you do anything more than use your talons.

I can't be worried that my huntsman will become a dragon behind my back and try to destroy me. You'll be able to track Lorelai and kill her easily enough in your human form. If she uses a harmful spell against you in self-defense, the magic in your collar will end her."

He seethed, the dragon's fire in his chest burning like an inferno, begging for release he couldn't give.

She leaned close. "*I* command you now. Your dragon heart obeys mine. Hold up your end of the bargain, and I will be bound by our blood oath to hold up mine." She placed the heart box on the table and for the first time seemed to notice the other Eldrians who had shifted and were trying to destroy the pillars with fire and the spikes on their tails.

Irina slammed her hand onto the tabletop and branches shot out of the wood, wrapped themselves around the Eldrians, and forced them away from the cage.

"He's beyond your reach now. His collar is warded against all who have dual hearts. If you touch him, he'll die. If you come too close to him, *you'll* die. He is mine now."

Trugg roared and strafed the branches that held him with fire.

Irina turned away. "I grow tired of you. Leave my castle. Stay away from my huntsman. If you come back, I will rip your hearts out, but unlike the king's, I won't keep yours safe."

"Safe?" Kol had to force the word out. It was as if without his human heart, he was nothing but dragon—all instinct and violence with no spoken language. His memories—of his parents, of Brig, of everything he loved about Eldr—were slipping through his fingers like water, receding behind a thick gray curtain that blocked him from everything that used to matter, leaving nothing to hold back the well of violent anger that had replaced his second heart. He grabbed for the memory of his mother's laughter, for his sister's smile, for anything that could give him a weapon to keep the rage at bay, but the images faded into darkness, and Kol was alone with the terrible beat of his dragon's heart.

Irina flicked her fingers and the branches that held Jyn and Trugg wrenched them into the air and hurled them from the room. Turning to Viktor, who stood silently on the far side of the room, his mouth set in a tight line, she said, "I've seen the face of the man who is helping Lorelai. He was in my huntsman's blood memories. Get me an artist. There's something familiar about this man's face. I want a name to go with it."

Turning to Kol, she said, "Find the princess. Bring me her heart, and I will restore yours."

He wanted to resist. To refuse to be her predator.

But the collar sent tiny shocks of power and pain into his skin, and his thoughts felt clumsy and far away. Irina waved a hand and the cage crumbled to dust.

"Go, huntsman."

He went.

TWENTY

It took four days for Lorelai and Gabril to reach the eastern edge of Duchess Waldina's estate. They traveled hard, pushing themselves from dawn to dusk as they hiked through thick stands of dying evergreens, climbed rocky ravines, and hurried through meadows of rotting grass. The strain was showing as Gabril's limp became more pronounced, the lines of pain that bracketed his mouth digging deep. Still, he refused to allow Lorelai to heal his leg, arguing that if the deer heart trick had failed, Irina could be coming after the princess herself. Lorelai needed all her energy just in case.

She stopped arguing with him on the second day. If his heart wouldn't submit to hers, she'd be exhausted from the effort, and he was right: she needed all her energy.

Just in case.

The Waldina estate rose above another long meadow of brittle, yellow grass. Fences of weathered oak hemmed in the enormous property, and horses already wearing their winter coats were scattered throughout the pastures, munching on piles of hay. Beyond the house, the village of Baumchen clung to the side of the first of three western mountains, but Lorelai had eyes only for the mansion at the end of the long cobblestoned road that bisected the meadow.

The mansion was enormous—an elegant monstrosity of marble columns, stone trim, scalloped shutters, and a hundred windowpanes gleaming in the afternoon sun. Multiple chimneys pierced the slanted roof, nestled between narrow gable windows, which were open to let in the fresh mountain air. Smoke rose from each chimney in thin ribbons of gray. The entire house was painted a bold yellow that reminded Lorelai of an egg yolk.

"We can't exactly walk up to the front door and knock." Gabril leaned against the fence that marked the border between the pastures and the forest they'd just hiked through.

"The horses look well fed." Lorelai scanned the pastures and then stared at the village beyond. "I wonder if the Waldinas are feeding their peasants as well as their livestock."

"I wonder where they're getting the hay for the horses since the ground here is just as bad as it is in the east."

"Being loyal to Irina must have a few benefits." Lorelai studied the mansion, gauging its security. Its weaknesses. Gabril was right—she couldn't just walk up to the front door and knock. Even if she gained entrance that way, the servants who opened the door would announce her to the duchess, giving the woman time to prepare herself.

No, what Lorelai needed here was the element of surprise.

And she'd just discovered her way inside the mansion.

"Wait out of sight in the trees. I'll be back as soon as I can, but don't worry if it takes a while."

"How are you getting in?" Gabril asked in a tone that really said, "Do you have a way back out?"

"Through the open dormer windows." Lorelai nodded toward the narrow gables whose windows were cracked open to let in the fresh mountain air. "I'll find the duchess's bedroom—"

"How?" His mouth was tight with worry.

"Trust me." Lorelai shrugged off her pack and handed it to him. "Nothing is going to stop me from getting what I need. I'll find the duchess's bedroom and wait. When she retires for the night, she'll get the surprise of her life."

"Be careful." He dropped her pack and pulled her against his chest. She leaned into him, his heartbeat a steady, comforting sound beneath her ear.

"You too."

He laughed, but there was no mirth in it. "I'll just be out here, worrying my fool head off while you take all the risk."

"My kingdom, my battle, my risk." She stood on tiptoes and kissed his cheek before turning back to face the mansion. "And save your worry for the duchess who aligned herself with Irina at the expense of Ravenspire. She's going to need all the help she can get."

Lorelai crept along the hedges and ducked behind trees as she made her way to the north wing of the mansion where the marked ostentation of the rest of the mansion was lacking and the windows were few and far between. The servants' quarters, no doubt. Lorelai glanced around but saw no one outside the mansion. Sasha flew overhead, sweeping the grounds in wide circles.

Do you see anyone I need to worry about? Lorelai asked as she sized up the wall she meant to scale.

Someone near the barn. Attack?

Lorelai craned her neck, but couldn't see the barn from where she stood. Which meant the person couldn't see her either. *Don't attack. Once I'm inside, guard Gabril until I call for you.*

Squirrels?

Yes, you can hunt some squirrels first, but be quick about it.

Share? Sasha sent an image of dropping a few spare squirrels into Gabril's lap.

Not squirrels. You can share a rabbit, but not squirrels.

Strange humans.

Lorelai rolled her eyes and then focused on the wall. She took a quick run at it, kicked off with her left foot, and scaled the wall in quick leaps. Holding on to the edge of the closest gable with one hand to avoid sliding off the steep roof, she hooked the fingers of her other hand around the open window and pulled until she could slide into the house.

She landed on a cot with a thin mattress, a thinner gray bedspread, and a lumpy pillow. A plain washbasin, an armoire that had seen better days, and a pair of scuffed work shoes needing a polish lined the wall beside the bed. Definitely servants' quarters.

Quickly, Lorelai pulled the window back to its former position and then hurried to the door. She peered out into a narrow hall. Empty. Easing out of the room, she closed the door behind her and moved down the corridor toward the main house.

It took several minutes of walking corridors and checking rooms before she found what she was looking for. In a room of polished wood floors and bookcases that stretched floor to ceiling, a maid was sweeping the hearth while behind the screen, a fire crackled.

Moving swiftly, Lorelai crept up behind the maid, pulling off her right-hand glove as she walked.

"Excuse me," she said quietly when she was directly behind the girl. The maid whirled in surprise, and Lorelai laid her bare hand against the maid's pale arm. "*Zna`uch*. Tell me what I want to know."

The maid's heart fluttered against the pull of Lorelai's magic for a second, but then the girl's eyes grew glassy, and she mumbled, "What do you want to know?"

"Show me where the duchess sleeps, but let no one see us."

The maid turned obediently toward the door. Lorelai kept her hand on the maid's arm as they went. The maid led her out of the library, down a staircase with iron railings, and through a hall covered in plush crimson rugs that looked expensive enough to have been woven in Akram. Every room they passed was empty, and a hush permeated the entire house.

"Where is everybody?" Lorelai asked softly as they rounded a corner and entered the west wing.

"Cook is in the kitchen finishing dinner. I couldn't say where the butler or Mrs. Alban are." The maid spoke in an eerie singsong tone that reminded Lorelai of the villagers in Nordenberg. Grief pricked her heart and ached in her throat at the thought of the place she'd lost Leo.

He would've loved this. Sneaking through a noble's mansion, bespelling a maid, and waiting in a duchess's bedchambers to scare her into giving up what she knew of Irina—Leo would've been in his element. He'd have agonized over a costume, while Lorelai was simply wearing the same thing she'd worn to trek across the mountains. He'd have insisted on code names in case they were caught and questioned. He'd have pretended to be an Akram noble or a broker from Balavata. He would've added *flair*, and he'd have done it perfectly while teasing Lorelai about her inability to ever be anything but her serious, straightforward self.

She'd give anything to hear him tease her again.

The gaping hole inside her that was Leo ached, a sharp pain that Lorelai felt in her bones. Her eyes stung, and the air in the opulent corridor they were walking through felt impossible to breathe.

"Who is Mrs. Alban?" she forced herself to ask through lips that trembled with grief.

"The housekeeper."

"Where is the rest of the staff?"

"We're all that is left. The rest were let go."

Apparently, being loyal to Irina fed your horses but didn't give you enough to keep a full staff employed. What were those jobless people doing for food this winter? Where were they living?

Lorelai's jaw tightened, and the thread of determination that blazed within her refocused her grief into purpose. No one else in Ravenspire should die because of Irina's irresponsible use of magic. Not if Lorelai could be stronger, faster, and better than the queen.

"Where is the duchess?" she asked as the maid's footsteps slowed outside a pair of doors with rose trellises carved around its edges.

"In the dining room awaiting her dinner."

The maid's singsong voice was scraping Lorelai's nerves raw. She stepped into a bedchamber decorated in brilliant blue, green, and yellow and turned to the girl.

"Go back to the library and sweep the hearth. Forget you ever saw me."

Removing her hand from the girl's arm, she shut the doors behind her as the maid turned back the way they'd come. A bank of windows on the western wall showed the sun disappearing over the edge of the mountain, leaving crimson streamers in its wake.

Lorelai settled into a chair in the corner beside the windows, the corner parallel to the door and therefore impossible to see until the duchess was already inside the room with the door shut, and waited.

Less than an hour later, the door swung open and Duchess Waldina entered the room. Her short, sturdy body was packed into a tightly corseted dress in the same brilliant blue as the curtains that framed her bedroom windows. Brown curls were piled atop her head, and her fingers were weighed down with jeweled rings. She shut the door, kicked her shoes off, and fumbled for the laces of her bodice.

Lorelai waited while the duchess unlaced her dress and heaved in a deep breath, and then she stood and said quietly, "If you scream for help, I will tear this mansion apart until nothing remains but the ground you built upon."

The duchess whirled toward the corner and opened her mouth, but Lorelai was already moving.

"Eee—"

Lorelai's gloved palm slammed over the woman's open mouth, cutting off her cry. Magic sparked in her bare palm, and the woman's brown eyes widened as Lorelai lifted a hand wreathed in white light and held it close to the duchess's face.

"I was very clear." Lorelai's voice was cold. "Scream, and I will bring this house down. You can see the magic in my hands. You're aligned with my enemy. Do you really think I'll hesitate to destroy everything you love?"

The woman shook her head in sharp, frantic movements that threatened to topple her tower of curls. For a moment, Lorelai was tempted to touch her with her bare palm and speak the same incantor she'd used on the maid, but according to news Gabril had gathered throughout the years from villagers on the duchess's lands, Duchess Waldina had spent significant time in the castle as Irina's guest. It was unlikely that Irina would allow someone to gain that much access to her without having put a spell or two in place to ensure her own safety. If Lorelai tried to overcome the spell, the duchess's heart would fight hers, and the physical cost would be tremendous.

Besides, Irina needed to believe Kol had killed the princess. Lorelai wasn't going to destroy that illusion until she was ready to launch an attack against the queen.

She met the duchess's frightened gaze, and bared her teeth in a smile that made the woman tremble. Maybe she couldn't use magic against the duchess herself, but the woman didn't need to know that.

"I'm going to remove my hand, and we're going to have a talk. You're going to answer my questions honestly, or I will use my magic to compel you to do so." Lorelai leaned close, her smile still in place. "If I have to use magic on you, Irina will know we've talked. That would displease me, and it would certainly displease her. I'm sure you understand the consequences of displeasing Irina."

The woman nodded again, her eyes darting around the room before returning to Lorelai. Slowly, the princess removed her hand and then gestured toward the bed.

"Sit down."

"Who are you?" The duchess's voice shook, and she rubbed her lips with her bejeweled fingers.

"We've met before, Duchess. Perhaps you remember? You gave me a bag of wintermint candy drops to keep me quiet while you curried favor with your new queen."

The duchess blanched. "That's impossible. You're dead."

"And yet here I stand."

Duchess Waldina pressed her hands to her cheeks and then fluttered them in the air like gaudily dressed birds. "Such a shock! I'm overcome. Of course, the queen must be told. She'll be so grateful to have part of the family she lost returned to her."

"Irina knows." Lorelai studied the woman's eyes, searching for the truth. "Only last week she sent a huntsman to kill me."

The woman's hands wilted, falling limply into her lap, and her eyes became guarded. "If Irina is against you, there is nothing anyone can do."

"Oh, I think you can do a lot for me, Duchess. Let's start with this. You know who I am and what I can do."

"You're the princess—"

"I'm a *mardushka*, and I am your true queen." Lorelai's voice was as unforgiving as the floor beneath her boots. "Irina is a usurper who murdered my father and tried to murder his children."

She clenched her fist as Leo's face blazed across her memory, and her power sparked, wreathing her hand in brilliant white fire. The duchess shrank against her yellow bedspread as Lorelai locked gazes with her.

"I didn't know. None of us . . . we had to take her word for it. We had to do whatever it took to survive."

"And yet many of the nobles across Ravenspire quietly defied the queen. Paying a measure of their peasants' taxes to alleviate the burden. Hiding those Irina's spies would condemn to death. Doing their best to keep their people safe and refusing to give their loyalty to one who used her power like a bludgeon." Lorelai took a step closer to the bed. "But not you, Duchess Waldina. You curried Irina's favor at the expense of everyone else. And look what it got you. Your land is dying. You have a skeletal staff, and I'm sure if I go into the villages on your land, I'll find people who are desperate and starving, who imagine breaking into this mansion with its tiny staff and stealing anything they might use to pay their way out of the kingdom. I'll find people who curse your name and wish death or worse for you."

"What could be worse than death?" The woman laughed feebly, but then scrambled toward the middle of the bed as Lorelai lunged forward, her bare hand raised.

"I am. I've lost my mother, my father, my brother, and my kingdom. The only thing left to lose is my own life, and that doesn't scare me." The truth of her words was a burning stone in her chest. "All that matters to me now is saving Ravenspire from Irina and the people who support her. People like you."

"No! I don't . . . That is, I was just pretending."

"Were you pretending when you sent a group of your own peasants to Irina's dungeon for the crime of begging you for help? Were you pretending when you housed known spies and then invited your fellow nobility for a weeklong house party that ended in nine of them being arrested for treasonous words against the queen? Were you pretending when—"

"How do you know about any of that?" The duchess demanded, her bravado as thin as the mattress on the maid's bed.

"I listen—and I know how to go unnoticed when I need to be. You'd be surprised what I've seen." The memory of the woman who'd killed her children to spare their suffering sent a flood of anger through Lorelai, and she clenched her jaw so hard it hurt. "Your crimes against Ravenspire are many, Duchess, and in a few short weeks, I will be your new queen. What can you tell me about my enemy that will convince me to spare your life?"

The duchess swallowed hard, and sweat gleamed on her brow, reflected in the brilliant light that wreathed Lorelai's hand. "Irina is in love with Viktor, her castle steward."

"What else?"

The woman took a deep, shuddering breath. "She never visits the castle gardens where your parents are buried."

Lorelai's heart ached, and she sharpened her voice. "None of this is helpful, Duchess. You have one last chance before I unleash my magic on you."

The duchess hesitated, and Lorelai snapped, "So be it."

The princess reached toward the sturdy wooden bedposts with her bare palm, and the duchess yelled, "No, wait! Wait.

There's one more thing. Irina is sick. Her heart. Whenever she does magic, especially a big spell, she has to take to her bed for days. That's all I know, I swear on my life."

Lorelai paused, magic burning her palm, her eyes locked on the duchess while her mind raced.

Finally, something she could use against Irina. All those years of forcing the land and its inhabitants to submit to her magic had cost both the land and the queen. A vicious sense of triumph welled inside Lorelai, and her smile made the duchess shudder.

If Irina weakened every time she used magic, if her heart was giving out, then Lorelai finally had a way to beat her. She could provoke the queen to use spells—huge spells. A weakened Irina would call on her army and her spies to help her defeat the princess, so the best way to incite Irina to use magic would be to work her way toward the capital, destroying anything Irina could use against her. She'd isolate her from her allies, tear apart the bridges, roads, and defensive positions that led to the capital so that no help would come for the queen, and provoke Irina to retaliate with magic at every turn. By the time Lorelai reached the capital, she'd be facing a queen too weak to put up much of a fight.

Without another word to the duchess, Lorelai left the bedroom, hurried out of the mansion, and raced to meet Gabril. They had two days' worth of ground to cover to get to Lorelai's first target.

TWENTY-ONE

FOR DAYS, TRAPPED in his human body, Kol had run through forests, forded rivers, and climbed the western Falkrain Mountains following the scent of his prey. He'd slept only when his legs gave out and refused to hold him. He'd eaten only when his vision blurred and a strange noise rang in his ears. The underbrush had clawed at him, low-hanging branches had swiped at him, and he'd lost his shirt when he'd tumbled down a hillside while trying to run at night. Through it all, the collar around his neck flooded him with pain, and the girl's maddening scent of evergreen, snow, and sweet burning wood remained tantalizingly just out of reach.

But now, Kol crouched beside an enormous evergreen tree and stared at the girl sitting with her back against a tree, his dragon heart thundering, his chest burning. The air in the northwest Falkrain Mountains was frigid, but even though he had on nothing but his pants, his boots, and a collar of thistle and bone, he couldn't feel it. All he felt was heat from the dragon fire trapped in his chest and a terrible pain that filled him until he could barely think about anything else.

He took a step, and her head whipped up. She met his eyes and smiled slowly.

"It worked." She sounded triumphant, but then she looked closer at him and frowned. "Where is your shirt? And why are you still wearing Irina's collar?"

He snarled.

The girl went still, her body tense. The wind teased her long black hair and brought her scent to Kol. He lifted his nose and tested the air. Evergreen, crisp snow, and the sweetness of burning wood, just like the coat his queen had given him to smell.

He'd found his prey.

No, not prey. She was . . . something else. Something he no longer had the words for. He shook his head, trying to think, to *remember*, but his dragon heart blazed within him, begging for blood and fire. For someone's pain to match the unending agony that circled his neck beneath his collar and spread through his veins like razor-tipped lightning.

The pain would stop when he killed her. He was certain of it. The collar seemed to whisper to him, words he couldn't understand but whose meaning he felt deep within his bones.

This girl's heart belonged to Kol's queen, and his agony would stop when he ripped it from her chest and returned it to the castle.

"What's going on?" the girl asked. Her voice reminded Kol of another girl who'd held up her chin and tried to speak without trembling as she begged Kol not to leave her behind in their castle. Not to die.

Another girl . . . she seemed far away now. Lost to the cloudy memories of a life before the collar. A life Kol knew he needed to remember but could only access in bits and pieces.

"You need to tell me what happened. I can help you fix it." The girl's voice shook a little, but there was a confidence beneath it. A certainty that she could face Kol and survive.

She couldn't.

No one could survive him. He was fire and blood and death. He was rage trapped in a human skin.

He reached for the knife tied against his belt.

The girl frowned and slowly inched her feet toward her body as if getting ready to leap to her feet.

The fury within him surged at the thought.

"Can you speak?" she asked, and this time all traces of fear had vanished from her voice.

The collar seemed to tighten and power poured out of it, searing his skin and adding more heat to the flames already raging inside him.

The knife fell from his fingers as he clutched his head with his hands and moaned. If he'd known the words to beg for his own death, he would've. His words, like his memories, felt trapped beyond the unending pain, beyond the shroud of smoke that had settled over his mind until only the whispers from the collar felt like truth.

He was a king. No, he was a killer. He was a brother.

He was fire, blood, and death.

And nothing would change until the girl in front of him was dead.

His head snapped up as the girl lunged to her feet. He locked eyes with her as his dragon heart beat fiercely. As he bared his teeth.

"Don't." She held up her hand like she could stop him. Like anything could stop him.

He clenched his fists as the fire in his chest spilled into his veins. Closing his eyes, he tried one last time to remember his reasons for not obeying the collar.

To remember himself.

"Run," he whispered, his voice more dragon than human, though he already knew it was too late. If she ran, his dragon would chase her. Catch her.

Kill her.

And he'd be free.

"No," the girl said.

He opened his eyes. Drew in a deep breath of evergreen, snow, and sweet burning wood. Felt the fire in his chest explode with a desperate need to hunt, punish, and destroy.

She shifted to the balls of her feet. Raised her hands as if to defend herself.

In one fluid movement, he scooped the knife off the forest floor and leaped forward.

Instantly, she sprinted toward him. He stretched out his hands to wrap around her neck and throw her to the ground, but then she was gone—somersaulting over him and racing toward the tree he'd been crouched beside.

He dug his heels into the ground and pivoted sharply, his dragon heart screaming for blood.

She scaled the tree in quick, graceful leaps, but by the time she was halfway up the trunk, he was already behind her. Grabbing her ankles. Flinging her toward the forest floor.

She did a front flip, tucked her head, and dove into a shoulder roll the moment her feet touched the ground.

Kol growled, his collar blazing, the pain wiping out every thought but one: kill his prey.

The girl was up and moving. She grabbed the knife he'd dropped as he scaled the tree and turned to face him.

He loosened his grip on the trunk and slid down it, ignoring the splinters that dug furrows into his bare hands and arms.

The girl flipped the blade around to face him and crouched, ready for his attack. "Just tell me what she did to you. Let me help you. No one has to get hurt."

She was wrong. He was already hurting, and it wouldn't stop until she was dead.

He lunged toward her, and she flipped to the side, narrowly avoiding his grasp; but this time, he was ready for her. Spinning to his left, he crashed into her, and they both went down.

She jerked her knees toward her chest, but he leaped on top of her and pinned her. She slashed wildly with the knife. Kol caught her wrist and twisted. She cried out in pain but refused to let go of the weapon.

He bent his face toward her and the fire inside him ignited into something blind. Feral.

Desperate.

Her heart. He just needed her heart, and then all this would stop.

He grabbed the knife by the blade, heedless of the metal's bite against his skin, of the blood that poured out of his hand. Wrenching it out of her grasp, he raised it above his head and aimed for her heart.

"No!" She raised her hands, palms out, to cover her chest, and the knife ripped into the gloves she wore, leaving a long, jagged tear.

He shoved at her hands, determined to get them out of the way. Once he sliced into her, once he removed her heart, the unendurable agony inside him would stop.

Once he removed her heart. He blinked as the image of his queen pressing her hand against his own chest to tear his human heart free burned in his mind. That was where the pain had started. Not with the girl. With his queen.

Hadn't it?

The collar whispered, the pain surged, and the memory was gone like it had never existed at all. He cried out in frustration.

"Wait." The girl lifted her hands again. "Just wait for a moment. Let's talk about this. Whatever you need, whatever is wrong, I can help."

He glared at her—this girl, this little, insignificant prey who was keeping him a prisoner of the agony of the collar—and plunged the knife toward her chest.

She deflected it with a sharp blow to his wrist. Off balance, he plunged the knife into the ground beside her, barely missing her. He yanked the knife free, still keeping her pinned as she kicked and struggled.

He was fire, blood, and death.

She was prey.

His pain was about to be over.

The knife streaked toward her heart.

She turned and slammed her hands into his chest.

The bare skin of her palm beneath the tear in her glove touched the bare skin of his chest.

White light exploded out of her hand and arrowed into him. The knife fell from his hands. The fire in his chest quieted. And the pain—oh, thank the skies above, the pain became a muted hum he could almost ignore if he tried.

The girl's eyes widened as the light found the empty space in his chest where rage existed instead of his human heart. Her magic felt like the comfort of a winter's fire. Like the purity of a field of unbroken snow. She looked at him like she'd uncovered his truth, and he desperately wished he could ask her to share it with him.

"What has she done to you?"

He didn't have the words to reply.

He suddenly realized that he was pinning her to the ground. That he'd hurt her wrist when he'd taken the knife from her.

That he'd treated her like prey.

Shame was a live coal lodged in his throat, heating his face and making it nearly impossible to meet her gaze.

What had he done?

I'm sorry. The words came to life in his mind, but his mouth could no longer form them.

She jerked as if he'd struck her, and her hand slipped from his chest. Instantly, the hurt crashed into him, and he doubled over as it stole his breath.

Pain. Nothing but unending agony and the terrible certainty that the only way he would ever be free was if he carved out her heart.

Please don't. Her voice, soft and certain, filled his mind, lighting a path through the clouds that obscured his memories.

He lifted his face to stare at her.

Can you hear me? She looked at him as if expecting an answer. As if the fact that her voice was echoing inside his own head was completely normal.

He nodded slowly while his dragon's heart pounded with rage and the collar whispered that she had to die.

She had to die.

Didn't she?

Her hand pressed against his chest again. The pain abated, and warmth that had nothing to do with his dragon's fire filled him again.

Better? she asked.

Yes. He thought the word and watched to see if she understood.

She held his gaze. *What have you become?*

He dropped his head. He was a predator. Fire, blood, and death. He didn't have the words for it, but the truth was an image of her destruction blazing across his mind.

That's not who you are. She slowly sat up to face him, her hand still pressed against his chest. *You don't really want to hurt me.*

He didn't. The clarity of her voice in his head felt like a beacon of safety. Like the only shore he still had left to stand upon.

Where are Jyn and Trugg?

The names felt familiar, but he couldn't make them fit the fractured bits of memory that slipped past the curtain of smoke in his mind.

They're your friends. A pretty girl with courage and attitude, and a boy who talks too much but who loves you enough to die for you. They would never have left you alone willingly.

He was alone. Imprisoned in his broken mind. Imprisoned

by the collar that would flood him with pain, with whispers. As soon as she removed her hand, he would lose himself to it.

The collar is causing your pain? Causing you to hunt me? the girl asked.

Yes.

She must have bespelled it. She studied the collar without touching it. *Our trick failed, and instead of letting your blood oath kill you, she found a way to force you to do her will anyway.*

He couldn't find her name, but the image of a delicate beauty with terrifying power filled his head, and the girl stiffened.

Irina.

Irina. He tried the word and found that it fit. That it matched the empty space inside his chest and the pain that spilled out of the collar.

She punished you. There was pain in her voice. Sorrow. But there was also anger, sharp as a blade and twice as strong. *She figured out that we tried to trick her, and she punished you by taking your human heart. My magic can feel the space where your heart used to be. We have to get it back, Kol. It's the only way to heal you.*

There was no healing for him. He was fire, blood, and death.

She shook her head. *If that was true, I'd be dead. You're at war with yourself. I can feel it.*

Yes. He met her gaze and willed her to see that no matter what he did after she removed her hand, in this moment, he understood that she wasn't prey. That she mattered for reasons far greater than a way to stop his inner torment.

We'll start by getting that thing off you.

His dragon heartbeat kicked hard against his chest, but he nodded.

Please. He watched her bite her lip as she tugged at the collar with the hand sheathed in the undamaged glove. *Please.*

The collar remained stubbornly in place.

"Lorelai?" A man's voice cut through the morning air, and her hand slipped from his chest as she turned to face the sound.

Pain was an inferno blazing through his body. Fury was the force that kept him alive. And the terrible stinging power from the collar flooded him, begging for the girl's beating heart in his hand.

"What is that boy doing back here without his shirt on? And where are his friends?" the man asked.

Kol whipped his head toward the man and roared, his fingers digging into the ground as he crouched beside the girl.

The girl who must die. Who must give her heart to him.

The girl who hadn't run, but had tried to reach him.

To save him.

"Get away from her!" The man ran toward him, his hand reaching for his sword.

"Wait!" The girl said as she stretched her hand toward Kol's chest.

The dragon inside him snarled in vicious triumph as her outstretched arms left her heart exposed.

Kol turned and threw himself away from the girl. Away from the knife.

Away from the temptation to destroy the one ray of hope he'd found since the pain began.

"Halt!" the man yelled. The cold rasp of a sword leaving its sheath scraped the air.

"No, wait! He doesn't want to hurt me."

But he did. He wanted it more than he had words to describe.

Come back. I can help you. Her voice filled his head, all comfort and beckoning light.

If he returned to her side, he'd kill her, and the pain would stop. But in the warmth that lingered where her touch had been, some part of him knew that the cost he'd pay for ending his agony was more than he could bear.

Kol turned his back and ran.

TWENTY-TWO

LORELAI STARED AFTER Kol's retreating back, her magic searing her palms, her breath coming in gasps, before leaping to her feet.

He'd run away from her, even though he desperately wanted to kill her. Even though the punishment for disobeying Irina was destroying him. Lorelai could feel his agony increase with every step he took. The part of him that had survived Irina's brutality was fighting to overpower his dragon heart, and he was paying for it with every razor-tipped breath, every fire-laced thought that burned from his mind into Lorelai's.

She'd underestimated his strength. She'd accused him of being without honor, when the truth was that he was trying desperately to save his kingdom at the expense of himself.

Trying desperately to save her—a girl who meant nothing to him—at the expense of himself.

Lorelai tore off her gloves and moved to follow Kol, although even in his human form, he was much faster than she'd ever be, but Gabril blocked her path, his sword still out.

"What is going on?" he demanded.

Lorelai met his eyes, and her voice trembled as she said, "We failed to trick Irina. And instead of letting the blood oath kill him, Irina took Kol's human heart and bespelled the collar around his neck to cause him incredible pain until he takes my heart back to her."

A muscle in Gabril's jaw clenched. "Without his human heart, he's a predator through and through—one focused solely on you. I know this isn't fair, I know the boy tried hard to act with honor, but we have to kill him. It's an act of mercy for him, and it's the only way to keep you safe."

Lorelai lifted her chin. "No one else is going to die because of Irina. Including Kol."

Die. Please. Kol's thoughts burned against hers, though they felt distant, as if the bond they'd formed was tenuous, and the farther he ran, the harder it was to hear the words that slowly formed in the tormented chaos of his mind.

I'm not going to die. Lorelai snapped at him while she scanned the grove of hemlock trees that spread along the western edge of the Falkrains, searching for movement. For the broken king of Eldr who wanted so badly to kill her and yet was holding himself back.

Not . . . you. Me.

You're not going to die either. Irina has taken enough from us both.

There was a flicker of gratitude from him before it was drowned out by a wash of agony that covered his thoughts in red and sent his dragon heart pounding.

"Are you listening to me?" Gabril demanded.

"I am now," she said, but part of her was tethered to Kol,

to the pain that screamed through him and the whispers that promised him he'd be better once he held her heart in his hand.

"Lorelai." Gabril's voice was gentle. "We can't save the boy. He's a predator now."

Yes. Kol agreed.

"He's not a predator. He's at war with himself. That means—"

"You don't know that. We can't assume any part of the boy we met still exists."

War . . . with you. An image of her broken chest spilling blood onto the ground while Kol tore out her heart filled his mind.

Stop that. Focus on something constructive. You and I aren't at war with each other, no matter what Irina wants.

" . . . have to do what needs to be done. You still aren't listening to me. Lorelai—"

Run. No. Chase.

"Both of you be quiet! Let me *think*." Lorelai whirled away from Gabril and began to pace.

"Both of us?" Gabril's voice was dangerously quiet.

Lorelai's cheeks heated. "I touched his chest with my bare hand and sent my magic into him. That's how I could feel the space where his heart used to be. How I know that he's at war with himself. There's a bond now." Because meeting Gabril's eyes felt impossible at the moment, Lorelai looked up, past the crease where the mountain met the valley they were in, beyond the point where the hemlock grove bled into the evergreens that covered the western mountain, and focused on the enormous command outpost for the section of Irina's army that was stationed in the north.

"And you're *talking* to him?" Gabril's voice rose.

"It would be rude to ignore him. Especially when he can't use his voice—"

"Because he's nothing but *dragon*!"

Dragon. Kol's voice was a snarl of rage and hunger.

You're more than a dragon. You're the king of Eldr. I'm the rightful queen of Ravenspire. And we aren't at war—

War. The hunger in his voice was a vast, violent longing that swept over Lorelai's mind in vicious waves.

She scowled at the trees, though she could no longer see him. *You listen to me, Kolvanismir Arsenyevnek. We are not at war with each other. Your collar is telling you lies. I'm telling you the truth, and you need to listen to me because I can help you.*

There was a long silence, punctuated by images of agony and struggle, and then he whispered, *Help.*

"What if he shifts? If he gives into his dragon completely, we're in serious trouble," Gabril said.

Why didn't you come after me as a dragon? Lorelai asked, and then mentally kicked herself. Putting that idea into Kol's broken mind wasn't one of her smarter moves.

She glanced at the tight line of Gabril's mouth and decided that he never had to know.

Kol sent back an image of the collar keeping him trapped in his human form. Apparently, Irina was worried about facing a vengeful dragon as well.

Lorelai met Gabril's gaze and said, "He can't shift. Irina's collar won't let him. And he's more than a predator sent to hunt me down. He's the king of Eldr, his kingdom is falling, and he's been trapped by Irina's treachery. I can save him, Gabril."

"The risks are tremendous." He sheathed his sword and stared her down, his implacable expression demanding that she back up her words with logic he could accept. "If he's at war with himself, he'll crumble eventually. Irina's magic has tainted him, and in my experience, that taint only grows more poisonous over time."

"Then I need to act quickly."

"If you use your magic to battle Irina's magic in the boy, you'll have revealed your true strength to her. She'll be more prepared, more informed, when you get to the capital. And you'll weaken yourself if his heart doesn't submit to yours, which will also give Irina an advantage—"

"I'm not just going to let him die! Not when I have the power to save him." Lorelai's words fell between them, hard as stones, and Gabril's eyes softened.

"He isn't Leo."

"No, but he's *somebody's* brother. Somebody's friend. And I made a promise to save Eldr if Irina didn't do it. Kol is part of Eldr." She raised her chin. "I keep my promises, Gabril."

Gabril crossed the space between them and pulled her close. "I know you do. And I'm grateful that's who you are. I just want you to be alive at the end of this. I can't bear the thought of losing you too."

She wrapped her arms around him and closed her eyes, letting the warmth of his chest and the familiar weight of his chin against the top of her head make her feel safe.

Not . . . safe. Kol's thoughts were a torment of fire, blood, and death. Her death.

I know, but right now there are more important things. She knew the risks of refusing to kill Eldr's king. Of setting her sights on Ravenspire's false queen and waging a war that would end with one of them on the throne and one of them in the ground.

Stepping back from Gabril, she said, "It's time to start. You remember what we discussed?"

He nodded, his stoic expression back in place. "If you get weak from the magic, I'm to get you to the next location even if I have to drag you behind me."

"Yes."

"A task made much harder by the presence of a dragon trapped in his human form who is dedicated to killing you."

"Use Sasha to keep him away until I wake up if you have to. Just get me off this mountain and down to the bridge that spans the Silber River and connects the Falkrains to the rest of Ravenspire before the army gets there. Irina will start using magic to try to stop us once she figures out what I'm doing. I need to be at the bridge or beyond it before that happens." She flashed him a little smile, though there was no mirth in it. "And pray that Ravenspire recognizes my intentions and lends me its heart without a fight so that nobody has to drag me anywhere."

"How do you plan to put a barrier between the ogres and the Eldrians if you can't actually touch the land in Eldr? Don't you need to touch the heart of the land if you want it to obey you?" he asked as they both turned to look up at the command outpost.

"I'll use the river our kingdoms share." She studied the way the outpost, with its thick stone walls and narrow towers, was carved into the side of the mountain itself.

Where is the armory? She sent to Sasha.

Kol sent back an image of confusion.

Sasha sent back an image of a massive building housed beneath the mountain.

It was going to get complicated having both of them listening to her thoughts.

How many people are in the outpost? she asked, and ignored Kol's fractured thoughts as Sasha sent her pictures of row upon row of soldiers standing at attention beneath the pale blue sky while a woman with multiple silver bars on the breast of her uniform yelled something to them.

Troop review. Most, if not all, of the people who lived in the bunker would be in the outer court. The army hadn't changed their schedule much since Gabril's days in the palace. That would make Lorelai's job a lot easier.

The bulk of Irina's weaponry and supplies were housed in the bunker that stretched from the outpost into the center of the mountain. The bulk of her northern army was stationed here as well—partially because Duchess Waldina owned the land and was loyal, and partially because this was close enough to the Morcant border to act as a deterrent in case King Milek decided to challenge his niece for the throne.

Destroying the outpost and the bunker would leave the northern army without the resources to fight Irina's battles from afar. Destroying the bridge that connected the Falkrain Mountains to the rest of Ravenspire would make it impossible for Irina to recall her soldiers to the capital for help once Lorelai arrived.

It made strategic sense.

It was also the biggest spell Lorelai had ever attempted, and she figured she had one chance to get it right before the threads of Irina's magic that ran through the ground reported her actions to the queen and provoked Irina to launch a spell that would save the outpost.

"Ready?" Gabril asked, the tension in his shoulders belying the composure in his voice.

"Ready."

She knelt in the dirt and thought of the woman who'd killed her children to spare them a slow, terrible death. The villagers who'd mobbed the Eldrians because they were desperate to avoid a choice like hers.

She thought of Leo, telling her to run while Irina's spell turned his veins black and stopped his heart.

Power flooded her body, streaking through her blood to fill her palms with the sting of magic. She raised her hands, wreathed in white light, and looked at the group of buildings jutting out from the middle of the mountain.

"Nakh`rashk." She slammed her palms against the dirt and sent her power deep underground. The heart of the mountain felt stubborn, slow, and unyielding, its power steadily syphoned off by Irina's magic. The second Lorelai encountered resistance, she stopped pushing and whispered, "I ask for the use of your heart, not for my own gain but to stop the one who is causing our land to die."

She let her magic rest within the land and willed her kingdom to respond to her. To help her. To see that she meant to heal Ravenspire instead of ruin it.

Nothing happened. The mountain refused to yield. Lorelai closed her eyes and whispered a plea. If she had to force the mountain's heart to obey hers, she'd be weak and exhausted for days, just as she was after healing Gabril. She didn't have time for weakness. Destroying the outpost was the first move in a carefully planned attack, and every piece of Lorelai's battle plan needed to happen quickly. She had to keep the queen on the defensive—scrambling to keep up by sending out spells of her own that would weaken her heart—and she had to strip all Irina's extra defenses away, or she risked engaging in a battle she might not be able to win.

"Please. Help me," she whispered. Her magic tingled and sparked, and then slowly, slowly the heart of the mountain moved toward the tendrils of her power that lay beneath its skin.

"Thank you," she breathed as the vast, stubborn strength of the mountain merged with her magic and became a tool she could shape to her will. "*Nakh`rashk*. Find the foundation of the army's outpost and shake it until every creature with a heartbeat has left its walls."

The mountain groaned and shuddered. Trees snapped in half and tumbled down. Puffs of dust rose from the outpost's compound, and then another shudder gripped the mountain, and the outer wall of the compound cracked in half.

Soldiers came pouring out of the compound's gate as the mountain trembled and shook. Lorelai kept her hands pressed hard against the ground as her heart thundered in her ears.

She'd known she was capable of great magic, but until this very moment, she hadn't truly believed she had the power to bring a mountain to its knees. The sight filled her with awe, but a streak of fear ran beneath it.

Irina was also capable of bringing a mountain to its knees, and look what the queen had done with the vast strength of her magic.

Tell me when all the people are out of the courtyard. She sent an image of a deserted compound to Sasha.

Running. Sasha's thoughts were full of soldiers stumbling out of the outpost as a spiderweb of cracks spread across the stone floor and raced up the walls.

Somewhere in the background of Lorelai's thoughts, Kol sent bits of words and fragmented images. Lorelai ignored him as she fought an inner war to quiet the fear that the magic she wielded would turn her into the enemy she was determined to destroy. She focused on the images in Sasha's mind of the soldiers scrambling for safety, and grabbed on to them like a lifeline.

Her power and Irina's power were alike, but that didn't mean their hearts were the same. If Irina had wanted this mountain destroyed, she'd have leveled it without once worrying about the human cost.

Clear. Sasha sent a picture of the last wide-eyed soldiers fleeing the outpost.

Lorelai stopped contemplating the nature of her power and drew in a deep breath as magic burned through her veins. Time for Irina to begin reaping what she'd sown.

Far beneath the solid, sturdy presence of the mountain, beneath the layers and layers of dirt, rock, and water, she found what she was looking for. Blistering heat turned a layer of rock into molten lava that flowed slowly through the deepest core of Ravenspire.

She gathered her magic and said, "*Kaz`zhech.* Open a channel to the fire below and let it consume the compound."

The mountain made a horrible grinding noise, like two enormous slabs of rock scraping against each other. A low rumbling shook the hillside, growing louder by the second. The trees trembled, branches clattering together. Leaves, pinecones, small stones, and dirt shook loose from the mountain and slid down its side.

Safe? Safe! Sasha demanded as she streaked across the sky toward Lorelai, leaving the compound behind.

I'm safe.

Kol snarled, and Lorelai whipped her head around to scan the trees, but the snarl had been in his thoughts, and she could find no trace of him.

The rumbling became a roar, and the scorching heat of the lava tangled with the threads of Lorelai's magic as it surged upward through the mountain's core. The compound shook violently, and large chunks of stone tumbled down the mountainside.

The ground beneath her hands heaved, and Gabril grabbed her shoulders to keep her from falling as long cracks split the mountain's skin and exposed the fiery veins of lava that flowed beneath.

"We need to get out of here," Gabril said.

"One more minute." Lorelai looked up at the compound and sent her will into the mountain.

The stream of molten rock that was rising within the mountain exploded into the compound and flooded the bunker. Steam hissed, stone cracked and crumbled, and the mountain trembled. And then the lava spewed out of the bunker and covered the courtyard, sending the remaining remnants of the wall sliding down the mountainside. The mountain shuddered once more, a violent ripple that tore through the land above the compound and sent it plummeting onto the courtyard below.

Lorelai whispered her thanks and lifted her hands from the ground. The roar of the lava became a distant rumble and then faded completely. She climbed to her feet and stared at the place where the outpost used to exist.

It was gone. Destroyed down to the last piece of stone. The bunker was sealed off, and every bit of weaponry had been consumed by the molten stone.

Lorelai's legs shook, and her fingertips were icy as she struggled to pull on her gloves, but she could stand on her own. Walk on her own. She'd done the biggest spell of her life, and because the mountain had agreed to be allied with her purposes, the cost to her body was small. She hoped that also meant the cost to the mountain's heart was small as well.

Must . . . hunt. Kol's words seared themselves in her mind along with an image of him digging his hands into a tree trunk, trying desperately to keep himself from chasing her.

Killing her.

"Let's go," she said as she looked over her shoulder for the huntsman who was losing his battle to spare her life. "It will take us at least three days to walk to the Silber River, and we need to get to that bridge before the soldiers find their bearings and become a cohesive unit again."

Gabril nodded and turned south. "And the boy?"

"He'll be hunting me soon. Let's put as much distance between us as we can while I come up with a plan to deal with him."

Gabril gave her a look that promised he had a plan of his own if hers failed. They started walking south while Sasha circled above them, and somewhere behind them, Kol fought to resist Irina's magic.

TWENTY-THREE

THE SUN TRACED the stone balcony with thin, golden fingers that did little to dispel the shadows spreading from the gathering twilight. Irina gripped the twisted metal balustrade with both hands and stared at the city—*her* city—spread out below her like a feast of plump cottages, pretty gabled inns, cobblestoned streets, and cathedral spires that pierced the sky like needles.

The soft glow of lanterns lit to welcome friends and family home dotted the cityscape like tiny golden stars. A gust of wind chased a thread of ice down Irina's spine, but she refused to shiver.

The sun's dying glow slid away from the balcony, plunging Irina into shadows. Her gaze followed the remaining light as it sank toward the ground, and her lips pressed together in a thin line when the light lingered in the castle's garden, sparkling against the white stone monolith that rose from a cluster of crimson flowers like a sentinel standing guard.

Her heart lurched, tapping against her breastbone like an

impatient fist. She pressed one pale hand against her chest in a futile effort to stop the painful pounding and tore her gaze away from the monolith.

She had nothing to grieve for. No one left to mourn. Instead, she had a kingdom at her feet and the ruthless power it took to rule it. Others might say they'd kill to be where she was, but they were liars.

Irina alone had proven capable of wresting the life she deserved from those who sought to keep it from her. She alone had taken the bitter dregs of failure and turned them into triumph. Soon Lorelai would be dead, her traitorous heart in Irina's hands, and Irina would find a way to renew her own heart. All would be as it should. The pain she was pouring into her huntsman's collar wouldn't let him fail her again.

Awareness curled along the edges of her power, stinging her veins as magic surged toward her hands.

Something was wrong.

She closed her eyes and focused on the threads of magic she'd laid throughout her kingdom.

To the north. Beyond the Hinderlinde Forest. Over the Sil-ber River and west.

Reaching out, she wrapped her bare hand around a vine of raven's rose that crept up the side of her tower. The thick, stubby thorns pierced her skin. Ignoring her cuts, Irina said, "*Prosnakh*. Find what I seek."

Her magic gathered itself and shot down the thorny plant in a stream of power that sounded like a clap of thunder when it merged with the ground. Irina closed her eyes and envisioned the mountains northwest of the Silber River. Duchess Waldina's land with its villages, its mines, and Irina's northern army command outpost.

The queen's heart pounded unsteadily as her magic merged with the heart of the thorny climbing rose plant and exploded into a vine of its own, snaking beneath the capital city, crossing the Hinderlinde Forest, and burning a path straight into the western mountains, far beneath the sparse villages that clung stubbornly to the mountains' unforgiving skin.

When the vine reached Duchess Waldina's lands, it burst into hundreds of tendrils that crawled beneath the ground, seeking answers. In seconds, the tendrils tangled with the lingering strands of Lorelai's magic, and the spells she'd used were revealed to the queen.

A vise of pain wrapped around Irina's chest and stole her breath.

Her entire command outpost was *gone*. Destroyed down to the last stone. Her weapons were buried beneath a lake of hardened lava, her communications towers with their signal mirrors and carrier pigeons were crushed, and her soldiers had fled to the nearest village.

But worse than all that were the threads of magic that wrapped around the heart of the mountain and repelled Irina's touch with implacable strength.

Lorelai.

Fury tinged with the bitterness of fear swamped Irina. She hadn't trained the princess to use magic like this—to merge with the heart of something and turn it into a weapon. It had taken Irina years to learn that skill. Either Lorelai had been practicing, training with a rogue *mardushka*, or the princess had more natural power than Irina had imagined.

Either way, the princess had just declared war, and Irina couldn't allow that to go unpunished.

Tightening her grip on the rose vine, Irina whispered, "*Nakh-gor kaz`lit*. Find the one I seek and punish her." Irina poured her intent, every strong-willed, vicious thought she'd ever had, into the incantors. Her arm throbbed, and her heart sent spikes of pain into her jaw as her power shuddered through the vine and then burst into hundreds of smaller threads that moved throughout the capital, the Hinderlinde, and across the Silber into the Falkrains.

Irina opened her eyes and swayed on her feet as the effort it took to gather power from the increasingly reluctant Ravenspire ground took its toll. Gripping the balustrade with bloody fingers, she smiled coldly as she gazed north toward land that was now connected to her as intimately as her own heartbeat.

Her huntsman would be closing in on the princess, driven wild by his need to rip out her heart and end his torment. Any day now, he would complete his task, and Irina would sleep well at night knowing the princess had paid for her betrayal.

But if he failed, the threads of Irina's power would not. The second Lorelai used her magic again, Irina's spell would attack, and Lorelai's foolish game would cost her everything.

TWENTY-FOUR

KOL'S HOURS WERE a blur of tree trunks, a pale sky that grew dark and star pocked before slowly giving way to dawn, and the torment that poured out of the collar and made him feel like every part of him was an inferno of unendurable pain.

The girl's voice was a lifeline that sometimes broke through the terrible whispers of his collar, but the longer he stayed away from her, the harder it was to hear her.

By the time the sun rose on the day after he'd left her behind, her voice was gone, and he was alone with the whispers. The pain. And the vicious beat of his dragon's heart.

He had to go after her.

He couldn't.

He had to rip her heart from her chest.

He wouldn't.

He wouldn't, but it was impossible to remember why.

Near midday, he stumbled, going down hard on his knees as the distance between him and the girl became liquid fire in his veins.

He was going to die.

No, *she* was going to die.

He wasn't a killer.

He was nothing but what his queen had made him to be.

The rage pumping through his chest collided with the power that surged out of the collar and became an unending stream of torment. Every breath he took was a razor in his lungs. Every move away from the girl was a knife that flayed him from the inside out.

He clutched his head in his hands and screamed until he was hoarse.

He had to go back. He *had* to. He was fire, blood, and death, and the girl's heart was his salvation.

Salvation.

His tortured thoughts grabbed on to the word.

He was a predator, and she was his prey. Once he held her heart in his hand, he'd be saved.

He looked up. Ahead of him, the cold, clear expanse of a lake separated him from the vast reaches of the eastern Falkrains. Beyond the mountains, something beckoned him. Something like home, if he'd ever had one.

If he ran, he could be in the eastern Falkrains by nightfall.

If he ran from his prey, the pain would tear him to pieces.

Kol dug his fingers into the ground beneath him, and closed his eyes. Fought to ignore the pounding of his heart and the whispers of the collar.

He would not be a monster.

He already was.

He was a monster, and nothing would change until he took his prey's heart.

The collar's whispers skittered through his mind, and red-hot pain poured into his veins, obliterating everything but a vicious need to hunt.

To kill.

To finally be free of this torment.

He threw his head back and roared, and the whispers became screams echoing inside his head.

He was fire, blood, and death.

And the girl was going to die.

He found her as the sun reached its midpoint in the sky. She was almost out of the mountains, almost to the open ground that led down toward the rushing river that separated the mountains from the forest that stretched between the north and his queen's castle. The man was with her, but his blade was sheathed. The bird was hovering, and the whispers in Kol's mind scraped until he was raw.

Identify the biggest threat.

Kill it first.

Kill them all.

The man's weapon was a threat, but the man couldn't run.

The bird was faster, but its beak and talons would do little but slow Kol down.

It couldn't stop him.

Nothing could.

He was a monster, and he'd come for his salvation.

The girl froze in the act of building a fire and looked at the trees around her. *Kol?*

His lip curled, and his muscles tensed.

Where are you? I know you're close. I can hear your thoughts.

Hunt . . . you. The words surfaced from the wreckage of his mind, and he curled his hands into fists. *Break . . . you.*

You don't want to do that. She looked confident.

Yes. He did. It was all he wanted. All he craved with every vicious heartbeat.

"He's back," she said as she slowly climbed to her feet. "And he's worse."

Gabril grabbed his sword as he lunged to his feet.

Hunt. Kol's voice was barely human. *Kill.*

I can help you. The girl's voice was calm. *No one has to die.*

The collar exploded into a frenzy of blistering pain, and he rose from his hiding place to lock eyes with his prey.

"He's coming." The girl glanced at Gabril. "Don't try to stop him. He'll kill you. He's lost control."

"Lorelai—"

"I never questioned your training methods, because you were the expert. Don't question me about magic." The girl lifted her bare hands, palms facing toward Kol. His heart thundered at the sight of her unprotected chest.

Her heart was his for the taking.

His pain was almost over.

"Point your sword toward the ground, take a few steps away from me, and try not to look like a threat," she said to Gabril. Then she gave the bird a stern look, and it shrieked at Kol as it settled into a nearby tree, its black eyes focused on him.

The man took a step back, pointed his sword toward the ground, and looked like an attack dog about to come off his leash as Kol exploded out of the trees and came for the girl.

Prey. He snarled.

Come to me, she said as she lifted her hands.

Kill you.

Come.

Her voice was a balm against the searing pain in his mind, and he shuddered to a stop, his breath heaving, his body shaking. The collar whispered, murmured, screamed. The pain scoured his body until he was nothing but fire.

Blood.

Death.

He clenched his fists around the collar and tore at it, but it didn't budge.

"Don't touch that collar," the man breathed. "Irina's magic is in there, and it might be a trap."

The girl nodded without taking her eyes from Kol's.

Kol released the collar and closed his eyes as her scent reached him. Evergreens. Snow. Sweet burning wood.

He was fire. His chest burned with every breath, and only the girl's heart would make it better.

Come to me, she said again, and his eyes flew open.

He snarled as he lunged for her, dragon talons extending from his fingertips.

She waited until he was almost upon her, and then dove beneath his outstretched arms, crashing into his knees and bringing him to the ground. He kicked out and whipped his body toward her. She elbowed him in the jaw, knocking him back. His talons scraped her shoulder.

He scrambled to get his feet beneath him again, and she leaped on top of him, her bare hands pressing into his chest and sending a bolt of magic straight through his dragon heart.

He threw her off him, sending her spinning into the under-brush. With a snarl of rage, he crawled after her, his heart screaming for her blood, the collar whispering until he could hear nothing else.

She watched him come for her, her hands raised as if to stop him. Foolish prey. He pulled himself into a crouch and leaped. Her bare hands slammed against his chest as he pinned her to the ground, and the brilliant heat of her magic arrowed into him.

He threw back his head, the cords of his neck standing out, his chest laboring with every breath as she sent her magic through him, cutting him off from the rage that lived in the empty space where his human heart had been and softening the messages of pain his body kept sending.

Help me. His voice, broken and raw, rose above the collar's whispers. He looked at her face and found fierce compassion in her eyes, resolute determination in the set of her mouth.

I am. Her thoughts spun quickly, almost too fast for him to follow. She was thinking of magic, of remedies, of how much pain she could take from him without Irina realizing she'd lost her huntsman.

Grab the tree beside us. I don't want to cause more damage to the land, but we don't have a choice. She jerked her chin toward the sickly looking maple. *Hold on to it with both hands, and whatever you do, don't let go until I'm finished.*

He didn't question her. Slowly, he climbed off her. She moved with him, keeping her hands against his skin. He turned, dug his now talonless fingers into the bark, and braced himself.

Taking a deep breath, she said, "*Nakhgor.* Find his pain. *Ja`dat.* Send it into the tree instead."

Her magic flared, his dragon heart pounded, and the collar was a band of agony.

"*Nakhgor. Ja`dat.*" Her voice rose as the magic surged through her and into him, rushing like a river that refused to be stopped. His dragon heart fought her, but Kol himself wanted to be saved, and the part of him that still survived bowed to the strength of her magic.

The brilliant light flowed through him, gathered the worst of his torment and sent it through his hands and into the maple.

Kol cried out as the tree shivered.

Power was an all-encompassing flood of light inside the girl, and it spilled over from her thoughts to his. It was pain and pleasure—freedom and a chain that bound her to an onslaught of weariness she couldn't stop if she tried.

He felt her struggle to push the weariness back. To do one last thing for him. Concentrating the last of her energy, she pushed her magic toward the thick gray shroud that kept him from his memories. Her voice trembled with power as she yelled, *"Nakhgor. Ja`dat."*

The shroud tore. The maple split in two with a tremendous crack. Kol's memories came flooding back, and with it the restraint he needed to gain control of his dragon heart.

The girl gave him a crooked little smile before she slumped toward the ground.

Gabril called out a warning, but Kol had already wrapped his arms around her. Already pulled her against his chest so that she wouldn't fall.

His mind was free from torment. The collar's whispers were muted, its pain a dull ache.

She'd saved him. Again.

He tried to say, "Thank you," but her eyes fluttered shut, and she slept.

TWENTY-FIVE

KOL WALKED AHEAD of Gabril, who had the unconscious princess carefully slung over his back as they made their way toward the Silber River that flowed from the western edge of Ravenspire to the eastern reaches of Eldr. Gabril said that Lorelai was going to use the river to keep her promise to help Eldr.

Lorelai.

Not *the girl*. Not *prey*. Not anymore.

Lorelai.

Kol's mind was finally clear, thank the skies, and though pain still pulsed from Irina's collar, though his dragon heart still longed for blood, the warm sense of connection he felt to Lorelai, even while she was unconscious, helped him hold the worst of it at bay.

Seconds after Kol had saved Lorelai from hitting the ground as she fainted, Gabril had lifted the princess away from him while warning him that, dragon or no, Kol was dead the second he even *looked* like he was thinking of hurting Lorelai.

Kol couldn't blame him. If someone had treated Brig the way he'd treated Lorelai, he'd have incinerated them where they stood.

Gabril stumbled as they climbed over a pile of loose gray stones that marked the border of a steep, grass-covered slope. Instantly, Kol pivoted, lunged toward the man, and wrapped his arms around the princess's waist to keep her from falling.

Gabril found his footing in seconds. "Remove your hands from the princess." The absolute authority in his voice would put Master Eiler to shame.

Kol steadied Lorelai against Gabril's back and then slowly stepped away. Her long black hair lifted gently in the wind, and the scent of evergreens, snow, and sweet burning wood made his dragon heart pound mercilessly in his chest, but he tamped it down and concentrated on the pale curve of her cheek, the sweep of dark lashes against her skin.

"If you're through memorizing the way she looks, I suggest you get in front of me again and start moving. And I swear on my life, if you are leading us into a trap set by Irina, nothing, and I mean *nothing*, will save you from me. Do I make myself clear, son?"

Kol tore his gaze away from Lorelai and nodded respectfully. It was a small miracle Gabril was tolerating his presence at all, especially considering the fact that Kol couldn't communicate with him.

Not that any of Kol's current thoughts were worth communicating to Gabril. Not when he was thinking about how desperately he missed his family. How much he longed to fly over Eldr's craggy landscape and walk the spacious bronze halls of the castle with Brig at his side. How fast he could wake Lorelai up so she could keep her promise and save Eldr. How he could get his heart back from Irina without losing himself to the torment of her magic again.

Maybe Lorelai would help him with that the way she was helping him with Eldr. Not that he had any right to ask. But she was Irina's enemy, and so was he. Which meant in a strange way that they were allies. He glanced at Lorelai again and noticed the way her dark lashes lay against the paleness of her skin and the way her red lips parted slightly while she slept.

His heart beat faster, and warmth unfurled in his stomach as he stared at her mouth and imagined thanking the courageous, beautiful princess of Ravenspire with a kiss.

Skies above, he sounded like an *idiot*. Eldr was still falling. Irina still had his heart and a hold on him through the collar around his neck. Lorelai was in terrible danger from Irina, he had no idea where his friends had gone, and his dragon heart kept agreeing with the collar's whispers that he would never be free until he killed the princess. This was no time to think about kissing a girl. Even one as intriguing as Lorelai.

Apparently, he'd recovered his memories just in time to lose his mind.

When Gabril stumbled again, going down hard on one knee, Kol raced to his side and lifted the princess from his back. He cradled her against the warmth of the dragon's fire in his chest, and waited for Gabril to get back up and curtly demand that Kol get his treacherous hands off Lorelai.

Instead, Gabril bowed his head for a moment, breathing hard, pain bracketing lines around his mouth. Kol looked at the distant line of hornbeam trees that marked the bottom of the slope and pretended he didn't notice.

Lorelai's scent stirred his dragon's heart, and it pounded viciously against his chest. He gritted his teeth and gentled his hold on her. He thought of Brig, trusting him to stay alive and to save Eldr, and of his friends insisting on following him and protecting him because he was their king and their friend.

He thought of Lorelai facing down a boy who deserved to die and choosing to save him instead.

The whispers from the collar urged him to hurt, punish, and kill, but he held fast to the memory of Lorelai's courage and stood steady.

After a moment, Gabril climbed to his feet, his hand pressing hard against his left leg. He studied Kol, his expression unreadable. Kol tried to look like he wasn't a threat, and almost wished that Gabril could see into his thoughts the way Lorelai could.

Almost.

Except not the thoughts about kissing Lorelai.

"It's getting close to nightfall. The last time she healed someone, she was out for two days. We need to find shelter for the night. Obviously we aren't going to camp in the open like this. If you're up to it, I'd appreciate you carrying her for a while." Gabril sounded begrudging, as if he was offering Kol an olive branch but might decide to smack him with it instead.

Kol nodded, and tried hard not to let himself react as Gabril drew his sword.

"You'll walk in front of me. My sword will be out at all times. If you try to hurt her, I will drop you where you stand." Gabril met his eyes. "Lorelai thinks there's something worth saving in you. Do your best to prove her right."

Kol adjusted his grip on the princess, tipping her head against his shoulder, careful to avoid having any part of her come in contact with the collar, and then set his sights on the hornbeam trees in the distance. Their thick trunks, low cradles, and profusion of gently twisting branches that stayed low to the ground would provide excellent cover. He jerked his chin toward the trees and looked to see Gabril's reaction.

The man grunted. "That will probably work. Let's get moving."

Kol had taken three steps when Lorelai's bird dove out of the air where she'd been flying in lazy circles and landed hard on his shoulder, her talons digging into his skin. He glanced at her, and she nipped at his face.

He leaned his face as far away from her as he could, and she slapped the back of his head with her wing.

Kol glanced at Gabril for help.

The man shrugged. "Don't look at me. That bird answers to Lorelai alone."

Sasha dug her talons farther into his skin and knocked her wing against his head again.

He glared at her. He was the king of Eldr. A Draconi warrior. He refused to be intimidated by a bird.

She bent her neck and shoved her face into his, matching him glare for glare.

Fine. Maybe he was a little intimidated. Luckily, he no longer had the words to share that humiliating fact with anyone.

Gabril chuckled, and Kol sighed.

They reached the hornbeams as the sun began its western descent. Gabril hovered over a small fire, cooking a simple dinner of beans with chunks of a rabbit Sasha hunted for them. Kol laid the princess on her bedroll inside the tent he'd helped Gabril erect. Then he settled down on a spare blanket and stared out the tent flap at the darkening sky while he thought of everything that was stacked against him now.

Somehow, he had to get his human heart back from Irina. He had to get this collar off his neck. He had to find his friends and pray that Lorelai woke up in time to help save his kingdom from the ogre invasion. If she didn't, his people would be gone.

Brig would be gone.

His throat ached at the thought, and even the warmth of the dragon's fire in his chest couldn't chase the chill of dread from his skin.

After everything he'd done, every piece of himself he'd sacrificed, he couldn't bear the thought of failing Brig.

Who is Brig? The princess's voice entered his mind.

He whipped his head toward Lorelai and found her eyes open, though she still looked exhausted.

My sister. I didn't know you were awake! Gabril said it took you two days to recover last time.

That's because last time I healed a stubborn old man whose heart refused to obey mine until I used everything I had to overpower it. It's easier when the person wants the same thing I want. Your dragon heart fought me, but there was enough of you left in there to make healing you easier than I expected. Your thoughts seem much clearer now. Congratulations on surpassing the vocabulary of my bird.

Very funny. The image of Sasha riding his shoulder while

slapping him with her wing and occasionally pecking at his face came unbidden to his mind. Instantly, he tried to think of something else, but it was too late.

She's protective. Lorelai sounded amused.

I was carrying you to safety!

Well . . . in all fairness, you did try to kill me.

He felt like she'd heaped burning stones onto his shoulders. It took everything he had to keep his eyes on hers. *I'm so sorry, Lorelai. I don't know how to apologize enough for that. Or for being in Nordenberg with Irina. I owe you a debt I can never repay.*

You didn't kill Leo. She sounded weary. *And I believe you when you tell me Irina twisted her words, forcing you into an agreement you never intended. As for trying to kill me after she took your human heart, it wasn't you. Not the true you.*

You risked your life to save mine. Again.

It's becoming an annoying habit of mine. She gave him a smile that suddenly reminded him how red her lips were against the paleness of her cheek.

He refused to pursue that line of thought now that she was inside his mind again. He had better things to think about anyway. Like how soon she could be ready to send a barrier into Eldr. And how long it would take to get there. And maybe—

As long as we're apologizing, I guess I should say I'm sorry for being aware of your thoughts long before I said anything to you, but—

Wait a minute. How long were you aware? His mind flashed back to wondering how it might feel to kiss her.

Her mouth dropped open and tiny spots of color bloomed on her cheeks. *I meant I heard you thinking about ogres and Irina and*

Brig. I didn't . . . Were you really thinking—

Oh, skies, no. Okay . . . maybe. Just for a minute. I'm a male. We do things like that all the time even when we should be thinking about something else. And I was thinking about other things. Lots of other things. That was just one stray thought out of many.

He was an idiot. He'd never stumbled over his words before with a girl. Never lost his ability to be charming while still keeping his distance from the many girls at the academy who'd wanted to kiss the prince so they could brag about it to their friends afterward.

How many girls have you kissed? She sounded curious.

The answer seared itself across his brain before he could bury it beneath thoughts of math equations and flight drills.

Seriously? That many? Was there some sort of competition you just had to win?

It was . . . There were a lot of girls at my school.

She rolled her eyes. *Well, keep your lips to yourself. I have more important things to do.*

He had more important things to do too. He had a kingdom to save, his heart to retrieve (if Irina had told him the truth about keeping it safe), and a sister who needed her brother to come home.

Grief, raw at the edges and weary in the center, filled him and flooded his thoughts before he could stop it. He was walking down the long hall that led to the throne room again, only this time he knew what waited for him. He was standing in the icy waters of Lake Skyllivreng, but the words he wanted to say to his family were too small to encompass what they meant to him. He was kneeling on the platform above the throne room while the head of the royal council placed his father's crown on his head and gave him the full responsibility for ruling a nation on its deathbed. And he was being crushed by the weight of it all. He was making decisions out of desperation, sacrificing what was left of himself so that he could do this one thing right. So that he could save Eldr.

Did the cost of Eldr's salvation have to leave so much wreckage behind?

Her breath caught, and he looked up to find tears in her eyes and an image of her brother—the boy with the irrepressible smile and the reckless light in his eyes—lying quiet as a statue in the meadow outside Nordenberg.

Part of the wreckage.

Leo isn't part of your wreckage. He's part of Irina's. Her own grief, just as raw as his, struck him hard, and he closed his eyes. Having something that was his alone pulled out of the darkest recesses of his mind and given to her without his permission was infinitely worse than having her see that he'd thought of kissing her. He was absolutely certain she felt the same about the grief that belonged only to her.

I can learn how to block you. She wasn't looking at him when he opened his eyes. *That's why you can't hear Irina's thoughts even though her magic has been inside you. She's touched so many people with her magic that she wouldn't have a secret thought left if she didn't block others. Gabril knows how to do it, and he can teach me. We don't have to be forced into sharing everything like this.*

Before he could filter it, he thought of himself, cut off from everyone, trapped with only his dragon heart, a collar whose power was barely held in restraint by Lorelai's, and the inability to share his thoughts with anyone at all if Lorelai blocked her mind from his.

She pressed her lips together, and drew in a deep breath, but he already knew what she was going to say before she said it. The truth was in the way her thoughts softened toward him. The compassion that unfurled in the midst of her weariness and grief.

He couldn't ask it of her.

Yes. Block me. He forced himself to focus on the words. To be resolute and to bury every shred of longing for his final piece of connection with another person. *That's what I want.*

You're a terrible liar.

He laughed, though it wasn't funny. He'd gone his entire life fooling everyone around him—with the possible exception of Brig—into thinking he was nothing but a charming daredevil who couldn't take anything seriously, because it had been easier to take his father's disappointment when Kol could tell himself he'd courted it on purpose. But there was no hiding from Lorelai. She'd already seen the worst he had to offer, and the longer they stayed connected, the more parts of himself he accidentally put on display.

You aren't the only one who is uncomfortably vulnerable here. She sat up and braided her long hair with swift fingers. *You can see me just as much as I can see you. If this is going to work—*

It doesn't have to work. Block me.

She rolled her eyes. *If this is going to work, we need some ground rules.*

Or you could just block me.

She stabbed a finger in his direction. *Stop arguing with me.*

I'm not leaving you trapped inside yourself with no one to talk to.

His thoughts warmed toward this girl who kept surprising him at every turn with the size of her heart and the strength of her spirit.

You keep rescuing me.

Don't let it go to your head. She gave him a crooked smile. *I'm sure one of these days you'll have the chance to rescue me instead.*

I hope not. He got to his feet and offered her his hand. *I hope you stay completely out of danger.*

She took his hand, her palm sparking against his with the tingle of her magic, and rose to face him. Her dark eyes were steady.

Ground rules. No poking into each other's thoughts on purpose. No digging deeper into things we accidentally show each other. And no dumb thoughts about kissing when we have so many other things to worry about. All right?

All right. He leaned away from her as his collar whispered to hurt, punish, kill, and the pain that lingered in the wake of Irina's magic throbbed dully.

And you have to immediately show me if the pain gets worse, or if you start to lose control. She flexed her fingers and looked at his chest, now covered with a shirt borrowed from Gabril. *Now, let's go eat. I'm going to need my strength.*

For the barrier in Eldr? He didn't bother trying to hide how much her answer meant to him.

Yes. Her eyes were on his again as he held the tent flap open, letting in a gust of cold air and a peek at an indigo sky slowly fading to black.

And then do you have somewhere safe to go? Somewhere to hide from Irina? You can always go to Eldr if you want.

She lifted her chin. *I'm not the one who needs somewhere safe to hide.*

Images spun through her mind—a bridge collapsing into the water, communications towers toppling, and Irina clutching her heart as every spell she used against Lorelai's onslaught weakened her further. His collar's whispers skittered and screamed as the princess's plan unfolded before him.

He met her gaze. *You're going after Irina.*

Once Eldr is safe, yes.

Lorelai, what you're planning . . . You're going to war.

Her eyes were fierce. *That's right. I'm going to destroy her defenses, provoke her to use magic so that she grows weaker by the day, and then I'm returning to my castle, and I'm taking it back.*

His dragon heart thundered, a vicious tempo that lit the fire in his chest. *Irina tricked me.*

Yes, she did.

She stole my human heart and trapped me with this collar.

Lorelai leaned close. *Want to help me?*

He bared his teeth in a smile every bit as fierce as hers. *I thought you'd never ask.*

TWENTY-SIX

IRINA CLENCHED HER mirror with a white-knuckled grip and glared at its surface. It was the morning of the seventh day after she'd flooded the Eldrian king with her magic, taken his human heart, and sent him, wild with rage and pain, back into the Falkrains to find and destroy the princess.

It had been a simple command. The strength of the collar's painful spell combined with the viciousness of his dragon heart should have compelled him to obey her.

And yet he defied her.

She hadn't been sure at first. She'd scryed the surface of her mirror several times a day, but she'd seen nothing useful. He'd been walking, sometimes crawling, sometimes hanging on to tree trunks as if he needed their help to stand.

Without allowing him to see her thoughts through the connection her magic had forged between them—something no one but Raz was ever allowed to do—she couldn't be sure of his intent. She'd assumed he was hunting the princess, slowed by the injuries she'd inflicted.

The truth set her blood ablaze with rage.

She stared at the mirror's surface, her teeth clenched so hard that little shocks of pain reverberated up her jaw as the swirling clouds of the mirror's surface parted to reveal the princess walking through a forest of hornbeam trees with the king by her side.

Not trying to kill her. Not ripping out her heart. *Smiling* at her when she looked at him, though he sometimes curled his hands into fists as if fighting the urge to hurt her like he was supposed to do.

"*Fool.*" Irina spat the word at the mirror's surface while her heart pounded and her palms burned.

He acted as though he wasn't under a blood oath to fulfill the task she'd given him. As if his kingdom wasn't on the line.

As if he could ignore her express orders without incurring any consequences.

Had he forgotten whom he was dealing with?

Irina's hands shook as she stared at Kolvanismir and Lorelai. The man who'd helped Lorelai escape wasn't visible in the mirror's surface. He hadn't been since the first time she'd seen the princess.

He was of no consequence. She'd had his sketch drawn from the memories she'd found in the king's blood. Viktor had recognized him immediately as Gabril Busche, the former head of the palace guard. She'd thought he was dead. She'd attended his funeral.

She'd be happy to attend it again.

But he didn't matter now. She could use him against Lorelai if necessary, but she didn't want to bear the strain that would take. Not when she'd already used so much power to create the perfect huntsman.

No, what mattered now was sending a reminder to the king that breaking an oath with a *mardushka* was not an option.

Not if he ever wanted to take another pain-free breath again.

Setting the mirror down on her vanity with a sharp click, she scooped up a blue velvet bag with a black ribbon drawstring. Loosening the ribbon, she poured the contents of the bag into her palm.

The moment the scraps of thistle and bone touched her skin, her magic flared, and she felt the connection to the king's collar.

She closed her fingers over the thistle and bone, locked eyes with the mirror's surface, and said, "*Kaz`lit*. May the punishment I deem worthy for his crime flood his body with pain."

Power poured out of her, sizzling against the bits she held in her hand. She felt the heart of the thistle she'd used for the collar surge beside the heart of the wolf she'd slain to harvest its bones. She'd conquered both hearts long ago. Now it was simply a matter of using them to conquer the king's heart as well.

And then Lorelai would die, and Irina would finally be at peace.

Maybe the king thought Irina couldn't hurt him if she wasn't beside him. Maybe he didn't understand that once the heart of a living thing had been conquered by a *mardushka*, any object created from that heart obeyed the *mardushka* as well.

Or maybe he was stupid enough to think the princess's magic would be enough to save him from the wrath of his queen.

"*Kaz`lit!*" She threw back her head, a vicious smile of triumph on her face as the magic connected with the hearts she'd conquered. "Flood his body with the punishment he deserves."

The magic spilled out of her. The thistle and bone did her

bidding. And when she looked down once more at the mirror's surface, the defiant fool of a king was on his knees, his expression full of agony, as he pulled frantically at the collar around his neck.

Irina concentrated, sending every bit of rage that flooded her body straight into the collar. Let him burn from the inside out. Let him *hurt* in places he never knew could feel so much pain.

Let him understand the cost of betrayal.

He fell forward, his body spasming, his mouth open in a scream Irina could enjoy even if she couldn't hear it. Talons grew from his fingertips, and she imagined the dragon's fire in his chest scorching him, begging him to shift though his queen refused to let him.

And then the princess was there. Falling to her knees beside him. Reaching for his chest and leaving her own heart exposed.

Irina clenched the bits of thistle and bone so hard, she felt them crack as she snarled, "Kill her. Kill her now, Kolvanismir. Use your talons to rip her heart out of her chest, and the agony will stop. Eldr will be saved. Just *kill her.*"

She pushed more agony into his body, and a stab of pain shot through her own chest in response.

The king opened his eyes and locked gazes with the princess.

There was nothing but hunger for blood on his face.

Irina smiled and used her free hand to push at the ache in her chest.

It was almost over. She'd broken him.

The princess leaned down.

The king dug his talons into the ground beneath him.

Irina gripped the thistle and bone, pushing pain into him

even while her heart stuttered and her chest burned.

And then Lorelai put her bare hands against the Kol's chest, her eyes never leaving his, and the pain that had been pouring out of the collar rebounded toward Irina like a whip.

The queen stumbled away from the vanity, her hand still clutching the remnants of her huntsman's collar, while fire streaked through her veins and her vision began to gray.

This wasn't possible.

It *wasn't*.

First the mountain's heart had yielded to Lorelai and now *this*.

It had taken Irina ten years of training, of searching out the black clan *mardushkas* willing to disobey King Milek's edict and practice the darker side of their nature. Ten years to learn how to force an unwilling heart to fully submit to hers.

And yet Lorelai was doing it as if it was nothing.

Irina gasped as the fire in her veins felt like it would incinerate her where she stood. It was a wolf's rage, a thistle's thorns, a queen's revenge, and a dragon's fire.

It was unbearable.

Releasing the thistle and bone from her shaking fingers, Irina stumbled against the wall and pushed her palm against her aching chest as the truth turned her knees to water.

She'd lost her huntsman. Lorelai had declared war against her when she'd destroyed the northern command outpost. If Lorelai was on her way to the capital, all that stood between Irina and destruction was the web of magic that lay beneath the ground and the strength of Irina's failing heart.

TWENTY-SEVEN

YOU BEAT HER. Kol stared at Lorelai, a wild light of triumph in his amber eyes. *You beat Irina.*

Lorelai stood beside him above the steep banks of the Silber River while Gabril scouted the area around the bend to the west where a massive bridge connected northern Ravenspire with the south. Power still gathered in her palms, and she tried to feel triumphant as well. She'd done it. She'd battled the magic that poured out of the collar, and she'd shoved it back toward Irina until it was once again bearable for Kol.

Irina had fought her for him, and Lorelai had won.

She hadn't been able to remove the collar, but still—she'd *won.*

Lorelai knew she should be thrilled, but instead she looked away from Kol and sagged slowly onto the damp clumps of river grass that clung to the rocky bank.

Lorelai?

She was stronger. She could beat the queen.

Her chest ached sharply as the truth sliced into her. She could beat the queen, which meant she could've saved Leo.

She stared at her hands while grief thickened her throat and shame sank into her heart like a stone.

Why hadn't she ripped off her gloves at the first sign of Irina? Why hadn't she stood alone in the street and faced the queen while Leo was safe in the blacksmith's shop?

She'd been so afraid to reveal herself, so sure it would be the end of everything, and Leo had paid the price.

Wait a minute. Kol knelt on the rocky soil beside her.

He died because we tried everything but magic. She couldn't look away from her hands. Powerful but useless the one time it really mattered.

Her vision blurred, and a shiver worked its way down her spine.

Lorelai—

If you're going to tell me that I couldn't have known I'd be stronger, or that I was right to be afraid of Irina, or some other useless thing that won't help, please don't.

It hurt to breathe. To feel the rush of her heartbeat and know that Leo's heart could still be beating too.

I was going to say that we always know what to do when we look back. I've replayed the moment my parents told me they were taking my brother to the war front a hundred times. And every time I find a way to change the outcome. His voice was quiet, but his thoughts were full of the loss that haunted him. *I convince them to wait a day. I get expelled earlier so that they have to stay and deal with that. I pretend I'm terribly sick. I run away so that they have to look for me. Anything to keep them from going to the war front. Anything to make the truth something I can bear.*

I can't bear this. The shiver that ran down her spine seized her body, and she trembled, teeth chattering. *I can't bear knowing I could've stopped Irina and saved my brother.*

I know you can't, but you don't have to bear it alone.

He sat quietly beside her, his thoughts an open invitation for her to see what he bore alone. How the weight of his responsibility and fear was crushing him. How he understood the terrible wound of hindsight and what it took to keep moving forward because that was the only road left open.

Something hot and feral churned through Lorelai. Magic sparked and burned in her hands, and she curled them into fists and pounded them against the ground until the skin broke and bled. She wanted to tear the world into pieces. She wanted to crawl into a hole and disappear.

She wanted her brother.

She was crying, choking on her tears. On the truth.

You aren't alone.

She leaned against him, the warmth of the dragon's fire in his chest chasing the chill from her skin. He wrapped his arms around her, his hold gentle, his thoughts full of confidence that she could keep moving forward when she was ready. And that she wouldn't do so alone.

She cried until the shame and grief had emptied out of her. Until she felt hollowed out from her head to her toes and exhausted in a way that felt permanent.

When she grew quiet, she realized that he was still on his knees, the rocky ground cutting into his skin. That the air had grown damp and cold, and he'd shifted his body to block the worst of it from touching her. She was suddenly, agonizingly aware that she'd practically crawled into his lap, and that she'd soaked the front of his shirt.

Nothing in Gabril's lessons on ladylike conversation was remotely helpful in knowing what to say next.

You don't have to say anything at all.

That was nice of you, she said even though *nice* wasn't the right word. He'd understood her grief, and he was the last place she'd expected to find peace.

Can I ask you something? His eyes met hers, steady and certain, while the wind tugged at his wild hair.

She saw the question forming in his thoughts, but was too weary to flinch.

Who killed Leo?

Her thoughts were a maelstrom of images and pain. Running over catwalks, Leo in her wake. Irina shouting an incantor. Monstrous vines exploding across the sky and hurtling toward the ground. Her gloves on as she desperately pulled Leo to the gate while his veins turned black and his heart stopped.

I should've taken off my gloves.

That doesn't answer my question. Who killed Leo? His voice was gentle.

I failed him.

Maybe in hindsight that's how it looks. But why were you in Nordenberg in the first place? Why did you have to run? What poison was running through his blood? He placed a finger under her chin and lifted her face until he could look her in the eye. *This is important, Lorelai. It's the difference between drowning and moving forward. Who killed Leo?*

She stared at him as the answer slowly bubbled to the surface. *Irina.*

He waited while the truth settled. While she found her equilibrium and her compass.

It mattered that Lorelai was strong enough to defeat Irina, and she'd spend the rest of her life wishing she'd known that all along. But it mattered more that she remember that Leo wouldn't have died if Irina hadn't decided that staying in power was worth sacrificing the lives of her people.

The exhaustion that swept through her dissolved into anger, which hardened into purpose once more.

She couldn't change the past. She could only move forward and make better choices now.

Slowly she climbed to her feet and then reached down to help Kol up. His hand was warm in hers, and she wanted to say thank you, but he already knew.

Gabril came around the corner, his face creasing into a scowl when he saw their joined hands.

"The bridge is clear for now. No soldiers in sight. Sasha scouted back the way we came. Since she didn't give me any warnings, it seems we haven't been followed."

"Because Irina will use magic against me when I make my next move," Lorelai said.

"Agreed." The scowl on Gabril's face deepened. "Are you going to stand there holding hands all day, or are we going to do this?"

Kol let her go. Cold air swept over her skin in the absence of his warmth, and she felt ridiculous for noticing the way his hair curled over his ears and the steady rise and fall of his chest as he breathed.

Careful now, he said as he brushed past her to follow Gabril.

We might need to add a ground rule about noticing inappropriate things at inappropriate times. He sounded amused.

I can't help that I'm an observant person. And speaking of being observant, we need to watch for Irina's counterattack. I'm hoping that when I use magic again, she'll be ready to send something nasty our way.

That's not really the kind of thing I'd hope for.

It's the whole point of this plan. The more magic she uses, the weaker she gets. Now let's stop the ogres in Eldr and start causing Irina more trouble.

How are you going to stop the ogres? His thoughts were a blaze of desperation bound with a thin thread of hope.

I'll ask the heart of the river our kingdoms share to do my bidding. If I can convince it to submit to me, then I can send a wall of water into Eldr and have it remain as a barrier between the ogres and your people.

I'm not sure water alone will do anything but slow the ogres down. There were flashes of horrifying scenes in his memory—children and elderly Draconi running from enormous, gray-skinned beasts who smashed everything to pieces—and he shivered.

It won't be just water. She met his gaze. *I'll bind my magic to the river's heart. As long as I'm alive, nothing will pass through the barrier. And if I die . . . just stay close to me. If I die, take my heart to Irina. Technically, you didn't agree to kill me. You agreed to bring her my heart. Her blood oath would force her to honor her promise. Either way, Eldr will be safe. Now let's get across this bridge so that I can get started.* They rounded the bend and came upon the bridge.

It was an enormous structure, wide enough for four wagons

to travel abreast at once. The ancient wood was bleached and weathered, but it stood sturdy, braced by crossbeams and thick pillars sunk deep into the river's bed. The water ran deep, its current strong. From her standpoint on the north side of the bridge, Lorelai could just see the bank on the south shore. Four pairs of statues of kings and queens long buried in the royal tomb stood guard at each end of the bridge, silent stone sentinels three times as tall as Lorelai.

There were other ways over the river—smaller bridges to the west, ferry docks to the east, but this was the avenue that connected the main road in the north to the main road in the south. This was the fastest way to get to the capital. Once this was gone, it would take weeks for Irina's northern army, currently stranded in the Falkrains, to reach her.

By then, either Irina or Lorelai would be dead.

You're not going to die. Kol's voice was fierce, and she heard the whispers of his collar crawling across his mind, urging him to destroy instead of protect.

I might. She didn't look at him as she walked past Gabril to study the bridge and plan her attack. She wanted to live, but she wanted the safety and well-being of her kingdom more.

I will lay down my life for yours. It's the least I can do.

She saw the resolve blazing through him, a brilliant light that filled him the way his determination to protect Eldr filled him, and her heart beat a little faster. The whispers from his collar grew louder, begging for her blood, but he fought to ignore them and focused on the debt he felt he owed her.

Eldr needs its king, she said as she walked between the first pair of weathered stone statues.

And Ravenspire needs its true queen.

She lifted her chin and met his eyes. *We're allies now. We'll just have to save each other.*

She moved through the next pair of statues, shivering a little as she looked up at the empty gray eyes of a queen with long hair and clasped hands that were missing most of their fingers.

This water flows through Eldr. There was longing in his voice. A sharp ache of loneliness as memories of wide bronze halls with rounded balconies, rugged mountains, and rooms filled with laughter and music swept over his mind.

And soon this water will make Eldr safe. She looked at the water and prayed its heart would submit to hers without a fight.

"Which do you want to do first? The bridge or the water?" Gabril said as he strode onto the bridge ahead of Lorelai.

Whichever one Lorelai chose would spark a response from the queen. And even though Lorelai had beaten the queen's attempt to punish Kol, she'd be performing two tremendously difficult spells, one after the other. If the river or the wooden bridge refused to submit their hearts to her, she'd be weakened and unable to fight Irina.

"I'll send a barrier into Eldr first." If the queen retaliated, and Lorelai was too drained to fight, she could flee. Leave the bridge intact and alter her plan. But her promise would be kept, and Kol wouldn't have to worry about losing anyone else he loved.

Thank you. He walked abreast of her as they passed the final pair of statues on the north side and began moving across the bridge.

I keep my promises.

And I keep mine. His fingers brushed against hers, and she saw the vow he'd taken to protect her at any cost. She saw the pain the collar was delivering in response. The way his dragon heart begged for her blood, and the way Kol forced himself to ignore them both so that he could be the boy he wanted to be instead of the predator Irina had created.

She saw, and her heart beat a little faster, a little harder, as together they walked out over the water.

TWENTY-EIGHT

LORELAI AND KOL were nearly to the other side of the bridge when Sasha swooped through the sky and settled on Lorelai's shoulder, her bright eyes staring at Kol while she clicked her beak at him.

Are we clear? Lorelai asked. *No one on the other side trying to get onto the bridge?*

Clear. Sasha gently butted her head against Lorelai's.

Keep watch over that side, please. I have something to take care of before I can destroy the bridge.

Sasha spiraled back into the air as Lorelai, Gabril, and Kol walked past the statues on the south side of the bridge.

"I have to touch the water," Lorelai said as she began climbing down the steep bank to the rushing river below.

Gabril gestured toward Kol. "Get down there with her, son. If the water's heart fights hers, she'll be too exhausted to keep herself from falling in. I'm trusting you to keep her safe. Don't let me down."

He didn't threaten my life this time. I think I'm growing on him.
Kol's words were light, but a heaviness lay over his thoughts.
Worry that the spell wouldn't work. That it would reach Eldr
too late. That he'd sacrificed so much of himself only to fail.

Lorelai had no words that could make it better, so she
plunged her bare hands into the frigid water. The cold was a slap
of shock that instantly numbed her skin. The swift-moving current dragged at her fingers.

And magic streaked through her veins to gather in her palms.

The heart of the water instantly surged toward hers. It was
merciless power, unyielding strength, and vast patience. Kol
wrapped his hands around her waist, anchoring her to the shore,
and she whispered her intentions to the water. Begged its heart
to see that she meant no harm. That she didn't want to force it
into submission and cause more damage to Ravenspire.

When the water's heart tangled with her magic until it was
hard to tell the difference between the two, she threw back her
head and let her magic burn through her.

"Tvor`grada." Her voice rang with the power that expanded
within her, pushing against her skin like she'd swallowed fire.
"Go forth into Eldr and rise until you meet the sky. Form an
impassable barrier between the Eldrians and the dark magic that
is destroying them from the south."

The water closest to her hands eddied and swirled, and the
bridge trembled as the river pulled away from its course and
flowed toward Lorelai. Beneath her palms, the water formed a
solid wall and began to rise.

She stood, the water rising with her, engulfing her hands and
then towering over her head. The river bubbled and churned as it

lifted toward the sky, a solid wall of water with brilliant threads of magic running through it.

"*Tvor`grada*," Lorelai yelled, and the threads of magic raced for each other, knotting together and spreading along the southern side of the river's wall like a tightly woven fisherman's net of blazing white light. Kol let go of her waist with one hand and reached to touch the water. Sparks bit into his skin as his fingers grazed the water, and he jerked his hand back.

"Now go! Stretch across all Eldr and keep the ogres from crossing your shores." Lorelai swept her hands to the east, and the wall of water rushed forward with a roar that tore chunks of rocky soil from its banks and sent them tumbling into its depths.

Lorelai kept her hands in the water as the river swept through the Falkrains and into Eldr. As it rushed across the craggy surface of Kol's kingdom until it reached the Chrysós Sea at the other side.

Whispering her thanks to the water's heart, she slowly withdrew her hands and tucked them into her sweater for warmth. The wall of water on Ravenspire's side of the border collapsed with a tremendous splash.

It's done. Nothing will be able to get past it as long as I'm alive. If the ogres use magic against it, my magic will fight them. I know it isn't a perfect solution, but—

He pulled her hard against his chest and wrapped his arms around her. His breath came in unsteady jerks, and the relief that threatened to undo him spilled over into her thoughts as well.

Eldr is safe now. Brig is safe. His hands shook and he fisted them into the back of her sweater. *I can't tell you how much that means to me.*

I already know. She leaned her head against the warmth of his chest because he seemed to need it, and because another warmth—bubbly and strange—was unspooling in her stomach and tingling with a magic of its own.

His thoughts spun too fast for her to catch more than glimpses, and she tried her best to give him the space he needed to collect himself by focusing on something else.

Like the way his heart pounded against her ear. Or the way he turned his face into her neck and sent the warmth in her stomach straight to her chest.

"Lorelai, down!" Gabril's voice was a whiplash of command that Lorelai obeyed instinctively.

Grabbing Kol's shoulders, she threw them both to the ground and rolled away from the river. An enormous foot made of stone smashed into the bank where seconds ago they'd been standing. Lorelai looked up to see one of the statue kings come to life, his blank eyes staring into hers as he raised his stone sword above his head.

Irina had made her move.

Kol wrapped his arms around her and rolled again as the sword slammed into the ground, slicing deep and sending a chunk of the bank sliding into the river.

She was leaping to her feet before the statue could pull the sword out of the damp ground. *Get to Gabril. Keep him safe. He can't run.*

She sensed Kol's dragon heart thundering viciously as the statue of a queen leaped from the bank above them and crushed the rocky shore beneath her feet. The queen whirled toward them, a stone scepter swinging at their heads.

They ducked, and the scepter struck the bank behind them.

I'll fight Irina. You protect Gabril. Go!

As Kol climbed up the bank to get to Gabril, Lorelai grabbed the queen's scepter with her bare hands, her magic blazing.

The heart of the stone statue was obstinate and indifferent and completely under Irina's control. Lorelai felt the whiplash of Irina's power sizzling against her own.

The king raised his sword as the queen's enormous hand closed into a fist. Lorelai let go of the scepter and ran.

She leaped over fallen rocks, skimmed across the muddy soil beside the river, and then snatched a gnarled tree root that protruded from the bank above her and swung her body toward the clumps of withered grass at the top. The statues chased her, their massive footsteps shaking the ground.

Gabril is safe. All the statues are coming for you, including the ones from the north. Get away from the bridge, Lorelai. Lorelai!

She focused on her goal, on the purpose that burned within her like a flame. *I came to destroy this bridge. She isn't going to stop me.* She reached the top of the bank and sprinted for the bridge as all eight statues on the south side of the river lunged toward her, weapons and fists flying. Her focus narrowed, her world nothing but instinct and training.

She leaped over a fist that crashed into the ground in front of her and skidded beneath a falling sword. Flipped backward to avoid the jagged blade of a queen with a gentle smile frozen on her face and was nearly impaled on the crown of another queen who'd gone down on her knees to reach for the princess.

They're converging. You have no way out. Kol's voice was furious. His thoughts raced with panic. With a desperate desire to shift into his dragon and smash the statues to pieces. *Use magic and get out of there. Or . . . oh skies, you used up your power on the river, didn't you? I'm coming. Hold on.*

Stay back. She dove between the feet of a king with a cropped beard and round cheeks and somersaulted onto the weather-beaten bridge. *Just be ready to help me if I need it.*

She didn't have time to overpower the statues' hearts with her magic. By the time she forced one of them to obey her, the other seven would crush her. She sprinted toward the middle of the bridge and scrambled to come up with another plan.

The wood beneath her heaved and buckled as the enormous statues from both ends of the structure ran toward her. She ran faster while she frantically catalogued her options.

Huge, heavy stone statues.

A wooden bridge with the hearts of heaven knew how many trees in it.

The river that already obeyed her.

Kol.

A plan with enough flair to have made Leo giddy for a month fell into place as she neared the middle of the bridge. Throwing herself to her knees, she slammed her hands against the wood beneath her as the bridge shuddered and creaked, and the statues thundered closer.

"Please save me from the one who abuses the heart of Ravenspire," she whispered. Power flared across her hands, and she yelled, "*Kaz`ja.* Heed my command and obey my wishes."

The hearts of the trees that had been used to build the bridge rushed toward her magic. A pair of kings lunged forward, their feet landing hard. Wood shrieked in protest, and a crack split the bridge beneath Lorelai.

"Catch me," she told the bridge as the kings raised their swords and swung them toward her.

Lorelai! Kol's voice was a blaze of desperate fear as she pulled her feet beneath her and then dove off the side of the bridge toward the swiftly moving river below.

A slender branch unfurled from a crossbeam beneath the bridge, wrapped itself around her waist, and held her suspended above the water.

She grabbed it, magic stinging her palms, and poured her power into the bridge. "*Kaz`ja!* Tear yourself free."

A queen smashed her fist through the bottom of the bridge and wrapped her fingerless hand around the crossbeam whose branch kept Lorelai safe.

"Now!" Lorelai yelled, and the bridge shuddered violently, sending a king to his knees.

Pillars split with a loud crack. Crossbeams curled away from their moorings. The crack that had begun in the center of the bridge split the structure end to end, and the bridge tore itself asunder with a tremendous clatter. Broken planks spun through the air and into the river. The two halves of the bridge twisted and sagged, and then the entire thing ripped free of the riverbanks and plummeted into the water, carrying the stone statues with it.

Lorelai sucked in a breath as the crossbeam holding her fell, and then she sank into the water, surrounded by debris. The current snatched at her, but there was too much wood, too much wreckage, for it to carry her very far.

You're going to be crushed! Kol sent her an image of giant stone statues crashing into the water on top of her.

The river's heart swept over her open palm and lingered. *Save me,* Lorelai begged the water, though she couldn't open her mouth to say the words aloud. She hoped that since the heart was already hers, already tangled with her magic, she wouldn't have to speak for it to know her intentions.

A shadow slammed into the water above her, and an impossible weight sank into her and pinned her to the riverbed. Kol's thoughts became a torrent of panic and furious desperation.

Her lungs ached for air.

Her muscles strained against the statue that anchored her.

And her magic blazed out of her hand, lashing through the water like a whip.

The river surged against her hand.

Please, she begged as lights danced at the edge of her vision. *Save me.*

The river's heart merged with her magic and became a ribbon of brilliant light. It sliced into the statue, and the stone exploded into a flurry of tiny pieces that tumbled around Lorelai before rushing south with the water's current. The ribbon of light wrapped around Lorelai's waist and lifted. She broke the surface and gasped for air while the river's heart gently pushed her to the bank where Kol had waded into water up to his waist, Gabril three steps behind him.

Kol reached for her, and she took his hands as he pulled her from the water. And then Gabril was holding her, his chin resting on her head.

"You just took ten years off my life," Gabril said.

You really did. Kol climbed up the bank and then reached back to help them. *That was the most terrifying, incredible thing I've ever seen.*

She held Gabril for an extra second, and then stepped back. "We need to get away from here before Irina sends something else to attack us."

"Still heading toward the intersection?" Gabril asked.

She nodded, and together they climbed the riverbank.

The intersection?

Where the main road leading east to west meets the road leading north to south. Those are the roads the rest of Irina's army will have to use to get to the capital. I'm going to destroy it, and I'm sure Irina will try to stop me.

Kol's smile lit something bright and burning in Lorelai's chest. *I bet my life she'll fail.*

I'm betting my life on that too.

TWENTY-NINE

HURT. PUNISH. KILL. The whispers trickled through Kol's mind, blood-hungry and ruthless, and he moved restlessly against the blanket he'd borrowed from Gabril. His dragon heart kicked against his chest, and his bones ached as the collar punished him for his refusal to obey its command.

His refusal to kill Lorelai.

She lay on the other side of the tent. Gabril's tall form stretched out on a bedroll between them. A tiny sliver of moonlight crept in through the tent flap and lingered against her face. Kol sat up, wrapped his hands around his knees, and studied her the way he couldn't when she was awake and aware of his thoughts.

In the days it had taken them to move from the ruined bridge to the intersection of the major roads that bisected Ravenspire, Kol had become as intimately familiar with Lorelai's thoughts as he was with his own.

He was fascinated by the way her mind worked—constantly

observing and analyzing every detail around her, making plans for handling danger in less time than it took most people to realize they needed a plan in the first place. He'd had classes on battle strategy, he'd had drills on instantly responding to dangerous situations, but he relied on what he knew—on solutions that were already proven. Lorelai looked for new information, new options, and instantly utilized them.

And the way she threw herself into danger because she had a plan—and sky forbid she back away from the goal she was trying to achieve—made something fierce and tender swell inside Kol's chest. Every time he turned around, she was assessing risk, not to avoid it but to take the lion's share of it herself.

She made him want to be a better warrior. A better king.

He stared at the way her skin glowed in the moonlight and admitted that, skies help him, he was drawn to her in ways he couldn't think about while she was awake and inside his head. There was nothing casual or ordinary about Lorelai, and there was nothing casual or ordinary about the way she made him feel. She was iron and fire, a warrior's spirit with a lion's heart. His parents would've loved her.

The thought of his parents hurt, and the four walls of the tent felt like they were shrinking around him. He needed wide, cool spaces and the endless starry sky. Careful not to jostle Gabril—last time he'd done that, he'd nearly lost an eye; skies only knew how that man slept with a sword in his hand without cutting off something he'd rather keep—Kol eased his way off his borrowed blanket and out of the tent.

They were camped in a small copse of ebony trees just north of the intersection that brought the main roads of Ravenspire together. Kol climbed the closest tree, swinging himself up the widely spaced branches with ease, until he reached the upper cradle. Settling in with his back against the trunk, he stared up at the sky and thought of Eldr, safe now because of Lorelai. Brig waiting for him to return. Trugg and Jyn, who were skies knew where after being thrown out of Irina's castle.

The collar whispered, and pain throbbed in his chest. Something dark and vicious crouched in the corner of his mind, but he focused on the stars, on holding fast to the person he wanted to be, until the pain lessened and the whispers were nothing but background noise.

You're getting better at that.

He looked down to see Lorelai standing at the base of the tree, her thick sweater wrapped around her to ward off the chill. *Why are you up?*

She looked toward the intersection, which was currently hidden from view by the gently twisting limbs of the ebony trees. A myriad of responses ran through her mind—*anxious, ready to get started, scared that you'd left us, wishing Leo were here*—but all she said was, *I couldn't sleep. And I figured it was best to destroy the intersection and the roads that lead to it during the night when the chance of hurting an innocent traveler is small.*

Why didn't you wake Gabril, then? We'll need to flee as soon as you use the magic or risk another nightmare like those statues coming to life when Irina retaliates.

I . . . wanted to check on you first. There was more behind her words—warmth and shyness and something deeper that Kol didn't know how to identify without pushing for things she was trying not to share with him.

I'm glad you did. He climbed down the tree and gestured toward a patch of grass that lay gleaming in the starlight between two trees. She followed him, and they sat side by side. Her thoughts raced, a rapid counterpoint to the slow, steady ache of missing Eldr that filled his.

You'll be able to go home soon. She clasped her hands in her lap and looked up at the sky. *I bet your sister really misses you.* Leo's face flashed across her mind.

He bumped her shoulder with his to take the sting of loneliness out of her thoughts. *You'll like Brig.*

I'm sure I would love her. She showed him everything she'd seen of Brig in his thoughts—her freckled nose and laughing eyes, her boundless curiosity and steadfast loyalty, and the firm belief she'd always had in Kol. *But you'll be going home, Kol, where you belong. I'll be here, where I belong. We're closing in on the capital. I'll destroy the intersection and the roads that lead to it tonight and then, as we enter the Hinderlinde Forest, I'll ruin the communications towers and armories that surround the capital until all Irina's resources are gone. Once we're through the Hinderlinde, the capital will be in front of us, and then it's just Irina and me.*

And me. His dragon heart pounded viciously at the thought of seeing Irina again.

Don't worry, I won't forget about finding your human heart and restoring it to you before you go.

I wasn't worried about that. I meant you aren't facing Irina alone. I'll be at your side. I may not be able to shift, but I can still call on my dragon's fire and speed. I'm still faster and stronger than a human, and Irina will have a hard time defeating both of us at once.

What do you mean you can call on your dragon's fire? She turned to face him, a tiny frown etched between her eyes. *Why didn't you use that against me when you tried to kill me?*

I live for the day when we can stop bringing that up in our conversations. He gave her a little smile. *I can't breathe fire anymore, but I can use it to heat my blood to a degree that would cause burns on humans.*

When did you figure this out?

When the statue fell on top of you in the water. Everything in me wanted to shift so I could smash it to pieces and rescue you. I was so . . . Terrified. Furious. He couldn't quite find the right word for how it had felt to watch Lorelai go under the water and not come back up. *My dragon's fire raged, and when I stepped into the river, the water sizzled against me.*

You didn't burn me when you took my hands.

I backed away from the dragon's fire. I won't hurt you, Lorelai. I'd die first.

You're willing to sacrifice yourself for everyone you care about.

He held her gaze and tried not to think about how much the understanding and admiration in her thoughts eased the sharp edge of disappointment he remembered in his father's eyes.

Her eyes reflected the starlight as she looked at him, her shoulder leaning against his. *And to think that you said you weren't even a very good prince.*

I . . . what? When? He looked at the images in her thoughts and saw himself standing before her after he'd nearly killed her in his dragon form, begging for her mercy for Eldr.

You think you're a poor substitute for your older brother. That no matter what you do, you'll still be a disappointment to your father.

Compassion softened her voice, but there was iron beneath it. *I think you're blind. You're a natural leader. All those pranks you somehow convinced the academy's top students to pull with you? All those friends of yours willing to follow you into the jaws of death without you even asking them to? It's because they know what I know—that you have the kind of bottomless strength and loyalty that will always put others first at the expense of yourself. You are exactly the kind of king Eldr needs right now.*

The fierce tenderness that swelled in his chest when he was with her expanded, pressing against Kol's skin until it almost hurt to be so close to her. *I never told you about my father's disappointment in me. Or about my friends following me to Ravenspire without me asking.*

She bit her lip. *I've seen your thoughts, even the ones you didn't mean to share.*

I've seen yours too. He met her eyes. *For example, I know that you think you're too serious, but that you wouldn't change it because it will help you be a good queen. I know you miss growing up with your mother to take care of you. And I know you hate the good memories you have of the time you spent with Irina after your mother died.*

It's weird to know so much about each other when we aren't even friends.

Who says we aren't friends?

We hardly know each other.

He raised a brow.

I mean . . . we know each other better than we should for the time we've spent together, but we only know the big stuff.

The stuff that usually doesn't come up in friendships for a long time. He bumped her shoulder again and gave her a smile. *How about if we make up for that?*

How?

By asking the questions that people usually ask when they want to get to know each other and don't have the pesky benefit of a magical mental bond getting in their way.

She laughed. *Fine. What's your middle name?*

He groaned inwardly. *It's Eilertolvanisk.* His words were accompanied by the image of Master Eiler standing beside his father, smiling proudly while Kol took his first steps.

You were named after the headmaster who expelled you from the academy?

He sighed.

Ouch.

I know it. What's your middle name?

Rosalinde Tatiyana. Rosalinde for my father's mother and Tatiyana for mine.

Favorite food?

Strawberry tart cake. Yours?

Cheese. Every kind of cheese. He looked up at the carpet of stars above them and searched for another question. Another detail to round out what he knew of Lorelai. *How did you get a gyrfalcon as a pet?*

Sasha would peck out your eyes if she knew you'd just called her a pet. Lorelai grinned at him.

Then please keep that breach of bird etiquette to yourself.

She leaned back, her shoulder still brushing his, and stared at the sky. *It was a few weeks after we'd run from the castle.* There was a darkness beneath her words, and Kol didn't have to look far to see images of her terror and grief when her plan to expose Irina fell to pieces and left her orphaned and homeless. *We were staying with an old woman in the Falkrains who was doing her best to treat Gabril's leg. I wasn't supposed to leave the cabin, but Leo convinced me to sneak out one afternoon so we could explore the woods close by. Sasha was just a baby, and she'd fallen from her nest. Her wing was crushed.*

I picked her up. She turned her hands over, palms facing up, and examined them as if she could still see the gyrfalcon lying there. *I held her in my bare hands, and the magic was just there, waiting. I spoke an incantor, and my magic entered Sasha's body and healed her.*

And that's why you share a mental bond with her?

She nodded. *I took her back to the cabin because she would've died out there on her own. She was too little to hunt. That's when Gabril decided I needed to start wearing gloves. He didn't want my magic to touch anything else in Ravenspire in case it had been bespelled by Irina.*

A wise man.

She smiled. *Yes, he is. But enough about that. What's your favorite memory?*

He thought it would be impossible to find an answer, but a memory rose to the surface unbidden. He was six, standing on the field behind the academy, the rest of his class lined up to his right, receiving a ribbon for the best flight time out of all the first-year cadets. Father was smiling proudly, his hand on Kol's shoulder, while his mother winked at him, her arm around Rag, who looked as superior and unimpressed as a nine-year-old could manage. Brig played at his mother's feet, unconcerned with the honor her brother was receiving.

That's a nice memory. She smiled at him.

It's the one time I remember my father being proud of me.

She met his eyes. *I'm sure he was proud of you far more often than you ever realized.*

He shrugged as though her words didn't matter, but he knew she could see the truth. *So what's your favorite memory?*

An image of Lorelai as a child sitting outside on a blanket eating berries while a woman with Lorelai's pale skin and brown eyes knelt behind her, braiding the princess's long hair. A boy who looked remarkably like his sister slept on the blanket beside Lorelai.

Your mother and Leo? he asked, though he could already see the answer.

She nodded, and they sat in companionable silence listening to the ebony boughs creak gently while somewhere in the distance an owl hooted. Finally, she stirred restlessly, and he could already see the plans taking shape in her mind. Wake Gabril. Pack the tent. Destroy the intersection and spread the damage wide enough to prevent anyone from traveling to the capital until the road was repaired.

Before she could say the words, he stood and leaned down to offer her his hand. She took it and allowed him to pull her to her feet.

I'm glad we're friends. Her tone was serious, her smile shy.

I am too. He watched her turn back toward the tent and let the warmth of their friendship push against the whispers that wanted him to destroy her.

THIRTY

IT WAS TIME to make her next move against Irina. Lorelai's pulse raced, and her stomach ached. Just days earlier, she'd provoked Irina by using magic and had nearly died, pinned underwater by a statue sent by the queen to kill her. There was no telling what spell would lash out or what creature would awaken and submit its heart to Irina's this time.

Maybe the queen had been so weakened in her battle with Lorelai for control over Kol that they were no longer in danger from her. Or maybe she still had enough strength left for another terrifying fight.

Lorelai needed to be ready to defend herself and the others. She needed to be ready to run if necessary. And she needed Kol and Gabril to be ready to do the same.

Which meant she had to win an argument that had been simmering for almost two weeks.

"Before I destroy the roads, I've got one very important thing to take care of." Lorelai locked eyes with Gabril as he hoisted his travel pack onto his back while Kol finished rolling up the tent in the silvery light of the stars.

"What's that?" Gabril asked.

"Your leg."

This should be interesting. Kol raised a brow and shoved the tent into its sack.

"I told you, you aren't wasting your energy on me when you need it for Irina." Gabril's voice was firm, and a spark of anger flared in Lorelai's chest.

"It wouldn't be a waste of energy at all if I didn't have to overpower your stubborn heart." She stalked forward and stood toe-to-toe with him.

"How do you know that?" he demanded. "Every time you've healed someone, you've fallen into a deep sleep for hours—sometimes days!"

"Not when I healed Sasha."

Hearing her name, Sasha swooped out of a nearby tree and perched on Lorelai's shoulder. *Stubborn human. Limp, limp, limp.*

I'm trying to change that. Lorelai glared at Gabril.

Bribe with treat? Mouse? Rabbit?

No bribery. He's going to bend to my will one way or the other. Lorelai lifted her chin and said to Gabril, "This is a stupid argument to have. I'm healing your leg."

He stepped back. "No, you aren't."

"Gabril—"

"What happens if using magic on me incites a response from Irina, only you're unconscious and can't defend yourself?" He matched her glare with one of his own. "I'm not going to be the reason you die."

"And I'm not going to be the reason *you* die!" She lifted her hands, and magic was already stinging her palms. "When I destroy those roads, Irina will attack. I have no idea what weapon she'll use, but we have to be ready to fight or to flee. You can't run, and I can't be distracted worrying about you."

"But—"

"This makes the most strategic sense." She took a deep breath and forced herself to sound calm. "If you submit to me, the cost to my body should be minimal. If Irina attacks after I heal you, and for any reason I can't defend myself, Kol can get me away from here."

I don't really think he's going to like the idea of sending me off alone with you. He sleeps with a sword between us, you know. I'm not high on his list of people he trusts.

This isn't about trusting you. This is about him trusting that I understand my limitations and my power.

You should tell him that. Kol hefted the tent's pack onto his shoulders and nodded toward Gabril.

Gabril took a deep breath of his own. "I appreciate your concern, Lorelai, and I love that you want to help me. But even if I submit to this, and even if it doesn't cost you physically, there's a chance that Irina will realize you've used magic, and that she'll retaliate before you're able to destroy the roads. What then?"

She held his gaze. "Then I'll use magic to destroy both the roads and whatever she sends at us. Or, if that's not a possibility, we'll flee and regroup, and I'll find another way to do what I've set out to do. Either way, your leg will be healed."

"Lorelai—"

"You need to trust that I know what I'm doing." Her voice

was firm. "If you can't trust me in this, how can you trust me to face Irina or rule an entire kingdom?"

Good point, Kol said quietly.

Gabril remained silent for a long moment, his expression as stoic as ever, and then he wrapped his arms around her. Resting his chin on her head, he said, "You're right, and that scares me more than I care to admit. I'm used to being the one who looks out for you, and knowing that I can't help you win this fight is hard to swallow."

She returned his hug and then stepped back, her hands wreathed in brilliant white light. "You'll help me by being at full strength. And by trusting me to know what I'm capable of."

He met her gaze and slowly wrapped his bare hand around hers, barely flinching as her magic licked his skin. "I trust you."

"Then come on. We're going to do this beside the intersection so that I can send your injury into the ground and give the command to destroy the road at the same time."

Together the three of them left the copse of ebony trees behind and walked across a field of brittle brown grass with clumps of bushes that smelled like rot. Sasha flew overhead, scouting the immediate area for travelers, though few would use the road at night when visibility was so poor.

The road was wide and paved with stones worn smooth over time and constant use. It cut the field into four equal squares and met in the middle. Lorelai led them across the point where the roads intersected and into the southern half of the field.

She looked at Gabril and tried hard to sound like she wasn't shaking inside at the thought of what Irina might send after them. "I'm going to take your injury into myself and then put it into the road. The second your leg is healed, I want you to run across the rest of the field into the Hinderlinde Forest. Kol and I will meet you there as soon as I've destroyed the roads."

"I'm not leaving you." There was no room for argument in his voice.

"Kol isn't going to hurt me. Since we can communicate through our mental bond, he'll be able to fight as an extension of myself. I don't know what's coming for us, or if I can convince the land to submit to me when it's been owned by Irina for so long. If I can't fight, Kol is faster than a human and—"

"This has nothing to do with the boy." Gabril held up their joined hands, and his eyes glistened as he looked at Lorelai. "I can't stop you from taking risks, and I don't want to. This is what you've been working toward for years. But I'm not leaving your side, no matter what it costs me."

You aren't going to win this argument. Kol's voice was steady, but she could see his fear of Irina's tactics in the way his thoughts skipped from one awful possibility to the next.

I want him to be safe.

He's your protector, and you're his queen. You asked him to trust that you know what you're capable of. Do you trust him the same way?

She did. This wasn't about trusting Gabril—the man who'd sacrificed his time with his family, his leg, and his safety to protect the prince and princess. To raise them to be just, loyal, and able to fight for what was right. This was about doing everything she could to keep the last person she loved alive.

The ache of missing Leo became a sharp pain at the thought of losing Gabril as well. Her breath lodged in her chest like a stone, and a tremor shook her as she stared at the road before her and considered her choices.

She could walk away. She'd be safe, and so would Gabril. They could leave the country. Maybe go to Eldr and meet Brig. Stay at the castle with Kol. Forget Irina and all the pain that lay in the past like so much wreckage.

But if she did that, she condemned the people of Ravenspire to a terrible fate. She left Leo's death, her father's death, and Gabril's sacrifice unanswered. And Kol would still be bound by a collar Lorelai couldn't remove. He'd still be missing his human heart. And Lorelai would live the rest of her days knowing that Ravenspire's pain, Kol's pain, were a responsibility she'd left behind.

Slowly, Lorelai straightened her spine and squared her shoulders, tightening her muscles until she no longer trembled at the thought of moving forward.

She could choose a different fate for herself, but she couldn't live with the consequences. She'd face Irina, no matter the sacrifice. She'd take the hit, fight the battle, and do her part to isolate and weaken the queen. And she'd do it even though it might cost her the last person she loved.

She was so caught up in her thoughts that she hadn't been paying attention to Kol's, and she jumped a little when he slid his hand into her free one and twined his fingers through hers.

Thank you, he said simply, but she could see behind the words. She could see the future he wanted for himself, the kind of king he wanted to become, and how none of it was possible if he was forever chained to Irina.

She squeezed his hand and let go. Turning to Gabril, she said,

"No matter what happens next, you stay alive. I don't care what you have to do to accomplish it, but you still stay alive. That's an order from your queen."

Without waiting for a reply, she knelt, pulling Gabril down with her, their hands still joined. "Ready?"

"Ready." Gabril sounded confident.

Ready.

Lorelai's magic burned against her palms, and she felt Gabril's heart surge to meet it. "*Nakhgor.* Find the bone that broke and mended poorly. *Kaz`prin.* Heal the break and send the damage through me and into the ground."

Instantly, Gabril's heart submitted to hers. Her magic pierced him easily, flooding his body and racing through his veins with the barest push of effort from Lorelai. When it came to the swollen knot of bone on his left thigh, light surrounded his leg, and there was a sharp crack as the bone straightened. Gabril cried out and slumped forward, but the pain was already rushing out of him and into Lorelai.

She clenched her teeth as his agony exploded into her body. It was a sharp, searing pain that left her skin clammy and sent her stomach crawling up the back of her throat.

Let it out now, Lorelai. Kol's voice was firm—a lifeline in the midst of the pain that was tearing into her. *Gabril's leg is fine. You did it. Put the wound into the ground.*

She tore her hand from Gabril's and slammed both of her palms onto the gritty surface of the road. The pain poured out of her and into the ground, and the stone beneath her hands cracked in two, revealing the ground beneath it. She pushed her hand into the crack, ignoring the sharp fragments of stone that scratched her skin, and pressed her palm against the dirt.

"Please lend me what strength you can," she whispered as her magic sank into the ground and waited. Her throat tightened, and her chest ached as she silently pleaded with her kingdom to recognize its true queen. "I seek to stop the one who abuses you. Will you help me?"

The heart of Ravenspire's land reached for her, tangling with her magic, but there was a taint to it. A streak of resistance that felt less like the ground and more like . . .

"Irina," she whispered as the threads of her power reached a web of magic that waited beneath the fallow ground.

She's already fighting you? Where? I don't see anything.

She has a trap laid beneath the ground. That means this place is important to her. And it means her response is going to weaken her. She looked up into Kol's amber eyes. *It also means we'll have to move fast, because the second I speak an incantor, her spell is going to react.*

I'm ready.

"Pros`rashk!" Her voice rang with power, and magic exploded out of her palms and into the ground, wrapping around the weary heart of Ravenspire and merging until they were united. "Scatter the stones that built this road and crumble them into dust."

For a moment, the ground resisted, the taint of Irina's magic pushing against Lorelai's. The princess's heart raced, and anger fanned to life in her chest. She wasn't losing this battle. She wasn't going to back down. Irina had controlled Ravenspire's ground for nearly a decade. It was time to sever those ties.

The princess threw her head back and yelled, *"Pros`rashk!"*

Power flooded her body, a fire lit from the inside and poured into the ground.

The field shuddered and heaved. The stones that paved the road cracked and crumbled, scattering dust and bits of rock into the brittle grass. A ripple began beneath Lorelai's hands and quickly sped along the roads leading east to west, leaving destruction in its wake.

Lorelai closed her eyes and pushed the magic, pushed the ground to go as far and as fast as possible. She needed the ruin to be widespread. She needed the capital isolated.

Power thrummed through her veins and roared in her ears, and then Kol had his arms around her waist and was hauling her to her feet.

Her eyes snapped open as he yelled, *Get away from the road!*

She stumbled back a step, and the ripple of destruction on the road disappeared into the distance. *What are you doing? I wasn't finished!*

Listen.

Gabril said, "We need to leave. Now."

She concentrated on hearing more than the thunder of her heartbeat, and nearly fell as the field twitched and bubbled like a pot of water left over a fire. Beneath the ground, something skittered and hissed, growing louder and louder until the grass trembled and cracks began splitting the land into pieces. The skittering and hissing poured out of the cracks, and Lorelai's throat closed in horror as swarms of beetles, spiders, and centipedes gushed out of the ground and raced toward her.

"Get to the forest," Lorelai said, and they ran south, leaping over cracks and crushing bugs beneath their boots.

They'd traveled half the distance between the ruined road and the forest when the ground in front of them disappeared, sinking out of sight and spewing a horde of insects the size of Lorelai's hands with long pincers that clacked and snapped as they crawled toward the princess.

Oh skies, we're surrounded.

Lorelai whirled to find the ground behind them had disappeared as well. She stood with Kol and Gabril on a slender circle of dirt surrounded by swarms of spiders and beetles that chittered and clacked as they raced forward.

It was Irina's favorite trick—dominating the hearts of multiple creatures so that there was no way Lorelai could overpower and subdue them all before being overcome.

Something crawled over Lorelai's boot, and she shook her foot as Gabril cursed and began stomping the ground. Kol stomped as well, but for every bug they killed, another five took its place. Sasha screamed in fury and dove, but she couldn't do more than sweep a few bugs away with the power of her wings, and more were already swarming to take their place.

A spider climbed over Lorelai's boot and onto her leg, and she slapped at it, but her boots were already overrun with multilegged centipedes, spiders in every size, and those awful huge beetles who chopped other bugs in half as they advanced on the princess.

She needed something to fight with—the heart of a living creature capable of defeating an insect horde. She needed a stone to crush them. A flood of water to drown them. A ball of fire—

Use me. Kol's hand wrapped around hers, and his dragon heart—vicious, powerful, and begging for blood—slammed against her magic and took hold.

Can you stay in control if we use your dragon heart? she asked, but she was already choosing her incantor as she used her free hand to shake off a centipede that was skittering over her bare arm. A sharp jab of pain pierced her heel as one of the monster beetles skewered her boot with its pincers.

I'll do my best. You can help me if I lose myself, but we're going to be eaten alive or dragged into the depths of the ground if we don't do something.

"Lorelai!" Gabril grabbed something off her back and threw it in the teeming mass that covered the field.

The ground beneath them heaved, sending them to their knees. Instantly, the bugs converged, swarming over them, biting, clawing, and skittering over the top of one another until the three of them were covered.

Lorelai shuddered and lost her grip on Kol. Flinging her arms out, she swept at the creatures crawling toward her face and then fell forward as another wave of enormous beetles gushed from the ground and raced up her body.

Pain lit into her in tiny, jagged pieces as pincers and fangs tore at her skin. Dimly, she heard Gabril cry out, but the whisper-hiss of hundreds of legs scrambling over the dirt, over her clothes, over *her* drowned out everything else.

They were tangled in her hair. Clawing at her stomach. Crawling up her neck toward her mouth.

She pressed her lips closed and struggled to find her footing amid the piles of slippery bodies that covered every inch of the trembling ground.

I've got you. Kol's hand found hers, and together they pulled themselves to their feet. Gabril was doubled over at the waist beside them, frantically trying to dislodge centipedes from his neck and back.

The ground beneath them was disappearing rapidly. If Lorelai didn't act *now*, they would be buried alive and then consumed.

Kol's hand gripped hers, and magic stung her palm. "*Kaz`zhech*. Bring his fire into me and punish those who harm us."

Violent heat surged through Kol's veins and into hers. She screamed as it gathered in her chest, a molten ball of fury and destruction that felt like it was turning her blood to vapor and her bones to dust.

Burn them, Kol shouted as he raised their joined hands where the white light of her magic had become a flame of orange and yellow that leaped toward the swarm at their feet. She raised her other hand, sucked in a breath that felt like razors against the heat inside her chest, and yelled, "*Kaz`zhech!* Punish them with fire."

Flames shot from her palms and scorched the ground, latching on to the brittle grass and sweeping outward in a blaze of orange with brilliant white at the center. The heat seared her from the inside out, and she shook, desperately holding on to the terrible strength of Kol's dragon heart as she turned to strafe the entire circle around them with fire.

Insects scrambled away from the flames but then curled up and turned to ash as the fire caught them. The scent of roasted bugs—bitter and pungent—hung heavy in the air, stinging Lorelai's eyes.

Her legs trembled, her teeth chattered, and every part of her body throbbed as the dragon's fire scalded her. The heat was a monstrous presence pushing, pushing, pushing against her chest until she could barely breathe. Until she thought her skin would split, and her bones crumble. She tried to keep her hands raised, but spots were dancing at the edge of her vision, and her muscles had lost their strength.

Kol let go of her hand and gently lowered her to the ground, though she could hear the collar whispering *hurt, punish, kill* while his dragon heart begged for more violence.

"You did it," Gabril said quietly as he crushed one last twitching spider beneath his boot. The field surrounding them was a smoking pit of insect carcasses and burned grass, but the fire, once it had finished the task Lorelai set before it, had extinguished itself.

The awful heat of Kol's dragon's fire seeped out of her, and she drew a breath of the pungent, smoky air. The pain was gone. She was still awake. Kol was still in control. And Irina had once again weakened herself without winning the fight.

Are you okay? Kol asked as he knelt beside her.

She was better than okay. Triumph was a radiant light blazing within her. She threw her arms around Kol and laughed.

We did it. She lost again. And now she's weaker, the road is destroyed, and we're one step closer to finishing this.

His arms came around her and pulled her close for a moment, his heartbeat a wild cadence beneath her ear. *We make a good team.*

The warmth behind his words made Lorelai suddenly, excruciatingly aware that she'd thrown herself against him. That she was still holding him. That her heart was beating as wildly as his.

She dropped her arms and got to her feet on legs that still shook. *I'm . . . sorry? Yes. I'm sorry. I didn't mean to . . . That was great. Really great.*

What was she doing? Had she lost her mind? She looked at Gabril's face, his brow raised at the two of them as Kol climbed to his feet. Thank heavens the starlight didn't show the blush that was heating her cheeks.

I'll pretend I don't know about it, then. Kol sounded amused.

It was just . . . You know what? I don't want to talk about it.

He grinned at her, the stars gilding his red-brown hair with silver. *Why not? It's kind of . . . fetching.*

She rolled her eyes. *Come on. Let's get out of here in case Irina recovers fast enough to send something else after us.* She hurried to catch up to Gabril, who was nearly at the edge of the Hinder-linde Forest, feeling the warmth of Kol's affectionate amusement behind her and the heat that still lingered in her cheeks.

THIRTY-ONE

THE TINY VOICE of doubt that had whispered relentlessly in Irina's ear since the night of Lorelai's betrayal had become a deafening roar.

How had Lorelai stopped the collar from torturing the Eldrian king? How had she taken control of the mountains, the water, and the land and defeated every spell Irina threw at her?

How had Lorelai thwarted Irina's will? Irina's *heart*?

Either she'd had training—unlikely since Irina had kept an eye on every semipowerful *mardushka* in all Morcant in case the princess tried to return to her mother's roots—or she somehow had more raw power in her fingertips than Irina had ever realized.

More power than she should possibly have.

Her deepest fear had become a reality: Lorelai was stronger than she was. There was no explanation for it. No reason that Irina could find, though she tried.

Had her birth been unusual? Had one of the fae from the

292

realm of Llorenyae fled its home kingdom and found succor in Ravenspire in exchange for gifting the princess with extraordinary power?

Irina's skin grew cold, and a finger of ice slid down her spine.

She needed answers about Lorelai's birth—about the magic that ran through the princess's veins—and there was only one person who could give them to her.

Her stomach roiled, and her heart beat in sharp, uneven bursts.

It was time to face what lay beneath the garden's monolith.

She swept through the hushed hallways of the castle, Raz clinging to her neck, and kept her expression cold and forbidding as her pulse tapped a frantic rhythm against her skin. She ignored the maids who ducked out of her path, the nobility who turned as if to speak to her, and the pages who scrambled to open doors before their queen reached them, and ignored as well the thread of fear that trembled along her spine. Her guards walked behind her, their hands on the hilts of their swords.

She burst into the castle's entrance hall, barely sparing a glance for the gleaming floor that had once been covered in blood and destruction.

She had no time for sentimentality. No room for the ache of loss and betrayal.

A page threw open the castle's front entrance, and Irina strode through, her spine straight and her head held high, though she shook as the chill of the early morning air settled against her exposed skin.

"Your Highness, perhaps a coat would be in order?" her guard asked.

She ignored him.

The path to the garden led down the front drive and then cut to the left and wrapped around the western turret. The monolith glowed beneath the morning sun, and the flowers that blossomed around it reminded Irina of blood against snow.

Tatiyana's blood.

Tatiyana, who no longer had a voice to speak or a will to overcome, but whose heart still lingered in her bones and would give Irina the answers she sought.

If she could stand to see what else her sister's heart contained.

"Leave me," she said to her guards as she forced her steps toward the monolith.

Her steps slowed as she left the crushed stone path to walk on the circle of midnight black dirt that surrounded the monolith. The flowers seemed to reach for her, their sharp edges eager for a taste of her blood. She bent to allow Raz to slither onto the ground, and then parted the flowers with her hands, heedless of the tiny thorns that left cuts scattered across her skin.

Her heart beat faster, and her breath came in sharp, unsteady bursts as she sank to her knees on the rich, black dirt, crimson flowers latching on to her hair and the sleeves of her dress. Facing the glittering white edifice that marked her sister's grave, she gathered her remaining strength, ignoring the weariness that was already pulling at her, and plunged her hands into the soil.

The ground was the same Ravenspire ground that had been grudgingly submitting its heart to hers since the moment she'd set foot in the kingdom over nine years ago. She'd mined its power and bent it to her will countless times, ignoring the drain she'd put on it for the sake of ensuring her reign.

This time, there was no ignoring the resistance she met. The depletion of the land's power that had once surged to the surface every time her bare skin grazed the ground.

She focused her power, her will, and magic exploded down her veins, out of her palms, and into the ground. *"Kaz'prin. Bring me what I seek."*

The soil bubbled and heaved. Irina held on to the soil's heart, exerted her will, and refused to falter even as she felt Tatiyana's heart slowly rise to the surface.

With one last shudder, the ebony casket ascended from its resting place, split in two with a tremendous crack, and then Irina was holding the bones of her sister.

Irina tried to speak, but her voice was caught in the suffocating thickness of the panic that closed her throat. The bones in her hand were from her sister's rib cage, the shelter of Tatiyana's heart, and the place where the strongest residue of what had once been a living being would still reside.

Murderer.

The thought was a whisper in the back of Irina's mind, and she nearly dropped the bones in shock.

It wasn't her sister's voice. It couldn't be. The dead were dead. Nothing could bring them back to life to speak new thoughts, new words. It wasn't her sister's voice.

It was Irina's own.

Her eyes stung, and she glared down at the bones she held. She wouldn't have had to kill Tatiyana if her sister had been less desirable, less lovable, just . . . less. Instead, she'd taken their father's love, their uncle's favor, and the kingdom that should've been Irina's—and she'd done it all without once acknowledging that she was leaving her older sister out in the cold.

That she was a thief. A selfish thief who deserved her fate.

Irina clung to the knowledge that she'd done what had to be done to right the wrongs stacked against her, but her throat didn't ease. Her eyes still stung.

And her heart ached in a way that had nothing to do with the toll of magic.

The bones seemed to burn her palms as she forced herself to say, "*Zna`uch.* Reveal to me the secret of Lorelai's power."

For a moment, it seemed her sister's heart would fight hers, but Irina was desperate, and Tatiyana had no will to exert. The queen blinked the tears from her eyes and raised her voice. "*Zna`uch.* Reveal the secret of Lorelai's power."

Images struck, faded and blurry at the edges. The ebony carriage entering Morcant. The evergreen crashing into Tatiyana and slicing her to pieces. Blood pouring into the pristine snow and carrying splinters of the carriage with it.

Tatiyana, lying on the ground and looking into the forest, where she locked eyes with her sister.

An understanding of what Irina was now capable of. Of what Irina would do.

A handful of ebony cradled in her sister's blood. A whispered incantor.

The heart of the carriage's ebony bowing before the power in Tatiyana's blood and sending that power, that magic, into the ground, where it raced away from Morcant like a streak of light that pulsed brighter and brighter as her sister struggled for air.

The light reaching Ravenspire's castle, burrowing into the stone, and searching for the one with lips as red as blood, hair as black as ebony, and skin as white as snow.

Lorelai, asleep and unaware. The light leaping from the stone, pouring over Lorelai's skin like a blanket, and then sinking into the princess's blood as Tatiyana breathed her last.

Irina dropped the bones, her hands shaking as rage obliterated the thickness in her throat and dried the last of her tears.

Even in death, her sister had managed to steal what Irina most wanted. Even in death, Tatiyana had stolen Irina's chance at a happily ever after.

Lorelai, the untrained half-Morcantian girl, possessed her own magic and every last drop of her mother's as well.

Irina couldn't fight that. Not with the Ravenspire ground turning against her. Not when her heart stumbled and burned every time she did the simplest spell.

Lorelai was coming for her, the Eldrian king by her side, and there was nothing Irina could do about it unless she found another source of power to bolster her own.

Another heart to bend to hers and give her its strength, its will.

A heart that wouldn't poison her blood as the hearts of those in Ravenspire all seemed to do.

She climbed to her feet and left her sister's bones lying scattered on her open grave. Tatiyana may have thought she could finish Irina by giving her daughter more power than any *mardushka* had a right to own, but Irina had a weapon her sister could never have foreseen.

She had the human heart of a Draconi warrior just waiting for a new chest to call home.

THIRTY-TWO

IT TOOK MOST of the day to travel halfway through the Hinderlinde Forest. All three of them were covered with scratches and bites. Lorelai had been so exhausted after using the weary heart of Ravenspire to destroy the roads and then using Kol's dragon fire to fight Irina that she'd been unable to walk on her own for the first few hours. They stopped in the late afternoon in an abandoned shack that Gabril remembered using when Lorelai's father went hunting for deer in the spring. The shack was small—maybe twice the size of their tent—and its lone window was covered in the same dusty grime that coated the floor inside, but it was well-built and had a fireplace.

Lorelai paced the floor, her thoughts racing, while Kol started a fire and Gabril readied a small pot with the last of their beans for dinner.

The longer she waited between attacks on Irina's infrastructure, the more time she gave the queen to recover her strength. If she really wanted to have the advantage when she entered the capital, she needed to hit Irina again.

Tonight.

The strength of Irina's response would give Lorelai valuable information about the queen's current state of health. Information that would help the princess decide if she should continue attacks from outside the capital or make her move against the castle itself.

It's a good plan, Kol said as she glanced out the window and considered her options, *but maybe you should eat first. Rest a little.*

Every second I rest is a second I give Irina to rest too.

True. But you had dragon's fire inside you today. And you barely slept last night. He held up a hand when she turned on him, her thoughts blazing into his mind. *I'm not saying I don't trust you to know what you're capable of doing. I'm just saying maybe some beans would be a good idea. Not just for your sake but for Gabril's. Whatever you do tonight, all of us have to be ready to respond.*

He was right. It had been a long, hard day for all of them, and if she provoked a response from Irina now, they would have to fight. They would have to run.

They had a much better chance of surviving if they'd eaten and rested for a while.

I admire the way you think. Kol smiled at her as he stacked the extra wood he'd gathered beside the fireplace and took a seat at the rickety kitchen table.

She gave him a look as she took a chair for herself. *What is that supposed to mean?*

He raised a brow as Gabril set the pot of beans down in the center of the table. *Are you always suspicious of compliments? I meant that I like the way you constantly analyze the situation, decide on a course of action that makes the most sense to you, and then just . . . do it. You want to go after Irina now, and if you had no one but yourself to consider, you would. But you don't do what's best for you. You do what's best for those you're trying to protect.*

So you're saying you and I are alike. Minus the fact that I've yet to try to kill you.

And I've yet to call you fetching.

And I'd never lock my headmaster in his toilet closet.

And I don't have magic. But otherwise, yes. We are a lot alike.
He grinned at her, and she smiled back until Gabril slapped a spoon against the table.

"Mind telling me what's so funny?" he asked as he spooned beans onto their plates.

"Nothing." Lorelai avoided looking at Kol.

"Then if nothing is funny, you two can stop grinning at each other like village idiots and start eating your dinner. I imagine tomorrow will be another difficult day."

And here I thought I was winning him over.

It would be easier if he could see into your thoughts like I can.

Oh, skies, no. That would be a disaster. A flurry of images raced through his head—Kol kissing girls in spacious bronze hallways, the wound his father's disappointment had left in him, and the night he'd stared at Lorelai's face while she was asleep. Lorelai's cheeks warmed as he said, *Don't look at those.*

Gabril gave them a look that said he knew something was going on and was determined to get to the bottom of it.

Lorelai shoved a spoonful of beans into her mouth. They were hot and tasteless. She swallowed quickly, and said, "Actually, I want to destroy the communications towers tonight. I can use the ground here to get to the ones in the capital and the surrounding area. Irina's response will tell us a lot about her current state of health, and it will help me decide if I should enter the capital tomorrow or keep battling her from afar for a few more days."

Gabril looked from her to Kol and back again before saying, "That's a good idea. How much rest do you want to take before we leave the shack and try it?"

She almost asked how much rest he needed, but swallowed the words before they could pass her lips. He'd tell her he didn't need any, and she wasn't going to argue with him.

"A few hours," she said, though the restless energy that filled her sent magic to her palms and made it hard to sit still.

Gabril nodded and kept a close eye on the two of them as they finished their dinner and spread their bedrolls out on the cots that lined the shack's western wall.

Three hours later, Lorelai was surprised to find that she'd slept, and that she felt more focused as a result. She pulled on her boots, braided her hair, and shrugged into one of Leo's thick sweaters—the closest thing she had to winter wear since she'd lost her coat in Nordenberg.

The sweater smelled like campfires and mountain air. She hugged her arms across her chest and imagined what Leo would say if he was with her.

He'd tell her they needed costumes before they entered the capital.

And that she needed to prepare a thunderous oration— heaven forbid he call it a simple speech—to deliver once she saw Irina.

And he'd laugh at the risk they were taking, a reckless gleam in his eyes as he stood beside her no matter what.

Her throat ached, and pressure built behind her eyes. For years she'd trained incessantly with one goal—to overthrow Irina and retake the throne. She'd never imagined doing it without Leo.

I would've liked him. Kol moved to her side and bumped her shoulder with his. *He sounds like someone who would've joined me in sealing the headmaster into his toilet closet.*

She surprised herself by laughing, though it came out sounding more like a sob. *Yes, he would've. As long as you gave him an important role to play and let him play it with all the flair his heart desired.*

I'm sorry he isn't here with us to play a role tonight. Kol walked beside her to the door as Gabril strapped on his sword and gathered up the travel packs. *We'll do this one with flair. For Leo.*

She smiled gratefully up at him, the hard knot of grief in her chest expanding into something softer. Something a little bit easier to accept. *For Leo.*

They left the shack and moved into the trees. Earlier in the day, Lorelai had noticed that while there were patches of rot, spots of crumbling bark, or soil that looked too pale, overall the forest was in much better condition than the Falkrains. Maybe Irina had pulled magic from the outer edges of the kingdom first, trying to protect the capital, and by extension herself, from the effects of the blight.

Or maybe the Hinderlinde Forest had never fully capitulated to Irina's will.

Either way, Lorelai hoped it boded well for what she had planned next.

"How are you going to do this?" Gabril asked when they'd put enough distance between themselves and the shack to have a place to run back to if Irina's counterattack required them to retreat.

Lorelai showed Kol her plan. *Is that okay with you?*

It's fine, but are you sure you want that much pain again?

It will be temporary. Lorelai met Gabril's eyes. "I'm going to use Kol's dragon fire again. Only this time, I'm going to see if I can send it underground and have it target the watchtowers only."

Gabril's mouth tightened, and he looked at Kol. "I can't see inside her head. If she's getting overwhelmed by the pain, you do something about it."

Tell him that was already my plan.

"He was planning on it," Lorelai said. Gabril grunted.

Hunt? Travel? Eat? Sasha swooped down and perched on a nearby branch.

Not yet. I'm going to do magic.

Rather eat.

Lorelai laughed as she flexed her fingers and felt the tingle of magic run down her arms. *Then go eat. I'll call you if I need you.*

Sasha flew away as Lorelai reached for Kol's hand and braced herself for the pain. Once again, his dragon heart leaped toward her power the second she sent her magic into him. Heat poured out of him and filled her chest until pain was a living creature trapped beneath her skin, thrashing and biting with jagged teeth. She clenched her teeth to keep from screaming.

Touch the ground, Lorelai. Send the fire where you want it to go. Kol's voice broke through the pain, and she fell to her knees and pressed her open palm against the forest's floor.

"*Zhech`pusk*. Destroy with fire. Allow all who have a heart-beat to get out of the tower unscathed." She accompanied her instructions with an image of a watchtower—tall and narrow, built of wood with signal mirrors along the top and a carrier pigeon roost to the side.

Fiery magic—orange and yellow with a core of white—burst from her palm and burrowed into the ground. She pressed hard, as much to stay in contact with the magic as to keep herself from curling up in a ball from the pain, and felt the threads of fire explode outward, hurtling beneath the forest floor until they reached a watchtower and then racing up the structure to engulf it in flames, always leaving the stairs and exit clear so that those who manned the tower could escape.

The fire found seven towers in all—two in the capital, one on the castle grounds, and one at each compass point surrounding the capital. While the seventh tower was crumbling to ash, Kol pulled his hand from hers and held her while the terrible heat of his dragon's fire drained away and left her shaking in its wake.

"Are you okay?" Gabril crouched in front of her.

"Yes," she said, though her limbs still trembled. She leaned on Kol as he helped her to her feet and then listened carefully.

The forest was alive with creatures rustling through the underbrush, insects chirruping, and the occasional mournful hoot of an owl, but there were no signs of Irina. No shuddering in the ground. No bugs or statues or anything else that looked like a weapon.

Lorelai had sent powerful magic through the ground only a day's journey from the capital, had destroyed all the capital's watchtowers, and Irina hadn't been able to retaliate.

She laughed and hugged Leo's sweater to herself, blinking in surprise as tears stung her eyes. "We did it. She didn't attack us, even though we burned down a tower on the castle grounds."

Gabril's teeth flashed white against his skin as he smiled. "You were right. I'm proud of you."

I told you we make a good team. And I think sending fire beneath the ground to incinerate every tower had plenty of flair. Leo would be proud too. Kol's hands at her waist kept her steady while her knees gained the strength to hold her again.

What about your brother? Would he have loved this too?

Rag? Kol laughed, though there was hurt behind it. *Not a chance. He was always serious. Always focused on doing things exactly as he'd been taught. His whole life was spent trying to live up to the responsibility of being king one day, and it took the fun out of him.*

Kind of like me?

Kol's fingers tightened around her waist, and he drew her a little closer. She could feel the heat of his chest, but instead of pain, it brought comfort. *There's no one like you.*

Kol's hands were still steadying her, though now it felt like she needed steadying for a different reason altogether. Her skin tingled with something different from magic, something that sparked along her nerves and shivered deliciously in her stomach. She smiled up at him, and he smiled back, and then Gabril cleared his throat.

"I may be old, but I'm not blind. I can see when I'm intruding." His hand wrapped around her shoulder and squeezed gently. "You two don't stay out too late talking, and don't do anything you don't want to tell me about in the morning."

Lorelai took a step back from Kol, and his hands dropped from her waist. "You're leaving us out here alone?"

"Would you rather I stayed?"

Skies, no.

"No! I mean . . . we'll be fine. We're just going to talk."

Gabril snorted. "That's what we called it in my day too." He looked at Kol. "If I can trust her to wage war against the queen, I can trust what she sees in you. And besides, if you try anything she doesn't like, she can turn you into a pile of ash."

Lorelai and Kol watched Gabril walk back to the shack in silence, and though they weren't touching, her skin still tingled with the memory of his.

THIRTY-THREE

As Gabril disappeared into the forest, heading back toward the shack, Kol faced Lorelai and closed the distance between them with a single step. She looked at him, her dark eyes glowing in the moonlight, her red lips parted, and Kol could think of nothing but her.

Are we about to break your ground rules? Kol leaned toward Lorelai slightly, giving her time to move away if she chose.

Ground rules? She looked at his mouth, and her breath quickened.

You remember. The list you gave me when you decided not to block me out of your head? He took one of her cold hands in his and focused all his thoughts on the way she sucked in a sharp little breath when he rubbed his thumb over her wrist. The way her pulse beat frantically against her skin.

What about it? She licked her lips, and he willed her to move toward him. To want this like he wanted it.

You make me want to break one of your ground rules every time you look at me like this. And, skies help him, waiting for her to decide if she truly wanted him or not was torture.

Her smile was a slow journey of warmth that lit up her face and lingered in her eyes. *You want to kiss me.*

Skies, yes.

For a brief moment, visions of the many other girls he'd casually kissed at the academy filled her mind, and he shook his head. *No, Lorelai. You're different. This*—he held up their joined hands—*is different. Search my thoughts, and you'll see the truth.*

He waited quietly while she looked and saw the way she shone a little brighter than anyone he'd ever met. The way she challenged him and thrilled him and made him want to perform some idiotic grand gesture to prove himself in her eyes.

A grand gesture like sparing my life even though it meant your blood oath with Irina would kill you?

He laughed, but his heart was pounding with something better than the need to hurt, punish, and kill. *I didn't do that for you. Not really. I didn't even know you at the time. I was just trying to keep my honor without condemning my kingdom.*

Still, it was a pretty grand gesture.

You think so? He leaned closer, and the scent of evergreens and snow and sweet burning wood made him want to drag her against him and show her just how different she really was from every other girl in the world.

"Yes," she breathed the word into the space between them, her thoughts full of anticipation and need. He took that as the permission he'd been waiting for.

Her lips were warmer than her hands as he gently pressed his mouth to hers, still giving her a chance to back away if she changed her mind.

I'm not changing my mind. She let go of his hand and grabbed the front of his shirt instead.

He ran his hand up her arm and tangled his fingers in her hair while still keeping the kiss gentle. Their first kiss needed to be perfect, and that meant holding himself back so that he didn't rush things.

Heat that had nothing to do with his dragon's fire filled him, pressing against his chest like he'd swallowed the sun, and he couldn't breathe without taking in her scent. Without hearing the tiny gasp she made as he deepened the kiss and pulled her closer.

Something brushed against his shoulder, and for a moment, he thought it was her hand. But then something bumped against him. Hard. He stumbled forward, grabbing Lorelai's arms to keep them on their feet, and turned to see that the Hinderlinde Forest had come to life.

Oh skies, we've got trouble.

The trees—hundreds of them, dripping moss and shedding leaves—were sliding toward them, their roots ripping through the soil and splaying out like tentacles. A horrible cracking sound filled the air as branches slammed against each other and trunks collided. They moved with a steady, relentless cadence that filled Kol with horror and sent his dragon heart thundering.

A walnut tree beside Lorelai raised its branches toward the sky and then slammed them down toward the princess's head.

Down! he yelled, but she'd already dropped to the ground and rolled away from the tree.

Away from him.

He lunged toward her, and a branch smashed the ground where he'd been standing.

*It's the same thing every time. You'd think she'd realize that tak-
ing control of so many hearts at once makes the cost of her magic that
much worse.* Lorelai sounded disgusted.

*Yes, she displays a true lack of originality. Maybe we can discuss
that further when we aren't in danger of being crushed by walking
trees.*

They're moving slow. We can outrun them. She flipped to the
side as a maple bent toward her, its branches swinging hard.

They're forming a fence around us.

Good thing we have dragon's fire and mardushka *magic, then.*
She grabbed his hand and pulled him away from a skinny hick-
ory that was wrapping its branches around his waist. Magic
tingled against his skin and then slid into his blood with a jolt.

They ran, stumbling over roots that lashed the ground,
ducking branches, and trying to find a path that wasn't already
blocked.

We're surrounded. Power filled her voice, and her eyes were
fierce as she looked at him. *And we aren't going to lead them back
to Gabril and the shack. It's me she wants.*

She isn't going to get you.

No, she isn't.

An oak swiped at her, and Kol pulled her against him. The
branch slid by, scratching Kol's hands as it passed. The sound of
roots tearing through soil, trunks creaking, and branches whis-
tling through the air filled the forest as the trees shuffled closer
and closer to Lorelai and Kol.

Sasha, path! Lorelai sent as she tightened her grip on Kol's
hand and muttered an incantor.

Fire spilled out of his veins and into hers, and her pain hit him a second later. Blistering agony, pressure that wrapped around her chest and threatened to cut off her air, and a shuddering weakness that tried to send her to her knees.

He wrapped his free arm around her waist and hauled her out of the path of an incoming maple. Branches lashed around them from behind and yanked them against a trunk. Roots tangled with their feet. His dragon heart pounded viciously, and he snarled as he struck out at the branches that were touching Lorelai.

Seconds later, the gyrfalcon shrieked from above, and Lorelai, her breath coming in desperate pants, said, *Path, Sasha. Find the river to the west.*

An oak lumbered close, striking at Lorelai with a thick branch covered in dying leaves. Kol tried to block it, but the branches wrapped around his chest shortened his reach. Lorelai threw herself against him, and the branch slammed into the tree that was holding them instead.

Sasha reappeared above them as the branches holding them began to squeeze the air out of Kol's lungs.

I've got the path. Time to burn our way out of here.

He bared his teeth as his dragon heart pounded a litany of hurt, punish, kill and poured fire into Lorelai through her magic. She made an awful sound of pain, but raised her free hand and grabbed the branches that were wrapped around them.

"*Kaz`lit*," she yelled, and fire blazed out of her hand and into the heart of the tree.

It shivered and creaked, smoke rising from its bark, and then it exploded into slivers edged with gold-tipped fire so blindingly white it hurt to look at.

311

Let's get to the river where the trees can't follow us, she said, but the pain from his fire was eating at her, and she could barely walk. *Follow the path Sasha sent to me. Can you see it?*

He saw it in her thoughts—a sprint southwest for more distance than he cared to consider given their current circumstances. He scooped her into his arms and began running west, twisting away from branches that came at him like clubs, and pausing briefly when their path was blocked so that she could incinerate the tree in front of them.

He was out of breath, his body scratched and beaten from branches he'd failed to avoid, when he heard a roar in the distance.

That's the river. Her voice was faint, her teeth clenched against the pain. *I hope you can swim.*

Almost as well as I can fly. Don't worry. I've got you.

I'm not worried. She slammed her hand against a branch that struck him in the side, and the tree exploded into flaming splinters with a terrible crack that was nearly drowned out by the roar of the river.

Good. No worrying. However . . . that sounds awfully loud for a river.

That's because it's a waterfall. She shivered, and the bare skin of her arms against his felt unnaturally hot.

You need to let go of the fire, Lorelai.

Not until we're safe.

I'll get us to safety. I promise. He crested a steep slope that was nothing but stubbles of grass and clumps of dying underbrush. Behind him, an entire army of trees shuffled faster, roots lashing like whips as they came. Throwing himself on his back, with

Lorelai cradled against his chest, he slid toward the jagged edge of the slope.

We're safe from the trees. Let go of the fire. Please, Lorelai. You don't need the pain any longer.

She released the fire and it pooled in his chest, its familiar warmth comforting.

Underbrush sliced into him, and the soil scraped his back raw as he slid. He braced himself, hit the rocks that lined the bottom of the slope, and scrambled to his feet, pulling Lorelai up with him. Above them, trees began shuffling down the hillside. Below them—he peered over the rocks and swallowed hard—a waterfall burst out of the solid rock that made up the hillside and tumbled into the river below.

Skies, he hoped there weren't rocks at the bottom of the drop because they had no other options. The trees behind them were gaining speed, and the quiet shush-shush sound of their roots digging into the ground, pulling them forward, and then ripping free again set his teeth on edge.

It should be fine, she said, though her voice still sounded weak from the pain of controlling his dragon's fire. *My magic will reach the heart of the river. Hopefully it will respond to me.*

Even if it doesn't, you'll be okay. I've got you. And, skies above, please let him be able to keep that promise. *Ready?*

She met his gaze. *Ready.*

He grabbed her hand and together they jumped.

THIRTY-FOUR

IRINA STOOD ON her balcony, her hands gripping the gold box containing Kol's heart while the capital shimmered before her in the pale moonlight. Below her, spread across the grass outside the dungeon's entrance, were the remains of today's failed attempt to take the years from someone else's heart and give them to her own. The pile of bodies included peasants from the south, gentry from the capital, a merchant from Súndraille who'd failed to pay his import tax, and even a member of the nobility from the western kingdom of Akram, who hadn't technically broken any laws but who had been necessary to prove Irina's theory before she dared to put the Eldrian boy's heart inside her chest.

Every time she tried taking the essence of a foreign heart, her body reacted as though she'd ingested poison. She'd come to believe that her magic, born and bred on Morcant soil with Morcantian blood running through her veins, would not accept the heart of anyone who did not also have Morcantian blood.

Every spell she used to fight Lorelai weakened her. Every

failure to stop the princess's onslaught sent bands of pain around her chest until the very act of breathing was torture. She needed to repair her heart, and there were no prisoners from Morcant in her dungeon. For all she knew, besides Lorelai, there were no other Morcantians within Ravenspire's borders.

Except one.

She had yet to decide if she could bear to sacrifice that one, even to keep the life she deserved.

The door to her sitting room clicked open, and Viktor's familiar steps moved across her floor. She turned to find him standing behind her holding a tray with soup and bread, his expression gentle.

"It's been a hard week for you," he said as he set the tray on a side table, beckoned her inside the room, and closed the balcony door behind her. His gaze fell on the gold box clutched in her hand, and slowly the gentleness in his face hardened into something like pain. "What are you doing with that?"

She looked at the box. "I need a new heart."

He frowned. "The boy will come through for you. He'll bring you Lorelai's heart, and this will all be—"

"He won't. He defies me. He's with the princess now, allied with her while she uses her magic to combat mine." She looked at Viktor and for once let him see the fear that ate at her night and day. "Lorelai is stronger than me. She's coming back to finish what she started." Her eyes stung. "I'm going to die, Viktor. Either because Lorelai will kill me, or because my own heart will give out."

As if to prove her point, her heart gave a sudden leap and pain spread along her collarbone to reside in her jaw. She set the box down with a sharp click and clutched at her chest. Viktor was at her side in seconds.

"Sit." He half dragged, half carried her into the nearest chair and kept his arms wrapped around her. His voice was heavy with worry. "You can get better. I know you can. Just stop doing magic for a while. Let yourself regain your strength—"

"I won't regain my strength." She caught his hand in hers and held it as her magic tingled in her palm, waiting to exert itself over his willing heart. "Not without help."

"I'll help you." He crouched beside her, his blue eyes earnest.

"I know a spell that will take the remaining years from another's heart and give them to mine. I've tried it over and over again on our prisoners, but it just makes me weaker. My magic refuses to accept a heart from Ravenspire."

"Maybe it isn't where they're born. Maybe you need nobility—"

"I've tried. Ravenspire nobility. Akram nobility. Gentry from my kingdom and others." She picked up the gold box again and cradled it as the boy's heart thumped steadily inside. "The only hearts I haven't tried are those from Eldr or Morcant."

She kept her eyes on the box as she waited for Viktor to understand what she already knew.

Viktor took her hands in his, box and all. "It's one thing to punish your prisoners. It's another to take more from the king of Eldr than he's promised you."

She tightened her hold on the box and met his gaze. "I told you. I'm dying."

"Then walk away from this." His eyes begged her to listen. "We'll go to Súndraille. I hear there's a fae in exile there who can perform miracles for the right price. We could get your heart cured and buy a ship. Sail the seas and find an island—"

"I'm not leaving." She pulled her hands from his and raised the box so that it glittered in the candles that lit her room. "I've fought too hard for this. Ravenspire is *my* kingdom, and I will not give it up. I'm going to try replenishing my heart with the Eldrian's," she said, and half believed it was true. She could try. Maybe this time it would work.

Or maybe Viktor, always dependable Viktor, would come up with a different solution so that she didn't have to suggest it— didn't have to even truly consider it—herself.

He held her gaze for a long moment, a myriad of emotions crossing his face, and then he said with quiet force, "No."

She stared at him. "What did you say to me?"

She'd expected agreement or a logical suggestion that would solve everything. Not resistance. Not from him.

He clenched his jaw, and his eyes seemed to be begging her for something. "I said no, Irina. You cannot ruin that boy's life any more than you already have. And if his heart proves as poisonous to yours as all the rest, you could die."

"I will do as I please. And when I'm finished, you and I will have a discussion about your proper place—"

"We will have that discussion now." Something wild entered his eyes. "In fact, we will discuss everything we've been leaving unspoken for years. Starting with the fact that you never loved King Arlen, that you might love me, and that even though I desperately want you to be safe and happy, I can't go along with this plan of yours."

"Not *now*, Viktor." She pushed a hand against his chest, but he refused to give ground.

"Yes, now." He ignored the icy glare she sent his way and leaned forward until she was pressed between his chest and the back of the chair. "I've devoted my entire life to you. I've given you my time, my energy, and my heart."

"I didn't ask for your heart."

"No, but you took it anyway. You take, Irina, from the land, from the people, from me. And because I understand why, I've held my tongue. I've swallowed my words and my pride, knowing it was the price I had to pay to stay by your side. I understand *you*." His voice gentled, and the pain inside it ripped at something Irina refused to let him see. "Unloved by those who were supposed to love you most. Passed over for the marriage and the throne that should've been yours. And then, when you did marry Arlen, he'd barely look at you, his children wouldn't trust you, and the gentry treated you like an interloper instead of like their queen. The wounds run deep—"

"I'm not wounded." Magic sped down her arms and gathered in her hands, looking for a target.

"You are. And the wounds others caused you are nothing compared to what you're doing to yourself. Irina, you don't have to destroy this boy and yourself to get to Lorelai. You don't have to keep everyone too terrified of you to dare lift a finger against you." He raised a hand and laid it softly against her cheek. "You don't need magic to be loved. You have everything you need to be a beloved queen—a beloved woman—right here." His hand dropped to press against her heart.

"Viktor . . ."

"I love you, Irina. Not because you wield magic. Not because you're the queen. In fact, I love you despite those things." He dropped to his knees and gathered her hands in his. "I love you, and I'm asking you to stop this. Please."

She tore her gaze from his and stared at the box that held her hope. For a moment, she tried to imagine a life outside Ravenspire. Alone with Viktor on a ship, searching for an island to call their own. But if she did that, her father would win. Milek would win.

Tatiyana, with her treachery, would win.

They would have everything, and Irina would be condemned to wander with no title, no kingdom, and no power to call her own.

She pulled her hands from Viktor's.

"Irina, please."

"I'm not leaving." She blinked tears from her eyes and pushed him away so she could stand. "I'm going to strengthen my heart, and then I'm going to finish what Lorelai started nine years ago. I'm going to keep what is rightfully mine."

"How can you be sure the spell even works? Maybe the hearts haven't been the problem. Maybe it's—"

"It worked on my father." She refused to look at him. "It works on a Morcantian heart. I just have to hope it also works on a heart from Eldr."

He slowly rose to his feet. "Do you love me?"

She stopped, her hand hovering over the box, as the question burned within her.

Did she love him? What would it cost her if she did?

He moved to her side, and repeated, "Do you love me?"

Slowly, she looked at him. At his pretty face, his rumpled cravat, and his blue eyes pleading with her to simply tell him the truth.

"Yes," she said softly before turning back to the box. "But I can't be happy with you if I don't defeat Lorelai and remain on Ravenspire's throne, and the only way I can do that is by replenishing the strength in my heart."

"And that will heal you? It will keep you alive so that you can defeat Lorelai, remain on the throne, and finally be happy?" The grief in Viktor's voice pulled at Irina.

She met his gaze and something shuddered inside her at what she found there. He knew the solution she'd been too afraid to put into words. "Yes. This will fix everything, and I will finally be at peace. I'll finally be happy."

She reached for the box, but he took her hand and pulled her against himself instead. Before she could speak, he covered her mouth with his. His kiss was wild—his lips claiming her, his teeth grazing her skin with a tiny bite of pain.

When he raised his head, he took the hand that had hovered over the gold box and placed it on his chest instead. "I meant it when I said I would not allow you to ruin that innocent boy's life. If you really need to take the remaining years from a heart, if that is what will truly bring you peace, then you can have mine. But you cannot have his."

She trembled as she stared at him. As the heart inside the gold box beat strongly while Irina's heart stuttered and ached.

She'd told him the truth. She wasn't leaving Ravenspire. Not after all she'd sacrificed to make it hers.

One more sacrifice, and then she'd be ready. She'd be powerful. She'd be unstoppable.

"*Ja`dat,*" she whispered, and the power burned in her hands. "Take what is his and give it to me instead."

"Irina, stop." Viktor sounded desperate. "Please."

Ignoring him, she raised her hand and let the magic coursing through her give strength to her voice. *"Ja`dat!* Take what is his and give it to me. Give it to me!"

Her hand, wreathed in brilliant light, slammed against his chest.

His head fell back, and he cried out in agony as her magic pierced his chest and surrounded his heart.

"No," she cried, but the spell didn't stop.

Her will was stronger than her foolish heart.

Her will desired Ravenspire.

Her will wanted Lorelai dead.

And so she watched with tears streaming down her face as Viktor's face aged, his hair grayed, and then he collapsed on the floor, his beautiful blue eyes cloudy and staring at nothing.

Her heart beat strong and fierce inside her chest.

Her magic coursed through her body like an avalanche of power.

Let Lorelai come for her. Let the Eldrian king try to defy her. She would crush them both. It would be Viktor's legacy.

She bent to straighten his rumpled cravat, allowing one sob to escape her lips as she clung to his chest, and then she dried her tears and walked away.

THIRTY-FIVE

I'VE GOT YOU. Kol wrapped an arm around Lorelai's waist beneath the water and pulled her toward the side of the cliff as the waterfall crashed above them. She kicked hard, and he pushed her upward until her head broke the surface. A second later, his head was above water too.

The curtain of falling water was behind them. A hollowed-out space in the side of the cliff was ahead. Lorelai looked at Kol, her eyes lit with something that made heat unfurl in his stomach.

We can hide there until we're sure Irina's trees are done looking for us. He looked over his shoulder at the curtain of water. *Of course, I suppose she could have monstrous fish coming after us.*

The river's heart is mine. Lorelai flexed her fingers. *I called to it the moment we hit the water.*

So we're safe for the moment?

Yes.

Sasha and Gabril too?

Her eyes darkened. *I think so. Sasha will look after him until we get out of here.*

Together, Kol and Lorelai found handholds in the rocky cliff side and climbed into the cave. The second she'd found her footing, he swept her into his arms and held her as if he'd never let her go.

You saved us, he said.

We saved each other.

He cradled her head against the warmth of the dragon's fire in his chest. *And you're sure we're safe?*

I'm sure. The water will tell me if we aren't.

Good. Then there's nothing to stop me from kissing you properly. His heart pounded at the look in her eyes. He could no longer tell the difference between the pounding of the waterfall and the pounding of his heart. He slid his hand up her back and tangled his fingers in her dripping hair. Her cheeks flushed despite the frigid water still clinging to her skin, and the tenderness that swelled within his chest felt like it would break him into pieces.

He bent his head, and the cave spun as he pressed his lips to hers.

This time, he kissed her like the world was ending, and she was his last chance at happiness. She held on to him, and her palms tingled and burned with magic as she ran them over his arms and onto his shoulders.

He tore his lips from hers and pressed them against the side of her jaw as she clung to him.

Her magic, as if obeying some secret incantor hidden within her heart, exploded out of her hands and wrapped the two of them in bands of blinding white light that tingled on the edge of pain.

Kol brought his lips back to hers and kissed her as if he meant to never let her go.

You healed me. Kol examined his arms and legs hours later as dawn was breaking across the sky.

Um . . . yes. Remember? I slept for nearly a whole day because of it? Lorelai gave him an amused look as she finger combed the tangles out of her still-damp hair.

He raised a brow. *No, I mean you healed me when you kissed me.*

I think it was you who kissed me. She gave him a cheeky grin that had him wanting to cross the cave and kiss her all over again.

So do it. Her smile widened, and he laughed though pain from the collar was starting to burn in a way that it hadn't for days. Lorelai hiked up her pant legs to examine her ankles and then looked over her arms as well. *It healed me too. That's a nice side effect. Plus it's far more enjoyable than using an incantor to pull your injuries out of your body.*

The whispers flitted through his mind—hurt, punish, kill— and he focused on Lorelai to drown them out. The collar wanted to list its wishes for Lorelai? Well, he had a list of his own. A list that kept him from seeing her as prey.

He had the image of her reaching for him, courage and compassion on her face, as he attacked. He had the way she tilted her head and squinted her gorgeous brown eyes when she was trying to figure something out. The way she lifted her chin when she was prepared to argue her point. The way her breath caught in her throat when he held her, and the red of her lips against her pale cheeks.

Cheeks that were now suffused with color.

He grinned. *Embarrassed?*

She concentrated on wringing water from her shirt. *You notice the strangest things about me.*

This from a girl who thinks my hair is both wild and adorable?

She laughed, but there were nerves behind it now. He looked to find the reason, and his stomach tightened. The capital loomed before them, just south of here. Irina was waiting, along with his human heart.

It was time to finish what they'd started.

The good news is that it took Irina a while to respond, and, while I don't ever want to be attacked by trees again, it wasn't as bad as the statues or the bugs. She shuddered.

You've weakened her.

Her smile made her look like the warrior that she was.

We have to go soon, while she's still trying to recover, she said. *This has been nice—*

Nice? You wound me with understatement.

She gave him a stern look.

The whispers in his mind seemed to grow louder.

Hurt. Punish. Kill. Let your dragon heart do as it pleases.

He shook his head and pushed against the voices. He'd won this battle countless times. He would win it again.

It's almost over, she said, and there was a shadow of fear in her usually confident voice. *If I don't survive, I want you to know that—*

You're going to survive. His voice was fierce as he stalked toward her, ignoring the streak of pain that wrapped around his chest. *Don't even think about the alternative.*

What if I don't? This time her fear was a palpable presence in her thoughts. He wondered if she realized that her fear was less about her survival than it was about letting down the kingdom that was depending on her.

Then I'll kiss you again, and your magic will bring you back to life.

Magic doesn't bring people back to life.

Then I will stay by your side to make sure you're safe.

He pulled her to her feet, brushed his fingers across her beautiful mouth and then kissed her until her magic flared and wrapped the two of them in bands of white light that tingled against his skin like he was standing beside a winter's fire.

He deepened the kiss, his dragon's heart pounding like a battle drum. Did she realize the effect she had on him? That her true magic had nothing to do with the power in her hands?

She had the courage of a Draconi warrior, the power of a Morcantian *mardushka*, and the heart of a true princess of Ravenspire. Irina had no idea what was coming for her.

Oh, don't I? A soft, cruel voice sliced through his mind, bringing a swath of unbearable pain in its wake.

Kol yanked himself away from Lorelai and stumbled back. His dragon heart thudded against his chest, viciously demanding blood.

Kol, what's wrong? Lorelai stepped toward him, and he lunged away from her.

Stay back! I don't want to hurt you.

Yes, you do. The amusement in Irina's voice was edged with anger.

You're scaring me. What's going on? Lorelai put her hands up as if to calm him and tried to approach.

He took a single step back. Pain, like fire-tipped razors, flooded his body. He fell to his knees on the rough cave floor and grasped the collar with both hands while agony squeezed the breath out of his lungs. Something dark and heavy fell across his thoughts, and suddenly Lorelai's warmth felt very far away.

You need my help. Lorelai dropped down beside him, and he could sense the power building in her hands.

He could also sense the specter of Irina in his mind, a shadow of menace that seemed infinitely more powerful than the magic Lorelai was offering to use.

Irina's laugh mocked him. *Oh, I am infinitely more powerful than your pretty little princess. Haven't you figured that out by now? I can come and go inside your mind as I please. I can give you pain and take it away. And lest you've forgotten our bargain, may I remind you that I hold your very fragile human heart in my hand?*

The space where his heart had been seemed to leap into flames. This was nothing like the comforting heat of his dragon's fire. This was a slow, agonizing death from the inside out, and he thought he'd do anything—*anything*—to make it stop.

He didn't realize he was screaming until Lorelai dragged him into her arms, her magic wrapping around him in brilliant strands. But this time her touch was like acid against his skin.

He shoved her away and tried to stand, but something far stronger than him seized his body and forced him to his knees like a supplicant before a throne.

What's this I see? Irina sounded curious, but he heard the rage underneath. *A magical bond created between you and the princess?* All pretense dropped from her voice, leaving nothing but fury and power. *I'll punish you both for that.*

Lorelai moved toward him slowly, as if trying not to spook him. *Kol, please. Just let me help you. It's the collar, isn't it?*

It's Irina. He forced the thought toward Lorelai. It was like trying to shove a pebble through a velvet curtain. He concentrated, and more pain exploded through his head, shooting sparks across his vision, but he felt the thought slip through.

Lorelai went still, her breath coming in quick pants as she stared at him. *Irina is in your head?*

Yes. He tried to show her an image of the pain Irina was sending him, the way Irina had somehow corrupted his bond with Lorelai so that the princess's magic only made the pain worse, and the curtain that seemed to separate his thoughts from hers now.

Lorelai's eyes narrowed, and she lifted her chin.

She was going to try to battle Irina for him, but he wasn't sure if he could survive the fallout.

Why don't we play a game? Irina's voice was a hiss of malice against his thoughts, and he clutched at his head as if he could rid himself of the sound. *It's called Which One of These Will the King of Eldr Kill? One match decides the entire game. Ready?*

Lorelai stepped toward him, her lips pressed tight, her hands extended.

He shook, both from pain and desperation, as Irina sent him an image of Lorelai, destroyed by the spell in his collar and lying lifeless on the cave floor while Kol, driven wild by Irina's power, ripped her heart from her chest.

His pulse raced, and he backed up as Lorelai advanced.

Hold still, Kol. She doesn't get to take you. She doesn't get to hurt you. I'm the one she wants. Let's see her try to take me instead. Lorelai's fierce expression matched her words, and Irina laughed in delight.

This is going to be easier than I thought, Irina said. *I made a mistake containing the curse to your collar. I'm going to rectify that the second she touches you. As I'm sure you felt when her magic brushed against you, I've all but destroyed the bond you shared with her. The two of us together are unstoppable, Kolvanismir. You will do as you are told. And if you even think about defying me again, I will squeeze the life out of your human heart and leave you with nothing.*

I won't kill Lorelai. He held the princess's gaze, trying to tell her with his eyes how much she meant to him as he waited for Irina to destroy him.

Lorelai shook her head vehemently as if she could see that he was waiting to die, and took another step toward him.

So then I guess we move on to contender number two in our little game. If you refuse to kill the princess, then you will go to the capital and kill this woman and her children instead. Irina showed him an image of a pretty woman with dark skin and black hair cut close to her scalp. Two boys, who each looked remarkably like Gabril, stood at her side.

Kol clenched his fists as the pain in his chest spread down his veins, and struggled to draw an unfettered breath. Skies, it hurt. Worse than anything he'd ever imagined. Worse than the torture she'd inflicted on him already. Worse than losing his human heart. His thoughts were fraying, and his dragon heartbeat was surging, viciously demanding its due.

I won't . . . Where were his words? He reached for them, and they floated away, awash in a sea of unendurable pain.

You will. Irina sounded satisfied. *I own you. I have your human heart in my hand. I have your little bond with Lorelai corrupted. I control what you can remember. I control the pain. I control YOU, and there is no one who can save you from me, Kolvanismir, least of all Lorelai.*

I won't . . . He closed his eyes and struggled to remember what it was he wouldn't do. Disobey his queen? That sounded wrong, but it was the only thought he could find that made any sense.

Don't disobey his queen. Make the pain stop.

"*Nakh`rashk.*" Lorelai's voice, full of fury and power, filled the cave. "*Nakh`rashk!* Find Irina's magic and scatter it to the winds." Her hands, ablaze with magic, wrapped around his, and he arced his back, his jaw locked helplessly against the waves of agony that swept over him.

Irina's laughter filled his head. *Lorelai gets to die first, but I think we'll go ahead and kill the others as well, just to make it a tidy little victory.*

He was consumed, every piece of him, with red-hot light. Irina's magic collided with Lorelai's and became a cage of brilliant flames that felt like they would burrow beneath his skin until they incinerated his bones.

Stop, he begged, but no one listened.

Irina was laughing.

Lorelai was saying her incantor over and over, her eyes blazing as she fought to push Irina's magic out of his body.

And his body . . . his body was fire. It was pain. It was more than he could stand.

Stay with me, Kol. Lorelai's voice was a soft caress within his tortured mind, and there was something he had to tell her. Some warning he needed to give, but it was lost in the unraveling of his thoughts. *I won't let you go. I won't let her take you.*

Irina stopped laughing. *Time to teach her whom she's dealing with.*

The collar around his neck seemed to tighten, and a wave of magic that felt thick as sludge slid out of the collar and over his arms.

He tried to pull away from Lorelai, but her magic was wrapped around his wrists, and she was determined not to let him go.

Please, he said but no one was listening. Irina was chanting words he couldn't understand, and they seemed to devour the last of his reason and deliver a terrible thirst for pain in its place.

He was fire, blood, and death.

No, you aren't. You're Kolvanismir Arsenyevnek, ruler of Eldr. You're stronger than she thinks. You can fight this. I'll help you, Kol. Fight this. Fight!

He fought. He strove to drown out the awful pounding of his dragon heart. To ignore the scathing fire that dwelled where he'd once been human.

To pull away from Irina.

He fought, but he was losing.

Lorelai was losing.

The tainted magic that seeped from his collar coated his wrists, slid over the bonds of Lorelai's magic, and then leaped for her hands.

She screamed, throwing her head back as the pain that lived inside Kol poured into her instead, leaving him as empty as a canyon with a river of magic rushing through it.

See? Irina whispered against his ear. *I'm stronger. I control you. And now because she tried to save you, because you both defied me, you get to watch her die.*

Let go, he urged Lorelai, but the thought refused to breach the curtain of Irina's magic. He was trapped inside himself, lost to the impulses of his dragon and the cruel wishes of his mistress. And Lorelai, the girl who had fought so hard to save him, was going to die.

He yanked at their joined hands, ferociously determined to break their connection as Lorelai's already pale skin went white with strain. Her voice broke, her breath was a sob in her throat, and tears streamed from her eyes as she met his gaze.

I'm sorry, he said, but she couldn't hear him. No one could.

No one but his queen.

Lorelai's back arced, and then she fell forward onto his lap, her body shaking uncontrollably.

He no longer had the words to tell her he was sorry. That she deserved better. That she should let go of his hands and leave him behind.

She was saying something, her lips moving though her words were mere breaths.

Time to finish this, Irina said. *We have more people to kill, Kolvanismir. Gabril Busche needs to learn what his betrayal will cost him. Kill the princess and let's be on our way.*

His heart thundered its agreement with this plan.

Hurt. Punish. Kill.

He was a predator. They were his prey.

He was fire, blood, and death.

Lorelai slowly pulled herself up until she was eye to eye with him. He snarled.

She leaned close and pressed her lips to his.

Magic shot out of her and surrounded him, cutting off the bonds of the curse and sending the pain that had been flowing into her back into Kol. Before he could move, she yanked her hands from his and pressed them on either side of his face. Pulling back from his mouth, she whispered, "*Nakh`rashk.* Scatter the queen's magic."

Irina shrieked in fury as Lorelai's magic surged into Kol's mind, found the thick curtain that obscured his thoughts from hers, and tore it to pieces.

Irina's cold voice said, *She can't get rid of me. The best she can do is hear your thoughts as I turn you into the predator you were meant to be.*

He had a brief moment of clarity, and he *knew.*

Lorelai might be able to tear through the curtain in his mind, but she couldn't break the collar. She didn't hold his human heart hostage. And she didn't control him.

Irina did.

Even now, his talons were out, his chest heating with his dragon's fire. He wanted to hurt, punish, and kill. He wanted it with a desperate hunger that roared through him until he felt like he'd never be satisfied.

With Irina in his head, it wasn't a question of if he'd become a killer, it was a question of when.

The only choice left to make in the last moments of his

self-control was whether he'd kill Lorelai or go after Gabril's family instead.

Kol, no. Lorelai's voice was full of horror as he pushed her away from him and turned toward the entrance to the cave.

Irina laughed as he dove into the water and began moving toward the capital.

THIRTY-SIX

LORELAI'S LEGS FELT too weak to hold her as she stumbled to the edge of the cave and peered into the thick sheet of water, still shaking from the remnants of the pain Irina had sent into her through her connection to Kol. She couldn't see Kol, but she could sense his thoughts—fragmented, full of agony, and poisoned by the presence of Irina in his head.

It didn't make sense. If Irina had so much power over Kol, why hadn't she used it weeks ago when she'd first taken his heart? Why let Lorelai heal him and create a bond with her magic?

Kol sent her an image of the vicious whispers of his collar. Of the way Irina's control over him felt far more powerful than it had before.

Lorelai sent back an image of her pursuing him as he raced to the capital with the speed of his dragon, and then ignored his instant objection as she tightened the laces on her boots. Just a few hours ago, she'd felt triumphant. Certain that she'd weakened Irina's heart to the point of ruin and that confronting her at the castle was a battle Lorelai could win.

Now, Lorelai had lost the battle for Kol, had lost an ally who could help her fight with fire, and was separated from Gabril while Kol raced to kill Gabril's family. She had no time to plan, no time to gather information and figure out how to swing the odds back into her favor. She had to act swiftly, or Irina would win the war before Lorelai even arrived at the battlefield.

Standing at the edge of the cave, droplets of frigid water misting her skin, she called up Gabril's face. The shape of his mind. The way he'd erected a barrier between his thoughts and hers.

Hours ago, Lorelai wouldn't have dreamed of destroying the wall he'd put up to keep his thoughts private from hers. But now she didn't have the luxury of asking permission or of hoping her magic was strong enough to do what she needed. If Irina could break into any mind she'd already bonded with, then so could Lorelai. She just had to *want* it. And right now, she wanted it with a desperation that burned through her body with every breath.

Clenching her fists, she thought of Gabril and felt her power tingle down her arms. She imagined tendrils of power leaving her body and seeking him out in the Hinderlinde.

"*Nakhgor.* Find the one I seek." Power burst from her palms, parted the waterfall, and blazed a path toward the forest.

Seconds later, she felt Gabril's mind, still steadfastly keeping her out. "*Pros`odit*," she said, and the wall in his mind cracked.

Gabril, don't block me out. We're in trouble, and I need your help.

There was a flash of shock, an instant of resistance, and then his calm, stoic voice said, *Where are you? How can I help?*

I'm in a cave under the waterfall to the west but—

I'm coming.

No! I'll come to you. It will be much faster.

Only you? Where's Kol?

For a moment, she faltered, her throat thickening with grief and her heart aching.

What happened? The sympathy in Gabril's voice snapped Lorelai back to her senses. He could see her thoughts. He'd felt her grief for Kol. She had to be careful what she showed him.

Irina broke into his thoughts—which gave me the idea that I could break into yours, and I'd apologize, but we have a huge problem. She's controlling him through the collar and through his hearts. I'm not exactly sure how because all I can see are his thoughts, not hers. But whatever she's doing, it's far worse than it was before. It's like she either finally decided to stop toying with him and to display what she's really capable of, or she found some way to increase her power.

Is he going to hurt you? The sympathy was gone and in its place was a warrior ready to defend his princess. She had to find a way to tell him that she wasn't the one who needed defending.

No. He fought her hard enough to get away from me without hurting me, but he only left because he thinks I can't help him. He thinks he's going to break and do her bidding. Already, I can feel his thoughts disintegrating, turning into a dragon controlled by pain—

He's going to be all right. Gabril's voice was a steady lifeline for her to cling to, but she couldn't.

He's going to be all right because I'm going after him, and so are you. Now show me an image of where you are.

She took a deep breath and flexed her muscles as Gabril

showed her a huge fallen oak tree lying close to the shack. Her muscles were stronger. Less shaky. The effects of Irina's curse were wearing off as her own magic coursed through her veins, lending her strength. It was time to tell Gabril the truth and put a plan into place that would save everyone.

Everyone but Irina.

I'm coming to you. She'd tell him the truth when she got to him. Otherwise, he'd race toward the capital without her, and that was exactly what Irina was hoping for. Gabril chasing down Kol. Lorelai chasing Gabril. None of them focused on the true threat.

None of them focused on Irina.

She raised her arms above her head and whispered, "*Voshtet.* Rise with me and fly."

Power burned in her palms as she dove into the water. Instantly, the force of the waterfall shoved her down, trying to crush her beneath its weight. She concentrated on the power rippling through her veins and opened her hands. Her magic struck the water, and a whirlpool swirled beneath her, moving faster and faster as it rose from the depths.

Be ready, she sent to Gabril as the whirlpool gathered itself and then shot upward, exploding through the surface of the water.

Ready for what?

For me. Almost there. She focused on the wild, untamed heart of the river and showed it Gabril waiting by the fallen oak. The river's heart surged toward hers willingly. The whirlpool turned on its side and arced toward the fallen oak with Lorelai standing on top of it as if it was an enormous silvery bridge made of water.

As it rushed forward, Lorelai said, *Hold your breath.*

My . . . what? Why?

Do it!

She felt Gabril's obedience at the same moment that she felt his utter shock as the bridge of water burst through the trees to rush past the fallen oak. Lorelai reached down, wrapped a hand around Gabril's and whispered an incantor to make him rise with the water. Then, as the river's heart responded to the new direction in Lorelai's, she pulled him up through the thick, churning wall of water until he was standing beside her, clutching her arms to keep his balance.

Sasha lifted herself out of a nearby tree and flew toward the princess. Lorelai winced as the heavy gyrfalcon landed on her shoulder, talons digging in. She'd left the brace behind with her travel pack.

The bridge of water streaked through the Hinderlinde, ripping leaves from the dying trees—that all looked as if they'd never come to life the night before and tried to crush Lorelai to death—until it reached the main road that led to the capital. It arced over the road, rushing above carriages and people heading back to the capital on foot. People screamed and dove off the road, but Lorelai didn't spare them a glance. The water was above them. They were safe.

And she didn't have a single second to spare.

Slow down. Let's make a plan and take a little time to focus. If we do this, Irina will know you're coming! Gabril's voice was a shout inside her head.

She already does. And now it was time to tell him the true danger. Her stomach ached and her hands trembled as she said,

She's sent Kol to kill Ada and your sons.

The sense of desperation coming from him was almost too much to bear.

I'll hold him back. I'm still connected to him. I haven't lost him completely. We'll go straight to your house and rescue them, and then I'll deal with Kol and Irina while you get your family to safety. Show me what your house looks like and where it is so I can tell the water where to go.

His chest rose and fell rapidly, and he let go of her hand to grab his sword instead. *I know you love the boy, Lorelai, but if he harms my family—*

He won't. Now show me the house and wall up your thoughts again so I can focus on keeping Kol from giving in to his dragon.

He sent her an image of a pretty brown cottage with a bright blue door and flowers in the window boxes. It was on the eastern side of the capital, well away from the main roads. She showed the water's heart where to go and then focused on Kol.

I'm coming.

His fragmented thoughts sped up, and she felt his frantic need to keep her away from him.

You aren't a killer, and I won't let her destroy you like this. Have faith in me, Kol. My heart wants to save you more than hers wants to hurt you.

Save . . . you. His voice was rough, mostly dragon, and she heard a steady snarl of *hurt, punish, kill* beneath his words, but Kol was still there. Still fighting to remain himself despite the queen's best efforts.

I don't need to be saved. She does. Is she listening to me?

Kol's terror was a bright flare in the darkness of his mind.

Can she hear me?

Hears . . . me.

Then make sure you respond to what I'm about to say, because it would be a shame for her to miss it. Lorelai's heart pounded, but not from panic. There was no more room for fear. She was an implacable force of nature, and she was coming to reclaim what was hers.

The water bridge twisted and dove beneath the iron arches of the capital's gate and plunged into the city, sending people scrambling for cover.

Are you listening? she asked.

Yes. His voice was faint, nearly drowned out in the insatiable bloodlust of his dragon's heart. Of the queen.

Then you let Irina see this. You show her my thoughts, Kol. You tell that lying, cowardly usurper that this is the last day she will breathe Ravenspire air. This is the last day she will look out on the kingdom she's ruined.

Ravenspire's true queen has entered the city, and Irina's time is over.

Kol was silent for an agonizing minute as Lorelai and Gabril plunged through the city streets, streaked around corners, and sped toward the eastern edge of the capital.

Angry. There was a shiver of fear in his voice, but there was pride too.

He was still there. Still Kol. Irina had once again underestimated the strength of a heart determined to withstand hers.

Her anger is nothing compared to the anger of this land and its people. Where are you?

He showed her the little brown cottage with the bright blue

door. The image pulsed with red as his heart screamed for blood, and the collar poured pain into his body until he could barely remember his name.

I'll be there soon. Don't hurt them.

Hurt . . .

No, you will not hurt them. You are not a killer. You are stronger than Irina thinks you are. Hold out a little longer. I'm almost there.

Wait. He seemed to be struggling to find another word. As the water surged around another corner and plunged down the cobblestones toward the cottage, he sent her an image of himself with a scarf tied around his mouth.

She won't let you tell me something?

The water arced gracefully toward the cottage's tidy lawn.

Kol was nowhere to be seen.

Gabril readied himself to jump as Lorelai spoke softly to the water's heart.

And then as the water deposited Gabril and Lorelai on the withered grass beside the blue front door and receded back toward the Silber River, Kol whispered, *Trap.*

"Gabril, watch out!" Lorelai cried as what looked like an entire regiment of the queen's soldiers, their eyes glassy and unfocused like the villager's eyes had been in Nordenberg, stood up from their hiding places behind trees, fence posts, and the surrounding cottages, and converged on Lorelai and Gabril.

Instantly, Sasha rose into the air and arrowed toward the closest soldier. Gabril pivoted, sword out to face the threat, and Lorelai caught a flash of movement inside the house.

Kol? Are you inside with his family?

Must . . . hurt. His voice broke. *No. I won't. Help . . . me.*

I'm going to help you as soon as I take care of the soldiers attacking us. She crouched and pressed her hand to the ground, careful to tell its heart that she wanted no injury to come to any of the soldiers. No one else in Ravenspire was going to die for Irina.

The ground rippled and shook, and thick strands of wiry grass shot out of the dirt to wrap around wrists and ankles, sending soldiers crashing down where they remained shackled to the lawn. With her back to the house, Lorelai focused on sending a snare toward each approaching soldier while also trying desperately to keep Kol focused on her.

"Gabril!" A woman's voice rose in panic, followed by screams of terror. Gabril wheeled away from Lorelai and ran toward his house.

Kol! What are you—

Kol sprinted around the corner of the house and launched himself in front of Lorelai as a group of soldiers, taking advantage of Lorelai's momentary distraction, cut themselves loose and attacked.

Why did Ada scream? Lorelai asked, dreading the answer until she saw that Kol didn't know. As soon as he'd seen that Lorelai was under attack, he'd abandoned his mission in favor of defending her.

So what had scared Ada? The sight of soldiers running toward her husband? Before she could figure out the answer, another wave of attackers rushed onto the property and straight for Lorelai.

Sasha screamed in fury and attacked, colliding with a woman and then whirling midair to dive toward another.

Kol was a blur of motion. He spun into one man and then

sent a woman to her knees. Lorelai ducked as a sword fell toward her neck, and then Kol was there, grabbing the sword with his bare hands.

She cried out a warning, but Kol didn't need it. The heat from the dragon's fire in his chest had spread throughout his body, and the blade melted as he held it.

Lorelai somersaulted beneath another sword and slammed her hands onto the ground again, desperately calling up more vines, trying hard not to use her magic to hurt those who were only fighting because a *mardushka* had bespelled them.

No matter how many vines she called forth, however, more soldiers kept coming. And not only soldiers, she realized. Nobility. Upper gentry. Peasants. Even children.

A chill swept over her. She couldn't defeat them all without injuring them. There were too many, and she didn't dare use up her strength when she still needed to face Irina. She had to stop fighting and start running.

It was time to flee this cottage.

Let's go, she said to Kol, but he ignored her in favor of launching himself at a well-dressed man in a silk cravat who was coming at Lorelai with an upraised cane.

These are innocent people, and we can't defeat them without hurting them. Are you listening to me? Kol!

She felt the change in him before she saw it. The darkening of his mind. The burn of agony that ignited his dragon heart. The cold, precise thoughts of a predator.

He turned toward her, his amber eyes feral.

Run. His voice was guttural and hoarse. *Prey.*

Don't let Irina have you. Fight this, Kol. Her heart pounded and magic screamed through her blood as she reached for him. She wasn't going to lose him. She wasn't going to lose another person she cared about to Irina. A flicker of awareness crossed his face as she stepped toward him, followed immediately by horrified fear.

And then his thoughts opened wide to her, and it wasn't his voice anymore. It was Irina's.

The Eldrian king is mine. Gabril and his family are mine. My guards have them halfway to the castle by now. You have no one left. You're a little fledgling mardushka, *and you are no match for me.*

Lorelai lunged for Kol, her hands reaching, but he was gone. Twisting away from her. Running toward the castle. Following the crowd of soldiers who'd already taken Gabril and his family to Irina.

THIRTY-SEVEN

"KOL!" LORELAI YELLED, but it was too late. He was too fast, and she was surrounded by a throng of bespelled people determined to kill her to satisfy their queen.

She threw herself to the side, narrowly avoiding a woman who came at her with an ax clutched in one hand and a baby on her hip. Three men old enough to be grandfathers lunged at her from behind, and she flipped forward only to dive into a shoulder roll when a girl who couldn't be older than twelve ran at her with a shard of metal in her hand.

Gabril and his family would be nearly at the castle by now. Kol's mind was a cold, dark place that refused to acknowledge her.

And the crowd around her kept doubling in size as more people thronged to the cottage, makeshift weapons in their hands.

Lorelai needed a way out. Fast.

Someone knocked into her, and she rolled forward, coming up on her hands and knees, only to be sent sprawling by a well-aimed boot to her back.

She whirled to avoid a sword, and it plunged into the ground beside her face.

Before she could move, a woman fell on her, and then two more piled on, pinning Lorelai to the ground as they grappled for her neck.

Lorelai shoved her palms against the ground and screamed, *"Pros'rashk!"*

The grass caved inward, an enormous, mouthlike circle with Lorelai at its center, and then exploded outward like a giant exhaling a gale force wind.

The throng that had been closing in on Lorelai flew backward, crashing into the cottage, the fence, and the trees, and lying dazed.

Lorelai lunged to her feet, cringing at the injuries she saw. Blood. Some broken bones. And already, the crowd that had been on the fringes was climbing over their fallen comrades and coming for her—a solid wall of people in every direction.

She couldn't afford another huge drain on her magic. Even when working with a willing heart, magic took its toll. She needed her energy for Irina.

Magic couldn't save her, but she'd spent the last nine years of her life saving herself without ever relying on the power that ran through her blood.

She could handle this. She just had to think like a warrior. Use her surroundings. Be unexpected.

First, she needed to know how deep the crowds were and which direction she should flee. As the horde clambered over the injured and came for her, she locked her gaze on a thick red-leaf maple that leaned toward the cottage's roof.

At least ten people stood in the way, and there were no branches low enough to grab with her hands, but it would have to do.

Sasha, path. She sent an image of the tree, and her bird whirled away from the cluster of men she'd been keeping at bay and barreled toward the tree, skimming the ground and crashing into those who stood between Lorelai and the maple.

The princess raced toward the tree, hurtling over prone bodies and grabbing a man's outstretched arms so she could push against him for leverage as she launched herself at the maple's trunk. She struck the tree with her right foot and pushed up and out. Three more leaps and she'd reached the lowest branches.

Sasha circled overhead, eyeing the crowd that was now crushing themselves against the tree as they fought to climb over one another and follow Lorelai into the branches.

Lorelai climbed until she was nearly eye level with the cottage's roof, the closest she could get before the branches became too slim to safely hold her weight, and then sidled out along a branch that was barely wide enough to allow her to keep her balance. Taking a deep breath, she judged the angle and then leaped for the roof.

She landed at the feet of a bespelled soldier.

He swung his sword, and she rolled to her left and straight into another soldier. More boots stood beside his, and when she craned her neck to take in the entire roof, her stomach dropped.

People were pouring onto the rooftop, using a twisted hemlock tree that grew close to the back porch. It was like Irina had seen what Lorelai was doing and had sent her bespelled army up the hemlock tree in a countermove that left Lorelai with very few options. She looked behind her to find an escape route.

Several peasants had clambered over the throng around the maple tree and were clinging to its trunk.

The yard below was so crowded, Lorelai couldn't see a single blade of grass.

Even her survival skills couldn't get her out of this. She was going to have to use magic and pray that she didn't kill any innocent people, and that she didn't have to overpower any hearts. She needed enough strength to face Irina before Gabril and his family died, and Kol was lost to her forever.

The man standing above her snatched her arms as she tried to spin away from him, and a woman who looked far too delicate to be so strong grabbed Lorelai's feet. Together, they moved toward the edge of the roof while Lorelai fought and bucked against their hands. She couldn't reach them with her palms. She couldn't reach the roof either. Her magic burned, begging for release that was impossible to give.

Help! she sent to Sasha but before the gyrfalcon could dodge the host of sword-wielding soldiers that crowded the rooftop and get to Lorelai, a tremendous roar of fury shattered the air.

Lorelai twisted to look past her captors and saw an enormous dragon, black as ebony, sweep the roof, knocking soldiers flying with the force of its wings.

"Trugg!" Her breath was a sob of relief.

Her captors skidded toward the edge of the roof, and then Lorelai was airborne. She flew toward the ground, back first. Twisting, she tried to correct her trajectory, but then something hard and sharp snatched her arms and lifted her toward the sky. She looked up into the face of a very angry-looking silver dragon with black wings and a line of glistening black scales running down its spine and tail.

Jyn.

Sasha shrieked in fury and dove for the dragon.

No! She doesn't mean me any harm. Follow, Sasha. Follow only. The bird pulled out of the dive and circled instead, but her thoughts were full of shredding dragon underbellies and poking out their eyes.

Jyn rose into the air, Lorelai clutched in her talons, and six other dragons were waiting for her—Trugg and five others in various combinations of purple, gold, green, and white.

A white and gold dragon gave Lorelai a look she couldn't decipher and then turned to lead them away from the pretty gabled cottages on the east side of Ravenspire. Once they'd cleared the cottages and left the bespelled crowd far behind, the dragons descended into a broken-down barn that was surrounded by trees and overgrown grass.

Jyn dumped Lorelai unceremoniously on the rough barn floor and shuddered. In seconds, the dragon's wings and ridges receded, and her scales softened into skin. Lorelai found herself toe-to-toe with the girl, whose dark eyes were brimming with anger.

"Where is Kol?" the girl asked. "What have you done to him?"

"Let's give her the benefit of the doubt, Jyn, before we jump to conclusions." The boy who'd been the white and gold dragon finished shifting and grabbed some pants from the pack he'd carried.

"I haven't done anything to Kol," Lorelai said.

Jyn slammed her foot against the floor "We don't believe you, *mardushka*. Where is our king?"

"Don't make me sorry I rescued you." Trugg finished shifting.

"I can put you right back where you came from."

Sasha flew into the barn and perched on Lorelai's shoulder, her beady eyes daring one of the Draconi to cross her.

The girl who'd been a purple and gold dragon grabbed the bag, pulled on some pants, and tossed various items of clothing at her friends. Then she faced Lorelai and said quietly, "I'm Freya. You've already met Jyn and Trugg. The other boys are Raum and Gerik, and the girl is Mik. Kol is our friend. We're here to rescue him, but the collar he wears is bespelled against those with dual hearts."

Trugg stepped forward, his hands fisted. "We know Kol found you again. We caught his scent when he came back into the capital and went to that cottage. But now his scent is gone, and you were the last person with him, *mardushka*."

Sasha clicked her beak in warning, but Trugg didn't spare her a glance as he hulked over Lorelai.

If the boy stepped any closer, Lorelai would have to give ground, and she didn't have time to play games to see which one of them was more intimidating. Straightening her spine, she put her palm against Trugg's arm. A bolt of power shot from her and sent him crashing into the sagging barn wall. Dust swirled in the air, and Jyn began shifting back into her dragon.

"I'm not going to hurt you. Any of you." Lorelai lowered her palms to make her point, and Jyn stopped shifting. "I'm not a threat to you or to Kol."

"Tell that to Trugg," Jyn said. "You just sent him into a wall."

Lorelai snapped, "Because he was trying to intimidate me. And also because once again he has yet to put on a pair of pants. I am already having a spectacularly difficult day. I don't need to add avoiding a pantsless Eldrian to the list of things I still have to do. Now, listen to me. Kol is in trouble."

Quickly she filled them in on what happened to Kol over the past few weeks. How he had fought to keep from losing himself to his dragon heart. How Irina had tortured him, Lorelai had healed him, and her magic had given them a bond that allowed them to hear each other's thoughts.

"That's kind of disturbing." One of the boys stepped forward. "But also useful. If you can talk to him—"

"Irina corrupted the bond. She's gained more power somehow—"

"Fantastic." Trugg turned and punched his fist into the closest wall. "We're going to lose Kol."

"We never should've come to Ravenspire. Trusting a *mardushka* is worse than facing the ogres." Jyn started pacing.

"It's not Kol's fault that *mardushkas* always find a way to make their blood oaths work to their favor," another boy said.

"It doesn't matter whose fault it is. We're going to lose Kol." The girl who'd been a green dragon looked like she was about to cry.

"No, you aren't." Lorelai's voice was fierce. "Irina isn't the only one with power. I'm going to the castle where she has both Kol and my family." Her throat closed over the thought of Gabril, sacrificing so much for her only to watch his family die at Irina's hands. Of Kol, lost to his dragon because he was desperate to be the king his people needed. "I'm going to destroy Irina and put Kol's human heart back in his chest."

Jyn's dark eyes narrowed. "Why would you care what happens to Kol? Last time you saw him, you wanted to punish him for making the blood oath."

Lorelai met her gaze. Her voice trembled as she said, "Kol and I have moved past that."

"Oh, skies, you're in love with him." Trugg shook dust off his shoulders. "Unbelievable. The boy is trapped with his dragon heart, unable to speak, and is determined to kill you, and *still* he manages to turn on the charm. Well, he's Eldr's, so don't go getting any *mardushka* ideas about him."

"I'm not in love with him. I've known him less than three weeks." Lorelai crossed her arms over her chest and glared at Trugg even as warmth heated her cheeks. "But you're right. I found his desperate struggle not to kill me very charming. The unbearable agony he was in and the constant fear that he was failing Eldr just added to the allure."

Trugg opened his mouth, but nothing came out.

"Are we done being ridiculous?" Lorelai asked, and then turned to include the other six Eldrians in her glare. "Kol thinks all he is to the outside world is a charming daredevil, but you and I know better, don't we? We see his incredible inner strength. His ability to put others first even at great cost to himself. We understand the depth of his loyalty and love. That's why you followed him to Ravenspire in the first place. You're willing to die for him, and so am I."

The Eldrians stared at her in wide-eyed silence.

"And another thing." She raised her finger and pointed it first at Jyn, who seemed to vehemently hate her for the power in her blood, and then swept her arm to include them all. "My name is Lorelai, not *mardushka*. I don't want to hear another word against my magic. Magic is an impartial force that obeys the heart of the one who wields it. If I wanted to harm Eldr, I wouldn't have honored my promise to Kol and sent a barrier between the ogres and your people. You should be grateful that I'm a *mardushka*, because you are going up against the most powerful woman who ever came out of Morcant, and the strength of my heart is the only thing standing between you and total destruction."

Trugg caught her eye, and a fierce smile cracked his face. "You'd make an excellent Draconi warrior."

"I'm an excellent warrior, period. Now, how much distance do you have to keep between you and Kol to avoid triggering the spell in his collar?"

"Queen Irina didn't say, but we don't dare get too close," the girl who'd been the white dragon said as she held out her hand for Lorelai to shake. "I'm Mik. It's nice to meet you."

Lorelai shook her hand and considered the problem. The castle would have magical traps set around it. Lorelai shuddered at the thought of more statues, more spiders, but whatever Irina had waiting for them, it was nothing compared to what Lorelai was going to do to the false queen.

Kol would be somewhere in the castle itself, but that would give the Eldrians room to fly to castle grounds and fight off whatever traps Irina had set so that Lorelai could get inside and rescue Gabril and Kol. Irina thought she'd isolated her enemies. She wouldn't be expecting them to launch a coordinated attack.

Lorelai looked at the Eldrians and lifted her chin. "Listen carefully. This is what we're going to do."

THIRTY-EIGHT

THEY APPROACHED THE castle from the south. Lorelai rode Mik and had to shield her eyes as the late afternoon sun glinted against Mik's white scales like brilliant sparks of fire. The Eldrians flew low to the ground, hugging the hills that marked the land south of the capital to make it harder for the castle guards to see them in time to sound a warning.

She'd sent Sasha ahead to scout so that the dragons would know where to fly, where to land. She couldn't afford for them to fail their part of the mission. They were her way past Irina's defenses—defenses surely designed to drain Lorelai's power before her showdown with the queen.

She'd stopped reaching for Kol's thoughts before discussing her plan with the Eldrians. He wasn't there. She'd found nothing but darkness, anguish, and Irina's cold, cruel voice mocking her attempts to find the Kol she knew and bring him back to her. It was better to ignore the connection and keep her thoughts to herself until the last possible moment.

Like the Eldrians, Lorelai couldn't afford to fail her part of the mission.

As they flew closer and closer to the castle, Lorelai drew deep breaths and forced her fear into a corner of her mind. She wasn't sure if she could defeat this newly powerful Irina. She wasn't sure if she could save those she cared about. If she could save Ravenspire.

But she didn't need to know the outcome to be sure of her heart.

She was the crown princess of Ravenspire, a powerful *mardushka* of Morcant, and she would right the wrongs against her people or she would die trying.

As the graceful spires of Ravenspire's castle loomed on the horizon, Lorelai's pulse raced, and her magic thrummed through her blood to gather in her palms where she held what she hoped would be the key to getting the dragons safely past Irina's defenses and into the castle grounds. The Eldrians crested the final rise, and then the castle with its gray stone turrets, its etched glass windows, and its sprawling gardens lay before them.

Trugg turned his huge black head and gave Lorelai a look that asked, "Are you ready?"

She nodded and raised her hands. Irina would have traps set. Shields up. Unnatural things like the snake-vine cage in Nordenberg created from her magic.

Lorelai had a plan she hoped would work. Every Eldrian had willingly given her a scale to hold, even though Lorelai could see that ripping a scale from their bodies had hurt. Through their scales, she could feel the fierceness of their hearts that were willing to serve her magic when she called upon them. She hoped that holding the scales would mean she didn't have to take their fire into her own body for her magic to use it.

The Eldrians flew in a solid line, seven abreast, as they streaked toward the castle wall.

Lorelai focused on the scales she held, letting her magic surround them, calling upon the strength and fury of their hearts. Guards, who were pacing the perimeter of the wall, drew their swords and called a warning as the dragons hurtled toward them. Lorelai waited until seconds before they crossed the wall and then yelled, "*Tvor`grada!* May the strength of each dragon's heart and the power in my blood be a shield for them so long as they need it."

Her magic burst from her palms and into the air, a shimmering net that encircled each dragon and sank into their scales, a barrier Lorelai desperately hoped Irina couldn't penetrate with ordinary spells. The princess had already warned the Eldrians not to test the shield by going after Kol. She wasn't certain her barrier could keep out a spell already enacted against the Draconi in the past, and she wasn't willing to lose one of Kol's friends to find out.

They flew over the wall, and a hedge of thorny bushes shot into the air, the thorns curling like claws, the branches reaching for the dragons as if the bushes had eyes. The dragons shifted course, flying vertically up the side of the hedge, trying to get to the top without being snagged by one of the grasping branches.

Jyn flew too close, and a whiplike branch full of thorns slammed into her. The force of the blow knocked her briefly off course, but Lorelai's shield held, and she remained unscathed.

Lorelai's relief that the hedge couldn't harm the dragons was short-lived as she realized what was happening.

"It's closing us out!" she shouted to Mik. The dragon flew faster, straight up into the air, while Lorelai clung desperately to her back. But no matter how fast Mik flew, the hedge was faster. It rose into the sky like it was trying to catch the sun, and Lorelai knew they'd never catch it. Never crest the top and dive into the castle grounds on the other side.

She needed another plan.

"Stop trying to catch it. Hover and face it instead."

Mik whirled into a sharp turn that had Lorelai's stomach pushing against her chest, and then they were facing the hedge head-on as it continued to rise above them. The other Eldrians followed Mik's lead.

Lorelai pushed her magic into the scales she held and yelled, "Give me fire!"

Heat ignited in Mik's chest. All along the line of dragons, smoke poured from their mouths as the fires in their chests roared to life.

"Now!"

As fire exploded from the dragon's mouths, Lorelai raised her hands. "*Zhech`pusk!* May the fire destroy any magic it touches."

Brilliant white magic shot through the fire, turning it into a blazing yellow-white ball easily twice the size of Trugg. Lorelai swept her hands forward and the fireball struck the hedge.

For a moment, nothing burned. The magic that had sent the hedge toward the sky held it steady.

But that was magic created out of bitterness and greed from a heart that knew only how to conquer instead of how to love.

Plus, Lorelai's heart wasn't alone in this fight. She had seven Draconi warriors willing to die for the cause as well. Leaning down, she whispered to the scales, to their dragon hearts, that she needed strength. Purpose. Courage to push past the hedge's magic and into the other side.

The dragons roared, and Lorelai felt their will, their resolve, slam into the magic that held the hedge.

The fireball ate through the branches, sending flaming bits of leaves and thorns raining on the ground far below. The magic in the hedge fought back, creating more branches, more thorns, but the Eldrians would not be swayed.

Lorelai would not be swayed.

The dragons pushed into the hedge, following in the wake of the fire that slowly consumed the barrier. Thorns raked at them, and Lorelai hid her face against Mik's side to keep from being sliced open. She hadn't created a shield for herself. She was absolutely certain shielding herself from other magic meant completely cutting off her Irina-tainted connection to Kol, and that was a risk she wasn't willing to take.

In moments, the fireball exploded out the other side of the hedge and streaked for the ground. The dragons followed immediately behind it.

"*Voshtet,*" Lorelai said, focusing on the fire. "Rise and fly before your dragon masters and obey their command."

On the castle grounds below, wolves prowled and trees shook gnarled branches at the sky before slamming them into the ground.

Leaning close to Mik's ear, Lorelai said, "When you face a threat that your regular dragon strength can't defeat, tell my fire spell what to do. It's part of your heart. It will obey you. You'll be okay."

Mik dipped her head in acknowledgment as the dragons

streaked down the south side of the castle, blasting fire into the trees that lunged for them, until they came to the entrance. The second the dragons touched the ground, the wolves attacked.

Trugg roared as the animals, foaming at the mouth, ran toward them. The ground shook and then erupted as spiders, centipedes, and snakes burst out of the dirt and swarmed toward the dragons.

"Help them fight!" Lorelai yelled as the other dragons smashed, burned, and tore into their foes.

Mik strafed the ground with fire, engulfing a pair of trees and a swarm of spiders that were racing toward them. Lorelai slid off her back, her knees shaking, but her hands steady.

Two more wolves stood sentry at the castle's entrance, their lips curled in vicious snarls.

Sasha, perch! Magic gathered in her palm like lightning as Lorelai lifted her bare hand into the air. Sasha swooped out of the sky and landed on Lorelai's palm as the wolves dug their claws into the ground and howled, foam dripping from their mouths.

The lightning in Lorelai's palm wrapped around Sasha, and the power coursing through the princess leaped for the threads of awareness that connected Sasha to the rest of the birds in the forest.

"*Hat'sja.* Come together. Come to me."

Sasha shuddered. The wolves locked eyes with Lorelai and dug their claws into the ground.

Lorelai braced her feet as power spilled out of her. The wolves leaped forward. Lorelai spun away from one, but the other slammed into her and sent her to her knees. The gyrfalcon shrieked with fury and raked the wolf with her talons as it snapped at Lorelai's hands.

"*Hat`sja!*" Lorelai yelled as her power pulsed with a multitude of heartbeats from the surrounding trees. Behind her, the dragons roared, and the thick, wet sound of battle filled the air, but Lorelai couldn't help them. She was too busy trying to survive long enough to get herself inside the castle.

Pain seared her, and she kicked at the wolf who was snapping at her, rolling to the side as it lunged for her and barely avoiding the jaws of the smaller wolf.

Kill them all. Kill, kill, kill. Sasha slammed into the biggest wolf and then shrieked in pain as the other wolf nipped her wing.

Lorelai kicked the larger wolf, sending it skidding over the ground, and scrambled to her feet. She turned toward the castle's entrance, where another pair of foaming, snarling wolves stood waiting. *Perch, Sasha. Hurry.* She held her hand in the air and sent her magic into the gyrfalcon the instant the bird settled onto her open palm.

There was an awful grinding sound as the bird's wounded wing knit back together, and then a rustle swept through the surrounding trees. It started as a whisper, a few leaves shushing together in the breeze, and then grew louder and louder until it sounded like a hurricane ripping leaves from branches and branches from trees.

The wolves behind Lorelai growled and stalked toward her, while those in front of her crouched, waiting. She braced herself to run, to fight, but then birds of every size exploded out of the trees and flew straight at Lorelai. The wolves behind Lorelai were battered from all sides, caught in the maelstrom until they were smashed against tree trunks and left discarded on the ground like crumpled toys. The animals at the castle's entrance lunged for her, but they were driven back by a wall of birds that circled Lorelai, a swirling funnel cloud of sharp beaks and bright eyes, and swept her from the ground until she seemed to float among them in midair.

The wolves howled as the larger birds left the funnel cloud, raked the animals with their talons, and then rejoined the rest of the flock only to do it all over again.

Kill? It was Sasha's voice. It was a hawk's voice. A robin's. A dove's. The strength of hundreds of birds speaking to her at once drove a spike of pain through Lorelai's head. She spun slowly within the funnel cloud, high above the ground, buffeted by wings on all sides.

Kill. She answered the birds. The flock lowered her to the ground and then swept toward anything that stood between Lorelai and the castle, tearing it to pieces. As the dragons battled behind her, Lorelai mounted the steps to the entrance hall and reached for Kol. She found darkness. Pain. And a terrible hunger for Lorelai's heart.

But she also sensed that he was close. Which meant either Irina had sent Kol out to fight Lorelai in her stead, or they were both waiting for her together somewhere in the castle.

There was only one way to find out.

The door to the entrance hall was heavy—the wood as thick as a horse's back with stone knockers and ornate iron handles—and Lorelai had to lean into it to get it open.

A page stood on the other side of the door, her mouth open in shock to see Lorelai step inside.

"Leave," Lorelai said softly as the echo of the door swinging shut behind her reverberated through the hall.

The girl's eyes widened, and she tugged on the collar of her uniform. "But I can't just . . . *you* can't just—"

Lorelai locked eyes with her. "I am Lorelai Diederich, daughter of Arlen Diederich the Third. This is my castle, and I am your queen. If you want the current usurper of a queen to spare your life in the upcoming battle between us, then you need to leave. Now. Go hide somewhere and don't come back until morning."

The page slowly backed away.

Lorelai turned as the girl disappeared into a side corridor. The entrance hall with its sumptuous marble floors, ornately curved staircase, and decorative benches gifted to Queen Rosalinde the First a century ago by the ruler of Balavata looked exactly the same as it did in Lorelai's memory.

She walked to the middle of the room and sank to the floor in the spot where she'd last seen her father alive. Where he'd told her to protect her brother.

Lorelai hadn't been able to save her father or Leo. But she could honor their memory now. And she could free the rest of Ravenspire, the people her father had pledged to lead and protect—the people he would've raised *her* to lead and protect—from the tyranny of its unlawful queen.

Her fingers tingled, and the cold, implacable heart of the marble stirred. Beneath it, Lorelai felt the barrier of mountain stone that had been used centuries ago as the foundation for the castle. It was her mountain, and the heart recognized her with a little surge of power.

She reached farther, pushing past the stone to the ground of Ravenspire itself, introducing herself to its heart once more. Telling it what she wanted and why she was asking.

Showing it that she meant to heal the damage it had endured all these years.

Lorelai pulled her magic back and let a single throb of grief for her father and brother ache in her chest before she lifted her hands.

She felt him—the terrible agony, the desperate need to hurt her—before she saw him.

"Kol." She looked up and there he was, his eyes bleak and feral, his neck raw from the collar he wore, and his dragon talons curved and ready as he faced her across the expanse of marble that stretched from one end of the hall to the other.

She'd save Kol first and then look for Gabril and Irina.

It's okay, she sent to Kol, even though she wasn't sure he could hear her. She stood and faced him, opening her arms. *My heart already belongs to you. Come and take it.*

Her magic flared, racing through her veins to gather in her palms like lightning. Something flickered in his eyes, and Lorelai leaned toward him, willing him to *see* her. To trust that she wouldn't let him become what he feared the most. That she would save him, no matter what.

"How absolutely touching. I do believe if I left the two of you alone, you might actually manage to rescue him." Irina's voice was sugar-coated knives, just like it had been in Nordenberg, but this time, Lorelai wasn't going to run.

She turned, putting her back to Kol, and found Irina standing in front of the door, Gabril bleeding and chained beside her while an enormous black viper coiled about his neck. Irina's hands were already wreathed in magic, her smile a slash of cruelty across her face.

THIRTY-NINE

Lorelai faced Irina, her magic burning in her palms, her knees shaking. Nine years of training. Hiding. Waking up screaming in the middle of the night with Irina's cold blue eyes blazing in her memory.

She'd been terrified of what the queen was capable of—she still was. But Lorelai knew what *she* was capable of. And she knew how far her heart was willing to go—how much she would sacrifice—to take Ravenspire's false queen off the throne.

It was time to end this. Looking Irina in the eye, Lorelai said, "I told you this was the last day you would ever breathe Ravenspire air again."

Irina's lip curled. "You disappoint me." She took a step forward. "You had so much potential. I could have trained you into a *mardushka* worthy of being my daughter."

"I already have a mother," Lorelai said. "One you tried hard to erase."

"Oh, I didn't just try, princess. I erased her very existence."

She took another small step toward one of the wooden benches that lined the wall.

"You can't erase someone when their memories live on." Lorelai lifted her chin and held out her hands, palms toward the floor. "I remember my mother. I remember my father and brother, too."

"You took Arlen from me." Irina's voice rose. "You took *everything* from me."

Lorelai slowly crouched toward the floor as Irina came closer to the bench. She couldn't allow Irina to touch the bench without having a spell of her own ready. She remembered the wooden vines from the night her father died.

"I took nothing from you that was truly yours." Lorelai's voice was steady. "Everything you have, you've stolen. You've misused your power to force others to give you the life you think you deserve. You've killed those in your way, tortured those who stood up to you, and destroyed the land with your insatiable appetite for power at any cost."

Irina stopped moving toward the bench. Her smile raised the hair on the back of Lorelai's neck. "And I suppose you think you're going to be able to stop me."

Lorelai's throat tightened, but she held Irina's gaze and said, "Yes."

Irina's eyes gleamed. "You're going to lose. Do you know why? Because you've already made the mistake that will destroy you." She extended her hands toward the bench, her magic reaching for the wood as Lorelai sank toward the floor. "You thought I was the biggest threat in the room. You were wrong. You really shouldn't have turned your back to him."

The queen lunged for the bench, her hands connecting. Lorelai slammed her hands onto the marble floor, her magic surging.

And then Kol struck Lorelai from behind, knocking her on her side.

She skidded across the marble, and Irina laughed wildly as shafts of wood exploded from the bench and became a mass of vipers writhing and hissing as they slithered over the marble toward Lorelai.

The princess grabbed the handful of dragon scales from her pocket and focused on the Draconi's hearts. The snakes coiled themselves, ready to strike, fangs already dripping venom. Lorelai shouted, *"Zhech`pusk,"* as the closest viper lunged for her face.

A bolt of white-orange fire shot from her hands and engulfed the snake. Lorelai swept her arm wide, and the fire leaped from snake to snake.

Irina pressed her palms to the polished cherry wall, and a hail of barbed wooden spears flew out of the wall and headed straight for Lorelai.

She threw up a hand to defend herself, but Kol was there, grabbing her hand and dragging her away. At first, she thought he was pulling her to safety, but soon she realized that he was taking her to Irina. His grip was like iron, and every surge of magic she sent into his hand met resistance as hard as stone.

Irina was right. She owned him now. The only way to save Kol was to kill the *mardushka* whose magic was poisoning his mind, body, and heart.

But she couldn't kill Irina if she was thrown, helpless, at the queen's feet.

The spears clattered to the marble floor behind her and

became thick, branchlike vines with serrated leaves and gaping teeth-filled mouths where flowers should be.

Lorelai bent double at the waist and shoved the back of Kol's knees with her free hand. He stumbled, his grip softening. She yanked her hand free and twisted away from him, her palms hitting the marble floor.

"*Rast`lozh*," she said, and the marble began expanding in a half circle around the princess, surging toward the ceiling like polished white hills and cutting her off from Irina.

Irina's vines slid over the top of Lorelai's barrier, their mouths snapping as they came for the princess. She spun to her left to avoid them. Kol snatched her waist and began trying to drag her up one of the slippery marble hills toward where Irina still stood beside the wall.

Lorelai looked past Irina to find Gabril's face a deep shade of red as the snake around his neck tightened its hold. Desperation blazed through her, and she struggled against Kol's grip.

Kol, listen to my voice. Hold on to me. I can help you. I can save you.

Irina laughed. "He can't hear you. He hears only the pounding of his dragon heart and the voice of his queen."

Lorelai whirled, planted her right foot against Kol's left thigh, and launched herself backward out of his arms. Snarling, he lunged for her. She spun into the air, hit him in the chest with a roundhouse kick, and sent him crashing to the ground.

Sprinting out of the half circle of marble, Lorelai dove for the floor, and spoke the incantor again the second her palm touched down.

The marble expanded once more, completing the circle,

rising like a loaf of bread until it was over Kol's head.

He was trapped inside a fence of marble.

He was safe.

Now it was just Lorelai and Irina.

The vines rushed for Lorelai, tangling in her feet and sinking vicious little teeth into her legs. She kicked at them as her skin burned and blistered from the venom in their fangs, but she didn't have time to think of an incantor to deal with them.

She needed to stop defending herself and start attacking.

"Do you really think you can take my huntsman out of the game?" Irina sent a bolt of magic into the floor and the marble circle cracked in half.

Kol burst through the opening and ran toward Lorelai, but she was focused on the arc of marble closest to the queen.

Pushing her palms against the floor, she whispered an incantor, and the thick half-moon of marble skidded across the room, slamming into Irina and pinning her to the wall. The marble knocked Gabril to the side, and he thrashed against the chains that bound him.

Irina screamed an incantor. Kol reached Lorelai, whose feet were still tangled in vines, as the windows that surrounded the door shattered and the glass teardrop chandelier fell from the ceiling to explode into shards against the floor.

The princess put one hand on Kol, desperately sending her magic into him, trying to smash through the barrier Irina had erected. With the other hand, she reached over a pile of writhing, snapping vines for the closest shard of glass.

Kol shoved her hand away, and Lorelai stumbled. Snatching at his shirt, she kept herself from falling as she bent at the waist and scooped up the glass. A vine lashed itself around her wrist and sank its little teeth into her arm. The pain was a brilliant flare that streaked through her veins and sent the room swaying, but Lorelai didn't hesitate.

Holding the glass, feeling the heart of the Ravenspire sand that had been sacrificed to make the chandelier, she said, *"Tvor`zhi."* It was the same incantor the queen had used to create snakes, but Lorelai had a different creature in mind.

Thousands of razor-sharp glass shards rose from the floor and hovered like a swarm of bees. As Irina shouted another incantor, and more vines peeled away from the wooden bannister to plunge toward Lorelai, the swarm of glass swooped through the air, gaining speed and momentum, and then dove for the queen.

Irina screamed as the shards arrowed over the top of the marble barrier and struck her.

Lorelai had no time to celebrate the victory. Kol was grappling with her, his amber eyes wild, his skin so flushed with heat from his dragon's fire that it hurt to touch him. She sent spells into him, shouted incantors, even tried to break his hold on her by breaking his arm, but he was a dragon trapped in a human body—impossibly strong, fast, and lethal, and she refused to do the one thing that would save her from him.

She refused to kill him.

Her chest burned from the vine's poison, and every breath tore at her throat like a knife blade as she struggled against him, pushing her power into him in desperate hope that somehow she could slow him down long enough to kill Irina and set him free.

"Kaz`lit." Irina's voice thundered throughout the hall, and Kol howled in agony as the pain inside him doubled.

The queen spoke another incantor, and the marble barrier crumbled into dust. The glass shards fell to the floor. And the cuts on Irina's skin knit back together again.

She began moving toward the far wall where the Diederich coat of arms, complete with a pair of crossed swords, was mounted.

"He's going to kill you, Lorelai. Any second now. It's the only way his body and mind can find any peace. But if he doesn't . . . I have something that will do the job." Irina's smile was cruel.

Kol lowered his shoulder and slammed into Lorelai, sending them both sprawling into the nest of writhing vines.

The vines whipped out and lashed themselves around Lorelai's arms, legs, and waist, pinning her to the floor. Their teeth were razors, their poison fire. Her lungs labored for every breath she took. Her pulse pounded in desperation as Kol yanked at the vines that covered her heart, heedless of the teeth that sank into his skin.

Across the room, Irina hefted the swords, one in each hand. Her lips moved, and the swords shuddered to life. Releasing the hilts, Irina smiled as the swords hovered in the air like hawks searching for prey.

Lorelai's eyes stung with tears as she met Kol's feral gaze. His talons tore at the vines across her chest. The swords began circling faster and faster. Weariness from Lorelai's constant use of magic was setting in.

Irina laughed in vicious triumph as she waited for the princess to die.

The last vine blocking Lorelai's heart snapped in two, and Kol roared in savage hunger.

The swords dove toward them.

And Lorelai *knew*.

She couldn't fight off both Kol and Irina. She had to choose.

There was no panic. No hesitation. There was only her heart willing to pay the cost of killing Irina and by doing so, save her kingdom and save Kol.

She gathered her remaining strength, stretched her palms flat against the floor, and called to the deepest core of Ravenspire. To secret depths unplumbed by even Irina.

The swords flew toward them.

Kol's hand curved into an open fist above her heart.

Irina laughed.

"*Hat`sja oyti*," Lorelai whispered. "Come together and rise. Take the one who hurts you."

Deep within the ground, something rumbled like thunder trapped in a cavern of rocks. Something bubbled and boiled and surged toward the surface.

"Please," Lorelai whispered, magic stinging her hands as it spilled into the marble and sank into the core of Ravenspire. "Help me."

The swords were almost upon them.

Kol's talons pressed against the skin around her heart as if he was gauging where to plunge his hand.

Irina shrieked her victory.

Leo's face blazed across her mind, the laughter in his eyes turning black with Irina's spell. Her father fell to the floor, already dying from the bite of the snake Irina had sent after him. The woman in the Falkrains sobbed over the bodies of her children before plunging her knife into her own chest. The land was rotting, the people desperately crying out for salvation; and Kol, an honorable king who'd only wanted to save his people, was lost.

All because of Irina.

Fury was a burning stone in Lorelai's chest. It was the power in her blood, the strength of her bones. It was the beat of her heart—the heart of Ravenspire's true queen come to save those she loved from ruin.

"Hat`sja oyti!"* Lorelai's voice rose as Kol struck, breaking the skin, tearing the muscle. *"Hat`sja oyti!"

Pain was a flash of blinding agony that seized Lorelai's entire body, but she kept her palms pressed flat against the floor, her magic pouring into Ravenspire with every furious beat of her heart.

The rumble grew louder. The marble shook, shivered, and cracked. And then the floor beneath Irina's feet fell away and a fiery river of molten lava gushed from the belly of Ravenspire and surrounded her.

Irina screamed an incantor, but there was nothing for her to touch except the blazing stone that already obeyed Lorelai. Her eyes met Lorelai's, and the fury in them dissolved into bewildered pain as the lava surged forward and dragged the wicked queen down into the depths of Ravenspire.

The swords dropped harmlessly to the floor, and the snapping vines disintegrated into dust.

The collar around Kol's neck snapped in two and fell from his neck.

The snake wrapped around Gabril's neck shrank until it became the harmless garden snake Leo had been playing with the night his father died.

Lorelai's blood poured from her chest.

Kol closed his eyes and shook his head, as if trying to understand where he was and what was happening.

This isn't your fault, Lorelai sent to him, and his eyes flew open as she used the last of her strength to say, *I forgive you.*

Horror filled his face as he saw his hand. Her blood.

He leaned toward her, but her strength was gone, and darkness claimed her.

FORTY

KOL JERKED HIS hand away from Lorelai's chest and stared in horror at the blood pouring from her. Her eyes were closed. Her body lay limp on the crumpled marble floor, surrounded by the dust of the things that used to be vines.

Skies, no. Lorelai? Lorelai! His heart thudded against his chest, but there was no call to hurt, punish, and kill because he'd already done it. He'd hurt her.

He'd *killed* her.

He'd killed the girl who'd saved him.

His hands shook, and his throat ached with unshed tears as he doubled over and pressed his forehead to hers. *I'm sorry, I'm sorry, I'm sorry, I'm sorry.*

It didn't matter how many times he said it, or how deeply he meant it. It only mattered that she was gone, and that he'd done it.

So what if Irina had driven him to it? It wasn't Irina's fingers covered in Lorelai's blood. It was *his*.

He didn't know how he was ever going to be able to shoulder the guilt.

The memory of her gaze and the kindness in her eyes as she told him it wasn't his fault and that she forgave him were blazing coals in his chest. He didn't want her forgiveness.

He wanted *her*.

He wanted her, but she'd done what she'd promised she'd do. She'd destroyed Irina. She'd set Ravenspire free. And she'd sacrificed herself to save Kol.

He choked on a sob and stroked her pale cheek. Ran his fingers through her long dark hair as grief ripped at him. Pressed his thumb against her red lips and jerked upright in shock as the faintest whisper of a breath passed her lips.

She was alive.

She was alive, and he wasn't going to fail her again. He couldn't call for help without his human heart to give him words. He refused to leave her side when he had no idea where to find a physician or how to make himself understood in time.

He'd have to save her himself. He stared at the wound in her chest and ordered himself to think. There was a solution, there had to be, and if anyone was skilled at finding unlikely solutions around sticky problems, it was Kol.

His dragon heart thumped in agreement, and its fire stirred in his chest.

His fire.

Quickly, he called the heat and let it blaze through him until it reached his hands.

If he could melt a sword with his touch, he could seal Lorelai's wound.

He lay his hands across the wound he'd made and prayed to the skies above that it would work. The heat sizzled against her flesh, cauterizing the blood flow.

Lorelai? Please . . . please wake up. Move a finger. Do something to show me you're still with me. He searched her mind, but all he could find were faded images of blood in snow and shattered pieces of what looked like an ebony carriage.

He'd stopped the bleeding, but she was still going to die if he couldn't find a way to mend what was broken inside her. If he could just get her to heal herself, she'd be fine. If he could just get her to use her magic . . . The memory of him stalking across the waterfall's cave, insisting that if she didn't survive her battle with Irina, he'd kiss her back to life blazed across his mind. Lorelai had said magic didn't bring people back to life, but she was still alive. Barely, but it was something.

Please let this work. Please. He bent toward her, framed her face in his hands, and kissed her.

Come back to me, Lorelai. Don't leave me alone. You promised you'd save me, but I'm not saved if I have to bury you and go home to what's left of Eldr. Please, Lorelai. Come back to me.

For a long moment, Lorelai remained limp and unmoving. Kol deepened the kiss and sent her his memories of her strength. Fearlessly choosing to save him in Tranke, even though he was a stranger to her. Choosing to help him try to break his blood oath, honoring her promise to save Eldr, healing him when he'd tried to kill her. Letting him into her heart, though she knew he was still bound to Irina. And finally, saving him by killing Irina even though it meant she wouldn't be able to stop Kol from tearing into her chest.

You're strong enough to come back to me, Lorelai. I know you are. Your heart just has to want it. Your heart has to want to live more than your body wants to die.

She stirred. A breath. A slight movement of her chest. And then her magic, in slow spirals of brilliant white, burst from her palms and surrounded the two of them, lifting them off the floor as it wrapped them in power that Kol could feel in his bones.

Her heart jerked once. Twice. Her nostrils flared. And then she threw her head back as her heart began beating in a strong, steady rhythm and the wounds on her arms and legs disappeared. The magic set them down again and dissipated.

Kol tried to say something, but the words wouldn't come. She was alive. He leaned forward and covered his face with his hands and tried not to show her how badly he was shaking.

She was *alive.*

He didn't realize she'd moved until she sat beside him and wrapped him in her arms.

You saved me, she said.

We saved each other. He turned to her and buried his face in her shoulder. *I'm so sorry. I don't know what to say to make it better.*

I already forgave you. Her voice was warm and sure. *We both know it was Irina making the choices, not you. Besides, far more important than the fact that an evil* mardushka *took control of you for a while is the fact that you figured out a way to save me.*

He raised his head and gave her a tiny smirk. *I did tell you I'd kiss you back to life if I had to.*

She smiled. *I'm sure it was a hardship for you.*

He tried and failed to smile in return. *I thought I'd lost you. I don't ever want to go through that again.*

She took his face in her hands. *My heart will always come back to you.*

Her kiss warmed him in a way his dragon's fire never would. He pulled her against his chest and held her for a moment while in the corridor above them, footsteps sounded as maids and pages crept to the bannister to peer at the devastation below and to wonder in whispers where the queen had gone.

Then the front door banged open, and Trugg stomped in followed by the rest of his friends, and, skies help him, even Sasha. The bird swooped down, took one look at the pool of Lorelai's blood on the floor beside them, and gave him a death glare.

Tell your bird not to kill me.

She's not going to kill you.

She is definitely considering it.

"Kol!" Trugg ran forward and snatched his king out of Lorelai's arms and swung him into the air. Setting Kol on his feet, Trugg slapped his shoulder, and Kol had to take a giant step forward to keep from falling to his knees.

Mik and Raum ran past him and bent to help Lorelai to her feet while Jyn and Tor unchained Gabril.

"Are you okay?" Mik asked Lorelai.

"I'm all right. Irina is dead. And I'm pretty sure Kol is a little jealous that you seem more concerned about me than about him."

Kol was mortified to realize he'd been thinking exactly that. He tried to give Lorelai a please-don't-share-every-intimate-thought-I-have-with-this-lot kind of look, but his friends surrounded him, thumping him on the back and hugging him.

"You did it," Gabril said quietly to Lorelai, and the image in her thoughts showed Kol how much Gabril's approval meant to her.

"We knew the moment the queen died," Raum said. "It was like an earthquake rolled through the ground, straight toward Eldr, and the nasty magical creatures outside stopped fighting and crumpled into dust. I think the queen's blood oath was satisfied and so her magic kept her side of the bargain as she died. Of course, we'll need to go to Eldr to be sure."

Kol felt like the crown of Eldr suddenly weighed nothing at all. *I need one of my friends to go ahead of us now and scout Eldr for the ogres so that so they can meet us on our journey home and let us know what to expect. Skies, it would be so much easier if I could just ask them myself.*

Don't worry. Lorelai sounded amused. *You're about to have the ability to share your thoughts for yourself.*

"That's enough of a reunion," Lorelai said, and Kol was amazed to see that his friends, even Trugg, instantly paid attention to her. "I need to find Kol's human heart and restore it."

"I don't know." Trugg wiggled his brows at Kol. "I think the fact that he can't order us around out loud is kind of fetching."

Lorelai punched Trugg's shoulder.

"What? Too soon?" Trugg asked.

Moments later, after placing her hand on Kol's chest and whispering an incantor, Lorelai had located the gold box that held his heart. She picked it up gently and looked askance at his chest.

"This is my first heart restoration. I honestly have no idea how to do this."

"I think you use your magic to put it back," Jyn said helpfully.

Lorelai narrowed her eyes. "You don't say."

Irina sent her magic into me first and then my heart just sort of appeared in her hand.

Let's hope it works just as well in reverse.

Her magic tingled in his blood, as familiar now to him as the beating of his own hearts. And then Lorelai, her face white with strain, was holding his heart in her hand and whispering an incantor over and over again as if she was terrified she'd get it wrong or it wouldn't work.

His human heart began to beat in time with his dragon's, and then it flickered like candlelight caught in a draft. She said her incantor once more, and his heart disappeared from her hand and returned to its rightful place inside of him. His human skin felt soft and malleable, no longer the iron cage that had held his dragon form at bay. His thoughts were clear, no more violent whispers from his dragon's heart, and words flowed easily to his tongue. He rubbed a palm against his chest and gave her a shy smile.

"Is this the point in our ongoing conversation where I tell you that you look—"

"Don't even say it." She smiled at him.

"I guess since we can have normal conversations now—"

"We should figure out how to block our thoughts?" Her smile slipped a little.

His did too.

Or not, he said. *I kind of like having you in my head. Especially since I have to rule Eldr and you have to rule Ravenspire, so we'll be spending time apart.*

Not too much time. She sounded stern, though her smile was back in place as she leaned against him. *I'm pretty sure I could find use for a dragon king—*

Could you now?

She laughed. *Of course. A dragon king to help me tour my kingdom—*

To kiss you senseless—

To save me time when I need to light a winter's fire—

He leaned toward her. *To kiss you senseless—*

To help me find—

He kissed her. Her lips parted for his, her hands, full of magic, pressed against his hearts, and though he was miles from Eldr and everything he'd ever known, he was home.

"I'm going to be sick. Do you hear me?" Trugg sounded grumpy. "The two of you make me want to vomit."

"Shut it, Trugg." Raum shooed the rest of the Eldrians from the room. "Kol has more than earned this happiness."

"I'd like a little happiness like that," Trugg said as he walked out the door.

"Then maybe don't talk about vomiting when there are girls present who might otherwise be interested in kissing you." Jyn followed him from the room.

"You're interested in kissing me?" Trugg sounded shocked.

"Not anymore."

Kol pulled back from Lorelai and smiled as the door shut behind his friends. "They're always like that."

"I love them." She took his hands. "And I love Eldr because it's yours. Whenever you feel strong enough to shift, we'll go there and make sure Irina's blood oath got rid of the ogres. If it didn't, I'll take care of it."

And she would because she had promised. And because she was strong enough to stand up when others couldn't.

He kissed her one last time, and then together they went out to gather the rest of the Draconi to head back to Eldr.

EPILOGUE

IT SEEMED WRONG to have her formal coronation ceremony without Leo there, critiquing the fashions, eating far too many of the appetizers, and charming one and all with his reckless smile, but it was time to assume the formal title of queen and wear the crown she'd fought so hard to take from Irina.

Formal coronation or not, Lorelai had been the acting queen of Ravenspire from the moment Irina had died. She'd visited Eldr to make sure Irina's blood oath had sent her magic to imprison the ogres once more—and to spend a little time with Kol in his own kingdom. She'd opened lines of communication with Ravenspire's allies. And she'd toured the land, building trust with peasants and nobility alike and doing what she could to heal the ravages of the blight while handing out food that Kol's treasure had purchased for Ravenspire from the merchants in Súndraille.

But spring was here, and with Ravenspire's crisis beginning to pass, it was time to face the ceremony she'd been putting off for so many months.

Lorelai stared at herself in the mirror. Leo would've loved this dress—it was bold and dramatic. Wearing it made her feel like somehow part of him was going to stand on the stage beside her like they'd always planned.

"Red is the perfect color for your dress, Your Highness." Her maid pursed her lips in concentration as she deftly swept Lorelai's hair into a complicated updo. "You'll be getting asked to dance by every nobleman in attendance."

"Thank you, Marlis." Lorelai smiled at her maid, but there was only one boy she wanted to dance with, and he was far away in Eldr.

Maybe you can pretend to be dancing with me. Kol's voice sounded amused.

While my feet are being trampled by some old nobleman with gout?

You can tell him he has adorably wild hair.

Don't make me sorry our connection works over such a long distance now.

He sent her a cheeky grin.

She knew how to fix that.

Of course, I believe most of the older noblemen are actually bringing their sons—only the ones eligible for marriage, of course— to dance with me. The consensus seems to be that I would make a pretty good catch.

You aren't going to marry a boring nobleman's boring son.

No?

No, because if one proposes to you, he'll be eaten by morning. Dragons have very healthy appetites.

Now it was her turn to smirk as Marlis finished her hair and slipped the sapphire earrings Kol had given her into her ears.

Draconi don't eat people.

I've been looking for a new hobby.

She rolled her eyes and stood. *Time for me to go face the crowd. You'll stay with me?*

I'm always with you.

He sent her a smile as she moved down the stairs, flanked by her guards, and headed toward the ballroom. She pressed her hands against the crimson silk of her dress, tugged on its tiny sleeves, and worried with the enormous floor-length skirt that felt like it weighed as much as Lorelai herself. She'd probably fall on her face if she tried to dance.

You'll be fine. He sounded amused but also something else. She looked harder and her brow rose. *Nervous?*

Maybe.

About what? she asked as pages opened the ballroom doors, and she swept inside.

About this.

The crowd parted, leaving her a clear path to the stage where the head priest from the capital's cathedral waited to place the official crown on her head and name her the queen of Ravenspire.

She began walking toward the stage, and there he was, wearing a black dress coat and a red cravat that matched her dress. His expression was solemn, though his hair was still unruly.

Surprise, he said.

You came. Her lips trembled as she smiled.

Of course I came. He matched her smile and held out his arm as she approached.

He led her onto the stage and then stepped back down as the

entire crowd curtsied and bowed.

The priest spoke for a few moments on duty to both the kingdom of Ravenspire and the higher power who ruled all kingdoms from the heavens above, but Lorelai had no idea what he was saying. She concentrated on not shaking. It helped a little to see Gabril standing tall and confident beside Ada and his sons, but when the strain of having hundreds of eyes on her got to be too much, she looked at Kol and felt steady once again.

Then the crown was on her head, and it was ridiculously heavy.

So is mine, Kol said as the music started and people began to dance.

I won't be able to dance with this thing on. I'm top-heavy. I'll fall over.

I'll catch you. He pulled her close to him, and the look in his eyes sent a flurry of butterflies into her stomach. Then he kissed her, and the warmth of his chest made her pulse race. Her breath caught while the magic in her blood called to Kol's hearts, and for the first time since she'd left Eldr behind, Lorelai was home.

INCANTORS

Hat`sja: come together and come to me

Ja`dat: take and give to another

Kaz`ja: command and take

Kaz`lit: pour punishment into

Kaz`prin: bring to me

Kaz`zhech: punish with fire

Nakhgor: find what I seek

Nakh`rashk: find and scatter

Oyti: rise

Prosnakh: request to find

Pros`odit: request to enter

Pros`rashk: request to scatter

Rast`lozh: grow or to levy

Tvor`grada: create barrier

Tvor`zhi: create life

Voshtet: rise and fly

Zhech`pusk: launch fire

Zna`uch: know/learn

ACKNOWLEDGMENTS

First and foremost, thank you to Jesus for sacrificing everything for me.

It takes one person to write a book, but it takes a team to help it see the light of day. The most important member on my team is always my husband, Clint, who is my biggest fan and supporter and who works with me to juggle our five children and very busy schedules so that I can always treat my career like a job instead of a hobby. I love you, Clint!

To my kids—Tyler, Jordan, Zachary, Johanna, and Isabella—you inspire me, motivate me, and fill my world with so many good things. I hope you grow up knowing that you can do anything you put your minds to.

To my mom for taking over my role as "mom" over Christmas break so that I could have long writing days to meet my deadline. To my sister for beta reading and for always being a huge fan of mine.

To my fabulous agent, Holly Root, who is both fiercely intelligent and incredibly kind. I'm so glad I have you in my corner.

I couldn't get through the drafting and revising process without the help of my writer BFFs. Thanks go out to Mandy Buehrlen for reading the beginning as I was putting the proposal together, for always encouraging me, and for being my spirit animal. To Jodi Meadows for critiquing the synopsis and beginning as I put the proposal together and for being ever ready to offer expert advice, bounce ideas around, and talk me off ledges. To Shannon Messenger for reading the beginning and finding the perfect missing ingredient to really make it shine. And to Lauren Thoman for beta reading like a BOSS. "Moment of silence for Viktor's cravat" remains one of my favorite comments ever.

Thanks also to Kat Kennedy for a last-minute beta read and for loving Lorelai so much. To Mireyah Wolfe, who stepped in on Twitter and helped me name Irina's snake (you suggested Kazimir, which eventually changed to Razimir). And to Rick Lipman, who reminded me that I am an author and I can just MAKE UP NAMES. ☺

Once a draft is ready to be turned in, the expert team at Balzer + Bray steps up. Many, many thanks to my immensely talented editor, Kristin Daly Rens, who always pushes me to deliver my absolute best and who believes in me and the story with rock-solid faith. I owe you a puppy and a trip to Scotland. My appreciation also goes out to my incredible publicist, Caroline Sun; my oh-so-talented cover designer, Sarah Kaufman; my rock star marketing team of Nellie Kurtzman, Jenna Lisanti, and Megan Barlog; the fabulous team at Epic Reads for their enthusiasm; and Kristin's insightful assistant editor, Kelsey Murphy. I adore my team and am deeply grateful for everything you do to make my stories shine.

Finally, to Lauren White. I hope when you read this book, Gabril's words take root in your heart and grow: "You don't go into battle because you're sure of victory. You go into battle because it's the right thing to do." Your courageous years-long fight against cancer is an inspiration, and so is your heart. You are a shining light to those around you, and I'm grateful I know you.